# SANDRIDER

# ANGIE SAGE

**BLOOMSBURY**
LONDON OXFORD NEW YORK NEW DELHI SYDNEY

Bloomsbury Publishing, London, Oxford, New York, New Delhi and Sydney

First published in Great Britain in October 2015 by Bloomsbury Publishing Plc
50 Bedford Square, London WC1B 3DP

First published in the USA in October 2015 by HarperCollins Children's Books,
A division of HarperCollins Publishers, 195 Broadway, New York, NY 10007

This paperback edition published July 2016

www.bloomsbury.com

Bloomsbury is a registered trademark of Bloomsbury Publishing Plc

Text copyright © Angie Sage 2015
Illustrations copyright © Mark Zug 2015

The moral rights of the author and illustrator have been asserted

A CIP catalogue record for this book is available from the British Library

ISBN 978 1 4088 6520 0

Printed and bound in Great Britain by CPI Group (UK) Ltd, Croydon CR0 4YY

1 3 5 7 9 10 8 6 4 2

*For Benjy Wishart*

# CONTENTS

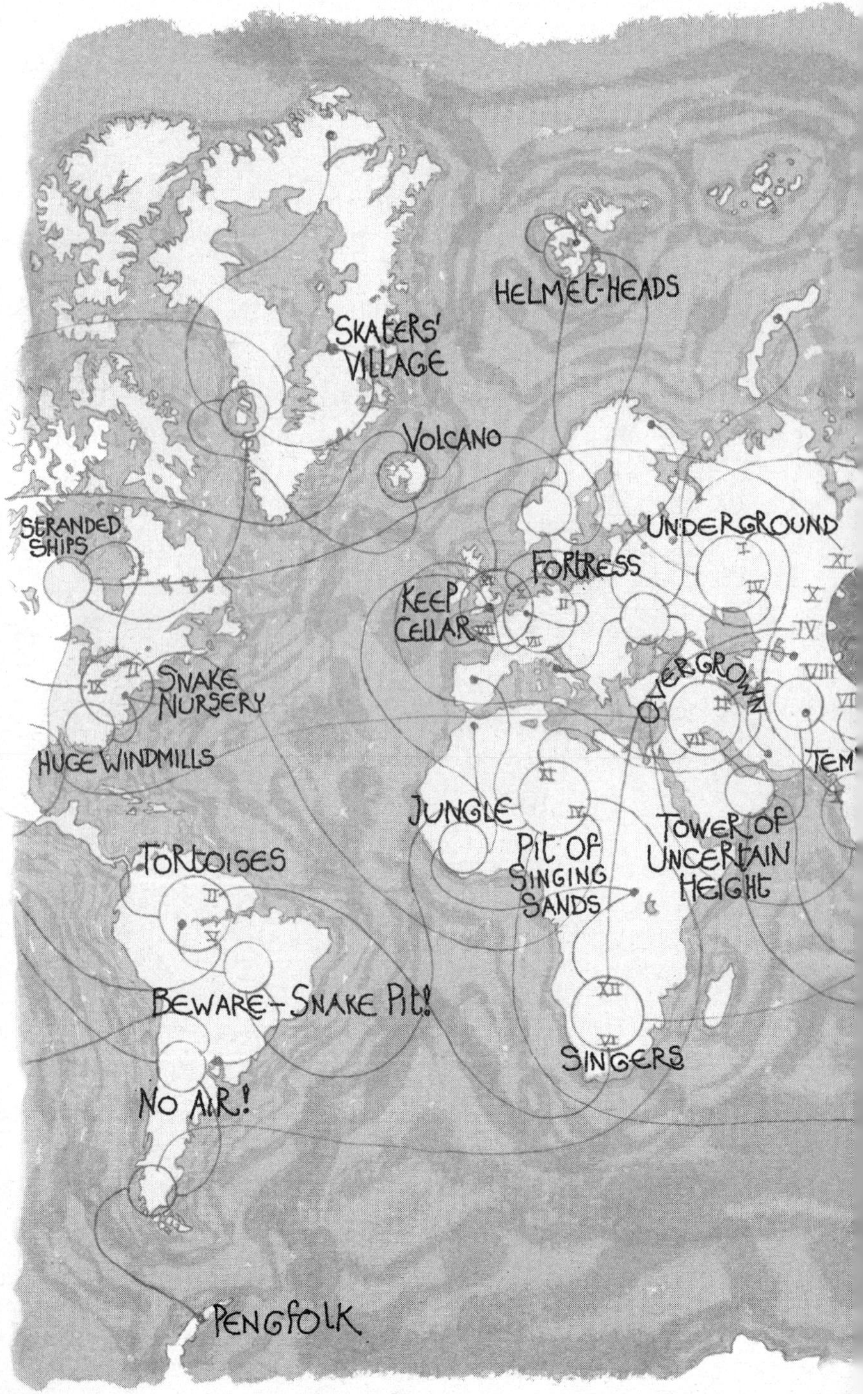

HELMET-HEADS
SKATERS' VILLAGE
VOLCANO
STRANDED SHIPS
UNDERGROUND
FORTRESS
KEEP CELLAR
SNAKE NURSERY
OVERGROWN
HUGE WINDMILLS
TEM
JUNGLE
TOWER OF UNCERTAIN HEIGHT
TORTOISES
PIT OF SINGING SANDS
BEWARE – SNAKE PIT!
SINGERS
NO AIR!
PENGFOLK

# MARWICK'S MAP
## OF THE
## ANCIENT WAYS

COMPASS DOESN'T WORK!

DEER TCH

SNOW & ICE

DEEP IN SAND

CAVERN

THE GREAT CLOCK

IND SENTINEL

MARKET PLACE

RAFT CITY

FLOODED

ISLANDS

PYRAMIDS

AVIARY

TEMPLE WITH PRIESTS EXPECTING GIFTS

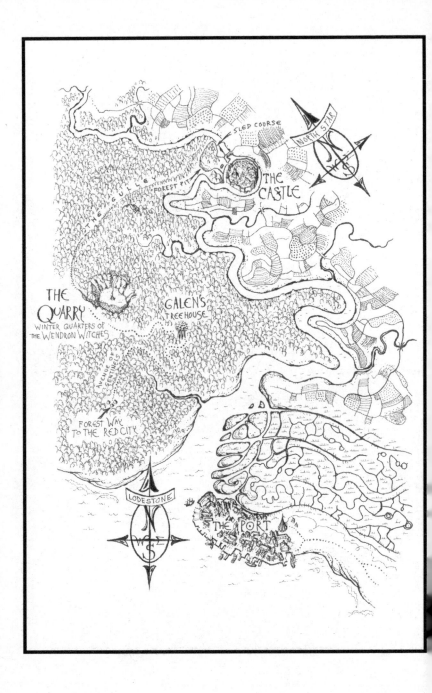

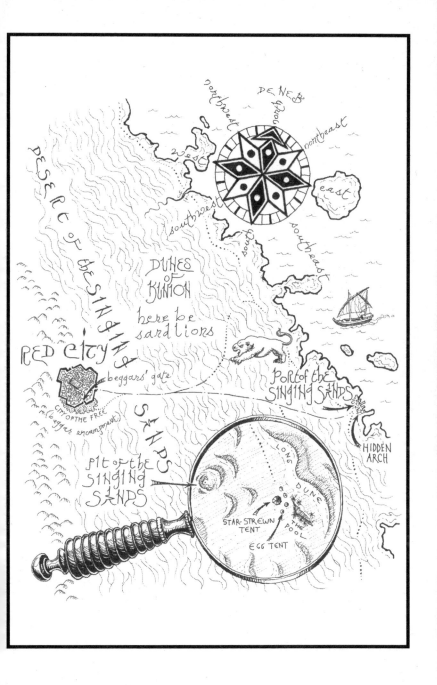

# THE GREEN SEAGULL

*A green dragon flew low across* the sea. Like a giant, infinitely annoying seagull, the dragon was following a beautiful blue-and-gold ship named the *Tristan*. Despite all manner of missiles hurled at him from the ship – including a large quantity of **Darke ThunderFlashes** – the dragon had not once lost sight of his quarry.

After long weeks at sea, the *Tristan* arrived at a small port on the edge of a vast desert. The dragon – much to the dismay of the Harbour Master – swooped in and landed on the roof of the tallest house on the quayside. Despite yet more missiles thrown at him (this time by the Harbour Master), the dragon did not move. He perched on the roof of the Harbour Master's house and continued to observe the *Tristan* with great interest.

"What's it watching for?" the Harbour Master asked anyone who was brave enough to come near. No one knew. Later, when someone told him that if you called a dragon by its name it would do whatever you desired, the Harbour Master asked, "What d'you think its name is?" No one knew that, either.

The dragon's name was Spit Fyre and he was watching for an Orm Egg. The final egg of the now extinct Great Orm, this was no ordinary egg. It was big enough to need carrying in both arms like a baby, it was heavy enough to make even the

3

strongest arms ache and it was covered in a leathery skin infused with brilliant blue lapis lazuli. Inside was an Orm embryo, the last of its race, stolen from its resting place in the Eastern SnowPlains by the sorcerer Oraton-Marr. Spit Fyre knew the Orm Egg was on board the *Tristan* and he was determined that wherever the egg went, he would go too.

The Orm Egg now rested on a soft blue cushion in the best cabin of the *Tristan*. Under Spit Fyre's relentless gaze, Oraton-Marr – a small man with short iron-grey hair – paced the deck above. He was accompanied by his sister, a large woman swathed in shining blue silk who was known to all as "the Lady". The Lady was an imposing figure. Despite her bulk, she moved smoothly along the deck, as though on little wheels. Her hair was bound in a blue cloth wrapped many times around her head, and on her hand perched a small, terrified bird, its leg tied to a wisp of silver chain that the Lady wore around her wrist. Behind the Lady, like a gloomy shadow, a square, flat-footed woman with the gait of an overweight duck followed. Her name was Mitza Draddenmora Draa; she kept a respectful distance but her narrowed eyes did not miss a thing.

The Lady was, to her brother's disgust, taller than he was. Usually the sorcerer wore spring blades upon his feet, which allowed him to tower over his sister, but after some undignified falls he had been forced to give them up on board the ship. The shorter version of Oraton-Marr and the Lady were discussing how to get the Orm Egg off the ship without Spit Fyre snatching it. The Lady had lapsed into bossy mode – which she always did when her brother was his natural height – but that afternoon the sorcerer was having none of it. He narrowed his dark green eyes and stared up at the dragon that had haunted them like a shadow through raging storms, blazing sun and starlit nights. "I shall set a trap," he said. "That dragon won't know what's hit him."

The next morning just before sunrise, Oraton-Marr dispatched half a dozen deckhands to hide on the quay in the shadows beneath the ship. All were brandishing nets and FireStix: long Darke spears with barbed ends of dull red metal – a weapon that the sorcerer had perfected during his time on board the *Tristan*. The barbs of FireStix were razor-sharp, designed to cut through dragon skin like a hot knife through butter, and then – Oraton-Marr was particularly proud of this – their sticky black tips were Primed to ignite on contact with dragon blood. The sorcerer looked up at Spit Fyre and smiled. The dragon would burst into flames, set alight from within. He was looking forward to that.

As the *Tristan* lay gleaming in the morning sun, from the top of the Harbour Master's roof – which was now sagging alarmingly – Spit Fyre eyed a shining lapis blue egg shape resting proudly on a soft blue cushion being escorted up on deck by two sailors in dress uniform. Spit Fyre's keen dragon eye also saw a movement in the shadows beneath the ship and the dull red glint of something sharp. He tilted his head to one side and considered the matter, watching as the cushion and its passenger were paraded down the gangplank. Spit Fyre gave a snort of contempt and turned his gaze back to the *Tristan*. He had no interest in an empty egg made from papier-mâché.

Despite the parading of the "egg" around the quay three times, Spit Fyre did not move. When Oraton-Marr realised his plan had not worked, he had a screaming fit and had to be calmed down by his sister. The "egg" and its cushion were abandoned in the middle of the quay and by evening had become a popular roost for gulls.

At the dark of the moon a few days later, Oraton–Marr tried another tactic. In the dead of the night, a rolled-up sail was taken down the gangplank by three deckhands. From his perch Spit Fyre watched with interest – he knew the Egg was nearby. The dragon gave a little jump of excitement and the Harbour Master's roof finally caved in. The three deckhands were so shocked by the snapping of timbers and the rain of falling roof tiles that they dropped the sail. Out rolled exactly what Spit Fyre had suspected: the true Egg of the Orm.

To the great dismay of the Customs Officer, Spit Fyre took up a new perch on the Customs House roof.

Oraton–Marr decided against a second screaming fit. Dragon or no dragon, he was not going to be thwarted a moment longer. He sent for a camel. Just before sunrise the next morning, the sorcerer shoved the Orm Egg unceremoniously into a sack and slung it into a bag on one side of the camel. Into the bag on the other side of the camel he put Subhan–Subhan, the cabin boy. Then, accompanied by his servant, Drone, and three deckhands armed with FireStix, he waved goodbye to his sister and her duck-footed companion, and climbed on to the camel.

To the relief of the Customs Officer, Spit Fyre took off from his roof.

Oraton–Marr headed out of the port. He ignored the long, straight road that led to the distant Red City just visible on the horizon, and set off into the wilderness of the vast desert of the Singing Sands. His navigator set a course for a small oasis and a star-strewn tent where an Apothecary and her two young daughters lived.

Spit Fyre followed, flying high enough to stay out of reach of the FireStix, but low enough to annoy.

When Oraton-Marr, bedraggled and sore, arrived at the star-strewn tent late that night, he never wanted to see a dragon or a camel again. Or a whingeing cabin boy or an egg. Or the three moaning deckhands. Or the craven Drone. But there was work to be done. Ruthlessly efficient, he took the Apothecary's baby daughter hostage and instructed the Apothecary on what to do if she wished to see the child again. He left before sunrise without the Egg, the cabin boy, the deckhands and, to his relief, the dragon. But he was stuck with Drone and a screaming toddler. And the camel.

Spit Fyre settled on a long sand dune above the star-strewn tent and the small encampment that had sprung up around it. As soon as Oraton-Marr was out of sight, the dragon attacked. He swooped down on to the tents and as the FireStix flew up towards him, he met fire with Fyre and destroyed them. But getting the Egg was not so easy. Subhan-Subhan was loyal to his Master and threw himself across the Egg as a shield so that Spit Fyre could not snatch his prize without injuring the boy.

Spit Fyre retired to the top of the dune to wait.

That evening as the sun set, the Apothecary climbed the dune and begged the dragon not to take the Egg. She told him that in twelve weeks the sorcerer would return, and if the Egg did not hatch – or there was no Egg to hatch – her baby daughter would die.

Spit Fyre bowed his head in defeat. But he did not leave his post. His time would come.

# THE COUNTDOWN BEGINS

*Oraton-Marr staggered up* the gangplank of the *Tristan* with Drone trailing behind carrying an exhausted toddler. The sorcerer instructed Drone to hand the hostage to his sister and went below to his cabin. He settled into his captain's chair, got up to fetch a cushion, sat down once more and took a mother-of-pearl box from a drawer in his desk. Inside the box was an assortment of origami shapes: birds, animals, ships and stars, all in pale blue. He picked out a paper flower, unfolded it, flattened it on his desk and smiled.

On one of his many walks around the quay trying to find a way to get rid of the dragon, Oraton-Marr had seen a flurry of pale blue papers blowing across the cobbles. He had picked them up because they were the perfect weight for his hobby of origami, and good paper was not easy to find. He had been very pleased with the quality of his beautiful blue paper, but was even more delighted when he had read the words upon it.

Once more, Oraton-Marr's mouth moved slowly across the words, savouring each one:

THE MAGYKAL MANUSCRIPTORIUM
AND SPELL CHECKERS INCORPORATED
NUMBER THIRTEEN WIZARD WAY, THE CASTLE.

As PREMIER ADVISORS TO THE FABLED WIZARD TOWER,
WE ARE PROUD TO OFFER A NEW GLOBAL SERVICE.
WE HAVE MANY THOUSANDS OF YEARS' EXPERIENCE.
WE CAN SOURCE MOST REQUIREMENTS.
WE HAVE AN EXTENSIVE STOCK OF
CHARMS, RUNES AND SPELL BOOKS
OR WE CAN REFURBISH YOUR OWN.
CONVENIENTLY SITUATED ON
THE ANCIENT WAY SYSTEM FOR
EASY ACCESS FROM ANYWHERE IN THE WORLD.

A smile spread across Oraton-Marr's thin lips as he thought about the "fabled Wizard Tower". The sorcerer took down his almanac, turned to the map section at the back and traced his long, pointy finger along the Ways that led to the Wizard Tower. Oraton-Marr was a great believer in signs and was convinced this perfect blue paper was the sign he had been waiting for – the Wizard Tower was his destiny. But the sorcerer was not a patient man. Drumming his fingers on his desk, he decided to get things moving as soon as he could. What he needed, he thought, was an Apprentice from the Wizard Tower. A senior one who knew all its secrets and fiddly little passwords would be ideal. Oraton-Marr smiled. There were twelve long weeks until the Orm Egg hatched, but he would spend his time well. He'd take a little trip to the Castle and get hold of an Apprentice so that when he was ready to take over, everything would go smoothly. Oraton-Marr sighed. He had had quite enough trouble already. He wanted to walk into the Wizard Tower with as little aggravation as possible.

The sorcerer closed his eyes and a strange name came to

him – ExtraOrdinary Wizard. He sat up, suddenly wide awake. *That was it.* That was the name of the top wizard in the Castle. He smiled. It suited him, there was no doubt about that: Oraton-Marr, ExtraOrdinary Wizard. He liked that. His face relaxed into a sickly, satisfied smile.

If it hadn't been for the Lady – annoyed by the crying of their tiny hostage – coming to tell him it was nearly midnight, Oraton-Marr would have missed the **Magykal** hour. Cursing, he rushed up on deck and sent a signal rocket burning brilliant green up into the sky.

★   ★   ★

Far away on his dune, Spit Fyre saw a green light on the horizon arc up over the sea. Also on the dune – at what he hoped was a safe distance from the dragon – was Subhan-Subhan, the cabin boy. Spit Fyre regarded the green sky-trail impassively, but the boy leaped to his feet and hurtled down to the encampment in a shower of sand. At the foot of the dune Subhan-Subhan threw the Egg of the Orm into a roaring fire to kick-start its incubation. As the Egg lay untouched within the flames, he took a small gold box from his pocket and from it he removed a tiny gold **Egg Timer**, of which one half was filled with minute grains of silver. Subhan-Subhan pressed his thumb on to the top of the timer and watched the first speck of silver fall through.

On board the *Tristan*, Oraton-Marr set his own identical **Egg Timer** running. The countdown had begun.

# PART II

NINETY-SIX
HOURS TO
HATCHING

# DRAGON WATCH

*It was just before dawn,* and Spit Fyre was on edge. This was the time when, in the dragon's experience, humans did secret things. From the top of his dune, Spit Fyre had a magnificent view. To the west, a gibbous moon was travelling through the star-dusted indigo sky, dropping slowly to Earth to meet the white ribbon of ocean that glimmered along the horizon. Silhouetted in the moonlight were the squat, square shapes of the port where, some twelve weeks ago, he had made landfall.

To the east, Spit Fyre saw the darkness of a vast, unpeopled desert. He knew that just over the horizon – for he had seen it as he had flown into the port – lay a sprawling city of red stone. A faint glow rose up from it, which at this time of night could easily be mistaken for the sunrise.

But Spit Fyre was not on his dune to enjoy the view. He was there to guard the Egg of the Orm – the egg that he had watched his Imprintor, Septimus Heap, pursue only to be struck down by a Darke Dart for his trouble. Spit Fyre had no doubt that Septimus would return for the Egg, and when he did Spit Fyre was determined that Septimus would find his dragon waiting. Over the long weeks of watching, Spit Fyre had gradually entered a trancelike state. He had stopped moving, eating or drinking. His scales had become roughened by the

13

sun and caked with sand, and it was now the opinion of those in the camp below that Oraton-Marr had turned him to stone. This suited Spit Fyre well. He would move when the time was right – and not before. It amused him to sit motionless while the occasional brave visitor wandered up to stare at him or even dared to pat his sandy scales. He had been less amused by one of the deckhands poking his belly with a stick, but Spit Fyre had restrained himself. Only his red-ringed, emerald-green eyes moved – and then only when he was sure no one was looking.

The dragon's eyes now surveyed the encampment below, lying in the moon shadow of the dune. It was inhabited by the usual range of humans: some good, some bad and some who hadn't yet made their minds up which to be. The humans lay sleeping in a motley collection of tents. In the centre was a large, circular tent of faded blue covered in silver stars. Like planets orbiting the sun, a scattering of smaller tents was ranged around it, dark colours all bar one, which was white and round like the moon. A well-trodden path led from the tents to a dark pool of water that welled up from a spring in the rocks deep below. In it the dragon saw the reflection of the stars, glittering silver in deep black. Beside the pool were a small vegetable patch, two olive trees, soft succulents and a broad, flat slab of rock where clothes were laid to dry.

Spit Fyre turned his gaze to the moon tent in which he knew lay the Egg of the Orm, accompanied by Mysor, the Apothecary's Apprentice, and Subhan-Subhan, who was known by all as the Egg Boy. The Egg now spent the day covered in hot sand, being turned every hour by the Egg Boy. At night the white tent was erected over the Egg, and Subhan-Subhan wrapped the Egg in furs and slept beside it, conserving its

14

heat, guarding the Egg with his life and – with the help of Mysor – waking to turn it every third hour, until the day it hatched. Only the Egg Boy and Oraton-Marr with their synchronised **Egg Timers** knew when this day would be. Even the occupant of the Egg was not entirely sure, although it was beginning to feel a strange restlessness.

That night, after its midnight turn, the Orm embryo had added another fold to its flat little brain and it now felt an itch on the end of its stumpy snout where the egg tooth was beginning to break through its skin. It would not be long now.

Outside, the desert air held its breath and Spit Fyre watched, still as stone.

# KAZNIM NA-DRAA

*Inside the star tent* the stillness was broken by the gentle rise and fall of a large mound of furs, beneath which Karamander Draa, the Apothecary, was sleeping. The only other occupant, the Apothecary's elder daughter, Kaznim Na-Draa, lay wide awake. Her gaze wandered around the peaceful space she knew as home. A single candle burned in a dish of scented water set in the middle of the rug-strewn floor. Its soft light showed books piled along the sides of the tent, a scattering of cushions around a low table on which a bowl of dates and a jug were set ready for breakfast. The jewel-like glass of blue and green potion bottles in neatly stacked boxes near the door glinted in the light of the steady flame and looked just like the jelly sweets from the Red City that Kaznim loved so much. She watched her mother's soft breathing for a while but avoided looking at the empty cot set at the foot of her mother's bed. Whenever she thought about her half-sister, Bubba, Kaznim felt as though she had swallowed a small cactus. It *hurt*.

After some minutes gathering her courage, Kaznim sat up, and, with several covert glances at her mother to check that she was still sleeping, she dressed quietly.

As a sliver of orange sun tipped above the distant horizon, Spit Fyre saw a movement in the wall of the star-strewn tent.

He saw a small, dark-haired girl in a long red coat wriggling out from underneath the canvas and hopping awkwardly as she pulled on a pair of leather sandals. She set off towards the Egg tent, stopped outside and stood with her head tilted in thought. She slipped off her sandals and then, to the dragon's surprise, she simply faded away. Spit Fyre blinked, wondering if he had just woken from a dream. But the sandals outside the tent told him otherwise.

In her hand Kaznim clutched the UnSeen Charm that the sorcerer who had brought the Egg and stolen her little sister had given her. It was beautifully wrapped inside a pale blue origami bird so that the opal pebble Charm formed the fat little belly of the bird. Kaznim loved the bird almost more than the Charm, even though she knew the sorcerer had made the bird himself with his own long, thin fingers and sharp, pointed nails. Kaznim knew it was a bribe to get her to spy on her mother. There was no way she would *ever* do that, but even so, she had accepted it because she had loved the little blue bird so much. Kaznim remembered how the sorcerer had presented it to her with the words: "For you, my dear. You can hide from anyone with this – except from *me*." She had taken the bird and stuffed it deep into her pocket where her mother would never find it.

Kaznim was looking for her tortoise. The Egg Boy had stolen it – she *knew* he had. She did not hold out much hope of finding the tortoise in the Egg tent, but she had to check. Kaznim stood UnSeen in the dim hush of the tent and listened to the Egg Boy's snuffles and the slow breathing of the Apprentice. She had never been inside the Egg tent before. Subhan-Subhan had sneeringly said that girls were bad luck inside a hatching tent and besides, her terrified mother had forbidden her from going in.

Now that she was inside, Kaznim did not see what all the fuss was about. The tent was hot and stuffy in order to keep the Egg warm through the cold desert night. All she could see of the Egg was a bump covered in a black fur with the Egg Boy curled around it like a fat white maggot. Her mother's apprentice, Mysor – whose thankless task was to wake the Egg Boy every three hours and bring him anything he wanted whenever he wanted it – was hidden beneath a pile of thick blankets beside the door. Kaznim tiptoed past him and looked at the fur pelt that covered the Egg. She longed to lift it and see the beautiful gold-streaked blue of the Egg's lapis skin, but she did not dare. She reminded herself that she had come for her tortoise, nothing else.

Kaznim dropped to her hands and knees and crawled across the rugs, patting them gently to see if there were any tortoise-shaped lumps. As she had expected, there were none. She got slowly to her feet and looked down at the Egg Boy, thinking that no one would ever guess how spiteful he was when he was awake. As if aware that he was being watched, the Egg Boy stirred and Kaznim stepped hurriedly back – on to something hard. She nearly screamed – *she had trodden on her tortoise.*

Kaznim dropped to her knees with a soft thump and Mysor opened his eyes. She froze, hoping that her UnSeen was still working. Mysor stared straight at her and did not react. Kaznim shivered; it was a strange feeling to have someone look through you. She waited until Mysor closed his eyes again and then, terrified of finding a crushed tortoise, she gingerly pushed her hand beneath the rug towards the lump, which was worryingly flat. Her fingers closed around something cold and sharp-edged, and she pulled out a beautiful gold box. Kaznim smiled with relief – it was not a squashed tortoise. The Egg Boy mumbled something in his sleep and Kaznim hurriedly shoved the box into the pocket of her tunic and slipped out of the tent. It served the Egg Boy right, she thought. She *knew* he had taken her tortoise, and so she would take his precious box.

Spit Fyre saw a square of gold float out of the tent and then one of the sandals rise into the air, quickly followed by the other. He watched the sandals walk away as if they had got tired of waiting for their owner, while a lone golden box hovered above them. The dragon closed his eyes for a few seconds and when he opened them the girl had appeared. The sandals were now covered by her feet and the gold box was hidden in a pocket in her long red coat. Spit Fyre watched the small, slight figure walk away from the encampment and head out into the emptiness of the desert and the sunrise beyond.

# TORTOISE HUNT

*Kaznim hurried on, looking* carefully for any telltale mounds of sand, which the long, slanting shadows of the sunrise would show. "Ptolemy ..." she whispered, pronouncing her tortoise's name: *Tollemy*. "Ptolemy, where are you?" Kaznim knew she had to be very alert to have any chance of finding the tortoise. Ptolemy was not big – he fitted comfortably in two cupped hands – and he moved fast. Once the sun had warmed the sand he would be awake and off for another day's hike. By the end of the day he would be miles away and lost for ever.

Kaznim had looked for the tortoise all the previous afternoon, but when at dusk she had returned tortoise-less to find the Egg Boy putting up the Egg tent for the night, his smirk told her that he had something to do with Ptolemy's disappearance. When Kaznim accused him of stealing her tortoise he had told her that that he had seen Ptolemy out by "the singing pit". Kaznim knew at once that the only reason Ptolemy would be so far away and in such a dangerous place was if Subhan-Subhan had actually taken him there. Or was the Egg Boy bluffing – was it a ruse to get her trapped in the sinking sands of the Pit of the Singing Sands? Either way there had been nothing she could do that evening. By now the tortoise would, in his own small way, be doing the same thing as the setting sun – digging himself into the sand for the night. She would never find him, and besides, it was far too dangerous with the sand lions waking for their night-time hunting. All Kaznim could do was to retreat into the star tent and plan Ptolemy's rescue and her revenge.

And now, she thought as her hand closed around the gold box, she had her revenge. Now the Egg Boy, too, would know how it felt to lose something precious. It served him right.

Kaznim walked quickly across the sand, leaving an unwavering line of footprints in her wake. On the far horizon she saw tall dunes rising like a swelling sea before a storm, dark against the strip of bright dawn sky. A little spooked by the vastness that lay before her, Kaznim turned to look back at her tent and saw the first rays of the rising sun catch its silver stars, sending them shimmering against the faded blue. She caught her breath. Her home looked beautiful. She thought of the hateful Egg Boy and she wished the Egg would hurry up and hatch so that her little sister would return and he would go away and leave her in peace with her mother, her tortoise, Bubba and Mysor.

Kaznim thought of her mother asleep in her bed of furs. She had left a note using the name she called her mother when no one was listening:

*Dear Ammaa,*
*I have gone to find my tortoise. I will be home soon.*
*Your daughter,*
*Kaznim*

Kaznim hoped that she would be back with her tortoise well before Ammaa read it. Ever since Bubba had been taken, her mother panicked if Kaznim went anywhere on her own.

The sun was rising fast now and Kaznim broke into a run. She knew she must reach the Pit of the Singing Sands before the warmth of the sun woke Ptolemy. The tortoise moved surprisingly fast, and soon he would look like just another distant rock shimmering in the heat haze. Ten minutes later, Kaznim had reached the pit. Once again, she looked back at the star tent; it seemed so far away that she felt a twinge of homesickness. She longed to be pulling back the door hangings, stepping into its cool shadows with her tortoise in her arms. *But first, Kaznim,* she told herself firmly, *you have to find him.*

# THE PIT OF THE SINGING SANDS

*The Pit of the Singing Sands* was a large circle of unstable sand – a treacherous place where no one trod for fear of falling through to who knew where. But the early morning sun made it relatively safe, for the slanting shadows showed where the solid ground beneath the sand abruptly stopped. That morning, the circle of the sand inside was quite a few inches lower than the solid rim and as Kaznim looked at it – hoping that Ptolemy had not decided to bed down there for the night – she saw the grains undulating as though some great beast was stirring below. It took all Kaznim's courage not to turn and run for the safety of the star tent. Heart pounding, she stood back from the edge and scanned the sand, watching for the telltale upwards push of sand that would herald a tortoise greeting a new day.

A sudden flurry no more than a few feet away caught Kaznim's eye and her heart leaped – *something in the Pit was moving*. A waft of fine dust puffed up into the gentle morning breeze and landed softly. There was another, more purposeful movement and at last Kaznim saw what she had been waiting for. A scaly, flat brown head with a perfectly round, bright black eye poked up from the white sand.

"Ptolemy!" Kaznim called out with relief.

Slow and deliberate in the cool of the morning, the tortoise pushed his way up and sat blinking in the sunlight. Kaznim squatted down and held out a small sliver of coconut, which she knew Ptolemy could not resist. "Ptolemy," she whispered encouragingly. "Ptolemy, come here. Come on, Ptolemy. Over here."

The tortoise stuck his head out and regarded Kaznim with a quizzical air. Then, very deliberately, he turned and stomped away – further into the circle.

Kaznim jumped up in frustration. "Ptolemy!" she called out. "This way. *Ptolemy!*" But the tortoise continued his onward trundle.

Carefully keeping firm sand below her feet, Kaznim circled the pit, heading for the other side, towards which Ptolemy was advancing at some speed. Tortoise and girl were converging when the singing began. A high-pitched keen drifted out of the pit: *"Aaaaaiiiiiiiiiiiaaaaaaaeeeeeeeee ..."* And like dancers whose tune had at last begun, the grains of sand on the top began to swirl.

Kaznim stopped dead. The hairs on the back of her neck rose. Late-night campfire stories of nightmare creatures emerging from the pit came back to her, and had it not been for Ptolemy, she would have turned and run. But the tortoise was still doggedly making its way to the edge of the pit. And so, going against all her instincts, Kaznim ran towards the Pit of the Singing Sands – away from her home, away from the place where she was safe, towards danger. She was not leaving without that stupid, pig-headed tortoise.

Dust rose in a fine mist, catching in her throat. Kaznim wound her long red cotton scarf around her mouth and nose, and crouching on the very edge of the firm sand, she willed Ptolemy to speed up and get near enough for her to reach.

The tortoise was almost there when he suddenly dropped, as if into a hole. It was no more than a few inches down, but it spooked him. He pulled in his head and feet and sat like a stubborn rock. Desperately, Kaznim threw the piece of coconut at him. Its only effect was to make the tortoise gather himself more tightly into his shell. A soft *sussssisssisssssisssussssisss* of sand began and to her horror Kaznim saw the sand within the pit begin to slowly swirl, like water going down a drain. Ptolemy began to sink.

Kaznim could bear it no longer. She threw herself forward as though she were diving for a ball. She sank deep into the soft sand but her outstretched hands caught hold of Ptolemy's cool, hard shell and did not let go. Snakelike, Kaznim began to shuffle backwards towards the safety of the edge of the pit, but as her feet touched the rim, the sand shifted beneath her and became as thin as water. Kaznim tumbled down, down, down through the sand, into the depths of the Pit of the Singing Sands.

# THE APOTHECARY'S TENT

*The Apothecary was woken* by the *Aaaaaiiiiiiiiiiiaaaaaaaeeeee-eee* ...
of the singing sands. She sat up fast, convinced that a
mischievous Sand Spirit had slipped into the tent. But as the
traces of sleep left her, Karamander Draa realised that this was
no Spirit. She had heard the sands once before and knew what
she must do – keep still and silent so that whatever emerged
from the pit heard no sign of human life.

"Kaznim," she whispered across to the mound of blankets
piled on to her daughter's bed. "Do not be afraid. Keep very
quiet. Lie still. It will soon pass." The blankets stayed obediently
quiet and still. A soft smile touched the Apothecary's face.
Kaznim was so brave, so calm in the face of danger – no one
would know she was there.

Some ten minutes later the wailing of the sands at last
subsided. "Kaznim," Karamander whispered in a low voice.
"All is well. You can come out of your burrow now."

But Kaznim's burrow was unresponsive. A worm of worry
twisted in Karamander's stomach – the bedclothes looked
wrong somehow. She got up and began to walk over to her
daughter's bed. By the time she was halfway across the rug-
strewn floor, Karamander was running. She already knew the
truth – *Kaznim was not there.*

"Kaznim! Kaznim!" Karamander pulled the blankets from the bed, threw them to the floor and raced to the door. With trembling hands she unlaced the door flap and stumbled outside into the early morning sun. Karamander ran from tent to tent, throwing open the door flaps, shouting for her daughter. She left the Egg tent until last.

Two figures, bleary in the stuffy atmosphere, sat up. "Wharr?" asked Mysor, his husky voice breaking as he spoke. The smaller figure jumped up guiltily. Mistakenly thinking he had overslept and was late for the first turn of the day, Subhan-Subhan leaned against the Egg and expertly twisted it through a quarter-turn.

"Mysor!" Karamander barked. "Out! Now!"

In seconds the dishevelled Apothecary Apprentice was blinking in the sunlight. Mysor was thin and tall with short, dark curly hair, clear blue eyes and a dislike for waking up.

"Kaznim's gone," Karamander said. "I need help."

Mysor was suddenly wide awake. "Gone?" he asked. "Where?"

"I don't *know* where she's gone," Karamander said desperately. "But the pit was singing."

"Oh." Now Mysor was as worried as his Master.

Karamander began to run. Her long red nightgown flowed out as her bare feet sped across the sand, heading towards the distant dust cloud that hung over the Pit of the Singing Sands. Mysor's long stride caught up with her easily. "Stop!" he said, in a commanding voice that surprised himself as much as Karamander. "I ask pardon, Apothecary. But we must be mindful. The desert gives signs to those who look. But they do not last long. Let us pause a moment and observe."

Karamander regarded her Apprentice with something near respect. "Yes. Yes, of course. You are right. Tracks. There will be tracks."

Mysor half closed his eyes and moved his head from side to side, scanning the sand. It was an old desert trick, designed to blur out the detail and show the structure below. Beneath the freshly blown sand he saw the ghost of a long, straight trail of footprints heading for the pit. He looked at the Apothecary. She had seen them too.

"So. She went to the pit," Karamander said flatly. She shaded her eyes against the glare. Beyond the dust cloud she saw nothing but empty sands. Her daughter had vanished. "But why? Why would she go there, of all places?"

"I ... I don't know." Mysor was not one to tell tales, but he knew that yesterday, Subhan-Subhan had walked to the pit. He had been up to something, Mysor was sure of that. Karamander followed his glance back to the Egg tent.

"If that brat has done anything to my daughter, I will ..." She trailed off, knowing she was powerless. The safety of her other daughter depended on the Egg Boy doing his job properly, and Karamander dared do nothing to jeopardise the hatching of the tyrannical Egg. With heavy hearts, Karamander and Mysor followed Kaznim's footprints as they headed towards the Pit of the Singing Sands. They both knew they were walking into emptiness.

Far behind them, a pale moon-face peered out from the Egg tent. The Egg Boy smiled. Stupid tortoise, he thought – so easy to take to the pit and toss in. And stupid girl, too – so easy to fool. The Egg Boy slipped back into the stifling heat of the tent and went over to the beautiful lapis-blue egg that only he, Subhan-Subhan, long-lost son of a tribe of Orm keepers, had the skills to incubate. At least, that was what the sorcerer had told him, and he believed it, even if no one else did. Subhan ran his hand over the Egg's smooth, warm surface. He was glad that the annoying girl would never see it hatch. She did not deserve to be in the presence of a Great Orm. He wondered how the little Orm inside would be changing today and reached beneath the rug to find his precious box.

*It was not there.*

Five minutes later all the rugs were heaped outside the Egg tent and Subhan was scrabbling frantically in the sandy floor. *Where was the Egg Box?*

On the edge of the Pit of the Singing Sands, Karamander Draa stared at the abrupt end of her daughter's faint, wind-blown tracks. She gazed at the mass of soft sand and the dust cloud hanging over it that they led into. There were no tracks leading away from the Pit, and the desert beyond was empty. There was no doubt about it. The Pit had taken her daughter.

Mysor waited silently while Karamander turned and gazed back at Kaznim's footprints, which walked towards her from the tent. He saw her watching them grow ever fainter as the early morning breeze blew away the last precious echoes of her child. When the footprints were gone, Karamander slumped to the ground and broke into cries so loud that even in the midst of his panic, Subhan-Subhan had to stuff his fingers into his ears.

# PTOLEMY

*Ptolemy was not as stupid* as Subhan-Subhan thought. From the
moment the Egg Boy had snatched him from his favourite
patch of milk thistle and thrown him up into the air like a ball,
the tortoise had understood that the boy wished him ill. And
when the boy had shoved him into his pocket – during which
Ptolemy had had the satisfaction of biting his finger – the
tortoise knew that something bad was going to happen. He
heard Subhan-Subhan check that Kaznim was still busy at her
lessons and then felt him hurrying away from the encampment.
Tortoises have been around long enough to understand that
not all human beings are well intentioned, and Ptolemy also
knew that human beings find tortoises very good to eat,
especially when cooked slowly in a deep sand oven. He knew
that Subhan-Subhan was always hungry, and the tortoise
gloomily expected this was going to be his fate. When at last
Subhan-Subhan took him out of his sticky pocket, Ptolemy
sighed and the air whistled into his nostrils like a tiny desert
squall. So when he had found himself flying through the air
once more and heading downwards towards the Pit of the
Singing Sands, the tortoise felt a sense of relief. He landed hard
and sank deep into the loose sand. By the time he had worked
his way up to the surface, his tormentor was gone and the sun

was sinking fast towards the horizon. Ptolemy decided to stay put for the night. He buried himself so that he was hidden from the night eagles (whose joy was to snatch up a tortoise, fly high into the air with it and drop it from a great height on to a rock) and settled down to sleep. He would set off back to the star tent as soon as the sun rose.

When Ptolemy awoke the next morning he saw Kaznim hovering beside the circle of treacherous sand. Ptolemy understood that the pit was dangerous for humans and he had tried to lead her away from the edge. He had very nearly succeeded, but humans do not have the patience of a tortoise. They are new and quick and the young ones in particular seem to act without any thought. And so, when the sands began to move and Kaznim jumped into them to rescue him, Ptolemy was not surprised. But he doubted it would do either of them any good.

Ptolemy felt Kaznim's hands close around his shell; he sensed their warmth and their strength — so different from the Egg Boy's spiteful grasp — and he felt safe. But it was short-lived. As tortoise and girl tumbled down through the sand, grit and the dust filled their ears, eyes and noses, and they began to choke.

Kaznim was too pleased to have her tortoise in her arms to realise her danger, and by the time she did, they had crashed to the ground. Kaznim pulled the tortoise close and rolled with the fall, just as she practised in her dune-diving lessons. But the sand that had spiralled up and opened to let them fall was now coming back to earth, and the cloud was getting so thick that Kaznim knew that soon she would no longer be able to breathe. She staggered to her feet, tucked the tortoise under her arm and pushed her way through the falling sand. She thought she could see the shape of an archway ahead. If only she could reach that, she would be out of this falling thickness; she would be able to breathe again.

But her breath was full of dust, her nose plugged with sand. Her head felt light and sparkles began to dance before her eyes. Kaznim knew she was about to pass out. And when she did, the sand would bury her and Ptolemy and they would be dead – and what would Ammaa do then? Kaznim took one last sand-filled breath and staggered towards the arch. Suddenly she saw two shadows appear. Four arms reached out, took hold of her and swept Kaznim and her tortoise into the darkness.

# MARWICK AND SAM

*Kaznim had the strangest sensation* of travelling at breakneck speed. For a moment she thought that she and Ptolemy had fallen into another pit, and she braced herself for the landing. But the strong arms still held her tight and Kaznim realised that she was not falling, but moving rapidly forward. She began to slow down, and moments later, she was in a tunnel walking towards dappled green light framed by the shape of an archway. The arms still held her tightly and Kaznim risked a glance at her captors. She saw two young men towering over her: one with dark matted hair and a wild look in his eyes; one – whose grip, Kaznim noticed, was much weaker – had fair, tangled curls and a deathly pallor to his skin.

Kaznim had heard many stories of desert children being taken for slaves, and her fear of falling was quickly replaced by the fear that she had been kidnapped. She readied herself to make a break for it as soon as she could. As they emerged into a circular garden with arches in its walls, the young men let go of her arms. Immediately Kaznim shot off, heading towards another arch.

"Hey!" yelled the young man with the matted hair. "Not that one! Jeez!" He raced after her and the next thing Kaznim knew, there was a hand snatching the back of her tunic and pulling her away. Kaznim kicked out. They weren't going to get her that easily.

"Whoa!" said her captor. "Ouch! Steady on. I'm only trying to help." There was something about the voice that made Kaznim stop struggling. It sounded genuine, like Mysor did when he was explaining something.

"Hey, that's better. If you run into that one you'll end up somewhere not nice at all. Here, sit down. You look rough, kiddo."

Kaznim thought the young man looked pretty rough himself. His clothes were bloodstained, ragged and filthy, but his brown eyes seemed friendly and she allowed herself to be led to a patch of soft grass where the other young man was already slumped. He did not look good. His tangled, straw-coloured curly hair was sticky with blood; his wispy beard was full of grit, but even so his bright green eyes had a faint smile in them. His companion hung back a little now, his dark brown eyes flicking to and fro restlessly, checking out the arches as if he were on guard. Both young men looked as though they had been in a fight and now Kaznim saw that the fair-haired one had a wide, heavily bloodstained bandage wrapped around his middle and a long gash on the outside of his right arm, which was bound with strips of twine, as if to keep the edges together. The dark-haired one seemed to have fared better. His face was bruised and there was blood on his tunic, but he had no dramatic bandages.

"You're hurt," Kaznim said shyly to the fair-haired young man.

He nodded and winced in pain at the movement.

"Would you like my tortoise?" she asked.

The young man managed a wan smile and slowly shook his head.

Kaznim did not feel brave enough to explain about Ptolemy. She put the tortoise down on the grass and all three fell silent as they watched him slowly uncurl and poke his head out into the sun.

Kaznim began to relax and take in her surroundings. The garden had obviously been neglected for many years, for it was very overgrown with creepers climbing up the walls and long, rough grass sprouting up from what was once thick paving. The walls rose high – about twenty feet – into the air and within them were many more arches like the one they had come out of, each with one or two letters inscribed into its keystone. Kaznim counted twelve altogether. It was a beautiful, peaceful place and had the air of somewhere that had once been much loved. The only slightly disconcerting thing was a regular rumble that came up through the ground every few seconds. It felt to Kaznim as though a great monster were breathing beneath them. But the breath was slow, so, she told herself, the monster must be sleeping.

In the middle of the circular garden was a small spring. It bubbled up into an old copper bowl around which were paving stones worn smooth by centuries of footfall. Kaznim was watching the dark-haired young man kneel down at the spring and fill a battered metal bottle with cool water, when suddenly a husky voice spoke beside her.

"Nice tortoise."

"He is called Ptolemy," Kaznim said.

"Good name ... for a ... tortoise. I'm ... Sam. Heap."

"Hello, Sam Heap," Kaznim said, slowly trying out the unfamiliar words.

"And I am called Marwick," said the young man with the water bottle, joining them.

"I am Kaznim Na-Draa." Kaznim smiled. She remembered how her mother would always tell her to make polite conversation after being introduced to people, but all she could think of to say was, "Where are we?"

"Good question," Marwick said. "Right now, I have no idea." He pulled a flimsy, much-folded piece of paper from his tunic and spread it out upon the blanket. On it was drawn a network of fine lines and tiny circles that made no sense at all to Kaznim. Marwick stabbed a long, dirty finger with a bloodied knuckle on to one of the circles. "We are here, I think," he said.

Kaznim peered at the paper. "But where is that?" she asked. "Where in the world, I mean."

"A small island far off the long coast of the Blue Mountains," Marwick said. "With any luck." He looked at Sam. "And if it is, there's no way they can get us."

Sam grimaced. "Let's hope ... not," he murmured.

Kaznim was puzzled. "But how can we be on an island?" she asked. "We haven't gone across the sea."

Marwick smiled. "Ah," he said. "But we have. We have travelled through an Ancient Way. You see, Kaznim, the Ancient Ways are –" The cry of a gull broke into Marwick's explanation, and he grinned. "Looks like I'm right, Sammo," he said. "And listen ... I can hear ... Yes, I can hear surf."

"What is surf?" Kaznim asked.

"It is the waves of the sea pounding on a beach," Marwick told her.

Kaznim now understood what the sleeping monster really was. She took a deep breath in and realised she tasted salt. Suddenly she felt a long way from home. She thought of her mother waking up to find she was not in her bed – which would, she thought, be happening just about *now*. Kaznim thought of Ammaa staring at *two* empty beds with both her daughters gone, and she could not bear to stay in the garden a moment longer. She snatched up Ptolemy – much to the tortoise's disgust, for he was halfway through a tasty yellow flower – and jumped to her feet. "Sam Heap and Marwick, thank you very much for rescuing me," Kaznim said rather formally. "I would like to go home now. I would be very grateful if you could show me which Ancient Way to take."

Sam's and Marwick's expressions told Kaznim that she had not asked for something easy. Or even possible. Marwick got to his feet. "I'm sorry, Kaznim," he said. "But you came through what we call an unstable Hub."

Kaznim frowned. "A what?" she asked.

Marwick waved his arm around their sunken garden. "This," he said, "is a stable Hub. It is in a place where people may come and go at all times. But not all are like this. Some Hubs have sunk beneath the ocean. Some are ice-bound, some are deep in snow and some, like yours, are full of sand. Of course, Hubs of ice or in the ocean can never be used, but those full of sand or snow will, in a wild Way wind, occasionally clear. But they soon fill up again. The Hub you fell into is an especially deep one. There is no way we can get back up through all that sand." Marwick shook his head. "No way at all."

Kaznim stared at him, trying to understand. "You mean I can't go home?"

"Well, of course you can go home. But we would have to figure out which Hub is nearest to you, and then you could travel overland from there. Where do you live, Kaznim?"

"In the star tent beside the Moon Pool, beneath the long dune."

Marwick looked puzzled. "So, where's that?" he asked.

"Um. In the desert," said Kaznim. "The Desert of the Singing Sands."

"OK … and whereabouts is that?"

Kaznim shook her head. "I … I don't know."

# GOING HOME

*Kaznim sat clutching Ptolemy tightly.* The tortoise's sharp-clawed legs churned powerfully against her stomach, but Kaznim took no notice. She was desolate – and mortified. How could she *not* know where she lived? What a baby she was. She had spent all her life that she could remember in the star-spangled tent at the foot of the long dune but she had no idea where in the world it was. Kaznim looked down at Ptolemy, who had now withdrawn peevishly into his shell. *It's all right for you,* she thought. *You have your home with you. I've lost mine. And I have* no *idea* how to find it.

Sam watched the tears spring into Kaznim's eyes – such a dark blue that they were nearly purple – and he sat up and put his good arm around her slight shoulders. She reminded him of his little sister at that age. "Don't worry," he said. "Me … and Marwick will look after you. We're … trying to find our way home too."

Kaznim was shocked. "Don't you know where you live either?" she asked Sam.

Sam lay back, exhausted by his effort. Marwick looked at him with concern.

"I'm OK," said Sam.

"No, you're not," Marwick retorted. "You need to rest,

Sammo." He turned to Kaznim. "We're like you," he said. "We know where we live, but we're not sure how to get there. We got lost a few years ago now."

*"Years?"* asked Kaznim, dismayed. It seemed that Sam and Marwick were as silly as she was. The thought that it might be years before she saw her mother again made the tears silently overflow and run down her cheeks.

"But it's only been years because we got stuck in a prison," Marwick explained hurriedly.

Kaznim stared at Marwick. "In *prison*?"

Marwick grinned. "Hey, don't worry, you're not stuck with a couple of murderers. We were prisoners of war. Got caught up in someone's battle. Never did understand what it was about, did we, Sam?"

"Nah," Sam muttered. "They were both ... as bad as each other."

"They were," Marwick agreed. "But it didn't help when you told them that."

Sam looked sheepish.

Kaznim smiled shyly. "It's good they let you go," she said.

Marwick grimaced. "They didn't. We escaped. Had a bit of a fight on the way out." He changed the subject. "Right, we need to get Sammo home. Let's have a proper look at that map."

Ptolemy stuck his two back legs hard into Kaznim's stomach. "Ouch!" she gasped, and put the tortoise back among the yellow flowers.

Marwick laid his flimsy map on the grass in front of Kaznim, then pulled a very battered, small notebook from his pocket and opened it. Kaznim saw that it was full of lists of letters, rather like the ones inscribed above the arches that led from the garden. She watched Marwick trace his finger along the lines on the map, stopping at each circle and writing down a number in his notebook. At last, when the list seemed very long, he stopped, sat up and said to Sam, "Fifteen Hubs. Can't do it in any less, Sammo. Sorry."

"No ... problem," Sam said.

Marwick frowned. Kaznim could see he thought fifteen Hubs *was* a problem. She guessed it meant that Sam would have to walk a long way. Marwick turned to her and said, "We're going back to the Castle. Sam needs to get proper help, fast." Kaznim nodded. She understood that. "Someone there will be sure to know where your home is," Marwick said. "And when we find out, I'll take you there. That's a promise, OK?"

Kaznim smiled. Marwick was a good person, she thought. If the Castle was full of people as nice as Marwick, it would be a lovely place to visit – but another time. Right now all she wanted to do was to get back home to her mother. She couldn't bear to think how upset she must be. "How long will it take to get to the Castle?" she asked anxiously.

Marwick sighed. "It's a tricky journey. The Castle lies on the edge of the system. And a lot of the Ways near there don't work any more. So let's get going. The sooner we go, the sooner we get there."

With some difficulty, Marwick helped Sam to his feet. The small amount of colour in Sam's face drained away, and he swayed precariously.

"You can lean on me," Kaznim offered.

Sam managed a smile. "Thanks ... but I'm fine."

41

"No, you're not," Marwick told Sam. "You lean on Kaznim like she said."

Once again Ptolemy was whisked away from his flowers and tucked under an arm. The tortoise drew in his head with a sharp hiss of annoyance. With Sam leaning on Kaznim's right shoulder and Marwick's left arm holding him up, they made their way slowly across the grass towards another of the strangely dark arches. Marwick stopped at its mouth and smiled at Kaznim. "Ready?" he asked.

Kaznim nodded nervously.

"We'll walk in together, just as we are now. We will go along a short tunnel and step into a weird misty patch. It will feel a bit strange, as though you are moving very fast, which of course you are, because you are travelling along an Ancient Way. But all you have to do is keep walking steadily, and hang on to Sam. Then we'll come out into another Hub – a place a bit like this, with twelve more arches. And then we'll go into another arch. We just carry on like that and if all my numbers work out we'll end up in the Castle. OK?"

Kaznim smiled. "OK," she said.

"I just hope that all the Hubs are navigable," Marwick muttered to himself, looking anxiously at Sam.

The trio walked beneath the arch and headed into the chill of a dank tunnel, moving slowly towards the strange white mist that hovered ahead.

"Here we go," said Marwick. They stepped into the mist and entered the Ancient Way.

Kaznim lost count of the number of Hubs they walked, waded, slipped and slid across. Marwick had to take them on two detours and it felt like hours later when he said, "Nearly there. Only one more Hub to go." But it was in the very last Hub that they hit their final and biggest obstacle. As they emerged from the mist and walked down the tunnel, the weight of Sam heavy on them both, they saw at the end of the tunnel a bright, shimmering purple light. As they drew close, Kaznim saw that the light was stretched over the arch like a skin. She thought she could hear a faint buzzing coming from it, like a fly trapped in a jar.

"Don't touch," Marwick warned. Gingerly, Marwick put out his hand to the purple light. Kaznim could tell by the way he rested his hand on it that the light had a physical presence – it actually was a tough skin stretched like a drum across the archway. Marwick spun around. "I don't believe it!" he said despairingly. "Marcia's **Sealed** it."

"Sealed?" Sam mumbled. "What, like a *Magyk* **Seal**?"

"Yeah," said Marwick.

With a soft groan, Sam Heap slid to the ground and slumped against the wall like a dummy with the stuffing half gone. His eyes were closed, and in the eerie purple light his face was a deathly blue.

Marwick dropped to his knees beside his friend. "Sammo," he whispered. "Sammo, wake up. *Please.* We're very nearly there." Kaznim watched Marwick put his hand on Sam's bandage and take it away again. It was dark with blood. "We're so close," he said. "*So* close." He gently tapped Sam's face and Sam's eyes flickered open. "Stay awake, Sammo. Stay awake for me. Please. *Please.*"

Sam struggled to keep his eyes open but Kaznim knew he was beginning to drift away. Marwick looked up at her in despair. "The Sick Bay is his only hope. And we can't get past this **Seal**." He got to his feet. "We'll have to take him around the long way." He shook his head in consternation, "At least four more Hubs to get back to where we are now."

As a daughter of an Apothecary, there were things that Kaznim knew that Marwick did not. Kaznim saw the dull film covering Sam's green eyes and she knew that Sam Heap had no hope of travelling through four more Hubs.

PART
III

SEVENTY-FIVE
HOURS TO
HATCHING

# SCRAMBLED EGG

*Alice TodHunter Moon, Apprentice to* the ExtraOrdinary Wizard, had been in the job for little more than two months. Alice – who liked to be called Tod – had spent most of that time feeling excited and confused in equal measures. Now she was headed for the early morning Wizard Tower Moot and a new feeling of apprehension began to creep over her.

The Moot was a weekly meeting that the ExtraOrdinary Wizard, Septimus Heap, had recently set up. It was held in the Great Hall of the Wizard Tower very early on a Monday morning so it did not interfere with the rest of the day's schedule. The idea was that the Moot would focus on one particular issue at a time until it was resolved. Septimus reckoned that any problem could be worked out if enough Wizards thought about it – but he was yet to be proved right. The conundrum the Moot was trying to solve was the whereabouts of the Egg of the Orm. However, so far not one Wizard had come up with anything useful.

Tod was waiting in the shadows at the end of the Apprentice corridor beside the silver spiral stairs. Her short dark hair was neatly combed – unusual for Tod – and her long elflock hung down her back, plaited and tied with a green ribbon. The ribbon matched her still-pristine Apprentice robes, which Tod wore in the new fashion as a short woollen tunic, fastened by a silver Apprentice belt and green leggings. She had adopted the Wizard Tower habit of wearing boots lined with sheepskin in the winter, and today, because Tod wanted to look like a good Apprentice, their laces were also green. In her hand she held a small blue folder that she had painstakingly painted to look like lapis lazuli, on which she had written two short words: *Orm Egg*. With butterflies flapping in her stomach, Tod watched the stairs – which were still on slow night-time mode – rotating downwards. They carried a selection of the more pedantic Wizards who enjoyed meetings, along with some reptile experts, none of whom were speaking to one another after a row the previous week about whether a newly hatched Orm ate its own egg sac. But it was not a good turnout; most Wizards had opted to stay in bed.

While Tod waited politely for a space on the stairs, she thought somewhat enviously of the other Apprentices in the junior dorms who were lucky enough to be having another hour's sleep. But as ExtraOrdinary Apprentice, Tod had much less freedom – she was expected to attend everything the ExtraOrdinary Wizard did. She was also expected to occasionally speak at meetings, and this was to be her first time. In fact, right then everything felt a little bit scary. There were rules she still did not understand and things she was afraid of doing wrong. The Wizard Tower sometimes felt like a big machine in which she was a very small cog. Resolutely, Tod pushed down a feeling of homesickness. At times like this she missed the simple life she had led in her PathFinder village far across the sea, but more than anything she missed her father, Dan Moon. And Tod knew he missed her too, far away in the house he had once shared with her and her mother, Cassi TodHunter Draa, who had died when Tod was little.

Tod's sad thoughts were interrupted by a friendly shout from above. "Alice, don't wait for me! Jump on!" It was Dr Dandra Draa. An imposing woman with short dark hair through which ran a striking streak of white, Dr Draa was the Sick Bay Wizard and Tod's guardian. Now that Tod was an Apprentice, Dandra insisted on calling her Alice, "It *is* your proper name," Dandra had told her. "And you should use it in your official capacity." But no one else called her Alice, not even the ExtraOrdinary Wizard – much to Dandra's disapproval.

Tod jumped on to the step just below Dandra.

Dandra smiled. She was pleased to see the blue folder and know that her protégée was taking her duties seriously, but she could not help being a little mischievous. "Ready for more scrambled egg?" she asked.

Tod grinned. "Scrambled egg" was the name the Apprentices had given the subject of the Moot. Now it seemed to have spread. "*Egg*stremely ready," said Tod.

"Alice, I do apologise," Dandra said, deadpan. She waited for a split second and then said, "I really shouldn't be *egging* you on."

Tod giggled. She loved Dandra's mixture of formality and fun.

The stairs took them from the dimness of the night-time lights in the domestic part of the Wizard Tower down into the shockingly bright arena of the Great Hall, an impressively vaulted space on the ground floor. Here, seven tall columns reared up to meet high above at a point in the centre of its shimmering blue ceiling, on which were scattered constellations of stars twinkling brightly. As Tod and Dandra progressed downwards, the blue sky faded into a pale green, which in turn morphed into brightly coloured pictures around the walls of the Great Hall. These showed scenes from the long history of the Wizard Tower and had been created with an ancient **Magyk**. They flickered in and out of focus, and where the **Magyk** grew thin, they faded into black and white. The Great Hall was achingly bright for so early in the morning and Tod wished that Septimus would – as he'd been requested to do by the more elderly Wizards – "turn it down a bit". But Septimus wanted everyone wide awake on this dark winter morning.

Tod stepped off the stairs and as her foot touched the soft, sandlike surface of the **Magykal** floor, the multicoloured words *GOOD MORNING, APPRENTICE* wandered through the grains at her feet and then *GOOD LUCK WITH THE SPEECH*, which was quickly followed by *GOOD MORNING, DR DRAA*.

Serious nerves attacked Tod as she and Dandra made their way over to a young man wearing the heavy purple robes of the office of ExtraOrdinary Wizard. Septimus Heap looked up from a long, narrow table where he was leafing through a stack of papers. His straw-coloured wavy hair was neatly tied back in a short ponytail and his bright green eyes flashed in the light when he smiled. "Tod, Dandra, good morning," he said. "I have a distinct feeling that today is the day we make the breakthrough. I sense a kind of …" He stopped and searched for the right word. "Er, *connection* with the Egg. As though it is somehow coming closer to us." Septimus became aware that Dr Draa was looking at him as though he had fallen prey to a rather nasty illness. "I am perfectly all right, thank you, Dandra," he said testily.

"I am pleased to hear it, ExtraOrdinary," Dandra replied. "Although I am aware that the Delusion Bug is back in the Port. A very nasty virus."

"I'm sure it is," Septimus said. "But I am perfectly well, thank you."

"The delusion of perfect wellness is one of its symptoms," Dandra said gravely.

A flicker of worry passed across Septimus's face.

"Luckily," Dandra added, "the very first symptom of all is a rash of tiny blue spots on the nose."

Septimus knew his nose was blue-spot free. He resisted the temptation to stick his tongue out at Dandra Draa, but contented himself with an irritable, "Huh!"

The hands on the new clock above the tall silver double doors that led out of the Wizard Tower showed six o'clock exactly. It was time for the Moot to begin. With an air of disappointment Septimus surveyed the sparse gathering: about twenty Wizards, three final year Apprentices who needed good attendance reports and Boris Catchpole, a thoroughly useless ex-sub-Wizard who was employed as doorman. Septimus did not include in his count the strange figure that lay upon the visitors' bench by the main door, fast asleep.

The sleeping figure – a long, willowy man dressed in beautiful white silk robes with gold sandals on his feet – had attracted a few amused glances from those at the Moot. He was, they knew, Septimus's jinnee, Jim Knee. Jim Knee was not usually seen in winter months due to his habit of going into hibernation under a large pile of soft quilts. But the previous night his Master had rudely awoken him from his deep sleep. Only the best gold upon his feet and the softest silk for his robes – and a risky relaxation of the rules between jinnee and Master, whereby Jim Knee was able to Transform into what he wanted, *when* he wanted – had persuaded Jim Knee to do as Septimus had commanded. Now, with his head upon his favourite goose-down pillow, the jinnee drifted back into a hazy doze, knowing that it was not going to last much longer.

Since becoming ExtraOrdinary Wizard, Septimus had discovered that it was only too easy to become overwhelmed by the huge amount of things he was meant to do. His solution had been to revert to his Young Army training: events were to begin and end *On Time, on the Chime* as the Young Army rhyme had it. Septimus had hated his time as a boy soldier, but he was surprised by how many aspects of his training he still found useful. The chime of the Great Hall clock having been silenced after complaints from those who lived immediately above, Septimus now picked up a small silver bell and rang it. The assembled gathering fell silent.

"Thank you for coming to the Moot," Septimus began. "I am sorry there are not more of us here." He paused and looked around. Aware that he needed to keep those who had bothered to turn up happy so that at least *they* would come to the next Moot, he continued, "But I see we have the pick of the crop here."

An appreciative murmur ran through the assembled group.

"And I am sure that with such great skill and Magykal talent gathered here this morning, we will find the answer we are looking for." Septimus smiled. "Since our Moot last week, my Apprentice and I have made some interesting discoveries. Tod, would you like to tell us all your results, please?"

Dandra caught her eye and smiled encouragingly. Tod fumbled with her blue folder and drew out a sheet of neat writing. Willing her hands to stop shaking, she read out the title.

"Conditions necessary to produce a successful human hatching of an Egg of the Great Orm." She looked up and wished she hadn't. All eyes were upon her. Behind the crowd she saw the tall silver doors from the outside opening and a figure in dark blue-and-gold robes hurrying in. It was Beetle, the Chief Hermetic Scribe. He nodded apologetically at Septimus and stayed quietly at the back. Flustered, Tod looked down at her piece of paper. She really liked Beetle and longed to impress him. Now she was even more anxious.

"I. Er. Um …" she floundered, overwhelmed by the expectant silence. It was a sudden sneeze from the Chief Hermetic Scribe that saved her. The noisiest sneeze that Tod had ever heard, it filled the Great Hall and all eyes turned disapprovingly on its owner. Another three sneezes followed fast upon its heels and Tod was surprised to see the Chief Hermetic Scribe turn a little pink.

"Ah … ahh … *TCHOO*! I'm sorry," he said. "Really *terribly* sorry."

Septimus frowned. "Never mind, Beetle," he said briskly. "Tod was just going to tell us what she has discovered about the human hatching of an Orm Egg. It's highly interesting and narrows the field tremendously." He turned to Tod. "Please, do continue."

Beetle's sneezes had blown away Tod's nerves. Her hands steady, she held the paper still and began to read in a clear voice: "The conditions necessary for a human hatching of an

Orm Egg are similar to those for the human hatching of a dragon egg, but there are important differences.

"For a human hatching of an Orm Egg to be successful it must, like that of a dragon egg, mimic the natural sequence of events. Three distinct steps are required. First there is the kick-start, which sets the hatching process in motion. Like the dragon egg, this requires fierce heat for twenty-four hours, but at an even higher temperature. Folklore tells us that a parent Orm would drop its egg into the crater of a volcano.

"The second stage is incubation. In the wild, the parent Orm would retrieve its egg and bury it in warm ash near the volcano. It would then wrap itself around the egg and using the muscles of its coils, would regularly move the egg to and fro, providing a rocking sensation. Like the young dragon, the baby Orm needs to know that a parent is present and awaits its hatching. Without movement the embryo would curdle and die.

"The third stage is hatching. Unlike a dragon egg, an Orm Egg does not need a touch of Darke to begin this process. It runs to a strict timetable and a much more rapid one: twelve weeks eggs–actly." Tod noticed she had raised a few smiles and her confidence grew. "The timespan for the incubation of the Orm Egg is surprisingly short. Because a dragon egg must be incubated for a year and a day we assumed that with a Great Orm being so much larger and slower than a dragon, the incubation period would be longer. But it was just yesterday that we discovered that incubation lasts only twelve weeks."

A few mutterings spread through the Hall at this surprising information and Tod hurried to finish what she had to say.

"The hatchling Orm will Imprint on the first living creature it makes eye contact with. This may be human or animal. The hatchling is almost identical to a hatchling dragon: it has wings, legs and a tail, and is very active. It can even fly. After twelve weeks in this stage it spins itself a cocoon, from which it will emerge in its adult state of a long, fragile tube with the ability to turn any rock into lapis lazuli. The larval Orm will break out of its cocoon with a sudden explosion. In ancient times, Orm cocoons were nicknamed time bombs." Tod paused and looked down at her notes. "And, um, that's all I have to say. Thank you very much." To the background of some concerned murmurs in the Great Hall, Tod put the piece of paper back into her folder. She felt very relieved.

"Thank you, Tod," Septimus said. "That was extremely interesting." He picked up a small, battered book from the table and held it aloft to show the Moot. "My Apprentice very generously says that 'we' discovered this. However, it was entirely her discovery. Tod tracked down this little book in the Pyramid Library – a book that has not seen the light of day for thousands of years, I suspect." Septimus refrained from adding the reason was because the book, *Orm Fanciers' Factoids*, was wrongly filed in the biography section under Oom: Francis Fa, the author. (Francis Fa Oom had once, briefly, been ExtraOrdinary Wizard.)

"I need not state the obvious here," Septimus said – although, looking at the blank early morning faces of the assembled Wizards, he thought that he probably did, "but it is over twelve weeks since the sorcerer Oraton-Marr stole the Orm Egg. However, all is not lost. I believe that it will have taken some time for the sorcerer to journey to a place where hatching will be possible. I feel we still have a good chance of being able to find the Egg before it hatches, but we must set about this at once. We must do all we can to prevent this evil sorcerer from Imprinting the Orm and thus acquiring the means to create an endless source of lapis lazuli. As you all know," Septimus said, flattering his audience (for he was none too sure they did know), "much of the Magykal power of the Wizard Tower stems from the fact it stands upon an enormous block of lapis, as indeed does much of the Castle. Possession of lapis lazuli enhances even a small amount of Magyk. Possession of an unlimited amount will render this highly capable sorcerer invincible."

Septimus paused to emphasise his point. "It is imperative that we find the Egg *as soon as possible*."

A rumble of concerned comments broke out and a shout came from the back of the Great Hall. "'S'cuse me!"

Septimus recognised the voice of one of his older brothers, identical twins Edd and Erik, who were both Senior Apprentices. Now that Erik had cut his hair very short it was easy to tell them apart, but their voices were still identical. Septimus took a chance. "Yes, Edd?" he said, squinting into the brightness.

"It's *Erik*." The reply was accompanied by some amused chuckles.

"Erik. What is it?"

"Isn't this all rather theoretical? I mean, we have no idea where in the world the Egg is, do we? And knowing how it hatches isn't going to help us find *that* out."

"On the contrary," Septimus said, trying not to show his annoyance with Erik. "Knowing the conditions the Egg needs to hatch allows us to narrow down the places it is likely to be."

"So where *is* it likely to be?" Erik shot back.

"Somewhere hot, where the Egg can be buried in sand, seems likely to me," Septimus replied. "I can't see Oraton-Marr risking living on the edge of a volcano. So we are looking for a desert."

"Any particular desert?" Erik asked with the trace of a sneer.

"We have narrowed it down to the three hottest at this time of year," Septimus said. "And we intend to explore each and every one until we find the Egg."

"How?" Erik interrupted.

"If you'd allow me to finish, Erik, you'd find out."

Erik leaned back against the wall and folded his arms. Septimus knew Erik was finding it hard to have his youngest brother in a position of power, but it did not excuse his rudeness.

"I propose to send my jinnee, Jim Knee, to all three deserts in quick succession to search for the Egg. As a Magykal being, Jim Knee will be able to travel faster than any human and will be protected from many dangers. I have given him permission to Transform into any creature he wishes, whenever he wishes. My Apprentice – who, as you all know, is a skilled PathFinder and understands the Ancient Ways – will show Jim Knee how to navigate them. We still have some final planning to do, but we hope to send the jinnee through today – there is not a moment to lose."

A murmur of agreement came from the Moot. "Now," Septimus said, "if anyone has any questions, please feel free to ask."

As if in reply, a loud snore came from the visitors' bench. It was followed by an outbreak of laughter from the Moot.

"I've got a question!" a shout came from the back of the crowd.

"Yes?"

"How do you plan to wake him up?"

"Oh, I'll wake him up all right," Septimus said. "Don't you worry."

# JINNEE FUSS

*Septimus and Tod retreated* to the Pyramid Library to work out the best routes for Jim Knee to take. As PathFinder, Tod – accompanied by Edd and Erik Heap as bodyguards – was to show the jinnee how to navigate the first route, then she and the twins would return. After that Jim Knee was on his own. It was not until late in the afternoon that Septimus and Tod had three long lists of numbers, one list for each desert and a number for every arch that Jim Knee must walk through.

Septimus sent a message to the Manuscriptorium to say they were ready, and they met Beetle in the Great Hall. Jim Knee respected Beetle – and Septimus knew he was going to need all the respect he could get. Beetle and Septimus looked down at the sleeping jinnee, who still lay dozing on the visitors' bench beneath his quilts. "Right," said Septimus. "Time to wake him."

Beetle grinned. "Good luck," he said.

"Jim Knee, wake up!" Septimus said in a commanding voice.

There was no response. The jinnee's eyes remained closed, his long, elegant hands folded peacefully over the top of the feather quilts. With the gaze of Edd and Erik upon him, Septimus was not going to let his jinnee get away with such disrespect. He took a small spiky red ball from his pocket and **Activated** it. The **Alarm** emitted a loud screech and began to jump up and down on Jim Knee's long, elegant nose. In a moment the jinnee was sitting up, an expression of outrage upon his face.

Septimus got in first. "Jim Knee, I Command you to find the Egg of the Orm."

"What, *now*?" asked Jim Knee.

"Now," said Septimus. "And I give you an overriding Command: keep my Apprentice safe."

"Will do," Jim Knee replied laconically. "And just to check. I do have free will to Transform?"

"Free will," Septimus agreed. "But only in pursuit of my Commands. Understand?"

Jim Knee reckoned that gave him plenty of scope. "Okey-dokey," he replied.

Tod led the way. She murmured the password in the offhand manner that all Apprentices soon acquired, then the tall silver doors to the Wizard Tower slowly opened and Tod stepped out into a beautiful winter scene. A hazy sun was already low over the rooftops of Wizard Way, sending rosy sparkles of light dancing on the frosty snow that lay on the courtyard before her. The Big Freeze had been long, cold and deep that year but Tod had loved every minute of it. The snow made her feel happy and optimistic, and as she walked slowly down the white marble steps, Tod felt sure they would soon track down the Egg of the Orm.

Behind Tod came the disparate trio of Septimus, Beetle and Jim Knee. The Chief Hermetic Scribe had a firm grasp on Jim Knee's right elbow, while Septimus had an equally firm grip on the left. Close behind them came Edd and Erik Heap in their green robes with purple Senior Apprentice ribbons on the cuffs of their sleeves. They were reassuringly broad and had a slightly wild look to them.

"I really can't see why you don't use our new Way in the Manuscriptorium," Beetle was saying. "It would be so much easier than going through Marcia's Hub. And you know what she thinks about Jim Knee."

"For security reasons we have agreed to keep that Way closed, Beetle, *as you know*," Septimus said. "I still wish you would let me put a **Seal** on it, just to be sure."

Beetle had been able to use the Manuscriptorium Way only once – when he and his deputy, Foxy, had nervously ventured to the other side of the world with a stack of leaflets advertising their services – before Septimus had insisted on it being closed. It was an open secret that the Chief Hermetic Scribe felt frustrated by Septimus's veto over what he saw as his own jurisdiction. Beetle had even joked among his scribes about declaring independence. "We are perfectly capable of policing our Way, thank you," Beetle said stiffly.

"Of course you are," Septimus said, trying to mollify his friend. "But you see, Marcia's Hub gives us much more choice. Eleven choices compared to one."

Beetle sighed. "I know. Just thought I'd mention it, that's all."

At the foot of the Wizard Tower steps they turned sharp left and headed for the **Hidden** arch, which Tod – unlike Septimus or Beetle – could see fitting snugly beneath the steps like a cupboard under the stairs. Jim Knee could also see the arch, but he was not going to give anyone the satisfaction of knowing it. The jinnee knew the Ancient Ways pretty well, having once routinely travelled them as part of his job as a runner for a wealthy merchant. But Jim Knee was still annoyed at having been dragged from his winter sleep and, while he would *eventually* obey his master as he was bound to do, he did not intend to make anything easy for Septimus.

The group gathered in front of a faint line of purple chalk tracing the outline of the arch that would take them to a Hub some fifty miles away deep in the bowels of the keep of an old castle. The Hub was familiar territory to them all, for it belonged to the previous ExtraOrdinary Wizard, Septimus's old tutor, Marcia Overstrand. Septimus was looking forward to seeing Marcia and talking his plan through with her. "OK, Tod," he said. "Take us in, please."

A sudden wail came from Jim Knee. *"Aieeeeee!"* With consummate drama, the jinnee slipped from their grasp like a wet fish and fell to the ground, apparently unconscious.

Septimus was not pleased. "Jim Knee, get up! At once!"

But the jinnee lay still, a streak of white upon the snow.

"I think he's too cold," said Beetle. "He's only wearing a thin silk robe and open sandals."

"Because that is all he *would* wear," Septimus said, staring down at his jinnee in exasperation.

"Not even *underpants*?" asked Beetle.

"Don't even go there, Beetle," Septimus said. "I do not want to think about Jim Knee's underpants, thank you."

Beetle smiled ruefully. "Underpants or no, it really is very silly of him. Jinn are notoriously sensitive to temperature changes."

Septimus had forgotten that. "Bother," he said. "He did it deliberately. Just to make things difficult."

"So what's new?" Beetle grinned. "When did Jim Knee ever make things easy?"

Septimus sighed. Despite his optimism in public, privately he knew the chances of Jim Knee finding the Orm Egg were not good – and if his jinnee was set on being so contrary right from the start, things were looking very bad indeed. "We'd better take him back inside and get him warm," Septimus said. He raised his voice in Jim Knee's direction. "But he needn't think he's getting away with this kind of behaviour. Any more trouble and he'll be hibernating in the **Sealed Cell**."

Jim Knee's eyes flickered. The jinnee had once spent some time in the **Sealed Cell** and he had hated it. It was horribly cramped and had reminded him of the inside of his last bottle. He decided to warm up in the Wizard Tower and accept Septimus's earlier offer of a fur coat. Then he'd get on with the job he had to do.

Septimus, Beetle, Edd and Erik lifted Jim Knee to his feet. The jinnee swayed and gave a weak groan. "He's putting it on," Septimus said.

"Very possibly," Beetle agreed, "but you can't be sure. Jinn are delicate creatures and with each new life they become more so. And if you believe half of Jim Knee's stories, he's had an awful lot of those."

"I suppose," said Septimus. He turned to Tod. "Would you mind going to warn Marcia we are coming? She's not a big fan of Jim Knee and it might be polite to let her know. Come straight back, OK?"

"OK." Tod smiled. She loved travelling the Ways on her own and she loved the fact that Septimus trusted her to go alone. Septimus watched his Apprentice place her hand on to the hard white marble below the steps, then he saw the shimmering shape of an archway begin to appear and the surface of the marble soften. Septimus was impressed by his Apprentice's skill. She was a good choice – unlike his jinnee.

# SHADOWS ON THE SEAL

*In Marcia's Hub three Drummins* were perusing the shimmering purple skin of a **Magykal Seal**. Drummins were very short, stocky, human-like creatures accustomed to living belowground. They had been caretakers of the Hub for three years now and they knew it better than they knew the suckers on the ends of their broad, flat fingers.

Using their preferred language of signing, Fabius Drummin signed, *There's something behind the Seal on Way One.*

Claudius replied, *Three humans, I think.*

*And a creature*, added Lucius.

*We should tell the boss*, signed Claudius.

Claudius and Lucius both looked pointedly at Fabius, who was on upstairs duties that day. *All right, all right, I'll go*, he signed grumpily.

Fabius hurried off, his bouncing strides taking him across the white stone floor of the immaculately clean Hub and up the winding stairs that led out of it. The remaining two Drummins stared at the Seal, watching for any sign of failure. They were looking so intently that they did not see the arch behind them – the only one **UnSealed** – light up with a golden glow and a slight figure in a green tunic and leggings come striding out. Tod stopped. She saw the Drummins were busy

64

and, not wanting to interrupt, she tiptoed over to them. "Hey," she whispered.

"Argh!" The Drummins spun around. "Don't *do* that, Alice," Lucius hissed, and using the Drummin sign for being quiet – one that everyone understood – he put his index finger to his lips.

Tod knew the Drummins were annoyed with her: they had called her Alice. "Sorry," she whispered. "I didn't mean to startle you. What's going on?"

*Trouble*, Lucius signed. Tod, being a PathFinder, also used signs, and although the PathFinder sign language lacked the complex grammar of the Drummins' language, many of the signs were similar. And "trouble" – the first two fingers of each hand folded at the second joint and twisted together – was easily recognisable.

*What trouble?* Tod signed.

Claudius proceeded to sign something much longer, but seeing Tod's look of incomprehension, he stopped and whispered, "There are creatures behind the Seal."

Tod's eyes widened in fear. "Not ... *Garmin?*" Garmin were nightmarish beings that the sorcerer Oraton-Marr had used to abduct, terrify and control people – including, once, Tod herself. The Seals were placed across the arches for good reason: to stop any danger of the Garmins' return.

Both Drummins shook their heads – it wasn't Garmin.

*Human*, Claudius signed.

Tod understood the sign for "human". Encouraged, she signed, *May I try?*

The Drummins respected Tod's knowledge of the Ancient Ways, and now that she was Apprentice they knew she would be careful with the **Magyk** protecting the **Seals**, so they stepped aside.

Very gently, Tod placed her hands on the delicate skin of the **Seal**. Beneath the thrum of the **Magyk** warming her palms, Tod could **Feel** the energy from something alive on the other side, but her skills were untrained and she had no way of knowing whether it was even human – let alone if it was a good human or a bad one.

On the other side of the **Seal**, Sam lay slumped against the cold stone of the wall, with Marwick and Kaznim on either side. And, for a reason neither Sam nor Marwick understood, the tortoise was now resting on Sam's wounded stomach. When Kaznim had first placed Ptolemy on Sam's sodden bandage, Marwick had been horrified. He'd snatched the tortoise off with the words, "Don't! It's filthy! Have you never heard of infection?"

Kaznim didn't like Ptolemy being called filthy but she took the tortoise quickly because Marwick had looked as though he'd wanted to hurl Ptolemy to the ground, and Kaznim had a horror of the tortoise breaking his shell. But then Sam had murmured, "Put it back. Helps with … pain." So Marwick had reluctantly replaced the tortoise and Sam had relaxed a little.

An awkward silence fell between Kaznim and Marwick and she occupied herself with gazing at the **Seal**, thinking of ways to break through. She was just about to suggest they stick a knife into it when she saw the shadow of two hands, not much bigger than her own, appear on it. "There's someone there!" she gasped. "Look! On the **Seal**!" Marwick looked up, hope springing into his eyes. Kaznim jumped up and placed her hands against the shadows of those on the other side. Her hands fit neatly inside the shape.

"Oh!" Tod snatched her hands away and jumped back. "There's someone there. Someone *touched my hands.*" She stared down at her palms as if trying to find out what they knew.

On the other side of the Seal, Kaznim saw the shadow of the hands disappear. "No!" she yelled. "Come back, please come back! We need help. *Help!*" She pummelled the unyielding Seal in desperation. Marwick sighed. It had been too good to be true, he thought. It was just a kid on the other side fooling around, nothing more.

In the Hub, Tod saw small, round shadows hitting the shimmering purple skin. "There's someone trying to get out," she whispered. "A child. Look how small the fists are. And how low down."

"It's a trick," said Lucius.

"A Darke trick," added Claudius.

Tod frowned. "It didn't feel Darke," she said. "Well, I don't think so. It felt more like a child to me. A frightened child."

"The Darke plays many tricks," Lucius said gloomily. "Impersonating a small human is but one."

"Particularly a frightened one," Claudius added for good measure.

Tod stared at the Seal. She could not shake off the feeling that someone on the other side was in desperate need of help. "I'll go upstairs and get Marcia," she said.

"Fabius has already –" Claudius began to explain, when the Drummin in question came thubbing down the stairs and bounced into the Hub. His gingery eyebrows were gathered into a frown.

"Boss has bloomin' gone," he said. Then, suddenly noticing Tod, he said, "Begging your pardon, Apprentice. What I mean to say is that unfortunately, Madam Marcia has left."

"She never said," Lucius growled.

"Left message with Cook. Caught ebb tide. Gone to wave the Captain off from the Seaward Quay."

"Huh. She's supposed to let us know first," muttered Lucius.

"Well, time and tide wait for no woman," said Fabius. "An' the Captain don't, neither. An' moanin' about the boss don't get us any closer to knowin' what be on the other side of the **Seal**."

On the other side of the **Seal** Sam's eyes were closing and his body was becoming limp. Marwick looked at Kaznim. "If we don't get out soon, Sam won't ..." His voice trailed away.

Sam stirred and groaned. A trickle of blood ran from his sodden bandage and Kaznim watched the dark red line slowly make its way along the pure white stone. When it reached the **Seal**, to her surprise, it ran through.

Kaznim turned to tell Marwick what had happened, but he was whispering something to Sam, and suddenly she felt like an intruder on something very private. She stared studiedly at the **Seal**. Behind her a stillness had descended. As an Apothecary's daughter, Kaznim knew what that meant. Sam's Leaving Time was near. She sat down, cross-legged by the **Seal**, and placed her palms on it once more. "Help us," she whispered. "Please. *Help us*."

★　　★　　★

In the Hub, Tod and the Drummins watched a dark liquid emerge from beneath the **Seal**.

"Blood," whispered Lucius.

"Murder," muttered Fabius.

"Most foul," Claudius added, shaking his head.

Tod could see the shape of two small hands once more pressed down low on the purple skin and she knew that, murder or not, someone was begging for help. "I'm going to get Septimus," she said.

The Drummins nodded. It was time to call in reinforcements. "Travel fast," said Fabius. "We will stand guard."

In less than five minutes, Tod was back with Septimus. His long purple robes and his impressive gold-and-platinum belt gave him an instant air of authority. The Drummins quickly jumped away from the **Seal** and let Septimus through. Like Tod, he rested his hands on the shimmering purple skin. Like Tod, he understood that there was someone in urgent need of help on the other side, but unlike Tod, he knew for sure that there was nothing **Darke** there.

★　　★　　★

Kaznim saw the shadow of two large hands on the **Seal**, high above her head. Then, while Septimus was explaining to Tod how to **Feel** the absence of **Darke**, Kaznim, with a sudden feeling of hope, jumped up. Stretching her hands high above her head and standing on tiptoe, she just managed to place her hands against the larger shadows.

"You are right, Tod, it is a child. And others, too, in great distress," Septimus said, taking his hands away – to Kaznim's despair. "Now, this is a serious step: I am going to override Marcia's **Seal**. One may only countermand another Wizard's **Seal** when a matter of life or death is at hand. I believe this to be the case right now. You understand?"

"Yes, I do understand," Tod said, feeling very relieved. She had wanted to break through the **Seal** ever since she had seen the small hands on the other side. Tod watched Septimus place his palms once more on the **Seal**. She saw two small shadows try to touch them and her heart did a little flip of pity – someone was desperate.

Under Septimus's instructions, Tod ushered the Drummins away from the **Magyk** and they watched from the other side of the Hub. They saw a bright blue mist flow from the ExtraOrdinary Wizard's hands; it spread across the **Seal** and Tod felt the familiar buzz of **Magyk** in the air. She had become used to the background of **Magyk** in the Wizard Tower but now, as concentrated **Magykal** energy flowed around the Hub, setting up eddies and swirls, Tod felt her old dizziness return. She leaned back against the wall, determined not to fall over. This was powerful **Magyk**, and Tod wanted to see it.

The purple skin across Way I was now coated with a shining blue mist that stuck so close that it looked as though the **Seal** was covered in wet paint. Tod watched Septimus stand back, bringing a thin stream of blue with him, which he took into both hands and formed into a ball. Then he muttered something and breathed on to the blue ball. At once, its colour changed to bright orange. The orange flowed along the strip linking to the **Seal** and then spread rapidly over it. Tod watched, fascinated, as the tight skin of the **Seal** began to dissolve and be replaced by a soft orange mist through which she saw three figures. Two were slumped to the ground, but a small one came hurtling out, yelling, "Help us, oh, please help! He's *dying*!"

Septimus hurried into the arch and Tod heard a sudden gasp. "Sam!" he cried. "It's Sam! And Marwick!"

# INTO THE CLIFF

*Tod was dispatched to* the Wizard Tower for two strong helpers
and a stretcher. Her choice of helpers was, Septimus thought,
exactly right. And so Sam Heap was carried home by Marwick
and three of his brothers: Septimus, Edd and Erik Heap. Behind
them followed Tod, holding Kaznim's free hand, while in the
other Kaznim clutched her tortoise, caught in the nick of time
as he fell from the stretcher.

Kaznim was startled when they emerged into a shockingly
cold whiteness over which a myriad of lights and colours
danced, reflecting off what she assumed was sparkling white
sand. She shivered in her thin cotton coat and held Ptolemy
close for comfort. Something told Kaznim that she was in a
place so far away that it would take many months to travel back
to her star-strewn tent. Tod saw the look of bewilderment on
the young girl's face and put her arm protectively around her.
She remembered the first time she had walked into the Wizard
Tower courtyard, how strange it had seemed and how the
onslaught of Magyk had been so overpowering that she had
fainted.

Kaznim, despite being from the **Magykal** Draa family, was
not particularly sensitive to **Magyk**, but she was glad of Tod's
comforting arm as she slithered and slid on the peculiarly

slippery, cold sand. As they reached the wide marble steps that led up to the entrance to the Wizard Tower, Kaznim looked in awe at the massive structure rearing above her – surely it was impossible that something so tall could remain standing. As she followed Sam's stretcher up to a pair of vast, solid silver doors, which were now slowly opening before them, Kaznim felt as though she were walking into the face of a cliff.

An outbreak of panic mixed with excitement greeted the stretcher-bearers as they hurried into the Great Hall. Kaznim watched wide-eyed as a sea of people in blue robes surrounded the stretcher, and the young man in purple took charge. She saw a flash of silver at the far side of the Hall, and something that looked like a giant corkscrew that went up into a star-filled sky above began to spin so fast that it reminded her of a whirling sand dancer. Suddenly a flash of blue appeared through the sky and rotated rapidly downwards; the next moment a tall woman with short dark hair through which ran a dramatic streak of white was jumping off and hurrying somewhat unsteadily across to the stretcher. Kaznim had an odd feeling that she recognised her, although she had no idea where from. She watched intently as the woman knelt beside the stretcher and placed two fingers on Sam's neck. Kaznim knew from her expression that the woman was expecting something very bad, but she looked up with a grim smile and said, "Faint, fluttering. He's alive."

Marwick made a strange choking noise and with renewed energy the stretcher-bearers picked up their burden and hurried Sam away to the back of the Hall. A sea of blue closed behind them and Kaznim could see no more.

Tod became aware that Kaznim was shivering violently. "Hey, you're cold," she said.

Kaznim shook her head. She was *something*, but she didn't know what.

Tod thought she knew. "You must be tired and hungry," she said.

Kaznim nodded even though she felt neither. All she felt was lost.

"I'll take you up to the Apprentices' common room," Tod said. "You can have some supper and I will find you a bed." Kaznim bit her lip. She didn't want to sleep in this strange place, so full of people, so heavy with stone, so bright with light. All she wanted was her own bed in the tranquillity of a starry tent with the soft breathing of her mother asleep in the darkness. Not trusting herself to speak, Kaznim allowed Tod to lead her on to the strange moving corkscrew.

Kaznim had seen stairs, but never any that *moved*. Numbly, she followed Tod's example. She stepped on to the silver platform and watched the ground drop slowly away. "They're weird, aren't they?" Tod said. "I remember the first time I went on them it was really scary."

Kaznim nodded uncertainly as the world spun around. As they rose up through the height of the Great Hall, towards the star-studded sky, she began to feel sick. And then, to her surprise, they passed through a hole in the sky and emerged into another, much simpler, smaller space with a floor all of its own.

"We need to get off soon," Tod said. "I'll go first and then you grab my hands and jump. OK?" Before Kaznim could say anything, Tod had stepped up on to the floor and was standing, arms outstretched, smiling with encouragement.

Kaznim froze.

74

"Come on," Tod said. "It's really easy. Just step off."

Kaznim shook her head. Her world was spinning out of control and she didn't know what to do. She clung to the centre post with one hand, held on tight to Ptolemy with the other and screwed her eyes shut.

Tod watched Kaznim rotate on upwards. She leaped back on to the stairs and broke Wizard Tower Apprentice Rule Number Fifty-Two: *Apprentices must not move between steps on the spiral stairs.* Tod didn't like to break the rules, but she reckoned that helping a scared girl and her tortoise was more important. Feeling very daring, she climbed the moving stairs and soon caught up with Kaznim.

Tod spent the next three floors trying to persuade Kaznim to open her eyes, but to no effect. As the stairs turned slowly on, ever upwards, Tod realised they were now approaching floor seven, where the Sick Bay was located. Deciding to make the best of it, she said, "Do you want to see how Sam is?"

"He's dying," Kaznim whispered.

"He's not dead yet," Tod said briskly. "Come on, Sam needs all the help he can get. This floor is the Sick Bay. Let's get off and see if there is anything we can do."

The only thing Kaznim wanted to do more than get off the horrible corkscrew was to help Sam. She let go of the centre pole, opened her eyes and wished she hadn't. The world was still spinning. She saw the floor travelling down to meet them and closed her eyes to stop herself from falling. The next thing she knew, Tod had grabbed her and lifted her on to something that, to her relief, *didn't move.*

Warily, Kaznim opened her eyes. The Sick Bay corridor was dimly lit and she couldn't see much. Clutching Ptolemy tightly to her, Kaznim allowed herself to be guided to some double doors at the end of the corridor, above which was a sign proclaiming in glowing red letters: *No admittance. Press green button and wait.*

Tod had never seen that sign lit before. She thought it did not bode well, but said nothing to Kaznim. She pressed the large button beside the doors and waited. After a very long minute, the doors opened a few inches and Edd peered out. "Tod – good timing!" he said.

"Oh?" Tod asked anxiously.

"Septimus wants you to fetch Marcellus Pye. As quickly as you can."

Tod knew that was not good news. Marcellus Pye was the Castle Alchemist but he also had a talent for surgery, which was something that Dr Draa thought was barbarous. Things must be bad for Dandra to agree to have Marcellus in the Sick Bay. "I'll get him right away," Tod said.

"Thanks." Edd began to close the doors and then remembered something. "And Septimus says, when you've done that, can you tell the rest of our brothers? That's Simon – you know, the Deputy Alchemist? And also Nicko, who'll be down at the boatyard, and Jo-Jo, who'll be … well, somewhere. Ask at Gothyk Grotto, they'll know. Is that OK?"

Tod was a little overwhelmed by the idea of rounding up the Heap brothers, but she was determined not to show it. "Yep. OK," she said, and turned to go. Quickly, before the doors closed, Kaznim pushed Ptolemy into Edd's hands. Edd Heap looked down at the creature as though Kaznim had given him a bomb. He had never seen a tortoise before.

"For Sam," Kaznim said. "He's an Apothecary tortoise."

Edd shook his head. "They don't allow animals in there."

"Tell them what he is," said Kaznim. "Then they will."

The tall woman with the white streak in her hair appeared at the door behind Edd. "Alice," Dandra said briskly. "We need Marcellus fast, please."

"Yes. Sorry. Just going," said Tod.

"Be quick," Dandra said and then, "Edd, what are you holding?"

Edd looked bewildered. "A Pothecary tortoise?"

Dandra looked amazed. *"Ptolemy!"* she gasped. "Give him to me!" She snatched the tortoise and hurried back into the Sick Bay. Edd stared down at his empty hands, shook his head, then turned and followed. The doors swung closed behind them.

"How did she know my tortoise's name?" asked Kaznim, staring at the closed doors.

"I have no idea." Tod was as bewildered as Kaznim. "Look, I've got to go. Wait here. I'll be back as soon as I can."

Kaznim watched Tod hurry to the silver stairs and press a large red button on the wall. A distant siren sounded a stair priority warning. Tod jumped on, the stairs sped up and in a sudden whirl of green, she was gone. Kaznim was left in the hushed dimness of the Sick Bay corridor, with its astringent smells that reminded her of a star-strewn tent so far away. She sat down on the waiting bench and a wave of homesickness washed over her.

# APOTHECARY TORTOISE

*Inside the Sick Bay* Dandra Draa and her old tortoise were becoming reacquainted. She held him up so that they were eye to eye and Ptolemy stuck his head out as far as he could. If he could have smiled he would have; it was good to see his old attendant again. He had wondered what had happened to her. Much as the tortoise felt great affection for his young attendant, he had, like all tortoises, a preference for maturer creatures.

Dandra felt as though her past had caught up with her and run her over. Her hands were shaking as she fought back a familiar feeling of fear. "Who brought this tortoise here?" she asked.

"Tod," said Edd.

"*Alice* brought it?"

"Er, well, there was a girl with her. Quite young. I think it belonged to her."

Dandra shook her head, puzzled. "I ... I don't understand," she muttered.

Edd nodded in agreement. He didn't understand either – Dandra never allowed animals in the Sick Bay, and here she was waving around a dirty rock with scaly legs and a cranky look in its eyes. *It will be peeing on the floor next*, Edd thought. "I'll get a cloth, shall I?" he offered. "Something for it to sit on."

Dandra looked impressed. "Yes, please, Edd. That's what we always do – but how did you know?"

Edd, who enjoyed helping in the Sick Bay, hurried away, pleased to be of use.

Sam Heap was in the Quiet Room, a small and peaceful space off the main Sick Bay. It was used for Wizards who were very ill or nearing the end of their lives, and after a nasty flu epidemic earlier that winter it was now home to six ghosts, all spending their obligatory ghostly Leaving Time – a year and a day after their death – in the place where they had entered ghosthood.

The ghostly old Wizards regarded Sam Heap mournfully. They all remembered him as a bright, noisy little boy, full of life. It seemed impossible that this thin and deathly still young man who was as white as the sheets beneath him – apart from the great gash of red across his stomach – was the same person.

"I'm surprised his parents aren't here," whispered one. "You know how obsessed Sarah Heap is with her boys."

"I heard that Sarah and Silas are away in the Forest," whispered another. "They went to stay with Galen for the MidWinter Feast."

"Whatever did they want to do that for?" came the reply.

"Silas didn't want to," said the first. "He was in here complaining the day before they went. But of course, you weren't here then. You were still ..." The ghost trailed off, embarrassed.

"Alive," the other ghost finished for him sourly.

There was an awkward silence – it was bad manners among ghosts to talk about Life and Death. "Well," said another, "even if Sarah and Silas are in the Forest, someone should go and tell them. It doesn't seem right not to know your boy's dying, does it?"

The ghosts nodded and sighed, sending a chill breeze ruffling the sheets. It was tough being stuck in the Quiet Room of the Sick Bay for one's Leaving Time. It was a small, gloomy place and it was crowded enough without having another ghost join them – especially a young one who had not expected to Leave his Life just yet. Those ghosts were always noisy and disruptive. And so – just like the Living who hurried in and out of the Quiet Room – the resident ghosts wished heartily that Sam Heap would recover.

But no one wished Sam to live more than Marwick. He sat beside the high, narrow bed, clutching Sam's cold hand. It seemed to Marwick that Sam was getting ready to Leave. His skin was sweaty, his breath came in rapid, shallow gasps and around his waist his fresh bandage was already showing a dark red stain of blood.

Dr Dandra Draa came in carrying Ptolemy on a starched white line square and very gently laid him on top of Sam's bandage.

The attendant ghosts looked at one another in disbelief. "She's gone mad," hissed one.

"Totally bonkers," agreed the others.

At the comforting presence of the tortoise, Sam's eyelids flickered and Marwick thought his breathing eased a little. And maybe his hand felt a little warmer. Maybe …

Ptolemy pulled in his legs and head and concentrated on what was beneath his shell. It did not feel good – the tissues felt damaged and disturbed and there was metal there, sharp and bright. This was not a job for a tortoise, Ptolemy reflected.

This was a job for a chirurgeon: something inside Sam needed to be taken out.

Dandra knew that too. She knelt down so that she was at eye level with her old tortoise. "Ptolemy. Show me, I pray, where the sharpness lies," she said.

Careful not to cause Sam any extra pain, Ptolemy put his legs out, raised himself up and moved around in a half-circle. Then, three times, very slowly, he dipped his head down and touched his nose to the sharp bright spot beneath the bandages.

Dandra looked at Marwick. "It is as I feared," she said. "There is something in the wound. But at least now we know where it is. And Marcellus Pye will be here soon to take it out."

"I knew it," Marwick mumbled. "I *knew* the blade had broken off." Marwick saw Sam's lifeblood oozing through the bandages and he knew that Marcellus Pye could not get there a moment too soon.

# PART IV

FIFTY-SIX
HOURS TO
HATCHING

# THE EGG BOX

*Forgotten in the crisis, Kaznim* sat alone on the hard wooden bench outside the Sick Bay. She watched a succession of people rush by: four Wizards staggering with a small, but clearly very heavy, ancient wooden chest, followed at intervals by three young men who all looked a little like Sam Heap. One wore black, one looked like a sailor, in navy blue jerkin and trews, and the last wore long green robes and looked to Kaznim just like the one to whom she had given her precious tortoise, except he had very short hair. People carrying piles of towels and large coloured bottles came and went. Silently Kaznim watched them all pass by with no more than a brief glance and perhaps a distant smile.

Suddenly a young woman wearing the most beautiful red silk robes and a simple crown, her eyes blurry with tears, hurried by. Kaznim stared in amazement. Enough Queens and Princesses had visited the star tent for her to recognise the real thing when she saw it. Like everyone else, the Queen raced by without noticing her and hurtled through the Sick Bay doors. But unlike the others, when the Queen came out she saw Kaznim and stopped. Kaznim smiled nervously. The Queen looked like a much younger version of a particularly unpleasant Queen who controlled the city nearest to her star tent. She even wore red, just like the Red Queen herself. But Kaznim could tell she was different; her eyes were friendly, not blank and cruel as her mother had once described those of the Red Queen – and besides, she was smiling, although a little sadly. It was said that the Red Queen never smiled except when she was about to cut someone's head off. And Kaznim was pretty sure this Queen wasn't planning on doing that. She didn't have a sword with her, anyway.

To Kaznim's utter amazement, the young Queen came over and knelt beside her. "Are you the little girl who came with Sam?" she asked.

Kaznim was speechless. She nodded and the Queen put her hand on hers. It was the first kind touch Kaznim had felt since Tod had disappeared, and tears sprung into her eyes. "Thank you," the Queen said. "I know it was because of you that they decided to open the Seal."

Kaznim's eyes grew wide. "Because of *me*?"

"They saw your hands through the Magyk."

Kaznim was in awe of the Queen, who was so beautiful with her long dark hair and violet-coloured eyes. At last she managed to stutter, "Is Sam … Is he all right?"

"Sam's not in pain," the Queen told her. "Thanks to your tortoise, I think. But he is very weak. There is part of a knife still inside him. We are waiting for Marcellus Pye. He is a chirurgeon. He will be able to take it out."

"And then Sam will be better?" asked Kaznim.

The Queen blinked away tears. "I hope so. I really, *really* hope so." She stood up quickly and brushed her hand across her face. "I must go," she said. "I'm going to find Mum and Dad. I *have* to tell them."

Kaznim nodded. So this must be a Princess, not a Queen, she thought. She was impressed that the King and Queen would want to know about Sam Heap. Most Kings and Queens didn't care at all if one of their subjects was ill. "It is nice of the King and Queen to care so much," she ventured shyly.

The "Princess" looked puzzled and then she smiled. "Oh, there isn't a King here," she said. "There's just me. I'm the Queen. I meant *Sam's* Mum and Dad, who are mine, too." The Queen reached down and held Kaznim's hand once more. "Thank you for helping Sam," she said, then she turned, ran to the stairs and jumped on. Amazed, Kaznim watched the light sparkle off the Queen's golden crown as the stairs took her slowly down.

Kaznim spent the next ten minutes occupied with wondering if Sam Heap was a prince. Surely he must be, if he shared his parents with the Queen. But if that was so, why wasn't Sam the King? In Kaznim's country a girl only got to be Queen if she had no brothers. It didn't make any sense at all. But then not much in this strange place did.

The Sick Bay corridor fell quiet and Kaznim sat in the shadows, bored and lonely. It was then she remembered, somewhat guiltily now, the gold box that she had stolen from Subhan-Subhan. Glad of something to do, she took the box from her pocket and ran her fingers over the ancient gold streaked with blue, the battered edges and dark metal hinges. Then she pulled open the clasp and looked inside. Nestling in a shaped bed of red velvet was the most exquisitely tiny hourglass that Kaznim had ever seen. Very carefully she lifted it from its bed and held it up. She had seen hourglasses before, full of sand, which ran through at a steady pace. But this one was different. Made of gold and lapis, it contained little silver grains that shone even in the dim lights of the corridor. It was exquisite. Entranced, Kaznim stared at it. There were many more grains of silver in one half than in the other, so she turned the hourglass so that most of them were in the top half and she could see them cascade down. To her surprise, they did not move. She turned it around, around, and then around again, yet not one of the grains dropped through. Kaznim was giving it one last go when, to her amazement, a grain of silver floated *up* from the bottom of the hourglass and buried itself in the mass of grains in the top. Kaznim nearly dropped it in shock. *It was **Magyk**.*

Kaznim stared at the hourglass. This must be what the Egg Boy called his **Egg Timer** – the one he'd boasted that the sorcerer had given him. Kaznim remembered now that the Egg Boy had said that a grain went through once every three hours. She looked at the small huddle of grains left. If only she could count them, she would know how long it would be until her little sister, Bubba, was safe. The hourglass was a frightening reminder of the power that the sorcerer Oraton-Marr had over her family. Someone rushed past into the Sick Bay and Kaznim quickly shoved the **Egg Timer** into her pocket.

Kaznim pushed away thoughts of her mother and sister. She blinked back tears and returned to studying the box. In two neat piles on either side of the empty hourglass bed were thick cards of different colours and shades. She took the cards out and saw a sprinkling of sand lying at the bottom of the box. Kaznim ran her finger across the sand, and felt even more homesick. She played with it for a while, letting it slide back and forth across the polished silver inside the box, then, afraid of losing the precious sand, she put the lid on the box and began to look at the cards.

There were twelve cards, ranging from a deep purple to bright, fiery red. Kaznim laid the cards out on the bench beside her and, beginning with the darkest purple card, she fanned them out and smiled – she had found a rainbow inside a pot of gold.

Kaznim looked at the cards more closely. On each one was a diagram of a cut-through egg with a small creature curled up inside it. She noticed that in each image the creature grew a little, beginning as a tiny shrimp and finishing as a perfect little dragon. Kaznim was so engrossed in the pictures that she did not notice the ExtraOrdinary Wizard emerge from the Sick Bay. The first she knew of him was when his shadow fell across the cards, like that of a sand eagle falling over a small desert creature. Hastily, she gathered the cards together.

"Ah," the ExtraOrdinary Wizard said. "Still here?"

Kaznim nodded. She wondered where else he thought she might go. She noticed that his gaze was fixed on the pile of cards.

"Nice pictures," he said. "What are they?"

Kaznim thought fast. "They're a card game. You … you play it on your own." She looked up to see if he believed her. It was hard to tell. His green eyes looked cloudy and he had a deep frown between them.

"I'm glad you have something to pass the time," he said. "It must be boring for you, stuck here."

Kaznim nodded. She felt bad about lying. But the pictures on the cards belonged to home, to her desert and the hot sands. Kaznim found she even felt proprietorial about the horrible

Egg Boy and the Egg. It was *her* world and it wasn't any business of the strangers in this noisy, heavy stone tower. Defiantly – for she could tell that the ExtraOrdinary Wizard wanted to look at the cards more closely – she put the cards back into the box and closed the lid with a *snap*.

The sudden wail of the emergency siren from the stairs stopped the ExtraOrdinary Wizard from asking anything more. The stairs sped up and he hurried over to wait beside them. Kaznim shoved the gold box deep into her tunic pocket.

"Marcellus!" she heard the ExtraOrdinary Wizard say. "Hurry. There's not a moment to lose."

Kaznim saw a youngish man in black and gold with his hair styled in a strange bowl cut stumble awkwardly off the stairs. He was carrying a small leather case that reminded Kaznim of her mother's Apothecary bag. The ExtraOrdinary Wizard grabbed his arm and hurried him along the corridor into the Sick Bay. The doors swung closed and once again all was quiet. Kaznim looked back at the stairs, expecting Tod to arrive, but there was no sign of her. There was nothing she could do but sit and wait. Which is what she did. Occasionally someone hurried into the Sick Bay but no one thought to come out and tell her how Sam was. Or to ask how she was.

Time ticked slowly by and Kaznim sat in the empty corridor, biting back tears. She felt utterly deserted.

# JO-JO

*Tod had been delayed* by searching for the last of Sam's brothers. She had eventually found Jo-Jo Heap moping alone in the rooms of his on-off girlfriend – a young witch named Marissa of whom not one of his family approved. When she finally hurried Jo-Jo along the Sick Bay corridor, Kaznim was lying curled up on the bench, asleep. A pang of guilt stabbed Tod as she and Jo-Jo slipped into the Sick Bay.

Marcellus Pye was sitting at the table packing a variety of small shiny instruments into his bag. He was surrounded by all the Heap brothers – except for Jo-Jo and Sam himself. Next to Marcellus sat Septimus, his purple robes splattered with dark stains of blood. Beside Septimus, Edd was busy writing up some notes for Dandra, then there was Nicko Heap, his sunburned face and brightly braided hair looking out of place in the sparse whiteness of the Sick Bay. Erik was talking in a low voice to the oldest Heap brother, Simon, who wore a similar black tunic to Marcellus although less encrusted with gold and, Tod noticed, less encrusted with blood too.

When Jo-Jo came in they all looked up at the same time and Tod had the odd sensation of five identical pairs of eyes acting as one.

"You took your time," Erik growled.

Jo-Jo looked flustered. He was still embarrassed to have been found tearfully waiting in Marissa's rooms. At the sound of Tod's footsteps on the stairs, Jo-Jo had thrown the door open and said, "Oh, Marissa, please –" and had then realised who it was. He had tried to close the door on Tod, and it was only when she had told him about Sam that Jo-Jo relented and agreed to come.

"Where's Sam?" Jo-Jo asked, trying to make up for his lateness. "Can I see him?"

"I'll take you through," said Septimus.

Tod and Jo-Jo followed Septimus into the Quiet Room. Sam was sleeping peacefully on his high, narrow bed, with, to Jo-Jo's surprise, a tortoise resting on a clean white bandage wrapped tightly around his stomach. Marwick was dozing in a chair beside him and on the other side of the bed sat Dandra, watching her patient, her fingers resting lightly on his wrist.

Dandra looked up and smiled wearily. "He's very weak," she said. "He's lost so much blood. But they got the blade out." She pointed to an oblong metal dish resting on a table beneath a small, high window.

Septimus picked up the dish and showed it to Jo-Jo and Tod. "Vicious thing," he said. A long, thin sliver of steel lay at the bottom of the dish, bright and sharp in a sudden shaft of moonlight. The ghostly inhabitants of the Quiet Room glanced at one another. Some of them were almost transparent, shocked by what they had recently witnessed.

Jo-Jo, too, was shocked. "Cool," he said, trying to hide his dismay at how ill his brother looked. "Yeah. Totally cool."

There was a strained silence and then Dandra said, "Alice, you look exhausted. Time for bed."

# SNEAK PEEK

*Tod wandered out through* the stillness of the night-time Sick Bay, past the subdued group of Heaps who had settled down for the night vigil, and slipped silently into the dimly lit corridor. She was so tired that she would have walked straight past Kaznim without a thought, had a small snuffle not alerted her to the presence of a curled-up form sleeping on the waiting bench.

*Bother*, thought Tod. The last thing she wanted was to have to wake Kaznim, get her back down the stairs and then find somewhere for her to sleep – which was not going to be easy, as the dorm was full. Sternly, Tod told herself not to be so mean. Kaznim was lost and alone in a strange place and she knew only too well how that felt.

Tod went over to Kaznim and shook her gently. "Kaznim. Kaznim … wake up." The girl stirred and her arm knocked something to the floor. It landed with a clatter and Tod knelt down to pick it up. It was a gold box. The lid had come off and some multicoloured cards had spilled out. Tod gathered the cards together and as she touched each one a faint buzz of alien **Magyk** fluttered through her fingers. Tod was surprised – she hadn't thought that Kaznim had anything **Magykal** about her.

In the dimness of the corridor's nightlights, Tod could not see if she had found all the cards. Not wanting to lose any of what was obviously Kaznim's treasured possession, she took a small FlashLight from her Apprentice belt – a thin green cylinder with a black spot at one end and a white spot at the other. Tod pressed the white spot and a beam of darkness shone from the black. Blearily, she pressed the black spot and a needle-sharp beam of light came shining out from the white. She scanned the floor beneath the bench looking for any stray cards and found a surprising amount of grit and two cards: a bright red and a pale blue. On the red card the FlashLight showed the diagram of a tiny dragon curled within an oval.

Intrigued, Tod sat down on the bench beside Kaznim – who was still deeply asleep – and looked at the cards. At first glance the drawing on each card looked very similar. They both had the outline of the oval within which a little creature lay. But the pale blue card showed a more simple shape, whereas the red one showed a perfectly formed tiny dragon. Tod gazed at them both for some seconds, and then with a jolt, she realised what she was looking at. It was a cut-through of an egg, and the blue card showed the dragon at an earlier stage of development. *Or was it*, Tod suddenly thought with a stab of excitement, *an* Orm?

With all traces of sleepiness now gone, Tod took the rest of the cards from the box and spread them out on the bench. She glanced guiltily at Kaznim. Something told her that Kaznim would not approve of this. In the beam of her FlashLight, Tod began to examine the cards, which were numbered from one to twelve. As she concentrated on putting them in order, the FlashLight beam strayed on to Kaznim's face. The girl's eyelids fluttered and suddenly she was awake. Kaznim sat up with a start.

"It's all right, Kaznim," Tod murmured, hurriedly shoving the cards back into the box.

Kaznim stared at Tod, for a moment wondering where she was – and then she remembered. She looked down and saw her box in Tod's hands. "That's mine," she said. "Give it back."

"Here you are," Tod said. "It fell on the floor."

Kaznim looked at Tod suspiciously, then she checked the box. Something was missing. "My sand!" she cried out, jumping down from the bench. "You've lost my sand!"

Tod realised what the grit actually was. "It fell out," she said. "There's nothing we can do about it now."

"Yes there is! We can sweep it up!" Kaznim was distraught. "It's my sand. From home. *My sand* ..." With that she burst into tears.

Tod kneeled down and shone her FlashLight beam on to the floor. She was still learning Basyk Magyk, and one of the simple spells she had read – although not yet practised – was a Collecting spell for small particles. Tod decided to try it. Anything was better than scraping sand off the floor at half past one in the morning with a grumpy little girl eyeballing her.

The excitement of trying some Magyk for a real purpose drove the sleep from Tod's fuzzy head. From her Apprentice belt, she took a small piece of ancient Magyk paper. She laid it on the floor and placed a grain of Kaznim's precious sand on the middle of it. Then, muttering, *"Like to like together spin, like to like gather in,"* Tod made a circling sign above the paper with her right index finger. There was a small blue flash and the

95

grains of sand began to whizz around in circles. In the beam of her FlashLight, Tod saw them heading towards the paper. "Like tiny ants," she murmured, smiling at her success.

Suddenly the sand stopped its orderly procession towards the paper. The grains began to run around the floor as though they had grown legs. Tod stared at them in dismay. What had gone wrong? And then she realised. She had forgotten that simple spells stay open until their task is done. The spell was now making the sand behave like tiny ants. Relieved that she had not likened the sand to spiders – Tod had a fear of spiders – she muttered, *"Like sand,"* and the procession resumed.

Triumphantly, Tod tipped the sand into Kaznim's gold box. She got no thanks at all. Kaznim snatched the box and looked at Tod with a new suspicion in her eyes. "Where's Ptolemy?" she asked.

"Who?" Tod asked, puzzled.

"My *tortoise*. Where is he? Is he still with Sam? Is Sam all right?"

Tod was relieved that they were on safer ground. "Sam is still very weak. But they took out a piece of a knife blade. Your tortoise is still with him. Dr Draa says Ptolemy will help Sam get a good night's sleep."

Kaznim frowned. "That's *my* name," she said.

"What is?" asked Tod. The Magyk had left her and she felt stupid with tiredness.

"Draa. I am Kaznim Na-Draa."

"What a coincidence. Well, tomorrow when you come and see Sam you will meet Dandra."

"Dandra?" Kaznim looked shocked. *"Dandra Draa?"* Dandra Draa was a name Kaznim had heard throughout her childhood.

And whenever it was said, it was accompanied by a downwards stab of the left thumb – the sign of the Eternal Curse.

"Yes, Dr Dandra Draa. She's our physician here. She runs the Sick Bay. She is really nice."

"Dandra Draa is *not* nice," Kaznim said very determinedly.

"Oh, I'm sure you'll like her when you meet her," said Tod, thinking what a strange person Kaznim was turning out to be.

"No, I won't," Kaznim told her. She balled her left hand into a fist, pushed her thumb out and jabbed her fist towards the floor in a movement that was full of hate. Tod stared at Kaznim, shocked. Defiantly, Kaznim returned the stare. And then, spitting out the words one by one, she said, "Dandra Draa killed my father."

# CARDS ON THE TABLE

*A year ago the Junior Girls'* Apprentice Dorm had had a makeover. Each bed now resided within its own private, tented space. Such was the dorm's popularity since the arrival of the tents that Apprentices who would have normally lived at home now queued up for a chance to "live in the Wizzer", as they called the Wizard Tower. It was rare for the dorm to have a spare bed, and that night as usual there were none. Tod was so tired that she could not think where else Kaznim could sleep, so she gave up her own bed. Kaznim seemed exhausted by her outburst against Dandra and as soon as she lay down she fell into a deep sleep. Wearily, Tod went to fetch some cushions and a spare quilt – there was enough space in the tent for her to sleep on the floor.

But Tod could not sleep. Her brain refused to switch off and thoughts whirled around her head like a merry-go-round. She lay staring up at the blue and green stripes of the silk that rose up above her, thinking about the cards in Kaznim's box, and about the sand from Kaznim's home. The more she thought, the more she was certain that Kaznim knew all about the Egg of the Orm. Maybe, Tod thought excitedly, she had even seen it.

Tod made a decision – she must show the cards to Septimus. *Right now.* And if she was going to have to be a low-down sneaky pickpocket to get them, then that was what she would be. Stealthily, Tod pulled back Kaznim's quilt and drew the gold box out of the sleeping girl's pocket. Careful not to spill any of the wretched sand, Tod removed the cards, replaced the box and gently covered Kaznim up again. Then she tiptoed out of the tent into the quiet of the dorm and made her way up to the seventh floor.

Tod burst into the Sick Bay. "Look!" she said. "Look what I found!"

Six Heaps, sitting around the central desk, looked up in surprise.

"Tod," Septimus said wearily, "it is two o'clock in the morning. You should be asleep."

Tod faltered for a moment. She felt like a child who was being told off for not going to bed. But she remembered what her father used to say to her: *"If you think something is important, Tod, then it is."* And so Tod pushed the cards into Septimus's hands. "Can you **Feel** something?" she asked.

Septimus held the cards and was still for a moment. "Yes," he said. "It's faint. But I can **Feel** ... echoes of **Magyk**. But not our **Magyk**."

Tod was excited that Septimus could **Feel** it too. Her confidence grew. "So now spread the cards out so that they run one to twelve, picture side up," she told him.

Septimus was amused that his new Apprentice had suddenly turned teacher. Obediently, he did as he was told so that a rainbow of cards ran across the desk.

"Cool card game," said Jo-Jo. "We should get some like that for the Grot." "The Grot" was the slang name for Gothyk Grotto, the shop where Jo-Jo worked.

"They're not pretend," Tod said scathingly. "They're for real." But Jo-Jo had sowed a seed of doubt and Tod began to be afraid that these might indeed be some kind of game.

"They belong to the little girl who came with Sam and Marwick," Septimus said. "I saw her playing with them. She did actually tell me they were a card game."

"Oh," said Tod. She suddenly felt very foolish. If Septimus too thought they were a game, she had made a really stupid mistake.

Septimus looked up and smiled at Tod. "I didn't believe her. I could see they were more than that. But we had other things to think about right then. Well done, Tod. I was wondering how to get a closer look without upsetting her." He examined the cards one by one, peering closely at each diagram detailing a growing embryo unfolding like a bud.

Nicko, the seafaring brother, spoke. "They're like gulls' eggs," he said. "I've seen the chick at all these stages." He pulled a face. "They taste revolting. You'd be surprised how crunchy the little bones are once it begins to look like a bird. And the tiny feathers get stuck between your teeth. Then, when you try to pull them out they break off and –" He stopped. *"What?"* he demanded. "What are you looking at me like that for?"

"Yuck," said Jo-Jo. "That is authentic *yuck*."

"The stuff you guys eat at sea is unbelievable," said Erik.

Nicko shrugged. "You'll try anything when you're starving on a rock," he said.

Septimus looked up at Tod. "This *has* to be the development of the Orm inside the Egg. Twelve cards, one for each week."

"And there was sand in the box too," Tod said excitedly. "She said it was from her home."

"Well, well, did she now?" Septimus murmured. "Sand from a desert ... It all fits." He shook his head. "But *why* has the little girl got them – what is her name again?"

"Kaznim Na-Draa," Tod said.

"Draa," said Septimus. "Strange coincidence. Why she has these with her is a mystery. We will ask her tomorrow."

"I don't think she'll tell us," Tod said. She explained what had happened outside the Sick Bay when the box fell on the floor, leaving out the tirade against Dandra. Recently there had been a campaign in the Wizard Tower against gossip. The catchphrase had been: *Mud sticks – so don't throw it*. Tod didn't want to throw any mud against Dandra, someone she admired and liked very much.

Septimus was thinking. "Draa ... Draa," he was murmuring. "It all fits. You know that Dandra lived in a desert before she came to us?" He got up and walked over to the Quiet Room. "Dandra, can you leave your patient for a few minutes?"

Dandra woke Marwick so that he could watch Sam and tiptoed out of the Quiet Room. "Alice!" she said very disapprovingly. "What are you doing here? Go back to bed at once."

"It's all right, Dandra," Septimus said. "Tod has brought us something rather important. And it won't wait. What do you make of this?" He showed Dandra the rainbow of cards.

"It is the embryonic development of a reptile," Dandra said. "In the later stages it looks like a dragon, but the early stages are significantly different."

"We think it is an Orm," Septimus said.

"Really?" Dandra put on a pair of small spectacles and looked closely at the cards.

"There's stuff on the other side, too," Tod pointed out. "Like a timetable. Look." She turned the cards over and spread them across the desk. The back of each card was divided into seven spaces and each space was split into eight. "It's like seven days of the week," Tod said. "And each day is split into three-hour slots."

"Like Watches on a boat," said Nicko.

"True," Septimus agreed. "Some task that has to be done at regular intervals, maybe?"

"Turning the Egg!" Tod said excitedly. "To keep it moving as though it were in its parent's coils – like it said in the book."

Septimus nodded. "Yes … yes, that would fit very well."

Tod felt thrilled to be taking an equal part in such an important discussion, and to be listened to because what she was saying actually mattered. She watched Septimus peer at the cards, frowning. She guessed what he was going to say.

"If that is the case," Septimus said, "then the task is very nearly complete. Look." Closer examination showed that the first eleven cards had all their boxes ticked. Card twelve – the bright red – had the first three days ticked and the first two boxes for the fourth day. The rest were blank.

Septimus picked up the red card and turned it over. It showed a tiny winged dragonlike creature curled into a ball. Its head was big, its eyes closed and its legs folded beneath its belly, with its tail wrapped around its body. On top of its nose was a pointed spike. "I am very concerned," Septimus said, "that this is the stage of development that the Egg of the Orm has reached. Which means that we have only … sheesh … *three days* to find it before it hatches."

Everyone stared down at the cards. No one spoke. And then Jo-Jo said, "Cool. A baby Orm. That is so *totally* cool."

"Shut *up*, Jo-Jo," chorused his brothers.

"Dillop," added Nicko.

"But it *is* cool," Jo-Jo protested. "Just think if we had one here. How amazing would that be?"

"Jo-Jo," Septimus said. "You are, as Nicko pointed out, a dillop. But actually, you have just said something rather interesting."

# PART
# V

FORTY-EIGHT
HOURS TO
HATCHING

# A DISSATISFIED VISITOR

*The next morning Tod woke* unusually early. It took her a few moments to remember why she was sleeping on the floor of her tent and some moments more to realise that the very reason for her being on the floor had disappeared: her bed was empty and Kaznim was gone. Tod leaped up in dismay, unable to believe her eyes.

The night before, as she left the Sick Bay, Septimus had said that her quick thinking had very likely saved them all from a highly dangerous situation. He was, he had told everyone, very proud of his new Apprentice. "Well done for putting Kaznim Na-Draa in your tent," he had said to Tod as he'd walked her to the door. "Keep a close eye on her from now on. Bring her up to my rooms for breakfast in the morning and we will all have a talk." Then he had smiled and said, "I'll leave it to you to ask her where the Orm Egg is. You have the magic touch." Tod hadn't been too sure about that, but she'd been delighted that Septimus trusted her so much.

And now Tod stared at the Kaznim-shaped space in her bed, horrified. She had blown it. All Septimus's trust was for nothing. Frantically, Tod threw on her clothes, raced out of the dorm and ran into the early morning quiet of the Apprentice corridor. She stopped at the spiral stairs, which were travelling slowly on night-time mode, heading downwards. Above, Tod heard the unusual sound of footsteps – someone was running down. To her utter relief she saw Kaznim approaching at top speed. Tod was amazed at how Kaznim had overcome her fear of the stairs. "Hey!" she called out.

"Go away!" Kaznim shouted as she rattled past.

Tod leaped on and clattered after her. "Hey, wait!" she said.

"Go *away*!" Kaznim yelled back and hurried on, whirling around like a top.

"Kaznim …" Tod was getting dizzy, but she dared not slow down. "Kaznim … please … What's the matter?"

Kaznim stopped and turned around, furious. "I hate this place. And I hate you. You stole my box, you stole my cards and if you had found it, you would have stolen my **Egg Timer** too –"

"No! No, I didn't steal anything," Tod protested a little guiltily.

"Yes, you did! You took the cards when I was asleep. I woke up in the dark and they weren't there!" Kaznim's angry voice echoed into the Great Hall as the stairs took them slowly down past the flickering pictures, bright in the dawn dimness.

"Shh!" It was not done to shout in the Great Hall, and Tod felt responsible for Kaznim's behaviour. "Look," she said quietly, "I didn't steal your box. *No way*. I didn't steal your cards, either. OK, I admit I borrowed them, but that's all. I'm sorry, but you were asleep and I couldn't ask you. I gave them back."

"So what!" Kaznim snapped. "It was *my* stuff and you took it. You're a nasty, sneaky pickpocket and *I hate you*."

"I'm really sorry, Kaznim, but you see –"

The stairs had now reached the ground and Kaznim – whose anger had driven away her fear of the stairs – jumped off without a thought. While the words wandering across the floor bid her GOOD MORNING, YOUNG GUEST, HAVE A HAPPY DAY IN THE WIZARD TOWER, Kaznim yelled, "You're all murderers and thieves!"

Tod jumped off the stairs to an accompanying wish from the floor – GOOD MORNING, EXTRAORDINARY APPRENTICE, HAVE A HAPPY DAY WITH YOUR NEW FRIEND – and hurried to catch up with Kaznim. "No, Kaznim ... wait. We're not thieves. And there's no way we're murderers. Honestly, we're not ..."

Kaznim stopped and spun around, her dark eyes blazing with anger. "Yes, you are! That horrible murderer woman has *stolen my tortoise!*"

Tod knew exactly who she meant. "Kaznim, Dandra hasn't stolen your tortoise. You *gave* it to her."

"I gave my tortoise to *Sam*," Kaznim yelled. "Not her!"

Tod was relieved to see that apart from Jim Knee wrapped in a fur coat, sleeping on the visitors' bench, there was no one in the Great Hall to hear Kaznim shouting. "Is that where you went just now? Up to the Sick Bay?" Tod asked, following Kaznim as she headed across towards the open doors, beyond which Catchpole was sweeping the snow off the top step.

"Yes. I woke up because I missed my tortoise ..." Kaznim's eyes filled with tears and made Tod feel very guilty. "So I went up to see Sam. There was no one there except for Marwick. I asked him if I could have Ptolemy back and he said yes. But then *she* came in and took my tortoise away from me!"

"Kaznim, please. I'm really sorry about Ptolemy –"

Kaznim did not want Tod's sympathy and she knew that the only way to avoid crying was to stay angry. "You're not sorry!" she yelled.

"I am, honestly. But I expect Dandra thought that Sam still needed Ptolemy," Tod said, wondering how to make things better. Behind Kaznim she could see Boris Catchpole coming in from sweeping the newly fallen snow off the top of the outside steps. Aware that the officious Catchpole was looking at them disapprovingly, Tod said soothingly, "Kaznim, why don't we go up to the Sick Bay together and I will talk to Dr Draa? I'm sure we can sort this out."

"I'm not talking to *her*," said Kaznim. Her voice went up a few more decibels, just as a group of elderly Wizards wandered in from the canteen. "Dandra Draa is a *murderer*. She killed my father and now she has *stolen my tortoise* and I *hate* her! I hate everyone in this horrible place – *every single one!*"

Tod and the elderly Wizards stood shocked as Kaznim spun around and set off at a run towards the slowly closing doors. Tod raced after her, but Kaznim was fast.

Kaznim reached the doors, wheeled around and yelled, "She'll be sorry! I'll be back with someone much more powerful than your stupid wizard and then you'll *all* be sorry!" And as the doors drew dangerously close together, Kaznim Na-Draa threw herself into the rapidly narrowing gap.

"No!" Tod shouted, afraid that Kaznim would be crushed like a nut in a nutcracker. But the small girl wriggled through and the next moment the doors settled together with their familiar soft *thunk*.

Quickly Tod gave the new day's password and, agonisingly slowly, the doors began to open again. Aware that she was

110

being watched by Catchpole, Tod hopped up and down impatiently, waiting for the doors to open wide enough for her to slip through. Tod did not like Boris Catchpole. He hadn't actually ever been mean to her, but there was something in his manner that told her he would not pass up the chance. And that morning he didn't.

# FUGITIVE

*The silver doors of the* Wizard Tower closed softly behind Kaznim and the cold hit her like a hammer. It was like nothing she had ever experienced; she could feel it seeping into her bones, thickening her blood, slowing her thoughts. She breathed in and the frosty air seared her lungs. Her thin red coat gave about as much warmth as a sheet of paper and her bare feet in her sandals ached. But Kaznim knew that there was no going back into the warmth of the Wizard Tower – at least not right then. But she would make good on her threat. She would indeed come back for her tortoise and she would not come alone. She would bring the sorcerer. Oraton-Marr was older, wiser and much more powerful than the two-faced young man with his soft blond curls and fancy purple robes. Then they would indeed be sorry.

Seething with anger and conveniently forgetting that the sorcerer she was lining up for a Wizard Tower takeover had actually stolen her baby sister, Kaznim took off down the wide, white marble steps. She headed quickly across a large courtyard lit by flaming torches, bright in the twilight of the winter dawn.

The courtyard was a strangely exotic place and had Kaznim not been running away, she would have happily wandered through, looking at the cold, white sand that was banked up against the walls as if blown into drifts, and the beautiful, dancing coloured lights. But Kaznim had no time to stop and stare. She hurried towards a massive archway that led out of the courtyard, her sandals flip-flapping as she went. In seconds she was going through the arch, glancing up at the beautiful blue lapis that lined it, reminding her of the egg at home. And then she was out. She turned briefly to check that no one had followed her, then ducked out of sight and stopped to catch her breath. Shivering violently, Kaznim stared at the scene before her, trying to make sense of it.

In front of her stretched a beautiful, wide avenue lit with flaming torches perched in tall silver torchposts that ran down its entire length. On either side of the avenue were low buildings of an ancient yellowing stone. Most of these housed shops and small businesses, somewhat obscured by a variety of stalls that were being set up in front of them. Straight down the middle of the avenue was an empty roadway, which was lined with banks of the strange, sparkling white sand. The surface of the roadway itself looked to Kaznim like white frosted glass. It was both beautiful and bizarre and she had no idea what it could possibly be.

It was the start of the course for the annual Manuscriptorium Sled Race. A wide racetrack of compacted, icy snow ran down the centre of Wizard Way, which led from the Palace to the Wizard Tower. All the preparation had been done the day before, and now, early in the morning, the people were beginning to venture out to begin what promised to be an exciting day. Stalls were being set up behind the racetrack walls, and a low buzz of excited chatter filled the air. A boy selling hot chestnuts was tending a brazier on wheels close to Kaznim. He had just set the first batch of chestnuts on the griddle when he noticed a wide-eyed, slight girl in the long red coat and bare feet in summer sandals. He wondered who she was; she looked so cold that he was quite worried for her. "Hey!" he said. "Come and stand by the fire. Get yourself warm."

Kaznim smiled shyly and shook her head. She was scared that any minute now, someone from the giant stone tower would be out to track her down. Relieved that the sneaky pickpocket Apprentice girl had not found it, she took the pale blue origami paper bird from her secret pocket and with shaking hands began to unfold it. From the bird's body Kaznim took the small opal pebble, clutched it in her fist and muttered the words the sorcerer had taught her:

*Let me Fade into the Aire,*
*Let all against me know not Where,*
*Let them that Seeke me pass me by,*
*Let Harme not reach me from their Eye.*

Once again, Kaznim felt the warm, buzzing sensation of ancient **Magyk** enveloping her. As it spread through her body, her shivering stopped and when the chestnut boy turned around to offer her a bag of hot chestnuts, he couldn't see her. It was strange, he thought, that he hadn't seen her go.

# SQUEEZE-THROUGH

*Inside the Great Hall*, Tod watched the doors to the Wizard Tower begin to open once more. "I hope you're not planning to do a Squeeze-Through like your young friend," Catchpole said. Running through the doors before they were fully open was known as a "Squeeze-Through", and Apprentices were banned from doing it. It was considered bad form even for Wizards not to wait until the doors had fully opened and settled on to their hinges.

Desperation made Tod brave. "I *have* to get out. It's an emergency," she said, edgily eyeing the doors, which always moved slowly in frosty weather.

"An *emergency*," Catchpole said mockingly. "Huh! And *I'm* a banana."

"You said it," Tod muttered under her breath.

The doors were now showing a gap just about wide enough for her to get through, but Boris Catchpole had planted himself in front of it with his broom held horizontally. He looked down at Tod pompously. "An ExtraOrdinary Apprentice is expected to set an example," he said. "She is not expected to have a slanging match in the Great Hall nor is she expected to play tag within the confines of the Wizard Tower."

"It's not tag!" Tod shouted in exasperation, and heard tut-tutting from the elderly Wizards who were now discussing the bad behaviour of modern-day Apprentices. "I *told* you, Catchpole. It's an emergency."

"Rules is rules," Catchpole said, doggedly holding the broom across the ever-widening gap. Tod saw that his gaze had shifted and was now fixed on someone behind her. "*You'll* have to wait an' all," Catchpole told whoever it was. Tod glanced back, expecting to see one of the elderly Wizards, but to her surprise she saw Jim Knee. He stood, tall and resplendent in his long fur coat, glaring at Catchpole. The jinnee, like all jinn who were at a Master's disposal, disliked authority. Jim Knee particularly disliked the Catchpole variety: the relish of enforcing petty regulations. He had had a few Masters like that himself, and he didn't like to see a young Apprentice being treated in this way.

"Let the Apprentice leave as she wishes," Jim Knee said. There was a threat in his voice that would have given most people a jolt of fear, but Boris Catchpole, who was not the most subtle of people, did not notice. He positioned himself firmly in front of the gap and held tightly on to the broom. "Let … her … leave," Jim Knee repeated.

"She can go out when the doors is fully open like everyone else does," Catchpole retorted.

Jim Knee stared at Catchpole with narrowed eyes. A long, low growl rippled through his body, making the hairs on the back of Tod's neck stand up. Jim Knee began to shiver and sway. There was a sudden flash of yellow and Catchpole screamed. Planted firmly in Jim Knee's place, teeth bared, muscles flexed, ready to pounce, was a long, low, yellow-and-black-striped tiger. A menacing snarl filled the Great Hall, a distant Wizard shrieked and Catchpole fainted – but not before Tod had seized her chance and raced out of the ever-widening gap into the frosty early morning air. She stopped at the top of the steps. It was as she had feared. The courtyard was deserted. Kaznim had gone.

# Unseen

*With the tiger bounding at her side,* Tod raced across the courtyard and through the Great Arch. Wizard Way was beginning to fill as arrivals from the early morning Port Barge mingled with the Castle stallholders. Tod scanned the scene before them. "I *have* to find her, Jim Knee," she said desperately. "She's our only clue to where the Orm Egg is. I promised Septimus I'd look after her, and all I've done is lost her."

In the shadows of her **UnSeen**, Kaznim, who was standing no more than a few feet from Tod, saw the tiger and froze. They had sent a wild beast out for her – *just as the Red Queen did for her father.* Kaznim prayed to the Sand Spirits that the tiger would not smell her scent.

The tiger was, however, far more interested in the scent of the hot-sausage-sandwich cart trundling towards them. It growled hungrily, opened its mouth and flicked its huge pink tongue around its black lips. A string of tiger saliva dripped on to the snow. Terrified, Kaznim shrank back against the wall.

Tod felt utterly deflated. Her only hope had been that Kaznim would be easy to spot. Not many people in the Castle wore red, partly because it was the Queen's colour and partly because it was the fashion to wear natural shades. Tod had also hoped that Wizard Way would be deserted, as it usually was at such an early hour, but today was the day of the Manuscriptorium Sled Races and she had not realised how early the preparations would begin. Before she had been asked to PathFind Jim Knee to his first desert, Tod had been due to represent the Wizard Tower in the Apprentice Race. She had put in a few practice runs and loved it. She pushed aside a pang of regret at the thought of her substitute having all the fun. Some things, she told herself, were more important than a sled race.

Aware that the seconds were ticking away fast, Tod scanned the hive of activity before her: people setting up stalls, Manuscriptorium scribes erecting barriers and hanging banners, marshals trying to keep the sled course clear and in the midst of it all, the hot-sausage-sandwich cart banging into everyone's legs and getting sworn at for its trouble.

Desperately, Tod searched the sea of greys, browns and muted greens for a flash of colour. A red scarf caught her eye but it belonged to Foxy, a lanky scribe who was tending the banks of snow that separated the sled course from the spectators.

*Where had Kaznim gone?*

From the safety of her UnSeen Kaznim stared at Tod and Jim Knee. *Please*, she silently prayed, *please let them go away. Please.* She did not dare move, for she knew they would see her footprints appearing in the cold white sand.

Tod now became aware of a feeling that she was being watched. Remembering what Septimus had told her about being still and listening to what she felt, she stopped searching the Way for a glimpse of red and concentrated hard. Suddenly she caught a tang of unfamiliar Magyk. She turned around and looked at the spot where it came from – a patch just in front of the courtyard wall where two small footprints were planted in the snow.

Kaznim saw Tod looking straight at her and she understood that it was all over. She closed her eyes and waited for the tiger to pounce. Suddenly there was a scream.

*"Aiiieeee!"* It was the sausage-sandwich cart boy, staring into the jaws of a hungry tiger. Kaznim opened her eyes to see the boy racing past her, scattering sausages as he went. She watched them roll across the white sand, bizarrely making it sizzle and turn to water. She saw the tiger wolfing up the sausages, while screams spread through the throng as people began to realise that there was a tiger on the loose. As panic spread and people scattered, Kaznim saw the pickpocket Apprentice girl grab hold of the tiger's scruff and say: "Jim Knee, stop it! You're scaring everyone. Transform now, please. Please, Jim Knee!"

The pickpocket Apprentice girl was, Kaznim thought, surprisingly brave – and oddly polite.

Tod had no option but to be polite. It was her only hope of getting Jim Knee to do as she asked – it was not for her to Command Septimus's jinnee.

However, Jim Knee was not about to give up the luxury of control over his own form and he had not the slightest intention of obeying Tod's request. Besides, now that he had eaten a few sausages, the jinnee was beginning to enjoy being a tiger. He loved the feel of his four softly padded, broad feet moving silently over the snow, the sense of the power in his muscles and the knowledge that they would take him wherever he wanted to go. The warmth of his fur in the frosty air was a delight and the smells that wafted towards his wide, sensitive nostrils were entrancing. He liked the smooth sharpness of his

120

strong white teeth, which did not ache in the cold like his ancient, crumbling jinnee teeth; and when he opened his mouth to catch a falling snowflake on his thick pink tongue, he loved the way everyone screamed. For a weedy jinnee, who was more used to being laughed at than feared, it was heady stuff. Why would he want to be anything else? He wriggled free of Tod's hold and took off down Wizard Way.

Kaznim watched Tod hurtle after the tiger, shouting out, "Stop, stop! Jim Knee, please stop!" and she knew that now was her chance. She must seize it before her UnSeen wore off and the Apprentice girl and her wild beast tracked her down. Quickly, Kaznim smoothed out the blue paper bird in which her Charm had been wrapped and once more read the words:

THE MAGYKAL MANUSCRIPTORIUM
AND SPELL CHECKERS INCORPORATED
NUMBER THIRTEEN WIZARD WAY, THE CASTLE.
AS PREMIER ADVISORS TO THE FABLED WIZARD TOWER,
WE ARE PROUD TO OFFER A NEW GLOBAL SERVICE.
WE HAVE MANY THOUSANDS OF YEARS' EXPERIENCE.
WE CAN SOURCE MOST REQUIREMENTS.
WE HAVE AN EXTENSIVE STOCK OF
CHARMS, RUNES AND SPELL BOOKS
OR WE CAN REFURBISH YOUR OWN.
CONVENIENTLY SITUATED ON
THE ANCIENT WAY SYSTEM FOR
EASY ACCESS FROM ANYWHERE IN THE WORLD.

Kaznim read the last line of the flyer again: *anywhere in the World*. A thrill of happiness ran through her. If the

Manuscriptorium could get messages all the way to her tent, then it could get *her* there too. As the wave of tiger-related screams rolled away into the distance, Kaznim followed a small signpost with a finger pointing to: *The Manuscriptorium*. It led her to a line of shops almost hidden behind the banks of white sand. As she walked towards number thirteen, Kaznim felt as though she were taking the first steps on her journey home.

# TIGER TROUBLE

*At the other end of Wizard Way*, Tod's troubles were mounting fast. People were not taking kindly to the presence of a tiger bounding through the middle of preparations for the sled race. Tod's chasing it, yelling, "Jim Knee, Jim Knee!" did not go down well either. Recently there had been a variety of pranks played by a rowdy group of Senior Apprentices who called themselves the Knights of Knee, in homage to their anarchic hero, Jim Knee.

"Jim Knee! Please! Transform!" Tod begged as she scooted after the jinnee. Jim Knee took no notice of her whatsoever. Every torchpost along that side of Wizard Way was now festooned not only with race banners but also with the more agile of the stallholders. A stampede across the sled racetrack had led to bodies sprawled across the slippery ice as though in the aftermath of a battle. And through the chaos loped Jim Knee, excited by his tiger-ness, loving the cool, sprung padding of his tiger feet, the smell of fear and the heady feeling of power.

Desperately, Tod tried to calm the panic. "It's not a real tiger!" she yelled. "It's only Jim Knee!"

But the mention of Jim Knee only led to shouts of "Shame on you, Apprentice!" and "You should know better!".

Jim Knee raced on, scattering people as he went, and Tod

knew he was loving every second. She at last caught up with the tiger at a bacon sandwich stall where he was demolishing its entire stock of bacon. Above him, at the top of a torchpost, the sandwich girl watched in dismay.

"Jim ... Knee ..." Tod puffed. "Please. That's enough ... Please, will you **Transform** now? Please!" The tiger turned around and stared at Tod, strips of bacon hanging from its mouth like a fresh kill. It crouched low and bared its teeth, spittle shining in the sunlight. Tod backed away, scared. There didn't seem to be much of Jim Knee left any more. She remembered what Septimus had told her about jinnee **Transformation** and how the nature of the creature that the jinnee had **Transformed** to would slowly take over. The tiger snarled a warning and shot off down Measel's Ope, the nearest alleyway. Tod went to follow but someone grabbed hold of her. "Tod, don't!" came a familiar voice.

Tod spun around. "Ferdie!" she gasped. "Hey, what are you doing here?"

Ferdie Sarn was the twin sister of Oskar Sarn; both were Tod's oldest friends from her home village. Ferdie smiled at the unexpected sight of her old friend. Ferdie's bright blue eyes sparkled in the wintery sun, and her red curls escaped happily from beneath her green woollen hat. "Well, what are *you* doing chasing after a tiger?" she asked, looking anxiously down Measel's Ope. "And what's a tiger doing in the Castle — they don't usually have them here, do they?" Ferdie grabbed hold of her companion, a blond-haired boy of about seven, and said, "No, William, you do *not* want to go down there."

William, the son of Simon and Lucy Heap, was squirming with excitement. "But I *like* tigers," he protested.

"And it would probably like you, too," said Ferdie. "You'd be really soft and squishy to eat."

William stuck his tongue out at Ferdie. "No I wouldn't," he said. "I'd be *crunchy*." But to make sure the tiger didn't get to find out whether he was squishy or crunchy, William hid behind Ferdie and gazed shyly up at Tod. He thought she looked very important in her green tunic and silver Apprentice belt.

"He's not really a tiger," Tod began to explain. "He's a –" Then she remembered she wasn't meant to talk about Jim Knee outside the Wizard Tower and stopped, feeling a little awkward.

"A secret," Ferdie finished for her. "One of your new *Apprentice* secrets. Some kind of tiger spell?"

"Well …" Tod hesitated. Ferdie was an old friend, someone she had known all her life, and she longed to tell her about the jinnee. In fact, she longed to tell her about the whole disastrous morning. But, like Jim Knee with his tiger-ness, the Wizard Tower code was seeping into Tod and she felt awkward sharing its problems, even with her closest friend. "Ferdie," she said, "I've got to go."

Ferdie looked sadly at her old friend. "OK. See you around, then."

"I mean, I've got to go because …" Tod trailed off. It struck her that the more people there were looking for Kaznim, the better. "I'm looking for a little girl in red. She was running away."

Ferdie looked surprised. "Running away? From you?"

"Well, yes, I suppose so," Tod admitted as she glanced around, checking for a glimpse of red. "Ferd, this is *really* important. I've made a massive mistake. I *have* to find her."

"I'll help you!" William said. "I'm good at hide-and-seek."

Ferdie was shocked at how upset Tod seemed. "Hey, don't worry," she said. "We'll both help you. A little girl in red will be easy to spot."

They hurried down the Way to the Palace Gates and then followed the racecourse as it took a sharp right along Snake Slipway. The ice glittered as the rays of the sun emerged above the snowy rooftops of the tall houses on either side of the winding street, and the banks of snow that lined the course shone a pristine white, smooth with the snowfall from the night before. There was a good view of the course as it ran down the actual slipway and took another sharp right turn on to the frozen Moat. On the opposite bank was an expanse of snow and beyond that, the tall, dark trees at the edge of the Forest. Tod scanned the scene for a glimpse of red while William drew faces in the snow bank.

"I don't think she could have got this far," Tod said. "Well, I hope not. She'll freeze. She's only wearing a thin cotton coat."

"Who is she?" Ferdie asked. "Or is that another secret?" she added a little tetchily.

Tod avoided the question. "Come on, Ferd, she must still be on Wizard Way somewhere. We'll go up the other side."

They slid across the icy course while William skidded around excitedly, then they hurried up the other side of the Way. As they negotiated their path through the line outside the Castle teens' favourite eatery, Wizard Sandwiches, Tod found herself fielding tiger-related complaints.

"Hey, Apprentice. Are you Wizards starting a bloomin' zoo up there?"

"Apprentice. It trashed my stall. I want compensation."

126

Impressed, Ferdie watched Tod politely apologising and telling everyone that the tiger was perfectly safe. Ferdie felt a little left behind by Tod. When they had been friends in their village at home, she and Tod had shared all their secrets and discoveries. But now Tod was learning so many new things that Ferdie knew she would never understand. Ferdie was not helped by the fact that her twin brother, Oskar, was also becoming immersed in Castle life. Oskar now helped out at the Manuscriptorium and was loving it. But all Ferdie was doing right then was helping William's mother, Lucy Heap. It was fun, but it wasn't quite in the same league as her best friend or even her brother.

Tod finished dealing with yet another complaint: "I'm sorry, but I haven't got any complaint forms. You can ask Catchpole at the door."

"You're really part of it all here now, aren't you?" Ferdie said wistfully.

Tod felt awkward. "Ferd, I'm an Apprentice here. You *know* that. So of course I'm part of it. But … it's not all as great as you might think. Today *everything* has gone wrong. You just wouldn't believe."

Ferdie felt the old Tod reappearing. She linked arms just as they used to and said, "Hey, Tod. Nothing can be that bad. And you've always got us. You, me and Oskie, we're the Tribe of Three – remember?"

"I do remember," Tod said. "Really I do."

They walked slowly up Wizard Way, looking out for any glimpse of red. While they searched, Tod remembered how she, Ferdie and Oskar had promised one another that they would track down the Orm Egg themselves. Tod realised that, with the excitement of the Wizard Tower being on the trail of the Orm Egg, she had forgotten her promise to the Tribe of Three. But now, she reflected, it didn't matter anyway. She had let the only chance of finding the Orm Egg slip away. She was, Tod told herself, rotten at keeping promises.

Ferdie was sad to see Tod so frazzled. Nothing was worth that, Ferdie thought, not even a swanky Apprenticeship with an ExtraOrdinary Wizard. She squeezed Tod's arm sympathetically. "Don't worry," she said. "It will be …" Ferdie grinned and made the PathFinder sign for "OK" – touching the top of her right index finger and thumb together to make an "O".

The sight of the familiar sign decided it for Tod. At least she could keep her promise to her friends. "Ferd," she said, "there's some stuff I really want to tell you, but …" She looked at William Heap, who was gazing up at them, listening intently.

"But later," Ferdie said with a grin. "Later, when I've taken William home."

"But I don't want to go home," said William. "I want to be in the Tribe of Three."

Ferdie smiled. "When you're older," she said.

William scowled. "You're just like Mum. She always says that when I ask to do stuff."

Ferdie laughed. She was more than happy to be just like William's mother. She liked Lucy Heap a lot. "See you later?" she said to Tod. "I'll be up at the Sled Shed with Oskie. You know he's racing the Manuscriptorium sled in the Apprentice Race?" she said proudly. A thought occurred to her. "Hey, are you racing in the Apprentice too?"

"I was going to be, but …" Tod trailed off.

Ferdie looked at her quizzically. "Another secret?" she asked.

Tod sighed. "Not for long, I promise. I'll see you up at the Sled Shed with Oskie before the race."

"Tribe of Three in the Sled Shed," Ferdie said with a smile.

"Tribe of Three," Tod replied, and she hurried away, preoccupied.

Before she had become Septimus's Apprentice, Tod, Ferdie and Oskar had made a pact that the Tribe of Three came before everything. But Tod's life wasn't so simple any more – she had loyalties to Septimus and the Wizard Tower now too. As Tod drew nearer to the Wizard Tower she found herself envying Ferdie with her more straightforward choices. But what was really bothering Tod was the thought of telling Septimus that not only had she lost Kaznim – and with her their precious clue to the whereabouts of the Orm Egg – but she had also lost his jinnee. In fact, she had single-handedly ruined any chance they had of finding the Orm Egg.

Tod slowly climbed the wide white marble steps that led up to the silver doors of the Wizard Tower. She spoke the Password, the doors swung open and Tod stepped into the Great Hall with a sinking feeling in the pit of her stomach.

She wasn't looking forward to seeing Septimus at all. She really wasn't.

# DARIUS WRENN

*Kaznim gazed up at a sign* that read: *The Magykal Manuscriptorium and Spell Checkers Incorporated*. Kaznim was a little disappointed. She had been expecting a building as big, shiny and **Magykal** as the Wizard Tower, but found herself outside a small, insignificant shop. She stared in the window, which was piled high with books and had a handwritten sign plastered across it proclaiming:

PROUD SPONSOR OF THE
ANNUAL MANUSCRIPTORIUM SLED RACES.
WE ARE CLOSED THIS AFTERNOON FOR THE RACING.
PLEASE NOTE: NO BETS ARE TAKEN ON THESE PREMISES.

Kaznim got rid of her **UnSeen**, took a deep breath and pushed the shop door. It opened with a friendly *ping* and she walked into a long, narrow office. Sitting on a pile of books opposite the door was a nasty-looking fat little ghost dressed in blue robes trimmed with faded gold. The ghost – the previous Chief Hermetic Scribe who went by the name of Jillie Djinn – glared at her and said, "What do you want, little girl?"

Kaznim had grown up with many spiteful Sand Spirits and knew well enough not to answer back. Careful to avoid catching the ghost's dark little eyes, she headed towards the large desk at the end of the office where a small boy sat, almost hidden behind it. He was nervously chewing the end of his pen.

The boy's name was Darius Wrenn. He was ten years old and small for his age. His short spiky, fair hair stuck out as though in shock, and his dark brown eyes had a permanently worried expression, which was accentuated by his nervous tic of blinking rapidly. Darius was from the Port orphanage and had recently been picked for the Early Starters Scheme at the Manuscriptorium. He wasn't enjoying the experience at all and that week was the worst so far. He was on duty in the front office, which scared him because anyone at all could walk in, and now the Chief Hermetic Scribe had gone to inspect the racecourse and left him all on his own.

"Just be helpful," Beetle had told Darius, rather unhelpfully. "Oh, and if any scribes bring in their younger brothers and sisters to show off where they work – which they are allowed to do today – you must make sure that there are no running games between the desks. But remember, today is the day when we want to make people feel that this is *their* Manuscriptorium and that we are here to help them with anything we possibly can. If someone asks for something you don't understand, ask Foxy." With that the Chief Hermetic Scribe was out of the door before Darius had time to tell him that Foxy was out on the racecourse too. In fact, *everyone* was out. As Beetle had closed the door, Darius thought its *ping* was the loneliest, scariest sound that he had ever heard. He sat behind the big office desk, shivering with the cold and dreading who might come in and expect him to help them.

And so when the door *ping* announced Kaznim, Darius was very relieved to see someone who was actually a bit smaller and younger than he was. He blinked nervously and in a shy squeak repeated what he'd been told to say. "Good morning. How may I help you?"

Kaznim was not sure how to begin. "Um. I've got this," she said, and pushed the much-folded blue piece of paper across the desk to Darius. He looked at it for barely a second – Darius could read a whole page in a single glance.

"Yes," he said.

"It is from here?" Kaznim asked nervously.

"Yes," Darius said. He was not sure if he was allowed to talk about the papers. The Chief and various scribes had told him so many different things. He looked anxiously at the ghost of Jillie Djinn. The ghost seemed unusually friendly. She nodded reassuringly and Darius's confidence returned. He smiled at Kaznim.

Encouraged, Kaznim asked, "Do you know the place where it went to?"

Darius remembered the excitement when Foxy and the Chief had returned from their amazing journey. They had not stayed long, but Beetle had made sure he knew where they – and the leaflets – had ended up. "We want to know where our first international customers come from," he had said, laughing.

"The Port of the Singing Sands," Darius told Kaznim proudly.

"Oh!" Kaznim gasped. "I live in the Desert of the Singing Sands."

Darius's eyes widened. "Wow. That's a *long* way away."

Kaznim bit back tears. "I know."

Darius possessed one precious book in the orphanage. It was called *The Wonders of the Seven Sands*. It had his father's name written inside it, lots of small dark type and three beautiful coloured pictures of people in long robes and desert tents. Whenever Darius felt cold in the orphanage – which was often – all he had to do was to open the book and he was warm again. "I love deserts," Darius said dreamily. "And tents."

"I live in a tent," Kaznim said.

"Wow …"

"It has stars all over it."

"Beautiful …"

"It is. And my mother – she's an Apothecary – she works there, and … I miss her. I just … *I just want to go home*."

Darius was speechless. He would want to go home too if he lived with his mother in the middle of a nice warm desert. Darius could just about remember his mother, although he tried not to. It made him too sad.

"But I don't know how to get home," Kaznim was saying. "I thought you might be able to help me. I thought you might know the way."

Darius did not answer straightaway. He was thinking about how he would so much rather live in a tent than the Manuscriptorium, which was just like the orphanage – full of rules that he did not understand.

Kaznim took Darius's silence as a refusal. She remembered how her mother had told her that if you wanted something from an official you must give a gift to show that you were serious about wanting it. So she reached deep into her secret pocket, took out the **Egg Timer** and showed it to Darius.

Darius's eyes widened. He had never seen anything so small and yet so perfectly made. "That's beautiful," he said.

"It's for you," Kaznim said. "To show you how much I want to go home." And she pushed the **Egg Timer** across the desk. With a feeling of wonder, Darius picked it up.

"What is it?" he asked.

"It's an **Egg Timer**," Kaznim said.

Darius thought it was far too beautiful to be given away. "I can't take it," he said.

Kaznim's face fell. "Don't you like it?" she asked.

"Of course I like it," Darius said. "But it's yours."

"I want you to have it," Kaznim told him. "Because I want you to tell me the way home. Please. I ... I miss my mother *so much*."

That did it for Darius. If someone knew a way for him to find his mother again, he would be devastated if they did not tell him. "All right then, I'll tell you," he said. "I can remember the numbers. If you like, I could write down the Ways to your home?"

"Oh, yes, *please*," said Kaznim.

Darius closed his eyes and the numbers he needed were there, as clear as if they were in front of him on a piece of paper. He dipped his beautiful new Manuscriptorium pen into the inkpot and carefully wrote out a series of symbols, *II-X-IV-I-XI-X-V-III-IV-VIII*, on to Kaznim's precious blue paper. He pushed the paper across the desk with a smile. "There," he said.

Kaznim was horribly disappointed. These were Way numbers. Even if she could get through the **Hidden** arch in the Wizard Tower courtyard she could get no further than the **Sealed** Hub beyond. "They're no use to me," she said miserably. "Everything's **Sealed**."

134

"Not *here*," Darius said proudly. "We have a Way here, and the Chief wouldn't allow it to be Sealed. You can go anywhere in the world from here."

At that moment Romilly Badger came through the Manuscriptorium door. Darius looked up and shoved the Egg Timer guiltily into his pocket. Romilly gave Darius a stern look. "I hope you're not talking about what I think you are, Darius," she said.

"No!" said Darius quickly. "No, I'm not."

"Good. Remember your Promise, now."

"Yes ... yes, I will," Darius said, blushing bright red. Romilly eyed the two children and decided they could not get up to much harm. She was already late for her duties on the racecourse. The *ping* of the closing door brought Darius back to reality. With Romilly's words ringing in his ears, Darius realised what he had just done – *he had broken the Manuscriptorium Promise*.

Darius thought fast. He had to get the numbers back, but one look at Kaznim tightly clutching her blue paper told him that it would not be easy. "I, er, I think I made a mistake in one of the numbers," he said. "I'll just fix it, shall I?"

Kaznim was not fooled. She saw Darius's flustered expression and she knew he was lying, just like everyone else in the horrible Castle. "No!" she said.

Desperation made Darius Wrenn brave. He raced around to the front of the desk and snatched the paper. Kaznim grabbed it back and gave Darius a shove, sending him flying backwards. But Darius was not giving up. One thing he had learned in the orphanage was how to fight. He ran straight at Kaznim and dived at her knees. Kaznim neatly stepped to one side and Darius crashed into the pile of books on which the ghost was sitting, watching the fight with some amusement. The books cascaded on to the floor and the ghost leaped up and set about kicking Darius. The kicks **Passed Through** him and Darius felt nothing, but it is always a frightening experience to be kicked by a ghost. Darius, however, was not to be deflected. He struggled to his feet and ran at Kaznim, who was heading rapidly for the door. He grabbed her shoulder and Kaznim swung around and punched him on the nose. It was the most painful thing that had ever happened to Darius. *Ever.* His hands flew to his face and he felt the wet warmth of blood streaming on to his palms.

As Darius stood clutching his nose, overwhelmed by pain, he did not notice the ghost of Jillie Djinn beckoning Kaznim to follow her into the Manuscriptorium. The next thing Darius did notice was the discreet *ping* of the door as the Chief Hermetic Scribe came back from his inspection of the racecourse.

Beetle stared at the books strewn across the floor and Darius with his hands over his face and blood dripping through his fingers. "What on earth is going on?" he asked.

Darius stared at his boss in dismay. Two fat tears ran down his cheeks and joined the drops of blood dripping on to the floor.

Beetle knew he should not have left such a new and timid scribe alone. "Hey," he said, putting his arm around Darius. "Don't take it to heart. It gets a bit rough here on race day. Were they the big boys from Gothyk Grotto?"

Darius shook his head. "It was a little girl," he whispered.

"A little *girl?*" To Darius's chagrin, Beetle sounded amused. "Well, I must admit, we do have some fierce ones in the Castle.

136

Never mind, Darius. I've just got the sled lane order to sort out and then we'll lock up for the day. OK? And you can have a nice glass of FizzFroot. How about that?"

Darius nodded and managed a weak smile. He didn't like FizzFroot – all the bubbles went up his nose and it tasted weird – but Darius didn't care. The girl had run away and the Chief Hermetic Scribe was never going to find out what he'd done. And he had a really cute Egg Timer, too.

# THE MANUSCRIPTORIUM WAY

*The ghost of Jillie Djinn took* Kaznim through a dimly lit room full of high desks and down some stairs. At the bottom of the stairs were some swing doors where the ghost paused, put her finger to her lips and whispered, "Shh. I will show you how to go home, but you must be quiet and take care no one sees you. There are bad people down here."

Wide-eyed, Kaznim nodded. She could believe that.

"So push the doors, then," the ghost said testily.

Tentatively, Kaznim pushed. The doors swung open so easily that Kaznim very nearly fell through and then, to her horror, they swung back so fast that they hit the ghost in the face. Aghast, Kaznim waited for the ghost to yell at her and bring the bad people running. But the ghost managed a strained smile and beckoned Kaznim onwards.

Kaznim followed the dumpy, shimmering figure in dark blue along a wide white corridor with a line of hissing white lights on the ceiling. It felt very exposed. There were workrooms none of them with doors – opening off the corridor. They all appeared to be uninhabited, containing only a table with a selection of objects indicating various projects in progress: glass cases, piles of paper, pots, brushes, small tools and, in one room, a large press. Kaznim would have liked to have stopped and looked, but she remembered what the ghost had said about the bad people and tiptoed carefully by, checking each room as she did.

To Kaznim's shock, the very last room before the corridor turned a corner was occupied. A boy with curly red hair was watching a strangely misshapen creature swathed in white doing something at a workbench. They had their backs to the corridor but as Kaznim tiptoed by, the boy noticed the movement and turned around. Kaznim froze. The boy looked very odd; he was wearing thick magnifying spectacles through which his eyes looked like huge blue marbles. He looked surprised and said, "Oh! Queen Jenna!"

The boy was Oskar Sarn. He pulled off his magnifying spectacles and hurried out to the corridor to see if the Queen was lost and he could be of any help. But all Oskar saw was a small girl in a long red coat. He thought nothing of it – the Manuscriptorium was full of scribes' younger brothers and sisters that day. Oskar put his spectacles back on and returned to helping the Conservation, Preservation and Protection Scribe, Ephaniah Grebe, put together a particularly complicated automaton.

The ghost of Jillie Djinn was waiting at the turn of the corridor, tapping her foot impatiently. "Hurry *up*," she said to Kaznim.

Kaznim did not need to be told. The boy had scared her and she was around the corner in seconds. To Kaznim's relief, the wide, exposed brightness gave way to the dimness of rushlights and narrow brick-lined corridors. Now the ghost picked up speed, seeming to almost fly along the passageways. The light grew ever dimmer as the rushlights became spaced further apart, and Kaznim had to concentrate hard to pick out the dark blue robes from the shadows.

After a reckless dash down some steep stone steps, Kaznim found the ghost waiting for her in front of an iron door with four massive bolts drawn across it. "Now, little girl, first we need the key. It is hidden behind that loose brick there. No ... down there. Where I am pointing, child." The ghost sighed impatiently.

Kaznim scrabbled at the brick and managed to free it. Behind was a long, thin key.

"Very well," said the ghost. "Now take out that brick up there. No ... *there*. Goodness, do you not have eyes?"

Flustered by the ghost's impatience, Kaznim fumbled awkwardly with the second brick, which she had to stand on tiptoe to reach. But she was determined to do it. At last she pulled the brick out and saw a metal plate with a keyhole set behind it.

"Put the key in there and turn three times to the right very quickly, then four times to the left," the ghost told her.

Kaznim did as she was told and she felt a mechanism inside the door shift.

The ghost seemed pleased. "The bolts are free now," she said. Kaznim went to open the lowest bolt but the ghost stopped her. "No, little girl. Did your mother never teach you to tidy up? Put the key back and the bricks. Leave it as you found it."

Kaznim hated how the ghost talked about her mother but she said nothing. Meekly, she put the key and then the bricks back and waited.

"Well, get on with it then," the ghost said snappily. "Pull the bolts back. You've only got ... ooh, let's see, about fifty seconds now until they lock themselves again."

Kaznim was horrified. She wrenched at the bolts – which luckily were freshly oiled and moved easily – and the door swung open.

Behind it was a brick wall.

Kaznim felt utterly wretched. "There's just a wall," she said.

"Ah. So you don't really want to go home," the ghost said. "I thought as much."

"But I *do* want to go home," Kaznim protested, very nearly in tears. "I do, *I do!*"

"Well, go through there then," the ghost said.

"Through the *wall*?"

The ghost looked annoyed. "Through the arch," she said, stabbing an impatient finger at the wall.

"Arch?" asked Kaznim. She stared at the blank wall, willing the tears to go away.

"But you can't see it, can you, little girl?" the ghost taunted.

Kaznim remembered what Marwick had told her about Hidden arches: *If you want to see them badly enough, you will. With practice. In time.* There was no doubt in Kaznim's mind that she wanted to see this arch very badly indeed, but she had no time to practise. It had to happen *right now*. So she stretched her arms out, placed both hands on to the rough brick and imagined she was Marwick – Marwick, who could see the Hidden arches and who travelled the Ways as easily as if they were desert paths. At last, after the longest twenty seconds in Kaznim's life, she began to see the shimmering shape of an arch glowing through the brick. Elated, she said, "I see it! I see it!"

"Be quiet, little girl," the ghost said. "The bad people will hear. Now show me your blue paper."

Keeping a very tight grip on her precious piece of paper, Kaznim held it up. The ghost peered at it closely. "See the first symbol on the list that that silly little boy wrote for you?"

Kaznim nodded.

"That is the number two, which is this arch here. You just follow the symbols and you get home. Understand?"

Kaznim understood more than Jillie Djinn realised. She understood that the ghost was taking a delight in not explaining the Ways properly and she correctly suspected that although the ghost clearly wanted Kaznim to **Go Through** the Manuscriptorium Way, it was for some nasty reason of her own, not because she wanted to help her. The fat little ghost was, Kaznim thought, as unpleasant as everyone else in the nasty Castle – except for Sam and Marwick. They were the only people she was sorry to be leaving. Kaznim knew that Marwick would have honoured his promise to take her home. But she also knew that was not going to be for some time, and she wanted to go home right *now*.

With an air of satisfaction, the ghost watched Kaznim step into the **Hidden** arch of the Manuscriptorium Way. "Close the door behind you," she said.

Kaznim did as she was asked – she didn't want the horrid ghost following her – and then, stumbling into the darkness, she walked bravely forward.

In the gloomy corridor, the ghost of Jillie Djinn folded her arms and waited. Within seconds the four bolts slid silently across the door and the ghost heard the locking mechanism slip into place. She wafted away up the steps, heading back to the Manuscriptorium where the scribes worked. Then she sat on the steps that led to her old rooms and waited, a triumphant smile on her face.

Kaznim's route was not an easy one. It took her through a nest of snakes, a giant spider's web, a tar pit, a circle of wailing spirits and many other strange and frightening places, but when at last she emerged into the evening sunshine that smelled of heat and the desert she knew she was home – or very nearly so. But as she walked across a quiet quayside, gazing up at the ships, Kaznim's luck ran out. A baby voice piped out, "Kazzie, Kazzie! See Kazzie!"

Kaznim looked up, amazed and delighted. She saw her baby sister on a beautiful ship, held tightly in the arms of a hard-faced woman. As Bubba pointed and gabbled excitedly, the woman hurried away. Moments later a familiar figure with cropped hair and a steely stare appeared at the ship's rail, and Kaznim locked eyes with the sorcerer Oraton-Marr.

"Seize her!" he yelled to the guards at the foot of the gangplank.

"Who, sir?" they called up.

"The child in the red coat. Yes, *her*. Get her!"

Five minutes later, Kaznim was prisoner on board the *Tristan*. Now the Castle and the Wizard Tower did not seem so bad after all.

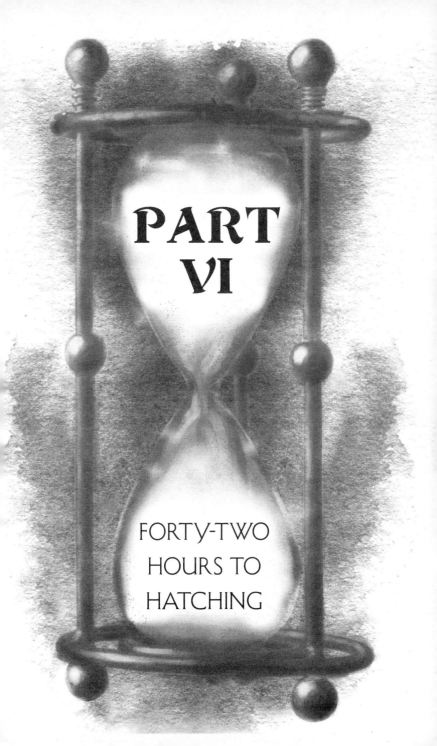

PART
VI

FORTY-TWO
HOURS TO
HATCHING

# CONFESSIONS

*That wretched Catchpole is an* officious prig," Septimus was telling Tod. "He was just as bad when I was a boy. I loathed him." He sighed. "I suppose you have no idea where Kaznim Na-Draa might be?"

Tod and Septimus were in the ExtraOrdinary Wizard's rooms on the twentieth floor of the Wizard Tower. Tod had just confessed that she had managed to lose not only their only clue to the whereabouts of the Orm Egg, but also the means of searching for it. Miserably, she shook her head. "I've no idea where she could be. She just vanished. It was almost as though she had done an **UnSeen**. In fact, I thought I felt something odd – a different kind of **Magyk** – when I first got outside the courtyard."

"She's too young to keep an **UnSeen** going for long," Septimus said. "But that is very useful to know. I'm sending all the duty Wizards out to look for her, and they need to know to track any echoes of foreign **Magyk**." He shook his head. "Though some of them would be hard put to track an elephant two feet in front of them."

"I'd like to go too," Tod said. "Seeing as I was the one who lost her."

There was an awkward silence in which Tod hoped that Septimus might tell her that it didn't matter and she wasn't to worry, but he didn't. What he did say surprised her. "If we don't find Jim Knee I expect you'd like to be in the Apprentice Race this afternoon?"

Tod was embarrassed. She hoped Septimus didn't think she had deliberately lost Jim Knee so that she would be able to be in the sled race. "Oh no," she said quickly. And then, when Septimus looked puzzled, she added, "I mean, yes, I would love to, but I must help you look for Kaznim. And Jim Knee."

Septimus considered the matter. "I think you should race," he said. "People expect the ExtraOrdinary Apprentice to run in the Apprentice Race. It will set alarm bells ringing if you're here and you don't race. The search party can go out right now and you can get down to the Sled Shed and tell your substitute he's off the race. And as for Jim Knee ... well, I don't want to Summon him but I may have to." Septimus sighed. "I am beginning to regret giving him power over his own form."

Tod could not help but feel a little sorry for Jim Knee. She wondered how it must feel to have no control over the most basic of things – the shape that one took in the world. She imagined being in the power of someone who could turn her into anything on a whim: a scorpion, a turtle, a little yellow crab. When Tod thought about it like that, she didn't begrudge Jim Knee his precious autonomy one bit. She just wished he had been a bit more helpful about what he did with it.

As Tod stood up to go, there was a knock on the door. Like a good Apprentice, she went to open it. Outside was Dandra Draa and her tortoise.

At the sight of Dandra, Septimus leaped to his feet. "Sam?" he asked anxiously.

"No, no, not Sam," Dandra said hurriedly. "Sam is sleeping and his temperature is stable."

Septimus could see that Dandra looked hollow-eyed and upset. She was clutching Kaznim's tortoise to her as though it was the most precious thing in the world. "But something *is* wrong?" Septimus asked.

Dandra took a deep breath. "Yes, it is. I, er, I have something, um, personal to tell you."

"I'll go now," Tod said diplomatically.

"Please stay, Alice," Dandra said. "Your mother knew my story and you should too. And you need to understand what – I mean who – your new friend is."

"New friend?" Tod asked, puzzled.

"Kaznim Na-Draa – the little girl with the tortoise. With *my* tortoise."

"She's not a friend," Tod said. She looked at Dandra, remembering what Kaznim had called her: *murderer*. No one who called Dandra such a thing could ever be a friend of hers.

"Take a seat, Dandra," Septimus said. "I'm sure it can't be that bad."

Dandra thought it could. She sat down on the exotic purple sofa and put Ptolemy carefully on her knee. The tortoise stuck his head out and stared impassively at the ExtraOrdinary Wizard. Septimus resumed his place in a low chair beside the fire and Tod sat on the edge of the sofa, at the other end from Dandra. They both looked expectantly at their visitor. Dandra felt so nervous that she seemed to have lost her voice.

"Would you like a drink of water?" asked Septimus.

Dandra shook her head. She took a deep breath and began her story.

"You know that I came to the Castle because I was invited by dear Marcia for my skills in **DisEnchantment**. Her summons arrived in the nick of time, as you say here. My life was in great danger."

Tod looked at Dandra, surprised.

"Some months before Marcia's message, Karamander Draa and her baby daughter, Kaznim, arrived at my tent. They were destitute, but even so I was surprised to see Karamander. I thought I was the last person to whom she would turn. You see, I was the cause of her husband's death."

"No!" Tod muttered under her breath. Surely Kaznim could not be right?

Dandra hurried to explain. "I did not desire his death – of course not. But it was my actions that led to it. I cannot deny that."

"We cannot always predict the effect our actions will have," Septimus said. "If they are performed in good faith, there can be no blame."

Both Dandra and Tod looked gratefully at Septimus. He had a way of making sense of things in a few words.

"Thank you, Septimus," Dandra continued. "It all began when I was assistant to the court physician of the Red Queen. I worked at the palace in the Red City – so called, they said, for the colour of the rock upon which it stood, but the people who lived there knew it was for the blood spilled within its walls. As assistant physician in the Royal Hospital I was relatively safe and I counted myself lucky. We were protected by the palace livery we wore and were not subject to the numerous acts of terror perpetrated by the city guards. Neither were we part of the court intrigues, which were the downfall of so many.

"We grew our medicinal herbs in the palace gardens and it was there that I met the Red Queen's son, Salazin. Salazin was fascinated by Physik, as you call it here, and he would ask me endless questions. Slowly, we fell in love. But it was hopeless. He was betrothed to another and even if he had not been, he would never have been allowed to marry a mere physician – despite the fact that actually that was what he himself dearly wanted to be. It was hopeless. We knew it was." Dandra paused and looked up at Septimus. "So we planned to run away."

"Yes," said Septimus, and then he remembered that he was not meant to know the story. In the confidence of the handover from one ExtraOrdinary Wizard to another, Marcia had told him absolutely everything. With his new diplomatic skills, honed by his year as ExtraOrdinary Wizard, Septimus decided to say nothing but to listen to what Dandra said next. He resumed his neutral expression while Dandra continued.

"We disguised ourselves as traders. I cut my hair short and we became a boy and his merchant master with trading packs. I put Ptolemy into the top of one of the packs and told him to stay still. Then, early in the morning, when a caravan of traders left the city we tagged along. Apparently no one noticed our absence until Salazin did not arrive for an important meeting; even then it was not much remarked upon. It was not the first time he had missed a meeting, Salazin found Court life very tedious. I had covered my absence by leaving a note saying that I had gone into the desert to find a rare plant. However, as night fell, people began to talk. It seems our love was not the secret we had thought. The Queen was furious. She sent out a runner to track us down. The runner was my cousin Karamander's young husband.

"The Queen ran a cruel regime. It was a terrifying thing to be chosen as a runner, for failure meant certain death. So I can only imagine what Karamander must have felt when her husband told her he had been chosen to go. Karamander's husband arrived at our caravan at midnight. I remember to this day seeing him silhouetted against the moon as he crested the nearby dune and cantered down to our encampment. Salazin and I knew we were in great danger and so I gathered all my **Magykal** powers and helped him use the **UnSeen** I had so carefully taught him. When I saw him slowly *Fade into the Aire*, I did the same **Unseen** so that we could still see each other." Dandra laughed, embarrassed. "Oh, I apologise, ExtraOrdinary Wizard. I forget myself. You know such things."

"A few," Septimus admitted with a wry smile.

"We moved a safe distance away so that no one would bump into us and sat watching Karamander's poor husband search for us. The people we had travelled with were as puzzled as he was, for once he had explained who he was after they knew it was us. Soon the whole camp was in uproar looking for us. I became concerned that our footprints would give us away, but we stayed still and prayed that the fuss of the search and the darkness would cover them. Our prayers were answered and we were not discovered. As dawn broke, we watched Karamander's unlucky husband head slowly for home, knowing he went to a terrible fate. I believe he was thrown to the Queen's lion that night. But what could we do? It was him or us.

"We dared not return to the caravan, so we stayed **UnSeen** and watched them pack up and leave. When they were gone we took our own way south, heading for a group of lakes where we knew good people lived. We had such plans ..."

Septimus saw tears glistening in Dandra's eyes. "It's all right, Dandra," he said. "You really don't need to tell –"

"But I *do*," Dandra interrupted him. "For my Salazin's sake, I do. So that at least someone will know how brave he was."

"Of course," Septimus said soothingly. "Of course."

"Our plans … Salazin would become my Apprentice and I would teach him all I knew so that he could fulfill his dream and become a physician too. We would be together. We would be happy. Simple dreams …" A tear escaped from Dandra's eye and landed on Ptolemy's shell.

"We travelled through the heat of the day and decided not to make camp that night but to carry on. We wanted to put a safe distance between us and the Red City, for we knew the long arm of the Queen stretched far. But as we walked wearily into the dawn of our second day of freedom, we were spotted by a new band of runners. Quickly we did our UnSeens once again. But this time it did not go well."

Dandra took a shuddering breath. Septimus felt great sympathy for Dandra. He still had flashbacks to his time as a boy soldier in the notorious Young Army, and even now a deep sense of fear would unexpectedly wash over him at odd times.

Clutching the tortoise to her like a comfort blanket, Dandra continued her story. Septimus and Tod heard how Salazin had bungled his UnSeen. They heard of Dandra's guilt that *her* UnSeen had worked. How Salazin had refused to give her away. How he had looked straight at her Invisible self and how the expression in his eyes had told her farewell. How she had watched him being taken away, tied on to a horse facing backwards, to what Dandra knew would be a terrible fate.

"I wandered UnSeen for days," Dandra told them. "In fact, I decided to remain UnSeen for the rest of my life. I didn't want to speak to anyone ever again. But after many days I came to a large, faded tent covered with silver stars, and from within came the sound of wailing. It was a cry of grief that I understood. I knew someone in there had died. A boy ran from the tent and he saw me. I will not trouble you with more details, but his father, an Apothecary, had died. Of course, you will guess what happened. I stayed to look after the boy, Mysor. I took over the practice and Mysor became my Apprentice. Things went well – until some months later, Karamander Draa turned up.

"I took her in. Of course I did. I felt I owed her *that* at the very least. All was good for a few months. Karamander was a willing helper and little Kaznim was a joy to be with. But then others began to arrive, people whom Karamander called cousins – although I recognised none of them. She asked me to let them stay a while and I felt unable to refuse. If I dared to suggest it was time they moved on, Karamander would break down in tears about her husband and the terrible death he had endured. Still more 'cousins' kept arriving, and I was soon vastly outnumbered and frightened by the amount of weapons the newcomers brought with them. My medical practice began to suffer as people who had trekked for miles to see me felt threatened. I began to suspect that Karamander had come to seek revenge.

"I was right. One morning I heard them plotting to kill me while I slept. That very day Marcia's message inviting me to the Wizard Tower arrived, and never was a message more welcome. Late that evening I left a note for Mysor – who I

154

knew would be safe, as Karamander clearly liked the boy – but I could not find Ptolemy. So alone once more I stole into the night and trekked to the Port of the Singing Sands. I took the first ship out the very next morning and as the land dropped beneath the horizon, I felt safe for the first time in years. But I was a fool to think I could run from this. Now Karamander has sent her daughter to take revenge and there is no escape. Not for me."

Septimus was not convinced. "But a mother would never send such a young child on a revenge mission – surely she would come herself. And from what Marwick says, Kaznim never intended to come here."

Dandra shook her head. "This morning, the child threatened to bring a powerful sorcerer to kill me."

"I think," Tod said carefully, "that Kaznim only wanted her tortoise back."

Dandra clutched Ptolemy to herself. "He is *my* tortoise," she said.

Tod and Septimus exchanged glances. The feud went deep.

Dandra continued. "The child clearly has access to a sorcerer, probably more than one. The Red City is riddled with them; they all vie to serve the Red Queen. Septimus, I am so sorry. I told Marcia my history and I should have told you, too. I have brought danger to your door."

Tucking Ptolemy under her arm, Dandra stood up. "I do not wish to bring trouble to the Wizard Tower. I will catch the afternoon barge to the Port."

Tod jumped up. "No! Please, Dandra. Don't go."

Septimus, too, got to his feet. "Dandra, you must stay. I do not believe you have brought trouble to our door. But even if you have, I would not wish you to go. The Wizard Tower is not a fair-weather friend. It is loyal to all within its walls."

Dandra at last understood that she truly was with friends. Not trusting herself to speak, she clutched her tortoise to her and ran out. As the door swung closed, Septimus murmured, "Who would have thought a little tortoise could cause so much trouble?"

Tod felt she had to be honest. "I think it was my fault, really," she said. "It was because I took the cards while Kaznim was asleep. Kaznim noticed and said I had stolen them. And she was right."

Septimus looked thoughtful. "Sometimes, Tod, you will find you do have to do things that are a little ... distasteful for the good of the Wizard Tower and the Castle. You did the right thing."

Tod shook her head. "I wanted it to be the right thing," she said. "But afterwards it didn't feel that way."

"You did what you felt was right at the time, for the right reasons – to find the Orm Egg," Septimus said. "And getting that egg *is* the most important thing right now, don't you agree?"

"Yes," Tod said – and then immediately felt bad because she had actually made it more difficult. "I'd do anything to find the Orm Egg," she said. *"Anything."*

Septimus did not like to see his new Apprentice so upset. He knew she blamed herself for losing Kaznim and Jim Knee. "Tod," he said. "If I had been thinking straight last night I would have put a guard outside the dorm to stop Kaznim from running off. Her disappearance is not your fault, OK?"

Tod nodded.

156

"And as for Jim Knee – well, I am that wretched jinnee's Master and as such I am, unfortunately, responsible for all he does. You do understand that?"

Tod nodded again.

Septimus stood up. "Now get yourself down to the Sled Shed and win the Apprentices' Cup for the Wizard Tower." He took a small card from his pocket and quickly scribbled something on it. "I hear Drammer Makken is your substitute," he said. "Give him that and he won't make trouble."

"Thanks ..." Tod took the card reluctantly. The sled race seemed rather frivolous after Dandra's story.

"And I shall look for that jinnee of mine. If I've not found him by the time the race is over – and you have won, of course – I will **Summon** him. I don't want to do that – it might damage him – but if it's a choice between a damaged jinnee and none at all, then I shall have to take the damaged one."

"Poor Jim Knee," Tod murmured.

"Indeed," Septimus said. "But don't forget, this life – or series of lives – was a choice she freely made."

*"She?"* Tod asked.

"Yes. I understand that Jim Knee was a woman married to a turtle trader when she decided to take the Path of the Jinn. Now, I have something for you." Septimus took a small purple cloth from his pocket. "For the runners," he said.

"Runners?" Tod asked, puzzled. She was still trying to imagine Jim Knee married to a turtle trader.

"For the Wizard Tower Sled. A secret weapon." Septimus grinned.

Tod eyed at the cloth uncertainly. "But the rules say that no new **Magyk** is allowed."

157

"Quite right too," Septimus said. "But it's not **Magyk**. It's just a normal cloth that Beetle – I mean, the Chief Hermetic Scribe – gave me some years ago. He knew every way to get the best from a sled. He was a terrifyingly fast sledder. Still is, believe it or not."

Tod did believe it. There was something boyish about the Chief Hermetic Scribe that she really liked. She often found herself about to call him "Beetle" and then remembered that a Year One Apprentice must be more respectful.

"The cloth removes even the smallest particle of dirt so the blade of the runner is as smooth as glass," Septimus explained. "You'll need to take more care on the ice at the start as you'll find the sled harder to control, but once you've got down to the deep snow on the other side of the Moat, you'll be amazed the difference it makes. Trust me, I won my last Senior Apprentice Race because of it."

Tod took the soft purple cloth and a swirl of butterflies fluttered through her stomach. Suddenly the race seemed very close.

"I will see you on the starting grid," Septimus said. "But now I must be off to find that jinnee. Time is ticking away."

# The Egg Timer

*The past few hours had* seen a huge change at the starting grid. As Tod emerged from the Great Arch she found a large race board had been nailed to the outside of the courtyard wall. Foxy was writing in the names of the sleds in his looping writing and Rose, his girlfriend and recently qualified Ordinary Wizard, was reading the list of races out to him. Rose smiled at Tod as she emerged from the blue shadows of the archway. "Good luck," she said.

"Oh! Thank you," Tod replied. Tod liked Rose a lot. They shared an interest in Charms but Tod had the feeling that when she was with Septimus, Rose avoided her.

"I'll be cheering for you," Rose said. "We all will. Everyone loves the Apprentice Race."

Tod smiled nervously. She was beginning to realise what a huge event this was. She pushed her way through the small crowd watching Foxy's loopy writing slowly reveal the lane order of the sleds, and headed across the top of the starting grid, now marked out in squares and bedecked with a huge banner reading *START* strung across the torchposts. Tod squeezed through a group of teens dressed in black – she guessed they were from Gothyk Grotto – and headed for the alleyway that led to the Sled Shed. This now had a rope

159

slung across it and Darius Wrenn was standing awkwardly behind it. He had a clipboard tucked under his arm and was gazing at the little Egg Timer glinting in his hand. Seeing Tod's gaze, Darius quickly shoved it into his pocket, picked up his clipboard and tried to look official. "How bay I help you?" he asked.

"Gosh," said Tod. "What have you done to your nose?"

Darius sniffed. "Nuffin," he said. "How bay I help you?"

"I'm racing," Tod said. "Can you let me through, please?"

Darius looked at Tod's very fine Apprentice belt and asked, "Are you the ExtraOrdinary Apprentice?"

"Yes. I'm in the first race."

Encouraged by his correct identification, Darius peered at his clipboard and frowned; something did not make sense. "You'll have to wait for the others," he said.

"Other what?" Tod asked, confused.

"Other … *people*?" Darius asked. Who knew what the ExtraOrdinary Apprentice might want to bring? Yesterday afternoon an Ordinary Apprentice had brought in a ShapeShifted cat in the shape of a large and very hairy spider and just dumped it on the desk.

"But there aren't any other people," Tod said.

"Oh. Right. So which one are you?"

Suddenly Tod understood. "I'm all of them," she said. "I am Alice and Tod and Hunter and Moon."

Darius looked impressed. "Wow. Four people at once. That is an *amazing* spell."

"So will you let me through now?"

Darius very carefully crossed all Tod's names off. "Yes, you can *all* come in."

160

Darius unclipped the rope and, emboldened by his success in letting in four people at once, said, "Excuse me. But, um, how can you tell if something is **Magykal**?"

Pleased to be asked something she could actually answer, Tod said, "Well, usually you can **Feel** the **Magyk** in it," she said.

"Can everyone do that?" Darius asked.

"Not everyone," Tod said.

"Can *you*?" Darius persisted.

"Yes, I can – well, most of the time," Tod said.

Darius took the little **Egg Timer** out of his pocket. "Could you tell me if this is **Magykal**?" he asked. "I think it might be, because the grains inside behave kind of funny."

Tod was surprised that such a scruffy little boy would have such an exquisite object in his pocket. "I'll have to hold it," she said. "Is that OK?"

Darius nodded and handed over the **Egg Timer**. A jolt of ancient foreign **Magyk** tingled through Tod's palm. "It is **Magykal**," she said. "And it's not from here. Where did you get it?"

"A little girl gave it to me," Darius said, feeling guilty. "I … I didn't want it. But she made me take it. Honestly."

Something that Kaznim had yelled at her as she had raced down the stairs came into Tod's head: *And if you had found it, you would have stolen my Egg Timer too.* "Was the little girl wearing red?" Tod asked.

Darius nodded.

*It had to be Kaznim*, Tod thought excitedly. "Do you know where she is now?" she asked.

Darius shook his head. "She ran away. I think the ghost scared her."

161

"Which ghost was that?" Tod asked.

"The horrible one we have in the Manuscriptorium," Darius said.

Tod knelt down beside Darius. She could see he was timid and she didn't want to frighten him. "You're Darius, aren't you?" she asked.

Darius nodded.

"Well, the thing is, Darius, that little girl has something very important that we need at the Wizard Tower. Something really, really important. And this might help us find it."

Darius knew he should never have accepted such a wonderful thing. "Please," he said, holding it out to Tod. "Please, you take it."

Tod shook her head. She didn't want to risk taking the Egg Timer on the sled race. "How about I tell the ExtraOrdinary Wizard?" she suggested. "Then you can give it to him and tell him about the little girl, too. OK?"

Darius looked horrified. The thought of the ExtraOrdinary Wizard himself asking him questions was too terrifying for words. He shook his head and thrust the Egg Timer into Tod's hand. "Take it, *please*," he said. "I don't want it. Really I don't."

Tod took the Egg Timer and, leaving Darius nervously clutching his clipboard, she hurried off along the cinder path that ran along the icy track towards the Sled Shed. Tod was longing to tell Septimus what she'd discovered, but she'd promised to meet Oskar and Ferdie and she mustn't let them down. With the Tribe of Three versus the Wizard Tower playing in her head yet again, Tod pushed open the sliding door to the Sled Shed and stepped inside.

# THE SLED SHED

*The Sled Shed was buzzing* with excitement. Large and newly built, it replaced the old Manuscriptorium boathouse. The care lavished on the interior, with its carved wooden beams and **Perpetual Frost** floor, reflected the Chief Hermetic Scribe's love of everything to do with sledding.

One of the first things Beetle had done when he became Chief Hermetic Scribe was to search for the long-lost Manuscriptorium sled **Charm**. This was a piece of **Magykal** wood that, when a sliver was shaved off and embedded into a sled, gave it the ability to move not only downhill but also uphill and along the flat. Beetle had eventually discovered the **Charm** by happy accident. It had been used to repair a chair on which a scribe named Colin Partridge sat. However, when Partridge decided to impress Romilly Badger by reciting the sled **Incantation**, his chair had shot off around the room, slaloming between the desks, leaping over piles of books, before other scribes thoughtfully opened the doors and allowed Partridge to go whizzing off down Wizard Way – watched by the entire complement of the Manuscriptorium, helpless with laughter. Once Partridge and the chair were rescued from the Moat, Beetle had extricated the **Charm** and set about commissioning a new sled from the Castle boatbuilder, Jannit

Maarten. Jannit discovered that sled-making was good practice for her Apprentices and one sled led to another. That morning, five of the finest sat beside the Wizard Tower sled and Beetle's old but much-loved Ice Tunnel inspection sled, known by all as the *Beetle*.

Oskar was racing the *Beetle* and he had great hopes for his sled; it had what he called "attitude". Watched by Ferdie, he was rubbing down a rough spot on the front of the runner when Tod came in. Oskar sat back on his heels and ran his hand through his springy red hair – a mannerism many of those who worked at the Manuscriptorium had caught from their Chief. "Hey, Tod," he said, and gave her the Tribe of Three sign – three raised fingers of the right hand.

Tod returned it. "Wow," she said. "It's amazing in here."

"Not bad," Oskar agreed.

The Sled Shed was dazzlingly bright. A line of brilliant white lamps hung from the roof beams and the **Perpetual Frost** floor glittered and sparkled. Seven sleds were lined up, each one gleaming as a result of much love and attention. The Wizard Tower sled was beautiful, but it was by no means the most impressive. As a boy, Beetle's hobby had been drawing fantasy sleds, and now the results of his drawings were there for all to see.

For the first race that day the five new sleds were raced by apprentices from the lucky shops, businesses or institutions that had won the Apprentice Race Draw. They also got to name and decorate the sled for that season. The Wizard Tower always raced its own sled, known as the *Wiz*, and the Manuscriptorium always raced the *Beetle*. In the last race of the day – the Midnight Massive – the Manuscriptorium raced all the sleds and Beetle always ran his old sled. It was the highlight of his year.

The *Beetle* stood nearest the door. One in from the door, guarded by a scowling Drammer Makken, was the *Wiz* – sleek and delicate like a racehorse, waiting patiently. The *Wiz* was made from a very dark, intricately carved wood, which was inlaid with strips of lapis lazuli. It sparkled in its Wizard Tower livery of purple, blue and gold. Its runners were narrow like skate blades, the metal was golden yellow with a thin strip of steel along the edge that had contact with the snow. At the front a gold bar ran between the two runners as they arched up towards the rider and on this hung a silver whistle, tied with a green ribbon. A long purple rope was also fixed to the bar and thrown casually across the seat. It looked much the same as it had when Septimus had used it in the Ice Tunnels below the Castle before the big Melt – except that the word "Wiz" was now painted along the side.

The next sled was a shimmering green with flashes of red. Raced by the new Palace Dragon Boy (employed in the hope of the return of the elusive Spit Fyre), it was, naturally, named *Spit Fyre*. The next in line was the *Sarnie*, raced by Wizard Sandwiches – a small and delicate sled like a fine spider, which looked as though it might fold up at any moment under the weight of its racer: the rather large washing-up boy. Next came Gothyk Grotto's sled in matte black, called – of course – *Grot*. This was to be raced by the mask technician, who wore a tight-fitting black suit and matching full-face cat mask. Jannit Maarten's boatyard was running *Bucket*, in honour of a little boat Nicko Heap had recently lost. *Bucket* was to be raced by the newest Apprentice, a girl from the port, who had painted two eyes on the front of the runners. Last came the *Spurius Fatuus*, in the hands of Doran Drew, a young apprentice from

Larry's Dead Languages. Named in honour of Larry himself, it was not a flattering tag, but the apprentice reckoned she was safe because Larry made a point of never watching the race. However, that year, Larry was secretly watching from an upstairs window.

Tod's substitute, Drammer Makken, glared at her. The newest Apprentice in the Wizard Tower, Drammer was a tall fourteen-year-old already gaining a reputation for being truculent. He wore a white bandanna around his thick brown hair. It should have read *The Best, Sucker!* but punctuation skills were not Drammer's strong point and he had left out the comma. Tod went up to him nervously. "Hi, Drammer," she said.

Drammer scowled. "What you doing here?" he demanded.

"I'm racing today," Tod said. "Sorry." She handed him the card Septimus had given her. It said: *Alice TodHunter Moon to race the* Wiz *in the Apprentice. Septimus Heap. EOW*.

Drammer looked at the card and swore under his breath. Then without saying a word, he strode out of the Shed.

Oskar watched him go, then turned to Tod. "I'm really glad it's you," he said. "That guy didn't understand the *Wiz* at all."

"Thanks, Oskie," Tod said.

"Hey, Tod," Benjy Pot, the Dragon Boy, butted in excitedly. "So you're racing? Sure you're ready?"

Everyone knew that the race really began in the Sled Shed, with the banter, the showing off, the technical tweaks. Tod was feeling increasingly nervous but knew well enough not to show it. "You bet!" she said brightly, slipping on to the *Wiz* and feeling for any looseness in the joints. It was not unknown for sleds to be tampered with – especially the *Wiz*, which was seen as "swanky". But the sled felt good and Tod could sense the energy within, waiting to be set free. She gave the runners a quick wipe with Septimus's purple cloth and then, acting as relaxed as she could, she got up and wandered off.

Oskar and Ferdie were waiting for her by the door. They exchanged signs and walked out into the chill of Sled Alley. Thoughts of Septimus and the Wizard Tower began to fade and Tod felt as though she had come home: the Tribe of Three was together again.

# TIGER EYES

*Septimus had found Jim Knee.* It had been relatively easy – all he'd had to do was to follow the screams. He had ended up in Gothyk Grotto, where the tiger was enjoying terrorising some young teens who had come to buy the latest craze: Death Wings. These were tiny black fluttering wings, which when thrown behaved like a boomerang and came back to the thrower. They had nothing whatsoever to do with death but Jo-Jo Heap had thought of the name and it had stuck. A mass throw was planned for the start of the Apprentice Sled Race. No one knew about the plan except the rider of the *Grot* sled, and it was hoped a shower of Death Wings would give the rider – race name: Daemon Kraan – a good start.

Septimus took his jinnee back on the end of a Gothyk Grotto rope-trick rope. As they walked towards the starting grid, Wizard Way fell quiet, all eyes following the young man in purple striding up the Way with his apparently faithful big cat. People were less impressed once it became known that the tiger was "only that daft Jim Knee", but even so, it was an arresting sight, and one that made the Castle people feel oddly proud. Where else would you find an ExtraOrdinary Wizard, a tiger and an Enchanted sled race on the very same day?

Suddenly Septimus caught sight of the Queen on the other side of the course, heading towards the Castle Walls. "Jen!" he called out.

Jenna gave him a wave, hesitated and then hurried over to him. As she drew nearer, she stopped. "You've got a tiger," she said.

"Yes. I found him at last. Jim Knee."

Jenna relaxed into a smile. "Ah. I see the yellow eyes now. But … are you sure it's Jim Knee? Don't all tigers have yellow eyes?"

"Do they?" Septimus looked down at the tiger, who lazily opened his mouth to display some very long teeth and then closed it with a growl. "Well, I'm pretty sure it *is* him. I mean, how many tigers *do* we have loose in the Castle right now? I suppose that's something the Queen always knows?"

"Goodness, Sep. None, I hope!" Jenna said. She put her arm through his. "You are a silly tease sometimes," she said. "I'm glad I saw you. I've been trying to get away all morning but there has been so much Queen stuff today, you would not believe."

"Well, you're just in time for the start of the Apprentice," Septimus said. "I've saved a seat for you in the stand."

Jenna shook her head. "I'm sorry, Sep, I'm going to have to miss it."

"But you *can't*. Everyone's expecting you."

Jenna looked miserable. "I know. I'm sorry. Don't be cross, Sep. Beetle's upset enough already. But there's only three more hours of good daylight and I want to get to Galen's before dark."

Galen, a healer who had taught Sarah Heap all she knew about herbs and healing and with whom Sarah and Silas Heap were staying, lived in a rambling treehouse deep in the Forest. Septimus was shocked. "You're not going into the *Forest*, Jen?"

"I'm going to find Mum and Dad. They need to know about Sam."

"But Jen, you *can't*. It's dangerous – and especially for you. You know, now you're Queen."

Jenna shrugged. "Queen or Princess, Sep, it makes no difference. Anyway, it's not as dangerous as you think. I've got ... connections there now."

"Connections?"

Jenna took Septimus's arm and walked him across the starting grid.

"Oi!" came a yell from a steward. *"Getoffthecourse!"* On race day, respect for the Queen came second to the sanctity of the track.

Jenna shouted out her apologies, then she steered Septimus and his tiger away. They headed up the steps beside the final ramp that swept down from the top of the Castle Wall towards the race finish. Once they had reached the battlements, Jenna glanced around to make sure no one was in earshot and continued walking. There was just room for the two of them on the cinder track that ran beside the polished icy snow of the racecourse.

"Sep," Jenna said, "you know how Morwenna from the Wendron Witches tried to kidnap me just before I was crowned?"

Septimus nodded. Jenna had got the better of the Wendrons' Witch Mother, but it had been a dangerous moment.

"And you know that if I ever have a daughter, the Wendrons will be after her as soon as she is born?"

Septimus looked at Jenna, shocked. "Jen, you're not ..."

Jenna laughed. "No, Sep. I am not planning on having a daughter just yet. But if I do I am determined not to be held to ransom by those witches. And so ..." Jenna dropped her voice and looked around to make sure no one was listening. "I have been making, shall we say ... arrangements. I have my own witches in the Forest now. Spies."

Septimus looked at Jenna with new respect. "Wow, Jen. How did you do *that*?"

"With this." Jenna drew back her red cloak, which was lined with white fur. Underneath she wore a Port Witch Coven cloak in deepest black.

Septimus looked disapproving. "You've still got that old thing?" he asked.

"Well, obviously I have still got it, Sep. This is why I am wearing it," Jenna teased.

Septimus pulled a face.

"Hey, don't be grumpy, Sep. It's very useful. A Queen needs a bit of an edge to her. And this is my edge." Jenna waved the cloak at Septimus. He stepped back and nearly slipped headlong on to the racetrack. "Oops, careful! Sep, don't look so worried. This cloak doesn't do much at all. I rely on other enticements – a promise of safe haven in the Palace anytime they need it. A bag of gold every MidWinter Feast and free food at Wizard Sandwiches."

"Free food at Wizard Sandwiches is an *enticement*?" Septimus grinned. "I'd have thought never having to go to Wizard Sandwiches would work better."

Jenna smiled. When she was with Septimus her cares dropped away and she felt like a teenager again. "You are so *mean*, Sep."

"As ExtraOrdinary Wizard I am supposed to be mean," Septimus replied with a smile. "It's part of the job description."

"Silly boy. But seriously, Sep, the thing with witches is that on a personal level, they don't have any money at all. Some of the covens are quite rich but it doesn't mean that the novices see any of it. And they are often hungry, especially in the winter. The newbies usually end up with just the bones and gristle at the bottom of the wolverine stew pot."

"Oh, yuck," said Septimus.

"So being able to eat for free is wonderful for them. And being somewhere warm. And of course Wizard Sandwiches is not the kind of place that asks questions."

"Most of them look like they belong to a coven anyway," Septimus said.

"Exactly," Jenna agreed. "So you are not to worry about me. My escorts are waiting and I'm going straight to Galen's treehouse. I'll spend the night there and bring Mum and Dad back tomorrow."

"But can't your witch spies just take a message to Mum and Dad?" Septimus asked.

"I am not having Mum upset by a couple of witches turning up and telling her that her son is dangerously ill. Really, Sep. *Think* about it."

"OK, Jen. You're the boss." Septimus knew when to keep quiet.

"Yep. You've got it." Jenna grinned.

With Jim Knee trailing disconsolately behind, the Castle Queen and the ExtraOrdinary Wizard wandered along the battlements, looking down at the bright pennants that marked the edge of the course blowing in the breeze. They walked on

172

in silence until Jenna said, "Actually, there is something you might want to know. Jo-Jo's girlfriend, you know, Marissa?"

"Oh, *her*," Septimus said scathingly.

"Hmm, her. Well, she's up to something."

"So what's new?" asked Septimus.

"It's probably nothing," Jenna said. "But my two, er, contacts say that she's working with Morwenna on something – and it's a big deal."

"What kind of big deal?" Septimus asked.

"They don't know. But Marissa told Jo-Jo that she's through with what she calls 'small fry' and she included not only him but *you* in that." Jenna gave Septimus a quizzical look. "I don't know why."

"Neither do I," Septimus protested. "I've had nothing to do with Marissa. Well, not for ages, Jen. Honestly."

Jenna raised her eyebrows. "None of my business, Septimus Heap. Anyway, I thought you'd want to know."

They had reached the end of the wall and now took the steps beside the sled ramp down to the North Gate. At the drawbridge Jenna gave the bridge boy a silver crown. Everyone else paid to get into the Castle, but the tradition was that the Queen paid to get out. There was no fixed price, but anything less than a half-crown would have been considered stingy.

"Bye, Sep," Jenna said. "See you tomorrow with Mum and Dad."

Septimus looked over at the Forest opposite. The tops of the trees were softened by snow and the contrast made the space beneath them seem even darker and more menacing than usual. He frowned. "Spies can't always be trusted, you know."

Jenna nodded. "I know," she said quietly.

Septimus hugged Jenna and felt the witch cloak hanging heavy beneath the fine red velvet. "Be careful," he said. "Please."

"I will," said Jenna. She stood on tiptoe and gave Septimus a quick kiss. "Bye, Sep." And then she was off, hurrying across the drawbridge.

Septimus watched her go and suddenly he knew he could not bear to let her go alone. And so, despite knowing he was playing with the safety of the Castle, he called out, "Jen! Wait!"

Jenna stopped and turned. She saw Septimus framed in the North Gate arch, his purple robes blending into the shadows. She saw him crouch down and talk to the tiger, and when Septimus untied the rope and the tiger began to pad towards her, Jenna knew what he was doing. She waited for the tiger to come to her. It sat down in front of her and gave a low growl. Jenna took a step back. It had a severe case of cat breath.

Jenna searched the tiger's deep yellow eyes for any sign of the jinnee within but she could find nothing. "You *are* Jim Knee, aren't you?" she asked warily.

The tiger put its head on one side and winked.

Jenna wondered if she had imagined it. "If you are Jim Knee, I command you to do that again."

The tiger stared up at her unblinking.

*Bother*, Jenna thought. *Not blinking on purpose is just the kind of thing Jim Knee would do.* Jenna glanced across to Septimus, who was watching from the shadows of the North Gate.

"He's yours, Jen!" he called out. "Send him back when you're safe!"

Jenna decided that Septimus must know his own jinnee. "Come with me, Jim Knee," she said. The tiger gave another low growl and winked – twice. That was good enough for Jenna. "Thanks, Sep!" she called out.

Septimus watched Jenna walk quickly away, her cloak red against the snow, the yellow-and-black tiger loping beside her. As they reached the edge of the Forest, the tiger began to disappear as its stripes blended with the trees. Septimus squinted into the shadows and thought he caught a quick flash of silver – the telltale sign of a Wendron Witch, for the young ones all wore a mass of silver rings – and then Jenna's red cloak was gone, vanished into the Forest.

Septimus watched for a while longer. He thought of Jenna moving through the Forest with the witches and despite himself, he was impressed. He knew that as ExtraOrdinary Wizard he should not approve of Jenna's contact with witches. The old saying that *"a Wizard and Witch shall never agree, that one and one and one makes three,"* was true. And yet what Jenna was doing felt right. She was venturing into the Forest on her own terms. She was making it hers. Maybe that was why the Wendron Witches wanted a Princess so much. Maybe they knew that one day, if they did not get their Princess, the Castle Queen would get *them*.

# THE TRIBE OF THREE

*As Septimus walked briskly* back along the Castle battlements, Tod, Oskar and Ferdie were sitting on the landing stage beside the old Manuscriptorium boathouse. The sky was blue and cloudless and the winter sun shone down on the icy Moat and its snow-covered banks. Bright blue and gold pennants fluttered in the breeze showing the path of the racecourse, which ran in front of them along the Moat to a ramp – known as Forest Ramp – that led up the opposite bank away to their right, marked by two tall flagposts. This took the sleds out on a long loop, routing them close to the trees some hundred yards away on the outskirts of the Forest. Although the treetops were covered with snow, the trunks were dark and the Forest beyond looked mysterious in its winter gloom.

From there the racecourse ran alongside the trees until in a breathtakingly steep dive it dropped into the Forest Pit – an old quarry. It then climbed out of the Pit and ran behind the old Infirmary before it took a sharp bend back towards the Castle and the North Gate drawbridge. After that a series of ramps took the sleds up on to the top of the Castle Wall – with a terrifying drop on either side – and then a steep descent down the final long ramp would send the sled hurtling down to the finish.

But Tod did not want to think about the race. She had Septimus to see and she had Tribe of Three business to sort out. She jumped straight in. "The Orm Egg is about to hatch," she said.

"What?" Oskar and Ferdie chorused. And then, "How do you know?"

Tod told them about Kaznim, the cards, Jim Knee and finally about Darius and the Egg Timer. She fished the tiny Egg Timer out of her pocket to show them.

"Wow ..." Ferdie and Oskar said together. "That is *beautiful*."

"Isn't it?" Tod said, letting the little gold-and-lapis hourglass lie flat on her palm and feeling the ancient Magyk once more. As they gazed at it they were all amazed to see a tiny, luminous grain of silver float from one very nearly empty chamber and burrow its way into the much fuller chamber. "I think," Tod said, "that this is some kind of Magykal countdown to when the Orm Egg is going to hatch."

"Then it's going to hatch pretty soon, by the look of it," Oskar said.

"I wonder how often a grain goes through," Ferdie said. "If it's just one a day, then there's still some time left. But if it's one every hour, then ..."

"There's hardly any time left at all," Tod finished for her.

Oskar had been thinking. "Tod," he said, "what exactly did Kaznim look like?"

"Well ... she was quite small. Dark curly hair and she was wearing a long red coat – thin, like a sleeping robe. Oh, and sandals on bare feet."

"*Pigs!*" Oskar said.

"Pigs *what*?" asked Ferdie.

There was something Oskar knew he should tell Tod and Ferdie, but he had made the solemn Manuscriptorium Promise, which meant he had sworn not to talk about anything he saw or heard in the Manuscriptorium. "We agreed that our promise to the Tribe of Three comes before anything else. Right?"

"You know we did, Oskie," Tod said. "That's why I just told you about Kaznim and the cards and the **Egg Timer**."

Oskar stared down at the Moat. He felt bad about breaking the Manuscriptorium Promise, but he knew what he had to do. "Kaznim didn't run away," he said. "She was downstairs in the Manuscriptorium. I saw her."

Tod and Ferdie looked at him, stunned. "You *saw* her?"

Oskar nodded. "She was in the corridor in the Conservation basement. I thought she was probably someone's little sister, but we were busy so I didn't really pay her much attention. But later, when I was leaving, I saw the ghost of Jillie Djinn in the front office and she seemed in a really good mood, even though Romilly's baby sister was lying on the floor having a tantrum. Jillie Djinn was laughing and saying over and over again that little girls will always get their own *way*. It was weird how she kept emphasising 'way'. It didn't make any sense at the time, but it does now. I reckon Kaznim went through the Manuscriptorium Way. And I think Jillie Djinn helped her," Oskar finished gloomily.

They sat in silence for a few moments until the high-pitched *ring-riiiiiiing* of a bell intruded on their thoughts. Oskar leaped to his feet. "It's the half-hour bell," he said. "We'd better go."

Ferdie was indignant. "Oskie, you can't still be racing," she said. "There are *far* more important things to do."

"But what *can* we do?" Oskar asked.

"I have to go too," Tod said. "I've got to tell Septimus about Kaznim and the Egg Timer."

"So what about us?" Ferdie asked a little sharply. "What about the Tribe of Three finding the Orm Egg?"

Tod sighed. "Ferdie, I can't keep Kaznim and the Egg Timer a secret from Septimus. It's way too important. You must see that."

Ferdie felt horribly disappointed. The Tribe of Three, she realised, was just a kids' game – there was no way it could compete with the Wizard Tower. "What I see," she said bitterly, "is that you belong to the Castle now. Whatever you may say, you don't really belong to the Tribe of Three. Your promise that we would all stick together and find the Orm Egg means nothing to you. *That's* what I see."

"But I can belong to the Castle and the Tribe of Three," Tod protested. "We *all* can. You belong to the Castle just as much as me, Ferdie."

"No I don't." With that Ferdie got to her feet and walked away.

"No! Ferdie, wait!" Tod called out, but Ferdie did not even look back. Tod watched her friend hurry up the steps and stalk off along the top of the Castle Wall, heading for her lookout post at the old Infirmary, where she was due to monitor the Apprentice race. Biting back tears, Tod turned to Oskar. "Oh, Oskie," she said. "I *have* to tell Septimus. You see that, don't you?"

Oskar nodded. He was learning fast how hard it was to have two loyalties. "When you think about it," he said slowly, "all that really matters is getting to the Orm Egg in time. It doesn't matter who gets there first – whether it's us or someone from the Castle – as long as it's not Oraton-Marr. And telling Septimus makes that more likely to happen. Not less."

Tod smiled. "Thank you, Oskie," she said, and she gave him a hug.

Oskar blushed. "Anytime," he said.

Tod cast one last look after the vanished Ferdie and said, "I'd better go and find Septimus."

"Hurry back," Oskar said. "You know we've got to be in the shed five minutes before Lead Out or the subs get to race. I don't want that Drammer sucker racing the *Wiz*. I want to race against you. And win!"

Tod grinned. "In your dreams, Oskar Sarn." And she hurried off.

# ON THE GRID

*With no idea where Septimus* might be, Tod decided to head for the Wizard Tower and hope to find him there.

A puzzled Darius unhooked the rope and watched Tod disappear into the crowd that was gathering for the start of the Apprentice Race. The sight of the ExtraOrdinary Apprentice pushing her way through caused many mutterings. *What was she doing? Wasn't she racing? What was wrong?* Tod heard them and realised how right Septimus had been about her racing. But some things, she thought, were more important than keeping up appearances. Frustratingly slowly, Tod pushed her way through the crowd. Suddenly someone barred her way. It was Drammer Makken.

"Hey," he said. "Look who it is."

"Get out of my way, Drammer," Tod said.

"Okey-dokey, pig-in-a-pokey." Drammer grinned and stepped to one side. His older brother, Newt, immediately took his place and Tod realised she was encircled by Drammer's friends. It was not a good feeling.

"Let me through, Newt," Tod said.

Newt looked lazily at his timepiece. "Patience, Alice," he sneered. "Of course I will let you through. In ten minutes and – ooh, let me see – twenty-three seconds. That's when the

Lead Out bell goes, isn't it? But until then we can just have a little chat, can't we?"

"No, we can't," Tod said. "Let me past." She went to sidestep Newt but the group pushed Tod towards the courtyard wall. Newt stuck his arm out between Tod and the wall so that she couldn't go forward. She tried to step back and found her way blocked. She was trapped.

"Get out of my way!" Tod yelled. Newt and his cronies burst into loud, forced laughter, drowning Tod's shouts.

The seconds were ticking by and Tod was getting desperate. Her chances of finding Septimus were rapidly disappearing along with her chances of racing the *Wiz*. Tod began to realise that there was no way she could get to Septimus in time now – wherever he might be. All she could do now was race the *Wiz*, as he had wanted her to.

Tod took a deep breath and yelled as loud as she could, "Get out of my way!"

"In a minute, little girl," said one of the larger boys, laughing.

"Little *Apprenticey-wentice*," jeered another.

Tod had had enough. She knew there was no way the gang was going to let her free. She was going to have to do something a little more dramatic than shout. Her hand moved surreptitiously to her Apprentice belt and she took out a **Scare Charm**, one of the basic **Charms** with which Septimus had loaded the belt when she had been Inducted as Apprentice. The Charm was not, he had impressed upon her, to be used lightly.

Tod slipped the **Scare Charm** into her hand, made a fist and squeezed the **Charm** as hard as she could to **Activate** it. Then, remembering that she must turn it on and tell it what she

182

wanted it to do, she yelled, "On! Set me free!" and opened her hand. There was a blinding flash of red light, and a small red ball bristling with needle-thin spikes flew out. It headed straight for Newt's arm. "Ouch!" he yelled. He grabbed hold of his arm and leaped away from Tod, leaving her with a clear space in front. The Charm ricocheted off the wall, bounced back and began leaping from one member of the gang to another. In the midst of the yelps and yowls, Tod pushed her way free and headed for the safety of Sled Alley.

Darius watched her heading towards him in alarm. "Argh!" he yelled. "There's a horrible red bug chasing you!"

Tod wheeled around to see the Charm bouncing after her like a faithful puppy. She scooped it off the ground and told it, "Stop." As an afterthought, she said, "Thank you." Tod wasn't sure if one was meant to thank Charms, but it seemed only polite. The Charm pulled its spikes into itself and its angry red light faded. In a moment Tod had a little rubbery red ball sitting quietly in her hand. She was exhilarated. The Magyk had worked brilliantly. "Thanks, Darius," she said. "Can you let me through, please?"

The sight of real Magyk had made Darius so in awe of Tod that all he could do was stare.

Aware that the seconds were ticking by fast to the Lead Out, Tod said urgently, "Darius, please. I have to get through."

"All of you?" Darius whispered.

"Yes. All of us. Thanks!" Tod scooted down Sled Alley and skidded into the Sled Shed to find Drammer Makken standing proprietorially beside the *Wiz*. Drammer looked shocked.

"Thank you, Drammer," Tod said coolly. "I'll take over now."

Drammer glared angrily, turned on his heel and stormed out of the shed.

"You cut that fine," Oskar said. "You had nine seconds left."

The Lead Out bell rang and the Sled Shed became quiet and tense. Each racer stood by their sled, and as Tod took her place beside the *Wiz* the Chief Hermetic Scribe appeared at the door, impressive in his ceremonial dark-blue-and-gold robes.

Despite his formal dress, Beetle was smiling broadly and looked as excited as any of the racers. He surveyed the line-up and looked particularly fondly at his old Inspection Sled. Under Oskar's care it had become a sleek, low-level racer, and Beetle was impressed. Its rough wood shone with a deep, polished shine and some new and very shiny levers on the front bar promised some slick manoeuvres on the racecourse.

Beetle began to speak. Tod listened with rapt attention as he complimented the racers on their sleds and wished them good luck. Tod smiled. She liked the way Beetle looked, how his shiny black hair flopped forward over his eyes, the way he always pushed it back when he was concentrating. She liked the air of seriousness he carried with him too, but today, Beetle had a carefree air that Tod had never seen before. He caught her eye and smiled. Tod smiled shyly back. She was so glad she had not run off to tell Septimus about Kaznim going through the Manuscriptorium Way.

Tod was right, Beetle *was* happy in the Sled Shed. When he needed peace and quiet in which to think, Beetle often retreated there and sat quietly with the sleds. It was not only because he loved the company of sleds, but also because it was the one place in the Manuscriptorium where the ghost of Jillie Djinn could not go. In life Jillie Djinn had never set foot in the

Manuscriptorium boathouse and now she had to obey the rules of ghosthood: "A ghost may only tread once more where, Living, she has trod before."

It was time for the Lead Out and traditionally, Beetle's old sled led the way, followed by the Wizard Tower sled. Feeling nervous, Oskar took his sled's dark blue rope and set off through the wide sliding door. The frisky sled came bouncing behind him, watched with a fond gaze by the Chief Hermetic Scribe.

Tod followed Oskar along Sled Alley. When all the sleds were out, Oskar stopped and the line drew to a halt. Beetle strode to the head of the procession and then Oskar led off behind him. As they moved through the shadows of Sled Alley in the wake of the dark silk robes of the Chief Hermetic Scribe, everyone fell quiet with the sense of occasion.

They followed Beetle out into the bright whiteness of Wizard Way. The thunderous roar of the crowd burst upon them like a wave, reminding Tod of the time she and her father had once almost lost their boat in the surf. Her thoughts were cut short by a piercing peep of a whistle. The seconds stepped forward, and when Tod's second – Romilly Badger – helped her guide the *Wiz* on to the grid, Tod felt as though she had been thrown a lifebelt.

"Someone spiked the FizzFroot," Romilly said. "They've all got a bit silly."

While the seconds were fussing with the sleds and making sure each was correctly in its grid box, Beetle's distorted voice came through the megaphone. *"Riders for the Apprentice Race, take your places on your sleds!"*

Tod sat on the *Wiz*, untied the whistle and put it into her pocket. She placed both feet on the front bar, took hold of the purple rope and felt Romilly rest her hands on the back bar, ready for the all-important push-start. Tod glanced over at Oskar, who had Colin Partridge as his second. Partridge was bent double like a spring waiting to uncoil.

The riders focused their gaze on the course that stretched out in front of them: a wide, straight line of shiny white ice that disappeared into a sharp right turn at the far end of Wizard Way.

Beetle's disembodied megaphone voice began to count down. "*Get set … Three … two … one … GO!*"

# THE APPRENTICE RACE

*A massively powerful shove* from Romilly took Tod by surprise. The *Wiz* shot forward and set Tod off balance; she leaned slightly to the left and, in a shower of Death Wings, she found herself heading straight for the *Grot*. Tod leaned hard over to the right and pulled the *Wiz* away from the black-spiked runners of the *Grot* in the nick of time. To her embarrassment, the *Wiz* continued on its diagonal track, now running fast towards the snow wall that divided the racetrack from the spectators. Panicking a little, Tod leaned too far to the left, the *Wiz* veered away from the wall and careered once again diagonally across the track, heading for the opposite wall. But this time there was no danger of crashing into any sleds – they were all well in front, heading down Wizard Way in a fine spray of ice. As Tod fought to get control of the zigzagging *Wiz*, she became aware of laughter and a triumphant yell from Drammer Makken: "Useless!"

Tod wished the snow would swallow her up. But as the *Wiz* once again shimmied over to the opposite snow wall, she heard Beetle's voice above the ever-increasing laughter. "Silence! Silence, or I shall restart the race. This is a normal start for the Wizard Tower sled. Do not disturb the rider's concentration."

187

Despite most of the spectators knowing that this was most definitely not the normal start for the *Wiz*, they fell silent. The relief from the laughter and Beetle's support gave Tod the clarity she needed. She leaned forward and whispered the words that were written on the little silver wings Septimus had given her when she had become his Apprentice: "Fly free with me." And then it happened. Tod felt the *Wiz*'s energy gather into its very centre and at last the sled became balanced. Concentrating hard, Tod steered the *Wiz* into the middle of the track and suddenly, they were off.

A gasp came from the crowd as the *Wiz* shot down the racecourse in a glint of purple and gold, trailing a rainbow spray of minute ice crystals behind. As the last of the six sleds in front shot around the first bend, the *Wiz* was rapidly making up lost ground and the crowd's laughter had transformed to cheers and whoops of excitement. No one had seen the *Wiz* go so fast before, and by the time it, too, had disappeared, it was generally agreed that the Chief Hermetic Scribe had got it wrong. Tod had been deliberately fooling around in order to give the field a decent chance – and provide an entertaining start to the race in the bargain.

The *Wiz* hurtled down Snake Slipway and as the sled swooped around to the right in a beautifully controlled turn and entered the Moat section of the course, exhilaration swept through Tod. She felt as she did when she was sailing her boat with the wind filling the sails and the white wake of foam running behind, but now – she dared to risk a quick glance behind her – it was a rainbow-coloured ice spray.

Tod took the *Wiz* across the track at the Castle bank to take advantage of the inner bend. Here the snow was clear from sled tracks but much deeper. It was now that the effect of Septimus's purple cloth became apparent – the *Wiz* cut through the snow like a hot knife through butter. As Tod leaned into the gentle curve of the Castle Wall, she became aware of cheers from the houses along the Walls and for the first time since the start, she risked a smile. With the swish of the snow loud in her ears, the wind in her hair and the spray curling up behind her, Tod headed past the East Gate Lookout Tower. A line of rats gathered on the roof waved enthusiastically, but Tod had eyes only for what was in front of her. And what she saw made her laugh out loud – she was catching up. Fast. No more than twenty yards ahead were three sleds: *Grot* and *Spit Fyre* neck and neck with *Sarnie* trailing. A few seconds later the markers for Forest Ramp came into view and she saw Oskar's sled heading across the Moat and up the ramp into the next section of the course. Not far ahead of him was the *Bucket* and in the lead was the *Spurius Fatuus*, raced with a supreme fearlessness. The *Spurius*, Tod thought, would be hard to beat.

It was on the wide Moat course that overtaking was easiest and Tod was determined to take advantage of that – there was no way she was going to be the last one up Forest Ramp. She leaned outwards, took the *Wiz* flashing across the tracks of the frontrunners and flew past the *Sarnie* in a shower of spray. Tod settled the *Wiz* into the tracks of the *Grot* and moments later was winging past the *Grot* and then the *Spit Fyre* in quick succession, both of whose riders looked shocked. Then she, too, was zooming up the Forest Ramp to the sound of cheers.

Tod and the *Wiz* were now entering the narrowest part of the course, which the riders called "the trench". There was really only room for one sled here, two if you were being reckless. The

189

track was U-shaped in profile with banks of snow so high that all spectators now lost sight of the sleds for some thirty seconds.

Ferdie was watching through a pair of **Enlarging Glasses** that Oskar had borrowed from the Manuscriptorium, *"So that you can see me win, Ferd."* She saw the *Wiz* disappear into the trench, closely followed by a furious *Grot*, which had edged the *Spit Fyre* off course and into the bank. Ferdie turned her attention to Oskar. Oskar had overtaken the *Bucket* at the top of Forest Ramp and somehow in the confines of the trench he had done the impossible. To her delight, Ferdie saw her twin emerge ahead of Larry's scribe, Doran Drew. The scribe looked wild. She was crouched down on the long, narrow sled, which shone silver against the snow, and was on Oskar's tail, so close that their runners almost touched. They were in the straight that headed to the Forest Pit and the snow was soft and loose. The *Beetle* was throwing up a stream of slush that covered Doran's goggles and every time she ran her hand across to clear them, she lost ground.

"Go, Oskie, go!" Ferdie yelled.

Suddenly a dip hidden in loose-packed snow caught on the *Beetle*'s stumpy runners and threw the sled to one side. Ferdie gasped. She watched Oskar struggle to pull the *Beetle* back into the smooth centre of the course. He managed it well, but Doran took her chance and now the *Beetle* and *Spurius Fatuus* were neck and neck, flying along the long, wide, straight track beside the Forest, heading for the Pit.

Catching up fast was the *Wiz*.

Ferdie put down her **Enlarging Glasses** and leaned out to get a better look at the whole course. Oskar and Doran had just disappeared over Dead Drop, the precipitous slope that went down into the Forest Pit. Ferdie watched the *Wiz* – closely pursued by the *Grot*, its rider crouched like a cat, his black robes streaming behind him – running down the long straight towards Dead Drop.

The straight was lined on the far side by the outlying trees of the Forest – tall, impassive spectators. As Tod sped beneath their overhanging branches, Ferdie caught a flash of silver from behind one of the trunks. Ferdie was not as technically **Magykal** as Tod, but she had a gift of **Feeling** the presence of people who were – or would be in the future – connected with her. And right then Ferdie **Felt** that there was someone in the Forest, watching. And not in a good way.

*   *   *

Ferdie was right, there *was* a watcher in the Forest. A young witch named Marissa was standing in the shadows of an ancient oak that the Forest witches (known as the Wendrons) called the Guardian, the most outlying of the Forest trees that allowed the witches to **Blend** with its shadow. Marissa wore her old dark green Wendron cloak despite the fact that she had fallen out with the coven and no longer belonged. (Marissa had also been a member of the Port Witch Coven, but she had had enough of them too. She was now what she called "freelance".) And so, as Marissa stood beneath the Guardian, her long brown hair held back by a plaited leather headband, her Wendron cloak wrapped around her, she was as near to invisible as it is possible to be without an **UnSeen**.

The glint of silver that caught Ferdie's eye came from the collection of silver rings that Marissa wore on every finger and both thumbs – and the reason they glinted was because Marissa's hands were shaking. For the first time in her life, Marissa was scared. Someone had made her an offer that she dared not refuse and she had to double-cross Morwenna Mould, Witch Mother of the Wendron Witches, in order to make it happen. Maybe, Marissa thought as she stood in the shadows of the Guardian oak, maybe being freelance wasn't such a great idea after all.

Tod was now hurtling towards Dead Drop. As if sensing her trepidation, the *Wiz* slowed and she heard the swish of approaching runners behind – the *Grot* was catching up fast. *"Go-go-go!"* Tod yelled, and the *Wiz* was gone, shooting over the edge of Dead Drop and plummeting down. Tod's breath seemed to be pulled out of her as she fell, and then with a jarring *thump* the runners caught the slope and the *Wiz* was off, shooting across the icy floor of the quarry. Another *thump* from behind announced that the *Grot*, too, had landed and Tod urged the *Wiz* on, gaining ground on Oskar and Doran, who were hurtling across the quarry floor, neck and neck.

The floor of the Pit was deep in snow and shadow. The winter sun never reached here and the chill struck through Tod's fur-lined cloak. Silent and fast, the silky-smooth golden runners of the *Wiz* gave it the advantage; it left the *Grot* behind and drew so close to the two leaders that their spray covered Tod in an icy dust. The steep incline out of the Pit now approached. All three slowed, but the *Wiz* less so. In the race up the incline Tod very nearly caught the leaders, but as they emerged into the warmth of the sun and the course levelled out, Oskar performed a very sneaky turn and cut across the line Tod was taking. Doran followed him, dropping back into second place, and Tod had to throw the *Wiz* sideways. Quickly she flung the sled back on track, slipped in front of the *Spurius Fatuus* and was away, hurtling after Oskar, heading for the shadows between the Infirmary and the Forest.

At her First Aid Post on the Infirmary veranda, Ferdie was relieved to see the *Beetle* and the *Wiz* emerge safely from the Pit. She watched the sleds rocketing along the darkest part of the course — the straight beside the escarpment at the edge of the Forest. The *Wiz* was close on the tail of the *Beetle*, and the *Spurius* was close behind. The *Grot* had just emerged from the Pit, the *Spit Fyre* and *Bucket* were still in it and the *Sarnie* was way back, teetering on the edge of the Pit in a fit of panic. Ferdie saw Tod take the *Wiz* to the edge of the straight and in a breathtaking turn of speed, she overtook Oskar in a daring loop. In another swoop, Oskar overtook Tod and they both hurtled on, and then Tod was once more ahead — the race was turning into an exciting duel.

"Go, Oskie, go!" Ferdie yelled.

As if in response to Ferdie's yell, Oskar once more took the lead. As he sped towards the sharp right-hand turn that would take him on to the drawbridge lead-up, Ferdie saw once more a flash of silver from the shadows of the oak. At the same time she saw Tod's sled suddenly slew across the track, hurtle over the snowbank and shoot into the trees beyond.

"Tod!" Ferdie yelled. Her fight with Tod forgotten, Ferdie leaped from the veranda and ran towards the course.

Out of the corner of his eye, Oskar had seen Tod's sudden change of direction and he knew from the way she was struggling to control the *Wiz* that all was not well. Without even thinking that with Tod out of the running he was very likely to win the race, Oskar skidded the *Beetle* to a halt and turned around, very nearly crashing head-on into the oncoming *Spurius*. Doran zoomed past with a whoop of triumph.

Ferdie ran towards Oskar, yelling, "Oskie, Oskie, wait for me!" In seconds she had jumped on to the back of the *Beetle*, yelling, "There's something in the Forest, Oskie. Something waiting for Tod!"

A chill of fear went through Oskar. He took the *Beetle* through the break in the snow embankment where the *Wiz* had ploughed through and headed into the trees.

On the course behind him, a nervous *Sarnie* wobbled by.

# OverRide

*All along the straight, Tod* had felt the *Wiz* wanting to pull towards the Forest and as they drew near an ancient oak, she saw a flash of silver in the shadows below the tree. A stab of fear shot through her – *someone was waiting for her.* Tod leaned forward to force the *Wiz* onwards, but suddenly realised she no longer had control of the sled. And then it happened – the *Wiz* shot across the track and through the snow embankment. The next moment Tod and the *Wiz* were bumping along the Forest floor and as they sped past the oak tree, out of the corner of her eye Tod saw a witch beneath the tree, watching her – but when she turned to look straight at her, Tod saw nothing but thick green shadows.

Tod felt very scared indeed. All the stories of the Forest that were told at night in the Junior Girls' Apprentice Dorm came back to her. As the *Wiz* slalomed through the trees, Tod clung to the sled, unsure whether she was more scared of falling off or staying on. The *Wiz* hurtled along, bumping over the stony ground, which was covered with only a thin layer of snow. A sheer rocky escarpment, dark and dripping with snow-covered moss, now rose up before her, and it seemed to Tod as though the sled was heading straight for the rock face, intent upon its own destruction. As she readied herself to jump off – a frightening prospect, as the sled was going extremely fast – Tod saw a fissure in the rock straight ahead and she knew that was where the *Wiz* was going. She must jump now ... *now* ... And then it was too late. The *Wiz* shot into the deep, dark narrowness of a sheer-sided canyon and Tod was with it. Where they were going she had no idea, but wherever it was, she and the *Wiz* were going together.

Marissa almost cried with relief as she watched Tod and the *Wiz* disappear into the gulley. She had forgotten to **Bind** Tod to the sled and had been afraid that the Apprentice would throw herself off it at the last minute, but it had turned out fine. Anyway, Marissa wasn't sure that she could remember the right **Bind** – there were so many different ones. Marissa's knowledge of **Magyk** was sketchy; she could never be bothered with the boring books that other witches seemed to enjoy reading. A smug smile spread across Marissa's face. Who needed stupid books anyway? Her **OverRide Enchantment** had worked like a dream.

A sudden yell of "Tod! Tod!" wiped the smile away fast. Marissa leaped back into the shadows of the Guardian and watched in dismay as a small wooden sled came rocketing through the trees in the tracks of the *Wiz*. On it rode a couple of wild-looking red-headed kids who Marissa did not recognise. She stared at them in panic. What should she do? She had enough to think about. She had the Witch Mother to fix, and the scary sorcerer was expecting her to deliver on her promise at midnight. There was no way she needed any more trouble, and those kids looked like trouble on runners.

Marissa looked over at the Castle. She saw the last stage of the sled race being played out along the top of the Castle

Walls – the *Spurius* was in the lead – and she heard excited shouts drifting towards her. A feeling of wistfulness for the companionship and safety of the Castle swept over Marissa. Her deal with the sorcerer was going frighteningly wrong. First Morwenna Mould, the Wendron Witch Mother, had stuck her nosy beak in and demanded to be part of it and now these screaming kids on a sled had suddenly appeared. Marissa's plans were getting out of control and she dreaded to think what the sorcerer would do if they didn't work out.

Marissa heard cheering from the Castle and it took all her willpower not to run for the drawbridge and hurry back to her cosy little attic room. But then Marissa thought of what awaited her back in the Castle: *that loser Jo-Jo Heap, a dead-end job in Gothyk Grotto and a load of idiots who treat you like rubbish. But if you get this right,* she told herself, *they'll all be terrified of you. And serves them right, too. So just get after those sleds and make sure it all works out.*

And so Marissa turned away from the lights and the cheers and hurried through the silent trees, heading towards the gulley into which two sets of sled tracks now ran. Using FleetFoot – the Enchantment that allowed a witch to move as fast as those she was following – Marissa covered the ground at speed, her feet a blur beneath her cloak. As she headed into the canyon she heard a roar greeting the winner of the Apprentice Race: the *Spurius Fatuus.*

The *Sarnie* crossed the finish line, and still Septimus and Beetle stood waiting for their sleds to finish. Their disappointment that they had not won – or even made a creditable showing – began to be replaced with a gnawing worry. Where were Tod and Oskar? *What had happened to them?*

197

While Septimus and Beetle were discussing what to do, Larry from Larry's Dead Languages rolled up to demand of his triumphant scribe whether all his teaching had gone to waste – *surely by now she could manage a decent insult in Latin? Any fool knew that* "spurius" *merely described a person whose father was not married to his mother.* "Nothus" *was what she should have used: someone whose father was unknown. The infinite subtleties of the Latin language were clearly lost on his idiot apprentice.* Larry stomped off again, leaving Doran wondering if maybe her tutor did have a sense of humour after all – albeit one a little different from most.

As Larry disappeared down Wizard Way, Septimus said, "Beetle, something's gone very wrong. We need to find them." Beetle needed no persuading. Accompanied by the two seconds, they hurried off along the course.

But the sleds and their riders were already deep in the Forest – and going deeper every second.

# PART VII

THIRTY-SIX
HOURS TO
HATCHING

# THE *BEETLE* AND THE *WIZ*

*The* Wiz *hurtled along the narrow gulley.* The sheer rock rose up on either side and was sometimes so close that it was hardly wide enough for the sled to fit. Tod was terrified – the *Wiz* was travelling with no care for her safety or for its own. Utterly reckless, the sled hurtled onwards like an iron filing pulled towards a powerful magnet.

Even though she was only few a months into her Apprenticeship, Tod knew that the *Wiz* was under an **Enchantment**, and the way it was being hurled from rock to rock made her fear it was a **Darke Enchantment**. She remembered Septimus telling her about a **Darke Summons** that had once happened to his eldest brother, Simon. Tod also remembered that Septimus had told her that many people did not survive a **Darke Summons**. Tod knew that he had been warning her that being an Apprentice was not all bright, coloured lights and happy **Magyk**, that it had its dangers, too. And now she was facing them for the first time.

With no choice in such a confined space but to cling on to the *Wiz*, Tod was bumped and shaken along the gulley like a marble in a box as the sled headed ever deeper into the Forest. The sharp rock walls bruised her as she was thrown against them, and low-level twigs and branches snagged and grabbed at her like snatching hands. Snow covered the ground, but it was thin in places and the rocks below jarred the *Wiz*, sending shockwaves through her.

It felt as though the gulley was going on for ever, but Tod knew that it must eventually come to an end. Pushing aside her fear that the end would simply be a blank wall of rock that the *Wiz* would smash headlong into, Tod decided that as soon as the sled came out of the gulley she would throw herself off it, wherever she was. Anything was better than being dragged helplessly towards something **Darke**. Tod knew she was not **Bound** to the sled, she could lift her hands from the bar and even stand up – if she dared. But for now she crouched down over the front bar of the *Wiz*, staring ahead, waiting for the moment the canyon would come to an end.

Tod had no idea that some distance behind her Oskar and Ferdie were on the *Beetle*, following her tracks. Oskar propelled the *Beetle* as fast as he dared, hoping to get a glimpse of Tod, but she was always just out of sight. However, the swinging branches and the showers of snow falling from them told Oskar that Tod was still ahead. But the *Wiz* was drawing ever further away and – fearless sled racer though he was – Oskar did not dare push the *Beetle* to the limits that the **OverRide** was taking the *Wiz*. He had Ferdie to consider too.

Far behind Oskar and Ferdie came someone who was used to considering no one but herself: Marissa, out of breath, dishevelled and footsore. She stumbled along, cursing her bad luck.

Far ahead of Marissa, Tod was gripping the front rail of the *Wiz* and staring ahead in horror. Just visible through the overhanging branches and getting closer by the second was a sheer wall of rock cutting across the gulley. It was the end of the road.

Tod was about to hurl herself backwards off the sled when she saw an opening in the rock, the round mouth of a tunnel with a light at the end. Tod dithered – should she risk throwing herself on to the ground, or stay on the *Wiz*? In that brief moment of indecision the *Wiz* left the gritty snow of the gulley and entered the cold, still darkness of rock. Its runners hit pure ice and the sled shot through the tunnel at breathtaking speed. Ahead, Tod now saw a circle of light – not dull greenish-white filtered through snow-laden trees, but bright yellow firelight. Tod had heard enough stories about the Wendron Witches to know that Forest firelight is not always a welcoming sight. Fire in the Forest usually meant the gathering of the Coven.

The *Wiz* careered out of the tunnel into the Wendron Witches' winter quarters – a wide, open space enclosed by the steep-sided rocks of an old quarry. The sled's runners hit bare rock and it ground to a halt.

Tod was welcomed by the collective **Scream** of the Wendron Witch Coven.

# THE WENDRON WITCH COVEN

*A coven* **Scream** *is a powerful weapon.* When timed right, in perfect unison and disharmony – as the Wendron Witches' **Scream** was – it renders the victim helpless.

Tod sat numbly on the *Wiz*, the **Scream** echoing around the quarry. Her hands were clamped firmly over her ears, but still the high-pitched drilling of the **Scream** bored into her head, drowning out all thoughts of escape. Tod could see nothing but a circle of faces with dark, wide-open mouths. On and on went the **Scream**, ricocheting off the rocks, while Tod sat in the centre of a whirlpool of noise, feeling as though she were made of glass and that any moment now she might shatter into a million splinters.

But even witches in **Scream** eventually run out of breath, and slowly the decibels began to drop, the echoes weakened and the sound began to drain away. When at last the gaping mouths were closed Tod was left shaking, feeling as though her ears were filled with glue and her muscles turned to jelly.

In the brief hiatus that always follows a **Scream**, Tod's surroundings began to sink in. Beyond the circle of witches in their dark green cloaks, beyond the roaring fire behind them, Tod saw the darkness of rock rearing up, topped by a fringe of Forest trees. If she had looked behind her, Tod would have seen a rock face peppered with small caves, some with ladders leading up to them, which was where the witches spent the long, dangerous Forest winter nights. But Tod did not need to look, she knew where she was; Septimus had described it to her in her Forest Knowledge tutorial. She was in the winter quarters of the Wendron Witch Coven.

Blinking as though they had just woken up and rubbing their ears, the circle of witches enclosing Tod shook themselves out of their Scream trance. Tod felt as weak as a newborn puppy; she could do no more than sit on the *Wiz* and watch. The circle began to open up and through the gap Tod saw a large witch swathed in a thick cloak of green, walking slowly towards her. She was flanked by two younger witches, on whom she leaned her not inconsiderable weight. Tod knew who this must be – Morwenna Mould, the Wendron Witch Mother.

Morwenna Mould stopped in front of the *Wiz* and looked down at Tod with an air of disappointment. "Is this it?" she said scornfully.

"It must be, Witch Mother," one of her supporters ventured.

"It looks very … *young.*"

"It is quite new, I think, Witch Mother," said the other supporter.

"It's too new to know much," Morwenna snapped. "I thought she was getting one of the older ones. He won't like it." Surprisingly light on her feet when she needed to be, Morwenna swivelled around to stare at the Circle. She raised her voice angrily. "Where is that Marissa girl, anyway?"

Her reply was a yell of surprise from the Circle. She turned, expecting to see the errant Marissa, and saw two small figures on an old wooden sled come bumping into the quarry. They were covered in snow.

Morwenna reacted quickly. "**Grasp** them!" she yelled.

Ferdie and Oskar were too chilled to react. The Witch Mother's helpers leaped forward, grabbed a twin each and held their shoulders in a **Grasp**. The coven stared menacingly at Oskar and Ferdie. There had been a rumour that Snow Sprites had been sighted in the Forest, and many of the witches – including Morwenna – assumed they had now made a successful sprite snatch. It was, the coven thought, turning out to be a good day, however new and useless the Apprentice might be.

Tod saw the look in the witches' eyes as they stared at Oskar and Ferdie and it frightened her. She stood up unsteadily and at once felt the weight of Morwenna's heavy hand descend upon her shoulder. A moment later she too felt the iron chill of the witch's **Grasp** leach into her bones and a feeling of fuzziness invade her mind, but Tod fought it, using a very basic **MindScreen** that Septimus had taught her.

Morwenna pointed at Oskar and Ferdie. "Take them to the cell cave," she ordered.

There was a shocked silence among the coven. The two witches who had Ferdie and Oskar in their **Grasp** looked at each other in dismay. Their job was to advise the Witch Mother – and it was a dangerous one. Morwenna Mould in her declining years did not take kindly to advice. However, Morwenna also did not take kindly to witches who were too frightened to give advice. Being chosen as a Witch Mother Supporter was seen as a poisoned chalice. The two current Supporters, Bryony and Madron, were close friends – unusual among witches – and had agreed to always act together.

"Ahem. Witch Mother," murmured Bryony.

"What?" snapped Morwenna.

"The, er, Snow Sprites," said Madron.

"Yes? What about them?" asked Morwenna.

"It is usually considered safer …"

"With Snow Sprites …"

"Who always hold a grudge …"

"When captured …"

"Or confined …"

"In any way …"

"For Forest's sake!" Morwenna Mould yelled. She flashed a look of exasperation that would have floored a witch acting on her own. "What are you trying to say, you mumbling idiots? Spit it out!"

Bryony and Madron glanced at each other, then they took a deep breath and said in unison, "Witch Mother. With respect. With captured Snow Sprites it is usually considered safer to … *kill them*."

# SNOW SPRITES

*"They're not Snow Sprites!"* Tod yelled. "Let them go!"

Ferdie and Oskar, already numbed by the cold, were now falling into the trance-state that is an effect of a powerful **Grasp**. With Bryony's and Madron's hands lying heavy on their shoulders, they stood stone-still, their eyes unfocused.

The coven turned its stare on Tod. "They're just covered in snow, that's all," she faltered.

"Of course they are covered in snow," said Bryony, who had Ferdie in her **Grasp**. "Snow Sprites generally are." A chorus of laughter greeted this.

"They're not Snow Sprites, they're my friends!" Tod yelled.

"Snow Sprites as friends, eh?" said Morwenna, whose hearing was not good. "Well, well. Maybe we underestimated you, Apprentice. Maybe you have a little more **Magyk** than it seems. Maybe you are not quite the mistake I took you to be. *Maybe* the sorcerer will be pleased to have you after all." The Witch Mother smiled. "And I'll have a few sprite bones to give him too, ha-ha. As long as we rake them out of the fire quickly."

The shock of Morwenna's words hit Tod like a blow: *Bones? Fire?* "Ferdie! Oskie!" she yelled. "Wake up!"

But neither Ferdie nor Oskar responded. Bryony and Madron grinned at each other. Their **Grasps** were clearly a lot more effective than that of the Witch Mother, and from Morwenna's sour expression they guessed she knew it too.

Desperately, Tod struggled to get free, but every movement made Morwenna's **Grasp** grow tighter and more painful. Soon Tod's shoulder hurt so much that she had no choice but to stay still. "You have learned your first lesson: do not fight the power of the Forest," Morwenna hissed at her. "Now your sprites will learn theirs."

"They are not sprites!" Tod screamed out. "They are human! Ferdie! Oskar! *Wake up!*"

But Ferdie and Oskar stared blankly into space.

"More wood for the fire!" Morwenna yelled.

In the centre of the quarry floor a fire crackled and spat. Now the witches scattered to the margins of the quarry where fallen branches lay stacked and hurried to bring them to stoke the flames.

From the margins of the Forest above, two young witches watched the activity below. These were Jenna's spies, Ariel and Star. They had just escorted their Queen safely to Galen's treehouse and had been waiting for a chance to rejoin the coven without being spotted. The frenzied fire-stoking gave them the perfect opportunity. As the flames rose higher, they ran quickly down the rocky path that led to the quarry floor. Ariel and Star slipped through the narrow gap in the rocks, picked up a branch, lugged it across to the fire and hurled it on to the flames. They grinned at each other in relief. No one had noticed.

As each witch added her fuel the flames rose higher, roaring up into the darkening sky. The heat was such that even though they were some distance from the fire, caked snow began to fall from Oskar and Ferdie and Tod at last began to feel warm. But the warmer Tod felt, the more scared she became. She watched her friends staring vacantly at the flames and she wondered if they had any idea what the witches intended to do. But most of all, she wondered how on earth she was going to stop the witches from doing it.

It wasn't every day that two Snow Sprites got thrown on to the fire, and the coven now began to form an excited Witch Circle around the fire and its victims-to-be. Star and Ariel joined them, unsure what was happening but doing their best to look as though they knew.

Like the drone of a swarm of bees, a low, rhythmic humming began – the renowned Wendron Witch Circle **Hum**. Something about its steady, expectant rhythm made Tod feel very afraid. The **Hum**, however, had a different effect on the Witch Mother – it was something Morwenna had noticed recently but had kept secret, for it was a sure sign of waning powers. It made her feel sleepy.

Tod became aware that the Witch Mother's **Grasp** had loosened. Her hand was now merely resting lightly on her shoulder. Tod longed to break away and run free, but she forced herself to stay where she was. If she ran now she would be leaving Oskar and Ferdie to their fate. She must stay calm and try to think. There *must* be something she could do ... but what?

The flames leaped higher and the **Hum** began to morph into a chant:

*Sprites burn bright!*
*Light the night!*

*Light the night!*
*Sprites burn bright!*

The chant jolted the Witch Mother from her **Hum**-induced daze. Completely forgetting her **Grasp**, she raised her hands in the air and shouted, "Coven, stop! Though twilight is falling it is not yet night. We will wait until Mother Moon rises over the Guardian Ash." She smiled. "We shall have our sprite bones soon enough, fear not."

Above the quarry, through the bare boughs of the tallest tree – which Tod guessed to be the Guardian Ash – she saw the white gleam of a full moon. The **Hum** began once more, growing louder and faster as though to speed the moon upwards and send her clear of its fine dark tracery of branches.

Star and Ariel looked at each other, aghast. The coven was about to burn two kids from the Castle. What would the Queen have to say about that? It would be goodbye to their free food at Wizard Sandwiches for sure. As the remorseless hum of the Witch Circle continued, Ariel slipped from the Circle and vanished into the shadows.

# MARISSA IN THE GULLEY

*Marissa stumbled along*, muttering the rudest words she could think of – she had a fine collection and many to choose from. Marissa could not believe how fast things could go wrong. She had gone to all the trouble of fixing a very successful **OverRide** and getting the ExtraOrdinary Apprentice into the Forest only to have two stupid kids on a sled get in the way. As she had raced after the Apprentice she had tripped over a branch and lost her **FleetFoot** and now the sled was too far ahead for her to get to it before it got to the coven's quarry. The Witch Mother would have her fat claws on the Apprentice by now. She was in big trouble. Cursing her bad luck, Marissa hobbled along as fast as she could, a stitch nagging at her side, the cold air making her wheeze and her twisted ankle jabbing at her.

Marissa had not wanted to involve the Witch Mother in her Apprentice snatch, but Morwenna Mould had found out and insisted on being in on the deal. Marissa had had no choice but to agree to send Tod to the quarry. However, she had not intended for Tod to actually get there. She had planned to catch her up with her **FleetFoot** and divert her out of the gulley well before she reached the coven. Marissa figured that by the time the Witch Mother realised what had happened, she and Tod would be far away.

212

But now, Marissa thought bitterly, everything was ruined. Morwenna Mould had her prize and all the power the sorcerer had promised her would go to that pig of a Witch Mother. It was so *unfair*. Marissa stomped angrily along the gulley, but when she came to the gap through which she had planned to take Tod, she stopped. Maybe, she thought, all was not lost. She could still go to the midnight meeting with the sorcerer, she just wouldn't have the Apprentice with her. But that didn't have to be a disaster. In fact, thought Marissa, things could turn out even better than she had planned.

Marissa smiled. She knew exactly what she would do. She would tell the sorcerer that she had been double-crossed. She would say that Morwenna Mould had kidnapped the Apprentice and planned to use her for her own benefit. She would fix it so that the sorcerer saw the Witch Mother as a dangerous adversary who must be vanquished at once. Marissa smiled. Yes, she could see it now ... marching into the Winter Circle with the powerful sorcerer at her side ... a quick ThunderFlash aimed at the Witch Mother ... maybe a Darke Dart ... or both. *Both*, thought Marissa. It served the old cow right. And when it had worked, when the fat old carcass of Morwenna Mould was lying on the ground having done all the nasty stuff it was ever going to do, then she, Marissa Janice Lane, would proclaim herself Witch Mother and that would be that. No one would dare oppose her with Oraton-Marr at her side. That would pay old Moldy Face back for all those nights she had spent scrubbing the burned wolverine stew off the bottom of the cooking pot. Marissa broke into a broad smile. She knew she could persuade the sorcerer to do as she wished – men usually did what she wanted.

Marissa slipped through a gap in the rock hidden by snow-covered ivy and in seconds was hurrying along the steep footpath that would take her around the top of the quarry and on the long journey to her meeting with the sorcerer. She wrapped her witch cloak around her for protection, trusting that she would not meet a pack of wolverines. That, thought Marissa, would be just her luck.

# THE QUEEN'S SPY

*As the moon moved slowly* up through the outer tracery of the top of the Guardian Ash, Jenna was climbing the ladder to Galen's treehouse, watched by the bright yellow eyes of a tiger hidden in the undergrowth. Jenna had released Jim Knee and told him to return to the Castle, but on principle the jinnee did not obey the command at once. He liked to retain the illusion of free will. And besides, though he would not admit it to himself, he wanted to see the Queen safely up in the treehouse, away from the night-time danger that always lurked on the Forest floor.

Galen's treehouse was a complex affair consisting of many platforms, pods, linking ladders and ropes spread across three ancient oaks. As Jenna stopped on the first landing and reached up to pull a vine to signal her arrival, she heard a sharp hiss from the Forest floor. She looked down to see Ariel's anxious face looking up at her.

"Queen Jenna," Ariel said, all in a rush, "you have to come! Something awful is going to happen in the Witch Circle."

Jenna had little interest in what was happening in the Witch Circle and absolutely no wish to go back into the night-time Forest. From what she had heard from Ariel and Star in the past few months, she understood that awful things often happened in the Circle. The less she knew about them, the better, Jenna thought. "It's none of my business," she said briskly, and went to pull the vine.

"But it *is* your business," Ariel insisted. "They're going to burn two Castle kids."

Jenna's hand froze in mid-air. *"What?"* she whispered.

"Please, Queen Jenna," said Ariel. "Come *now*. There isn't much time."

# THE MOON OVER THE ASH

*The moon broke free from* the last tracery of the Guardian Ash. All witches' eyes were upon the Snow Sprites, who, now that all their snow had melted, looked worryingly like real children. But not one of the witches said a word – some because they dared not and many because they didn't care. They were having a great night, so why spoil it?

Star glanced anxiously up at the small gap in the trees where the path ran down to the quarry, but she saw nothing. Around her the sprite chant grew ever louder:

*Sprites burn bright!*
*Light the night!*
*Light the night!*
*Sprites burn bright!*

Tod had managed to sneak a **Charm** from her Apprentice belt and she was now clasping a tiny silver snail shell. This was for an **UnSeen** that gave her the highest protection possible from harm – and Tod reckoned she needed all the protection she could get. Silently, she began the **Incantation** and to her relief, Morwenna – despite her heavy hand resting on Tod's shoulder – did not notice, for Tod's substance was unchanged.

Many of the witches saw the ExtraOrdinary Apprentice slowly disappear, but not one dared mention it. Some actually felt relieved – at least one of the children might survive the night.

Ferdie and Oskar, still under the fearsome **Grasps** of Bryony and Madron, were mercifully unaware of what was in store. As the two witches slowly walked Ferdie and Oskar towards the fire, Tod carefully lifted Morwenna's hand from her shoulder and stepped out of her reach. The Witch Mother, enthralled by the chant and the sheer excitement of the moment, did not notice.

As Bryony and Madron propelled Ferdie and Oskar nearer to the flames, within her **UnSeen**, Tod was so close that she could have reached out and touched them. The chanting was drawing to a crescendo and Tod knew there would come a moment when the two witches must release Oskar and Ferdie from their **Grasps** in order to hurl them into the flames, and at that point she would have to act with lightning speed. Stealthily as Jim Knee himself, Tod padded beside Oskar and Ferdie, matching them step for step, waiting to pounce.

All eyes in the quarry were on the witches and their victims as they creeped ever closer towards the fire. Tod's gaze did not leave Ferdie and Oskar for one second. By now they were so close to the fire that the heat was searing. Tod braced herself. *Any moment now*, she told herself. *Any … moment …*

It happened fast. In a sudden, synchronised movement, Bryony and Madron released their **Grasps**.

Ferdie and Oskar saw the flames. They screamed

Tod pounced. She pulled them back from the fire, yelling, "It's me, Tod! Run! Run!" Bryony and Madron lunged at them, **Grasping** hands outstretched, but Ferdie and Oskar were racing away, with Tod's voice behind them shouting, "Run! Run!"

But they were not free yet. The Witch Circle had closed ranks. The Tribe of Three were now surrounded by a steely necklace of blue witchy eyes.

*"Rush them!"* yelled Tod.

The Witch Circle joined arms like a chain-link fence and began a strangely pulsing Hum: *thrummer-thrum-thrum, thrummer-thrum-thrum,* spinning a web around them, making them dizzy. Ferdie and Oskar stopped at the witch fence, bewildered, like sheep reaching the boundary of their pen. They turned to Tod just in time to see her UnSeen slowly leave her.

Morwenna Mould's deep laugh cut through the Hum. "Ha! I see the Sprites have some spirit!" she said. "And I see the Apprentice has too. Well, well, let us have some fun with them, let us see them *really* run." The Witch Mother walked over to the fire and drew out a burning branch. "They will run fast with this behind them!"

A brave, lone shout came from the Circle. "Witch Mother! The Apprentice is meant for the sorcerer!"

"And he can have her – when we are done with her – and some nice, toasty sprite bones as an extra gift."

With the burning branch in her hand, the Witch Mother walked very slowly towards Tod, Oskar and Ferdie, enjoying her power.

"I'm sorry," Tod said.

"What for?" asked Ferdie.

"Because I should do something. But I don't know what."

"Scream?" Ferdie suggested.

And so they did – all three together.

The Witch Circle laughed and screamed back. Once again, the Scream of the Wendron Witch coven rang throughout the Forest.

# THE TIGER, THE WITCH AND THE RED ROBE

*Jenna, Jim Knee and Ariel* were heading for the path that led down to the quarry, when the **Scream** began. It drifted up, eerie and piercing, and caused a fluttering of night owls rising from the trees in panic. Ariel's hearing was acute, she had already heard the brief screams of Ferdie, Oskar and Tod and she suspected that the witch **Scream** was being used to cover up the sound of genuine screams, which did sometimes upset the more sensitive witches. Ariel feared it would all be over by the time they arrived at the Circle, but she dared not tell Jenna that.

Ariel glanced around to check that the Queen and her tiger were still following. Jenna saw the fear in the young witch's eyes and felt sick. The path wound endlessly ahead and she knew that at the end of it they had to scramble down the steep, rocky path into the quarry. There was no time left.

"Ariel, stop!" Jenna called.

Ariel swung around and looked at the Queen. So she, too, knew it was all over. "I … I am so, *so* sorry –" Ariel began, but Jenna cut her off.

"I shall send my jinnee," she said.

Ariel looked blank.

"The tiger. He's a jinnee."

Ariel's eyes widened in surprise. This Queen was worth keeping on the right side of. "Oh," she said. "Yes, I knew that."

"You know the way. Show him. You will be faster than I. If the Castle kids need any help you must give it. And I don't care what you have to do, OK?"

Ariel nodded.

Jenna kneeled down beside the tiger and searched for a hint of understanding in its yellow eyes. She saw none, but she knew she must assume the best. "Jim Knee," Jenna said. "I command you to follow Ariel with all speed. She will show you the way to the Witch's Quarry. Go as fast as you can. You will find Castle children there. I command you to bring them to me safe and well." Jenna stood up. "Go!"

Jenna watched the tiger bounding after the young witch, who glanced behind her and looked, not surprisingly, a little anxious.


Tod, Ferdie and Oskar had linked arms and were facing the witches. Like an ever-tightening noose, the Witch Circle was closing in, pushing the Tribe of Three back towards the flames. The hypnotic pulse of the Hum made each step towards the heat of the fire feel oddly unreal.

Suddenly the voice of Morwenna hissed in Tod's ear, sharp against the blur of the Hum. "You're a little fool," she said. "You should know better than to ally yourself to two sprites. If it wasn't for the sorcerer I would throw you in as well." Tod looked up and saw a flicker of enjoyment cross the Witch Mother's face, and she understood that the witches were playing with them in the way a cat plays with a mouse. A wave of anger replaced the fear and Tod swung around and landed a

221

wild punch somewhere in the middle of the vast softness beneath Morwenna's thick green cloak. Morwenna reeled backwards, the **Hum** turned to a gasp and the two nearest witches broke the circle to catch their Witch Mother before she fell to the ground. They were a fraction too late and Morwenna's bulk brought them crashing down with her.

The Circle was broken and with it the power it was casting over the witches. Many began to realise the enormity of what they had been about to do. Some hugged each other in dismay and others stood with their hands over their faces, staring at the fire through their fingers.

As Tod, Ferdie and Oskar made a dash for the break in the circle, Morwenna Mould's voice echoed around the quarry: "Stop them! Stop them!" But no one rushed to obey. The three reached the gap and as two of the older witches made a halfhearted move to grab them, a tiger leaped out of nowhere. It stood snarling, its teeth bared, its yellow eyes glittering in the light of the fire, daring anyone to move.

Under the shocked gaze of the Wendron Witch Coven, the tiger escorted the two Snow Sprites and the Apprentice away from the circle. Not one witch raised so much as a finger. Even when a cry of "I said stop them, you fools!" came from their beached Witch Mother, no one moved. Silently the broken Witch Circle watched the tiger escort their three ex-captives across the quarry floor. They had just reached the gap in the rock where the path led up to the Forest when the Apprentice turned and ran back. The two Snow Sprites tried to stop her but she ignored them.

The witches shrank back. What **Darke Magyk** was the Apprentice about to visit upon them? Even the Witch Mother, who was now back on her feet and propped up by Bryony and Madron, did no more than watch warily. But all the Apprentice did was pick up the ropes of the two sleds, then turn and walk away, pulling the sleds behind her.

As she headed towards the waiting tiger that was guarding her friends, Tod felt the hairs prickle on the back of her neck – she was being followed. Tod had a small **Celebrate Charm** in her Apprentice belt. Septimus had given it to her that morning. It was, he had insisted, to be used only if she won the race. But Tod hoped Septimus would understand her disobedience. Suddenly, she swung around to face the Coven. It was just like Grandmother's Footsteps. The witches who had been rapidly creeping up behind her froze. With one fluid movement, Tod took the **Charm** from her belt and threw it up into the air, calling out the **Incantation** as she did so: *"To the Victor, the Spoils!"*

The **Charm** exploded into sparks, prickling and crackling red and green in the night air. It was beautiful, but to the witches, who had no idea what it was, it was terrifying. Overexcited by too much **Screaming** and the prospect of a sprite-burning, the witches scattered with shrieks of fear.

Morwenna Mould knew she was defeated. Left virtually alone in the Quarry – apart from Bryony, Madron and a few of the older witches too creaky to run very fast, the Witch Mother watched her prey disappear into the gap between the rocks where the path led up into the Forest. Even if she had wanted to, there was no way Morwenna could follow them – she could no longer fit.

Morwenna spat on the ground in disgust. She was sure she knew who was behind this – the double-crossing, two-timing little trollop Marissa. Marissa would be sorry, she would make sure of that. And then, as Morwenna Mould stood fuming, a flash of gold in the trees at the top of the path caught her eye. She looked up and saw the distinctive red of the cloak of the Castle Queen, A surge of fury ran through her.

"Queen Jenna!" the Witch Mother yelled, her deep voice echoing around the quarry. "You will regret this. When you have a daughter I will come for her. You will never have a moment's peace. Never!"

Jenna looked down at the furious figure below, its squat shape silhouetted against the firelight. "You take on a Castle Queen at your peril, Morwenna Mould," she muttered. Then, with the tiger at her side and her two witches on guard behind her, Jenna led Tod, Ferdie and Oskar through the night-time Forest to the safety of Galen's treehouse.

# PART VIII

## THIRTY-FOUR HOURS TO HATCHING

# GALEN'S TREEHOUSE

*Many years ago Galen had* taught the teenage Sarah Heap all that she knew about herbs and healing. Now Galen was elderly and frail and living an increasingly precarious life in her Forest treehouse. Sarah Heap worried about her much-loved old mentor and had decided to spend the winter looking after her, which was why Silas Heap, unwilling to let his wife brave the Forest on her own, had found himself spending an uncomfortable and boring winter up a tree eating what he described as "rabbit food".

But that evening Silas was – as Sarah pointed out – smiling for a change. He had his daughter with him (who had arrived with two very pretty young witches) and he had just learned the wonderful news that his son Sam was back home. Both Silas and Sarah had feared they would never see Sam again. Even though Silas could tell from Jenna's careful answers to Sarah's questions that Sam had been injured, he had great faith in the talents of Dandra Draa and her Sick Bay team. Just to know for the first time in four long years where Sam actually was that night was a tremendous relief to Silas. The icing on the cake was that tomorrow he and Sarah had a perfectly acceptable excuse to leave this cold, nut-strewn, shrew-infested treehouse and return to civilisation. Even the shirt woven from smelly, unbelievably scratchy goat hair that Galen had given him for a MidWinter Feast Day present (and that Sarah made him wear so as not to hurt Galen's feelings) no longer itched quite so badly that night.

The largest group that the treehouse had played host to for some time was gathered around the fire basket, which was suspended above a circular hole in the middle of an open platform. Silas, Sarah, Galen, Jenna, Ariel, Star, Tod, Ferdie, Oskar and a yellow-eyed tiger were sitting on rugs strewn over the rough wooden planks. Silas threw another log on the fire and tongues of flame leaped up into the branches above.

"Careful, Silas!" Sarah shouted. "You'll burn us to the ground!"

Silas threw a bucket of water on the flames and watched the glowing cinders drop through the fire basket to a huge pile of ash on the Forest floor far below. Then he took some skewers of meat from the outer embers of the fire and offered it to their guests. Galen pulled a face at the sight of what she called "flesh".

"Anyone for roast squirrel?" Silas inquired cheerily.

Everyone, apart from Galen and a loyal Sarah, was very much for roast squirrel. Tod, Ferdie and Oskar were ravenous. Jim Knee – who Jenna had decided to keep as protection – eyed the tiny pieces of meat with disdain and slunk away. There was good hunting to be had in the Forest, he could smell it.

Tod gazed up into the dark tracery of branches above. She saw the moon riding high in the star-filled sky and a shiver ran through her as she remembered the last time she had looked at the moon through the trees. She glanced at Ferdie and Oskar, who were sitting wrapped in blankets, quietly talking to each

228

other. Tod reckoned that they still didn't totally understand what had so very nearly happened to them. Which was, Tod thought, for the best.

At the end of supper Ariel and Star reluctantly got to their feet. "We must go now," they said.

"Oh, *must* you?" Silas said, sounding very disappointed.

"You heard what they said, Silas," Sarah snapped.

Ariel smiled at Silas. She liked his mischievous blue eyes. "We are sorry to leave you, Silas Heap. But it would not be good for us to be absent tonight."

"No, it wouldn't," said Sarah.

Jenna helped Ariel and Star drop the ladder down and handed them an extra gold coin each for their night's work. As they went she gave them a message for Septimus, telling him she, Tod, Oskar and Ferdie would be back the next morning. Jenna watched her witch spies descend the ladder, pleased with them and their night's work. She was still shocked by what had so very nearly happened. How right she had been to keep a close watch on the Wendrons, she thought. If she had not … Jenna shook her head to clear the thought from her mind. It did not bear thinking about.

# The WitchFinder

*Jenna returned to the fireside* to see Galen taking a small brass tube from one of her many leafy pockets and handing it to Sarah, saying excitedly, "You must see how well your wonderful gift works. It really is a genuine WitchFinder."

Sarah took the tube and went to the edge of the platform, where she put it to her eye like a telescope. Galen, slower on her feet, joined her. "Oh!" Sarah gasped under her breath. "I can see them both. Look, there's Ariel running … and Star just behind her. They blend into the night so well. You could never see them without this. Never. And did you know it shows their footprints, too?"

Galen smiled. "There's no hiding place for witches with a WitchFinder," she murmured.

"It's amazing," Sarah breathed. "I can see them all the way through the trees. Their cloaks kind of glow and the trees almost disappear." She turned to Galen. "I'm so glad it works. You can never be sure when you buy at the Port Magyk Market."

"I knew it worked when I caught sight of Morwenna a few nights ago," Galen said, smiling.

"You don't need a fancy gadget to see Morwenna," Silas commented, joining them. "She's what you might call obvious."

"Silas, you are *so* rude!" Sarah sounded rather pleased. There had been a time – many years ago now – when Silas had thought Morwenna Mould rather wonderful. And Morwenna had felt much the same about Silas. But those times were long past, as was the truce that had then existed between the Wendrons and the Castle. Sarah gave the WitchFinder back to Galen. "Galen, I do wish you would come back to the Castle with us," she said. "It feels so much more dangerous than when I lived here."

"Times change, Sarah dear. That was nearly thirty years ago."

"Exactly," Sarah said. "And you are not getting any younger."

This did not go down well with Galen. "Be that as it may, Sarah Heap, I belong in the Forest and this is where I intend to stay. I will *not* be hounded out by a coven going to the bad." Feeling that she had been a little harsh with Sarah, Galen added, "Anyway, dear, thanks to your WitchFinder I shall be well prepared for any trouble."

The rest of the evening passed happily. It reminded Tod of the beach fire gatherings she, Oskar and Ferdie used to have at home in their PathFinder village. It ended in much the same way too, with people telling increasingly scary ghost stories while the moon sank slowly, the night air began to bite and everyone's thoughts turned to how much warmer it would be in bed.

The accommodation in the treehouse consisted of a collection of pods made from woven willow branches bent into spheres and covered with fir fronds. They perched like huge nests high in the canopy of the three tall oaks and were connected by rope walkways and precarious arrangements of ladders and planks. Galen roosted like a large scruffy hen in a tiny pod precariously placed at the top of the middle, tallest oak. Silas and Sarah had one of the pods nearest the platform because Silas did not enjoy balancing along the ropewalks.

Galen now set about settling her guests for the night. She gave Jenna her own pod next to Silas and Sarah. Tod, Ferdie and Oskar, to their delight, were directed to a large pod high up in an outer oak, with its own platform and private ladder to the Forest floor.

The pod had a circular opening over which hung three wolverine skins. Inside it was knee-deep in dry leaves and moss on which was placed a neat pile of yet more wolverine skins and some brightly coloured blankets that smelled of goat. The pod felt warm and safe, as indeed it was. Galen took care that the outer branches of her three oaks never touched those of any other tree. Any creature that wished to invade the treehouse – right down to the smallest leaf leeches and tree shrews – must ascend the trunks and get past the rings of fiendishly sticky bark glue, which Galen had painted around her trees. And so Tod, Oskar and Ferdie had the luxury of being in the middle of the night-time Forest while feeling perfectly secure.

Drained by the events of the day, Ferdie and Oskar wrapped themselves in the goat blankets, curled up in the soft, springy leaves and fell asleep at once. But Tod was not tired at all. Despite the terrifying experiences of the Witch Circle she was excited to be out in the Forest and away from the urban feel of the Castle. She sat in the entrance of the pod, looking out and thinking how good it was to be free from the rules and regulations of the Wizard Tower and back in the middle of nature once more. The fresh smell of the air, free from the damp mouldiness of the Forest floor, made her feel wide awake.

Perching in the canopy of the Forest felt not unlike being out at sea. The swaying of the topmost branches in the breeze felt like the rocking motion of a small boat and set Tod wondering what her father, Dan Moon, was doing that very moment. Was he out on a night fishing expedition watching the sky just as she was? Was he thinking of her right then, just as she was thinking of him? Tod longed to show Dan all she was doing and she hoped that one day soon, when all was safe from Oraton-Marr, he would be able to come through the Ancient Ways to the Castle once again.

Thinking of the sea reminded Tod that Galen had loaned her the WitchFinder for the night. "Keep a lookout for Morwenna Mould," she had said. "She's up to something, mark my words." Tod put the WitchFinder to her eye like a telescope and began to Watch the Forest.

It was strange seeing the Forest through the WitchFinder. The trees became quite insubstantial: their thick, dark trunks looked pale and gave the appearance of being almost transparent. In contrast Tod saw that the animals – and what a wonderful variety there was – were sharply defined, and seemed almost ultra real, as though someone had carefully drawn around them with a thick black pen. It was fascinating. Tod spent a happy ten minutes Watching a family of tree shrews fight over a supper of a large leaf leech and then, having dropped most of the creature on to the Forest floor, settle into their nest with much fussing and petulant nipping.

Slowly, Tod grew sleepy. She was about to reluctantly put the WitchFinder away when a faint green glow appeared on the edge of her circle of vision. Tod held her breath with excitement – *it was a witch*. She was coming along the path and she was heading this way. Remembering how Galen had twisted the thick brass cuff of the WitchFinder to get a close-up view, Tod did the same and found she was looking straight into the bright blue eyes of Marissa. She almost dropped the little brass tube in shock and was about to pull down the wolverine skin door flaps when she remembered that there was no way Marissa could see her. Tod was safely hidden in a pod at the top of the tree and was hundreds of yards away, which was way too far for even the most skillful of witches to Feel that she was being watched.

Fascinated, Tod Watched Marissa wind her way along the Forest path, the WitchFinder picking out the witch's cloak and making it glow a bright greenish yellow. Marissa was hurrying along the path, glancing over her shoulder every now and then, and it seemed to Tod that the witch feared she was being followed. Marissa was up to something, of that there was no doubt.

Soon Marissa was below, rushing past the broad foot of the first of Galen's great oaks. The witch glanced upwards and Tod held her breath, even though she was pretty sure that Marissa was more worried about being seen than seeing, for the witch pulled the hood of her cloak up and shrank into it as she hurried by.

Marissa hurried on through the trees and Tod was impressed by how silently she travelled. Sound from the Forest floor travelled easily upwards, yet she heard not the faintest whisper of a footfall. As Marissa drew away and ever more trees obscured the view, the bright glow of her cloak in the WitchFinder eyeglass began to grow dull, and Tod had to concentrate hard to follow the witch. After some minutes Marissa was no more than an occasional vague glimmer – and then she was gone.

Tod was sure that Marissa was up to something. She remembered the Witch Mother's comments about the sorcerer and the deal she had with Marissa. Tod had the strangest feeling that the sorcerer might be Oraton-Marr and if that was the case, then here was another link to the Egg of the Orm.

Tod made a sudden decision. She knew she was being foolhardy, but she didn't care. She shoved the WitchFinder into her deepest pocket, pulled a wolverine skin around her for warmth, then dropped the emergency rope down. She felt the weighted end hit the ground, then with the practised movements of one used to climbing up masts and the sides of tall houses to hang nets, Tod was down the rope in seconds, before she had time to talk herself out of what she was doing. She stood for a few moments on the Forest floor and looked up at the treehouse complex, seeing the friendly glow from the embers of the fire. Tod felt a brief flicker of fear and pushed it aside. She had a witch to follow. And fast.

# IN THE NIGHT-TIME FOREST

*Tod pointed the* **WitchFinder** *at* the ground. She told herself that if it did not find Marissa's footprints she would climb straight back up the rope and forget the whole thing. Tod was not sure whether she was entirely pleased when a glowing outline of a foot sprang into the **WitchFinder** eyepiece. Not more than eighteen inches in front of that print was another, then another. Left, right, left, right. There was no excuse now – before her lay a clear trail.

Heart beating fast, Tod set off. She had learned from Oskar how to travel silently through a forest but she was not as skilled as he, and every time a twig snapped under her foot her heart jumped in fear. Her way was clear at first because Marissa had followed a well-worn path, but soon Tod came to a large, round rock where the path continued but Marissa's footprints did not. Tod stepped off the path into the mulch of thousands of years' leaf fall, across which Marissa's footprints glowed like a line of beacons. In the deep softness, Tod's footfalls were silent, and she soon became aware that all around her was silence too. A feeling of awe crept over her; she felt as though she was walking through a very ancient space.

Tod was now approaching a close-knit line of trees that presented a solid wall of trunks and branches. She stopped in front of two extremely tall, straight trees that stood remarkably close together, like sentinels. Marissa's footprints passed between them and Tod knew she must do the same, but her way was barred. Two great boughs were growing across her path, and a tangle of smaller branches formed a tightly woven net. Tod wondered how Marissa had managed to slip through – it did not seem possible.

Unable to rid herself of the feeling that the trees were staring down at her, Tod looked up at them. "Please," she whispered. "Please let me pass." In the tops of branches Tod could hear a rustling that spread far in front of her, as though the trees were talking to one another. "It's really important," Tod said. And then it came into her mind to say, "I mean only good for the Forest."

The rustling above increased as though a strong wind was blowing through the treetops, and Tod began to feel scared – something very eerie was happening. Suddenly she felt very alone and exposed. What was she *doing*, following a witch deep into the night-time Forest? Was she totally crazy? Tod's certainty left her. All she wanted to do was to get back to the treehouse. Fast.

As she turned to run, a movement of the two sentinel trees caught her eye and Tod stopped in amazement: *the great boughs blocking her way were beginning to rise*. To see a tree moving was awe-inspiring. As the arms of the trees lifted, Tod saw those of the pair of trees behind beginning to do the same and she knew she must go on. She stepped between the first two trees and moved slowly forward down the avenue of towering trees. Ahead of her she saw the rising branches rippling like a long wave. As she moved down the long, straight avenue she became aware that the branches were lowering behind her. There was no turning back now. A sense of awe stole over Tod as she followed Marissa's glowing footprints through the trees. She understood that she had been allowed to enter a very private space. She was not sure why, but she did remember Galen saying that the Forest had its way of knowing what was good for it.

Tod had been prepared for something magnificent at the end of the avenue – some kind of tree temple, maybe. But as she stepped beneath the last of the raised boughs she found herself in a small clearing in which there were what appeared to be three large and unruly heaps of wood partly covered with turf, each with a ramshackle door in it. They looked, Tod thought, like the kind of camps she, Ferdie and Oskar used to build on the edge of their own forest, the Far, back at home. They certainly did not look like anything special. And where was Marissa? Tod put the WitchFinder to her eye and saw the witch's footprints leading to the middle heap. Puzzled, Tod stared at the ramshackle door and the random piling of the log and branches. Was this where Marissa lived? She supposed it must be. A wave of weariness came over Tod. She had been so sure that Marissa was up to something important. Now it seemed that all she had done was risk the dangers of the night-time Forest just to follow Marissa back to her scruffy dump of a home. How stupid was that?

Tod watched the door for some minutes but the little hut was silent. Marissa was clearly already fast asleep. Feeling very foolish and not just a little scared at the thought of the journey through the Forest back to the treehouse, Tod turned to go. The first pair of tall trees stood before her, impassive. Their branches hung low, the two huge boughs barring the path back along the avenue, their twigs intertwined in a tangled net. "Please ... let me pass," Tod whispered, spooked by the sound of her voice in the deep silence of the clearing. But the boughs did not move. Tod tried not to panic; she told herself that she had had to wait a few minutes for them to move before. And so she stood there, waiting patiently, but nothing happened. "Please," she whispered. "Please let me pass ..."

It was then that Tod heard behind her the creak of a door opening. She swung around to see Marissa gingerly stepping out. In the shadow of the sentinel trees, Tod froze. Marissa had yet to see her; the witch was looking back over her shoulder and speaking to someone. Her voice sounded strained. And then Marissa was out and stepping aside to let whoever was in the little hut come out too. How two people had fitted inside, Tod had no idea. The hut was tiny.

Marissa cast her witchy glance over the clearing, searching for danger – and saw Tod. The witch's blue eyes lit up so bright that they seemed to glow inside her head. "Stay right there," she said to Tod in a low, urgent voice. "Do not move. Do not say a word. It will be all right, I promise."

Tod stared at Marissa. She knew enough about the witch not to trust any of her promises. She glanced behind her but the boughs with their twisted network of twigs were as impenetrable as ever. Tod had no choice but to stay where she was anyway.

Marissa was now helping someone out of the hut and as the figure stepped into the clearing Tod could not suppress a gasp. There was no mistaking the close-cropped steel-grey hair and the deep-set, dark green eyes. It was the sorcerer, Oraton-Marr.

Marissa shepherded Oraton-Marr – resplendent in blue silks – into the clearing. "It seems," she said, "that my threats have worked. The Witch Mother has thought better of her double-crossing plot. See, she has left the Apprentice here for you. As I suspected she would."

The sorcerer eyed Marissa suspiciously. "You never said you suspected that," he said. "You told me she had the Apprentice captive and wanted to do a deal with me. And I told you –"

"That you do not do deals with witches," Marissa finished for him. "And why should you, Your Highness, when the very mention of your name clearly strikes fear into their hearts?"

"Quite," Oraton-Marr replied. His eyes narrowed as he stared at Tod, half hidden in the shadows. "But she's just a child. She'll know nothing of any use."

"This is the *ExtraOrdinary* Apprentice, Your Highness," Marissa said. "I assure you, she knows a great deal."

Oraton-Marr did not look convinced. "It's a start, I suppose," he said. "Bring the Apprentice to me. The deal was that you handed her to me, remember. So do it. Hand her over."

"Oh … yes. I'll go and fetch her."

Marissa set off towards Tod, then she suddenly stopped dead and said a very rude, unwitchy word. *Tod had disappeared.* Marissa stared at the spot where Tod had been standing only a few seconds earlier and began to creep towards it as if somehow hoping to surprise her. Tod, amazed that her panicked UnSeen had actually worked, stepped to one side. But she had not fooled Oraton-Marr.

"She's over there, you idiot!" he yelled at Marissa, his harsh voice cutting through the soft silence of the clearing.

"Where?" Marissa darted desperately from side to side, flailing her arms like a windmill in a vain attempt to grab hold of Tod. It would have been funny if Tod had not been so terrified.

While Tod moved slowly enough not to make a sound, but fast enough to keep out of Marissa's clutches, she became aware of two more figures emerging from the hut. How many more could it hold? And what was Marissa doing with them all? The first to emerge was another one she recognised: Drone, Oraton-Marr's servant. And struggling in his grasp was a small girl.

"Kaznim!" Tod breathed – and Marissa heard her.

After that everything happened so fast that later Tod could never remember exactly how it all came together. But it did. The sequence of events went something like this:

Marissa grabbed hold of Tod.

Tod kicked Marissa.

Marissa let go of Tod and yelled.

Tod's **UnSeen** evaporated.

"Get her!" Oraton-Marr yelled to Drone.

Drone let go of Kaznim and set off across to Tod.

Marissa screamed.

Kaznim, now free, pulled a stick from the hut and swung it at Oraton-Marr's feet.

Oraton-Marr fell over.

Drone lunged at Tod.

Marissa screamed.

Tod kicked Drone.

Drone fell over.

Kaznim jumped on him.

Marissa screamed, "Wolverines!"

At the edge of the clearing Tod saw the yellow eyes of a pack of wolverines. "Please!" she yelled at the sentinel trees. "Please let me pass!"

But Tod had no need to shout. In front of her the avenue was once again opening up. As Tod hurried forward she saw Drone try to grab Kaznim, so she grabbed her first. And as Tod and Kaznim made their escape, the avenue unfolded before them like a wave of green. Holding tightly on to Kaznim's hand, Tod pulled the girl along with her, scrambling beneath the rising boughs. Behind them she was aware of the boughs dropping to the ground unusually fast, like a portcullis guarding a castle. As Tod and Kaznim ran along the avenue they heard the screams of Marissa, the yelling of Drone and the curses of Oraton-Marr grow ever fainter until they faded away. At the last pair of sentinel trees, Tod stopped and watched the boughs slowly come to rest. "Thank you," she said. "Thank you for saving us."

Kaznim stared at Tod, totally confused. The Apprentice girl who had chased her with a tiger had just saved her from the evil sorcerer and now she was talking to trees. Kaznim noticed that Tod no longer had hold of her hand – she was free to run away if she wanted to. But Kaznim did not want to. Something told her that the Apprentice girl did not mean her any harm, and so Kaznim stood patiently beside Tod watching the last two great boughs settle back into their sentinel position. As the trees relaxed, they gave a satisfied groan, knowing they had done right by the Forest.

# FOREST STRANGER

*In the depths of the Big Freeze*, when the winter mornings were dark and cold, the Forest slept late. And so it was in the treehouse. As the pale light from the sun crept around the wolverine-skin door flaps of the pods, their occupants all felt that it was much more sensible to stay curled up beneath piles of furs and goat blankets.

Galen was the first to emerge from her pod. Silently she set about making goat milk porridge laced with honey and setting the water on to brew Forest coffee, which Galen made from dried acorns – although Silas Heap was convinced that she actually used dried goat dung. The pleasant smell of the porridge drifted up through the trees, wandered into the top pod and woke Ferdie from a deep, leafy sleep. Slowly, Ferdie opened her eyes and remembered where she was. The soft morning light filled the pod with shifting shadows and Ferdie's gaze wandered around the cocoon in which she had spent the night. She loved the pod. It felt safe and yet exciting at the same time. As her eyes became used to the dim light, Ferdie counted her companions: there were three sleeping, breathing bumps of blankets.

*Three?*

Ferdie sat up fast. Who else was with them? A host of ghostly tales from the previous night flooded into her mind. Was it a witch child? A tree spirit? Or maybe even a were-wolverine, creeping into Forest beds at night and eating its bedfellows at the dawn of the new day. An awful thought occurred to Ferdie. Maybe *all three* bumps beneath the blankets were were-wolverines. Maybe they had already eaten Tod and Oskie and were now waiting for her to wake up. In fact, maybe they had already eaten *everyone in the entire treehouse*.

Ferdie, still jittery after the Witch Circle, panicked. *"Aaaargh!"* she yelled.

Three figures leaped up. Not one of them was a were-wolverine.

"Oh," Ferdie said, somewhat embarrassed. "Sorry. I thought ..." Her voice trailed off. What she had thought seemed so stupid now. She looked at the young girl with the dark curly hair and wide-open eyes, and tried to remember seeing her the night before. She was sure she hadn't. And from Oskar's expression, he hadn't seen the girl either.

"This is Kaznim," Tod said. "I was looking for her in the Castle. Remember?"

"You found her *here*?" Ferdie asked, puzzled.

"Well, not here in the pod, exactly," Tod said evasively.

"So *where*, exactly?" asked Oskar, who always knew when Tod had something to hide.

"Um. Well, somewhere really weird. In the Forest."

Ferdie and Oskar stared at Tod. "You've been into the Forest? While we were asleep?" asked Ferdie.

"Um. Yes," Tod admitted.

"Well, you might have taken *me*," Oskar said. "You know I wanted to explore."

"Like Ferdie said, you were asleep," Tod said. "Anyway, it was an emergency."

Ferdie and Oskar looked unimpressed. "What about the Tribe of Three?" they both said.

"I know, I know," Tod protested. "But you were *asleep*. Snoring, in fact. OK?"

"OK," Ferdie and Oskar said reluctantly.

"Well, tell us then," Ferdie instructed.

And so, while they all sat wrapped in blankets and furs and the warmth of their breath misted the chill morning air, Tod told them about her time in the night-time Forest.

As she drew to a close, Oskar and Ferdie looked dumbstruck. *"Oraton-Marr?"* they exclaimed.

"Yes," Tod said. "It was him." She turned to Kaznim, who had listened silently to the conversation so far. "Could you tell my friends what you told me last night?"

"She understands what we say?" Oskar sounded surprised.

"I am not an animal," Kaznim told Oskar crossly. "Of course I understand what you say."

"I'm – sorry," Oskar stammered, embarrassed. "I … I thought you might speak another language."

"I am a Draa," Kaznim said proudly. "Kaznim Na-Draa. Draa speak many tongues."

Ferdie smiled at Kaznim. "Hello, I'm Ferdie."

Kaznim smiled uncertainly.

"And this is my twin brother, Oskar."

"Sorry if I was rude," Oskar said. "I didn't mean to be."

Ferdie continued, "I was helping Tod to look for you in the Castle yesterday. We couldn't find you anywhere. You just vanished."

Kaznim looked at Tod. "Your tiger was chasing me," she said accusingly. Tod laughed and Kaznim looked offended. "It was not funny," she muttered.

Tod hurried to explain. "I wasn't laughing at you, honestly. But the tiger wasn't a real one. It was a jinnee. Called Jim Knee."

Kaznim looked at Tod in awe. "You have your own jinnee?"

Tod shook her head. "He's not mine. He was helping me, that's all."

Kaznim was still impressed. To have a jinnee helping you was a sign of great power.

"I'm sorry he frightened you," Tod said. "He didn't mean to. He's nice, really." She paused and then said, "So … where did you go?"

Kaznim took out her precious blue piece of paper. "Here. To this funny little shop with the long name."

"It *is* a funny shop," Ferdie agreed. "I go there to see Oskie. He helps out downstairs."

Kaznim nodded. "Yes. I saw him there. He had insect eyes."

Oskar grinned. "I did. And I saw you too, once I took my insect eyes off. You were brave being with that horrible ghost. She can be really nasty at times."

Kaznim nodded. "I could tell. But she said she would show me the Way out, so I followed her. And I went into the Hidden arch and through lots of Ways, just like I did with Sam and Marwick. The boy on the desk was nice at first and he gave me the numbers, you see, so I knew where to go."

"Was it a long way?" Tod asked.

"It was," Kaznim said. "And some bits were really scary. But

I didn't care. I just wanted to go home to my Ammaa. But ..."
She trailed off and bit her lip. Tears welled up in her eyes.

"Didn't you find your Ammaa?" Ferdie asked gently.

Kaznim shook her head. "The sorcerer got me."

"Oraton-Marr?" asked Tod.

Kaznim nodded. "He was on a ship in the Port of the Singing Sands. I didn't know that was where he lived. I thought he would be in the Red City where they have lots of nasty sorcerers. Bubba saw me and called out. Then he got me."

"Who's Bubba?" asked Oskar.

"My little sister. The sorcerer stole her so that my mother would make sure the Egg hatched."

Ferdie, Oskar and Tod exchanged glances. This must surely be the Orm Egg.

"The Sorcerer does that kind of thing," Ferdie said. "He stole our little brother."

Kaznim looked at Ferdie with fellow feeling. "Did he give him back?" she asked.

"No," Ferdie said. "We *took* him back."

Kaznim looked at Ferdie with disbelief. Ferdie put her arm around the girl. "And we will take Bubba back too. You'll see. Come on, let's go down and find some breakfast."

But first there was something Tod really wanted to know. "So ... why did the sorcerer bring you into the Forest?" she asked.

Kaznim gulped. "He was cross because I had stolen the Egg Boy's box, but I gave it back because he said I would never see Bubba again if I didn't. And then when he opened it he saw that the Egg Timer was missing and he was so angry ..." Kaznim stopped and looked scared. "I told the sorcerer that the nasty

247

boy in the shop had the **Egg Timer**. I hoped he might go and find the boy and scare him. But then the sorcerer told me that *I* had to take him there."

Tod's hand closed over the **Egg Timer** in her pocket. She remembered Septimus's conversation with Beetle about the importance of not using the Manuscriptorium Way and she was now totally on Septimus's side. The thought that Oraton-Marr could just walk into the Manuscriptorium whenever he felt like it was horrifying. So why had he ended up in the Forest instead? Tod was about to ask exactly that when Kaznim began to speak once more, her voice trembling.

"So I went back to the little alleyway where I had come out and there was nothing there," Kaznim said. "The arch had gone and I was so scared that I couldn't see it however hard I tried. The sorcerer got very angry. He said he would take me to the Red City and then I was even *more* scared. I thought he was going to give me to the Red Queen for her to kill. She likes doing that, you see. She killed my father."

Tod looked at Kaznim, surprised. "But you said that Dandra Draa killed your father."

"Well …" Kaznim looked embarrassed. "He died because of what Dandra Draa did. But the Red Queen was the one who swung the sword that cut off his head. Not Dandra Draa."

"The Red Queen did that *herself*?"

"Yes. After she had thrown him to her lion just for fun. You are lucky you have such a nice Queen here. I don't think she would ever cut off anyone's head, however cross she was. But in the Red City the Queen does that every week. So I thought she would do the same to me.

"I asked to say goodbye to Bubba but the sorcerer just laughed. And then everything went very fuzzy and I didn't know where my hands and feet or even my head was; I felt like I was falling apart. The ground seemed to disappear and the next thing I knew, I was somewhere else and I was being sick all over the sorcerer's pointy feet. I knew I was in the Red City because the ground I was being sick on was covered with dark red sand. I guessed some horrible spell had brought me there."

"You're right," Tod said. "It was a really horrible spell." She knew enough **Magykal** theory to understand that Oraton-Marr had done a **Darke Transport** – he had taken a living person with no **Magykal** skills on his own **Transport** with no regard for her safety. No wonder Kaznim had been sick, Tod thought. She was lucky to still be alive.

"We walked along some alleyways and we came to an iron door in a wall. There was a woman standing there with a green headband and a long green cloak. I thought she was one of the Red Queen's guards and the door led to where the lion lived. But when she saw us, the green woman looked almost as scared as I was. And even more scared when Oraton-Marr asked her where the Apprentice was."

"Apprentice?" Tod asked.

"Yes. The woman said there had been some trouble with some mould or something. The sorcerer grabbed her by the throat and said lots of the bad words that I used to hear the Egg Boy say when he thought that no one was listening. He told the green woman to open the bad-word door and he would go and get the bad-word Apprentice himself, seeing as everyone else around him was so bad-word useless. Especially bad-word witches. And then I understood that the woman was a witch, not a guard, and that I wasn't going to be eaten by a lion. So I felt a lot better. She opened the door and we went into a nice courtyard with a palm tree and a fountain. We walked over to the palm tree and then something really strange happened. It got cold and dark and smelled funny, and suddenly we were in a tiny hut. And then I came out of the hut, and I was in the Forest." Kaznim looked at Tod. "And so were you."

Oskar, Ferdie and Tod looked at one another. There were so many questions they were longing to ask Kaznim about the Orm Egg, but at that moment a bell rang far below and they heard Sarah yell, "Breakfast!"

Kaznim yawned again. "I am so tired," she said. Like a small animal she lay down on the leaves and curled into a ball, and her eyelids fluttered closed.

The Tribe of Three left Kaznim to sleep and slowly climbed down through the trees, discussing what to do. By the time they reached the fire-pit platform they had agreed on two things. First, they would tell no one about Kaznim or what had happened the night before in the Forest. And second, they would be going through the Forest Way into the Red City as soon as they could.

# SLIPPING AWAY

*They found Galen stirring a* bubbling pot of porridge. Tod gave her back the WitchFinder and Galen put it in her pocket with a smile. "Find any witches?" she asked.

Tod hated to lie so she said, "Yes, I did. Marissa Lane."

Galen looked surprised. "She's trouble, that young woman," she said.

"She is," Tod agreed.

Galen's green eyes looked up keenly and Tod felt as if Galen knew exactly what had happened the previous night. But Galen did not comment. She turned her attention to the porridge, which was sticking to the bottom of the pan. "They're nasty baggages, those Wendrons," Galen said. "You want to keep out of their way, you know. Especially at night."

Sarah and Jenna joined them for breakfast. Both sat quietly. Sarah was concerned about leaving Galen alone. Her old teacher seemed so frail in the morning light, her fragile hands shaking as she spooned out the porridge. Jenna was tired; she had not slept well in her pod. Silas, anxious to be away as soon as possible, had skipped breakfast and was busy packing their bags.

Tod was sipping her hot porridge, trying to work out how they were going to get away from the treehouse without being

251

noticed, when a soft *whoop-whoop* came up from the Forest floor. Jenna hurried over to the edge of the platform and gave an answering *whoop*. Turning back to Galen, she said, "Ariel and Star are here. Can they come up?"

Galen did not like witches in her treehouse, but she knew that Ariel and Star were a little different. She nodded and picked up two more bowls. Witches were always hungry.

"Thank you, Galen," Jenna said, and let down the ladder.

In the confusion caused by the arrival of Ariel and Star, Silas Heap's sudden appearance, his overeager helping of the young witches on to the platform, and Sarah's consequent irritation, Tod, Ferdie and Oskar slipped away. In a moment Ferdie and Oskar were shimmying down the rope to the Forest floor and Tod was climbing up to their pod. Quickly, she wrote a note: *Please do not worry. We are fine and will be back at the Castle very soon. Alice TodHunter Moon, Ferdie and Oskar Sarn*. She placed it in on the pile of blankets where it could be easily seen, then she woke Kaznim and hurried her down to join the others on the Forest floor.

Ariel and Star had a message from Septimus saying that he wanted Tod and Jim Knee back *as soon as possible*. While Jenna busied herself getting Sarah and Silas – who were on the verge of an argument – ready for the journey home, she had no idea what was happening fifty feet below on the Forest floor. Four guests – one of them uninvited – were leaving.

Oskar was looking doubtfully at the sleds. "But there's hardly any snow under the trees," he whispered. "They will slow us down." Tod knew that Oskar was right. Reluctantly, she pushed the *Wiz* and the *Beetle* into some bushes and hoped they would be safe. Then, under the cover of Sarah's raised voice in which the words "witch" and "silly old man" could easily be heard, Tod led the way along the path that she had taken the night before, while the sounds of Silas's indignant responses faded into the distance as they moved through the trees.

Some ten minutes later, as they stood before the first two sentinels of the avenue of trees, they heard more voices. This time it was their names being hallooed in the distance, with Ariel and Star's exuberant, whooping the loudest. The calls sounded anxious and Tod felt bad. She was for a moment tempted to head back, but as the towering trees slowly raised their branches, she was overcome by the sense that they were on an essential mission, and calling voices or no, they were going to complete it. They would return to the Castle with the Orm Egg. And then everyone would understand.

# THE FOREST WAY

*They walked through the* avenue with a feeling of awe as the boughs rose before them in a magnificent wave. The previous night Tod had not seen the astounding height of the trees nor understood how strange it was to see branches move like limbs of a massive beast. Now, as she walked silently along with Kaznim, her feet padding on the soft carpet of fine fir needles, Tod had goosebumps running up and down her neck. Behind her came Oskar and Ferdie, staring up in amazement at the moving cage of boughs. The last two trees raised their branches and Tod led the way into the clearing. "Here we are," she whispered. "It's the middle one."

Oskar and Ferdie looked disappointed. "It's just a pile of sticks with a door," Ferdie said.

"I know," Tod agreed. "But that's what everyone came out of. That's right, isn't it, Kaznim?"

Kaznim nodded cautiously. She wasn't sure she wanted to go back into the hut. Suppose the sorcerer was waiting for her? Suppose this was all a trick? She could not help remembering that the Apprentice girl had picked her pocket while she slept. How could she trust someone who did that?

Tod saw the mistrust in the girl's eyes and guessed the reason. "Kaznim," she said. "I'm sorry I took your cards. But I did it

254

because the cards were our only clue to where the Orm Egg is. You see, Oraton-Marr is waiting for the Egg to hatch and when it does he will Imprint the baby Orm so that it belongs to him. And then, when it grows up it will begin to eat rock and turn it into lapis lazuli for him and Oraton-Marr will become the most powerful sorcerer ever."

Kaznim frowned. "Why?" she asked.

"Because lapis lazuli makes Magyk powerful."

"Even Darke Magyk?"

"Especially Darke Magyk," Tod said.

Now Kaznim understood why the Orm Egg was so important, and why Tod needed to find it before it hatched. But that did not make things any better for her. "The sorcerer said that Bubba will die if he does not hatch the Egg and get the Orm," she whispered.

"We won't let your sister die," Tod said. "No way. Will we?" She turned to Ferdie and Oskar for support.

Ferdie put her arm around Kaznim. "We will keep her safe. We will rescue Bubba just like we rescued my little brother, Torr."

"We promise," Tod said. She looked at Oskar and Ferdie. "A Tribe of Three promise."

"You really do promise?" Kaznim asked, still doubtful.

"We promise," Ferdie, Oskar and Tod repeated together.

Tod knew there was one last thing she had to do to be totally honest with Kaznim. She took the Egg Timer from her Apprentice belt and held it out to Kaznim, who stared at it in surprise.

"Darius, the boy in the Manuscriptorium, gave it to me," Tod said, "but I know it belongs to you really."

Kaznim stared at the jewel-like hourglass nestling in Tod's palm, but she did not reach for it. "It is not mine," she said. "I stole it."

"So, we're even," Tod said with a smile, pressing the **Egg Timer** into Kaznim's hand.

Kaznim looked down at the tiny hourglass. She watched a grain of silver leave its few companions in the nearly empty section and burrow its way through the centre to submerge itself in the sea of grains on the other side. She knew that another grain gone meant it was three hours closer to the Egg hatching, three hours closer to her sister being safe.

"Shh!" Oskar suddenly hissed. There was a sound like a distant wind in the avenue of trees and they could hear the soft creaking of the branches rising once more. "There's someone – some*thing* – coming!" Oskar whispered.

"We've got to go," Tod said. *"Now."*

She headed towards the middle hut and with some trepidation, pushed open the door. It moved easily on well-greased hinges. Leaves crunched under her feet as Tod stepped into a conical space not unlike Galen's tree-pod. She stopped and waited for the others to follow. Oskar was last. He quickly closed the door and at once the atmosphere inside the hut changed. The sounds of the Forest vanished and a fierce light and heat replaced the damp chill. Tod took another two steps forward and she, Kaznim, Ferdie and Oskar walked out into the heat of the sun.

# PART IX

## TWENTY-TWO HOURS TO HATCHING

# GHOSTLY GLOAT

*Back at the Wizard Tower*, Septimus had a visitor. He had come back from visiting Sam in the Sick Bay and had walked into his rooms to find a small, round ghost in dark blue robes sitting on the purple sofa. She was happily swinging her feet, which did not quite touch the floor.

Septimus was not pleased. "Good morning, Miss Djinn," he said stiffly. "This is an unexpected surprise."

"You mean an un*welcome* surprise," Jillie Djinn replied tartly – and correctly.

Septimus remained standing by the door as if waiting to usher the ghost out, even though he knew there was nothing he could do to make her leave. "A ghost will go where a ghost will go," was a saying wearily repeated in the Castle by those who could not get rid of unwelcome ghostly visitors.

"Don't worry," the ghost told him. "I'm not staying. I've come to say what I've come to say and then I will go."

"What *have* you come to say?" Septimus asked. From the little smirk playing around the ghost's lips, he guessed it was not something that would be welcome.

"I consider it my duty to tell you that yesterday the Chief Hermetic Scribe violated the solemn agreement he made with you."

"What solemn agreement?" Septimus asked, his heart sinking.

"The solemn agreement to keep the newly discovered Hidden arch, the third Castle entrance to the Ancient Ways, untravelled. Yesterday, on his watch, a child Went Through."

*"What?"* Septimus was immediately annoyed with himself. He had been determined not to give Jillie Djinn any satisfaction, but the news had caught him totally by surprise. He had never, *ever* dreamed that Beetle could betray his trust in this way.

The ghost's small, neat features wore a quiet look of triumph. "I will not repeat myself," she said. "Once said is quite enough. I don't like to gossip." With that, still in a sitting position, she rose vertically from the sofa and then straightened up and walked out, her feet so high off the ground that when she passed Septimus – now leaning against the doorway in shock – she was actually taller than he was.

"I like to do my duty, ExtraOrdinary Wizard," Jillie Djinn said, looking down at him. "*Someone* has to."

Septimus stared at the ghost as she wafted down the corridor. "Wait!" he called out after her.

Greatly enjoying the drama of the moment, the ghost stopped and slowly turned around.

"Who Went Through?" Septimus asked.

Jillie Djinn shrugged. "Oh, just a little kid. Going home, she said. I expect she got lost." The ghost could not suppress a smirk.

Something made Septimus ask, "Was she wearing a long red coat?"

"Hmm. Let me think now … I rather suspect she was." And with that Jillie Djinn stepped on to the silver spiral stairs and travelled with them as they slowly wound their way down.

Septimus heard a few shouts of surprise drifting up and a distant yell of the classic warning cry: "Bewares, bewares, ghost on stairs!" (It was considered bad luck to ride the stairs when a ghost was on them.)

Septimus waited until the shouts had died down, then he took a deep breath and set off for the Manuscriptorium.

# SHOWDOWN

*In the Manuscriptorium, the* scribes were finding it difficult to settle to work. They were sitting at their desks quietly, but longing to discuss the excitement of the previous day's races and the unprecedented loss of the two sleds complete with riders. Unnoticed by all, the ghost of Jillie Djinn had sidled in and was lurking in a dark corner. She was biding her time, waiting for her plans to bear fruit.

Beetle was trying to set a good example by quietly discussing the finer points of an old translation of a book of Charms with Romilly Badger, although neither had the heart for it. Suddenly, the door in the flimsy partition to the front office burst open, sending the windowpanes rattling. It was the ExtraOrdinary Wizard and he looked furious. A smile of pure glee appeared on Jillie Djinn's face, and she settled down to enjoy the show. It was beginning well.

Open-mouthed, the scribes watched the ExtraOrdinary Wizard stride across to their Chief. "I want a word with you," he snapped. "Right now!"

Beetle looked up, stunned. "What?" he said.

"You heard," Septimus told him.

Beetle had been Chief Hermetic Scribe a good deal longer than his old friend had been ExtraOrdinary Wizard, and he was used to being treated with respect. There was an old rivalry between the Wizard Tower and the Manuscriptorium. Beetle's professional pride was not going to put up with such rudeness from the ExtraOrdinary Wizard, whoever he might be. He glared at Septimus. "ExtraOrdinary Wizard. The Manuscriptorium is a place of work and study and you will respect it as such. If you wish to speak to me in private, I suggest you follow me to the Hermetic Chamber."

Septimus did not want to follow the Chief Hermetic Scribe anywhere. "On the contrary," he snapped. "*You* will follow *me*. To the *basement*." With that he strode through the ranks of desks – his every move followed by the gazes of silent scribes. They watched the angry purple robes disappear down the wide steps that led to the Conservation Scribe's domain and heard the *flap-flap-flap* of the swing doors as he pushed through them.

Beetle was also good at power games. He made no attempt to follow Septimus but resumed his conversation with Romilly in a studiedly natural manner, well aware that Romilly wasn't hearing a word he said. Beetle then made a show of checking up on other scribes' work and only when he could find nothing else he could reasonably do did he finally head purposefully down to the Conservation basement.

Silence fell in the Manuscriptorium. It was so quiet that when a pin actually did drop, everyone jumped – and then went back to listening. What, they wondered, was the boss meant to have done?

As soon as the doors at the foot of the steps had stopped flapping, the hiss of whispered conversations broke out in the Manuscriptorium. No one dared talk too loudly for fear of missing any clue to what might be going on in the basement. They did not have long to wait. Soon Beetle's angry voice came loud and clear.

"How dare you come marching into the Manuscriptorium like you own the place? How *dare* you speak to me like that? I will not have the office of Chief Hermetic Scribe treated with such disdain. If, in your capacity of ExtraOrdinary Wizard, you have something to say to me, you will say it in private, not in front of my scribes. I would never, *never* speak to you like that in public in the Wizard Tower."

Up in the Manuscriptorium approving glances were exchanged along with whispers of: *You tell him, Chief!*

Septimus's voice came sharply in response. "And *I* would never go back on a solemn agreement and put the entire future of the Castle at risk. *Never.*"

"And neither would I, Septimus."

*Of course he wouldn't* susurrated around the Manuscriptorium.

"Oh, but you *have.* Yesterday you allowed someone to travel the Manuscriptorium Hidden Way – the very Way you promised me faithfully that you would keep closed to all. I took you at your word, Beetle. I trusted you. But yesterday you allowed our only chance of finding the Egg of the Orm before it hatches to walk away – *through the Manuscriptorium Way.*"

"What *are* you talking about?"

*Rubbish. He's talking rubbish,* the scribes whispered.

"I am talking about Kaznim Na-Draa – the girl who came with Sam and Marwick. The girl whose home is, Beetle, in case you didn't know, the very place where the Orm Egg lies. She was our one chance to find the Egg in time."

264

*Why is he talking about eggs? He's flipped. Egg-flip. Ha-ha.* The scribes grinned at one another.

"But – but this is ridiculous," Beetle protested. "This just did not happen."

"Unfortunately, Beetle, it did. Yesterday, not only did you allow Kaznim Na-Draa to travel through the Way, but you actually *watched her go!*"

"I most certainly did not!" Beetle spluttered.

*Yeah, you tell him!* Beetle's fans upstairs gave one another thumbs-up signs.

"I have a witness who saw it," Septimus said.

"Who?" Beetle demanded.

It was at that moment Septimus felt a little less confident of his ground. "Jillie Djinn," he said, lowering his voice.

Upstairs the scribes were whispering: *Who ... Who did he say ... Did you hear who it was?*

At this point Romilly got up and walked out to the office where Darius Wrenn was sitting, shivering. He jumped up guiltily when he saw her. "Darius," she said. "I think you have something to tell the Chief, don't you?"

Darius nodded. He got up and trailed miserably through the Manuscriptorium in Romilly's wake, acutely aware that every scribe was watching him.

# BOLTED

*Beetle and Septimus were standing* in front of the heavy
iron door that covered the Hidden arch of the Way. With
four automatically relocking bolts drawn across it and the
key and its lock separately hidden behind secret bricks,
Septimus was forced to admit that Beetle's security looked
good.

"So what exactly did that wretched ghost say?" Beetle was
asking.

"She said …" Septimus searched his memory for Jillie Djinn's
exact words. The impressive state of the door and Beetle's
utter incredulity had shaken Septimus's confidence. He was
beginning to wonder if he had acted too precipitously. "She
said it had happened on your watch."

"Well, that is totally different from me actually *watching* it,"
Beetle pointed out.

Septimus had to admit that was true. "But it doesn't change
the fact that our only chance of getting to the Orm Egg has
walked out through here and it must have been with help from
someone in the Manuscriptorium. There is no way Kaznim
could have done it on her own."

"But no one knows where the keys are – apart from myself,"
Beetle said. He was beginning to understand the enormity of

what had happened. "Septimus, I am as horrified as you are. And that wretched ghost was right about it being on my watch. *Everything* is on my watch. Night and day, it is *all* my responsibility." Beetle sighed. "But I just can't work out how a little girl who had never been here before would know about the Way, let alone know how to open the door."

Septimus, who had noticed Jillie Djinn lurking on the steps, remembered the expression of glee on her face. "Following instructions given by a spiteful ghost, maybe?" he asked.

Beetle looked horrified. "Surely not. Surely not even she would compromise the Manuscriptorium like that."

Septimus shook his head. "I don't know. It seems to me that some ghosts who went unwillingly into ghosthood – as I suspect your ex-Chief did – do take a delight in messing up the lives of those who come after them. Especially if they may not have had, let us say, a particularly happy relationship with that person during Life."

Beetle nodded. Jillie Djinn had once sacked him. "Well, she's certainly not made life easy for me since I've become Chief. I hate to say this, Septimus, but I think you are right." Beetle shook his head. "But how a former Chief Hermetic Scribe could betray the Manuscriptorium is beyond me. Oh! Romilly, hello."

Romilly had just appeared around the corner. She was pushing Darius in front of her like a reluctant trolley. "Excuse me, Chief. Darius Wrenn has something to tell you."

Darius blinked a few times.

"Haven't you, Darius?" Romilly prompted.

"I gave the Kaznim girl the – the numbers," he stammered.

Beetle was puzzled. "What numbers?" he asked.

"The numbers for how to get to … to where she wanted to go. It was the place where we sent the leaflets before the door was locked."

"But those are secret," Beetle said. "You should never, *ever* have told her."

Darius hung his head. "I know. I am really sorry. But she wanted her mother. And … I wanted to help her."

"So, Darius," Septimus said briskly. "Did you see Kaznim go into the Way?"

Darius shook his head. "No! Honestly I didn't. I didn't know she came down here. I thought she had run outside with the horrible ghost. They both disappeared together."

"Ahem." A gentle cough interrupted him. It was Ephaniah Grebe, the Conservation Scribe. Ephaniah, half man, half rat, had lost the power of human speech, but he understood it perfectly well. He handed Beetle a hastily scribbled-upon piece of paper. His deep brown human eyes looked anxiously from his furry face as he watched Beetle read his writing.

*Oskar Sarn saw the girl. He wanted to check what she was doing, but I called him back. Did not realise importance. Very very sorry.*

"You have no need to apologise, Ephaniah," Beetle said. "The fault is mine and mine alone."

At that Darius began to relax. Maybe he wasn't going to lose his job after all.

"Did *you* see the girl, Ephaniah?" Septimus asked.

Ephaniah nodded. He took a large pad of paper from a pocket deep in his voluminous white robes and began to write. Fascinated, Darius watched the long, delicate rat fingers holding the pen forming Ephaniah's beautiful looped script.

*Briefly. Small child. Dark curly hair. Long red robe. Oskar got better view. I will tell him to speak to you. He is here today. Is late. Unusual for him.*

"Ah," Septimus said. "Oskar Sarn had a bit of trouble on the sled run yesterday. He'll be back soon. Queen Jenna is bringing them all back from the Forest. They should be here any minute now, in fact."

Ephaniah's face showed human emotions as much as any not mixed with rat. It wore a puzzled look. He was about to scrawl a few lines asking why the Queen was going to all the trouble of bringing Oskar to work, when the sound of running footsteps coming along the passageway made them all look around. Colin Partridge appeared, flustered. He flashed a quick smile to Romilly and then said, "Queen Jenna is in the front office, Chief. She wants to speak to the ExtraOrdinary Wizard. At once."

Up in the front office, Jenna waited anxiously. As the door opened and Septimus and Beetle hurried out, she took a deep breath.

"Septimus," she said. "Tod is gone."

"Gone?" Septimus asked, puzzled. "Gone where?"

"I've no idea, Sep. I saw her at breakfast in Galen's treehouse, and then she vanished, along with her two friends. You know, those PathFinder kids. She left this." Jenna handed Septimus Tod's note.

Septimus read it, frowning. "What does she mean, *we are fine*? They will most certainly *not* be fine on their own in the Forest. Those witches will get them for sure."

Jenna put her hand on Septimus's arm. "No, Sep. I happen to know that the Wendrons don't have Tod. Or Oskar and

269

Ferdie. Oh – and just to make everything really great, Jim Knee's gone too. He ran off when we were searching and *he's* not come back either."

Septimus looked flabbergasted. "I don't believe it," he said. "I just don't." He sat down on a pile of books, which wobbled dangerously. "My Apprentice, run off in the Forest. My jinnee's gone goodness knows where yet *again*, and every second that wretched Egg is getting nearer to hatching. It's a nightmare."

Jenna looked distraught. "I'm so sorry, Sep. We searched everywhere. I … I don't know what to say. All I could think of doing was coming back to tell you myself."

"Thanks, Jen. I appreciate that," Septimus said.

The Queen, the Chief Hermetic Scribe and the ExtraOrdinary Wizard looked at one another, each remembering times when they were younger and had been in the middle of all kinds of troubles. Then all things had seemed possible, but now that they were older, nothing seemed possible. They weren't sure if they liked being older very much.

Jenna spoke first. "We have to prioritise," she said.

Septimus and Beetle looked at her expectantly.

Jenna took a deep breath. She wasn't sure how they were going to take this. "Castle first. Apprentice second. Jinnee third."

There was a silence, and then Septimus spoke. "You're right," he said. "But I'm still sending out as many Wizards into the Forest as I possibly can. And as soon as I've done that, I am **Going Through** the Manuscriptorium Way and following Kaznim Na-Draa."

"And I am coming with you," Beetle said.

Jenna longed to say the same but she knew she could not. With the ExtraOrdinary Wizard and the Chief Hermetic Scribe gone from the Castle, it was her job to stay behind. *Sometimes,* Jenna thought, *being Queen is not a lot of fun.*

Septimus smiled at Beetle. "Thanks," he said. "I really hoped you'd say that."

PART
X

TWENTY-ONE
HOURS TO
HATCHING

# THE RED CITY

*Tod walked into the blazing* heat of the sun. She breathed in the hot, dry air – shocking after the chill damp of the Forest – and watched Kaznim, Ferdie and Oskar emerge, blinking, into the light. Buoyed by the familiar smells of hot sand and spices, Kaznim laughed. "Welcome to the Red City!" she said.

Tod, Oskar and Ferdie shrugged off their wolverine cloaks like sloughed skins and took stock. They were in a deserted courtyard, surrounded by high red walls made of smooth mud. The only sound was a faint trickling of water from a little culvert that ran alongside the wall to their left. Above them the backs of tall houses – a patchwork of pinky-red – reared up, the expanse broken only by a few tiny windows covered with metal grilles. The sun was almost directly overhead and the place hummed with heat, the walls surrounding them like those of a kiln. Beside them rose a tall, thin palm tree, its long trunk reaching up to the sky, with a few ragged leaves at the top. It cast little shadow, but what there was had a strange shifting quality to it – this was the entrance to the Forest Way.

"Phew," Oskar said, wiping his forehead. Both he and Ferdie felt the heat far more than Tod.

"It is cooler outside," Kaznim said, heading off towards a door set deep in the thick wall. The polished wood was completely smooth, with only a tiny keyhole giving a clue as to how to open it. Kaznim turned around, her face a picture of dismay. "I don't have the key," she whispered.

"Oh, Oskie will fix that," Ferdie said confidently.

Oskar was not so sure. One look at the tiny keyhole told him it was going to be trouble. He was right. For ten long minutes Oskar worked methodically through the layers of the weirdest lock mechanism he had ever encountered. At last Oskar heard the delicate *tic-ick* of the final cog clicking into place, and the door into the Red City swung open.

They headed out into the cool shadows of an alley. Ferdie took a tiny green felt dragon on a purple ribbon from her pocket and placed it carefully on the ground. "So we know it's this door," she said. Then, turning to Kaznim, she asked, "So now where?"

"We have to go to Beggars' Gate," Kaznim said in a half-whisper. "It's the best way to get to the road that goes to my tent."

"A road all the way to your tent?" Oskar said. "Wow, that's great. Easy-peasy."

"Peasy?" asked Kaznim.

"It's just Oskie's silly talk," Ferdie said. "He means it's going to be really easy to get to your tent, as the road goes straight there."

Kaznim looked a little embarrassed. "Well, it doesn't quite reach my tent," she said, "But it's fine because at the end of the road you can see it. Well, usually. As long as there isn't too much haze. Or wind blowing the sand."

"Ah," Oskar murmured.

"And we need to hurry, as it's a long way and it's not good

to be in the desert at night. Because of the sand lions," Kaznim added.

Oskar mentally downgraded the journey from Easy-Peasy to – in Manuscriptorium scribe-speak – a Ton of Trouble.

"Okey-dokey," Tod said in a determinedly cheerful manner. "You lead the way to Beggars' Gate. We're right behind you."

Kaznim set off along the alleyway. It was bounded by tall walls made from red mud decorated with sparkling pieces of glass and mosaic. The alley wound like a snake between walled gardens, past locked doors and tiny windows set high in walls. A few thin, dusty trees rose up from the gardens and from some came the trickling sound of water, which made them feel thirsty in the dry heat. Smaller walkways branched off, winding away into deeper shadows and canyons of impossibly narrow spaces between houses. Kaznim ignored these and carried on, heading along the main alley, glancing from side to side as if searching for something.

They followed Kaznim – who, Tod thought, had an uncertain look about her – and now found themselves walking beneath bright red paper streamers looped across the alley and wound around tall posts upon which lamps were precariously balanced. Behind them now they heard the muffled sound of drumming and rhythmic chanting echoing off the walls and surrounding them with noise.

The air was stifling and stuffy, and Tod, Oskar and Ferdie felt increasingly uncomfortable in their heavy woollen winter robes. Tod noticed that Ferdie's and Oskar's faces were almost as red as their hair, and she could feel the dampness of her own dark hair as it stuck to the back of her neck. But in front of them, Kaznim moved like a stream of cool water, her faded red coat flowing as she glided silently over the red sandy ground.

As they rounded yet another bend they heard a strange new sound – high-pitched, tinny piping – not far ahead. Kaznim, Tod noticed, had slowed down and looked uncertain. Ahead of them was a tall gatehouse, its pillars straddling the alley. Kaznim walked uncertainly into the shadows beneath and stopped dead. "Oh!" she said.

Beyond the gatehouse was a vast square festooned with red banners. It was almost empty but it was clear that a big event was going to take place soon. The tinny piping came from four soldiers in silver chain mail and long red cloaks. They stood at the corners of a central platform, which was covered in gleaming gold cloth and protected from the sun by a red-and-gold-striped awning. Four tall poles, each with a golden crown perched upon the top, rose up from each corner, and like ribbons from a maypole, bands of paper – from palest pink to deepest blood red – streamed out to other, smaller poles planted around the square so that a great network of red cast stripes of shadow across the ground. Kaznim stared at the scene before them, her hands over her mouth in dismay.

"What's the matter?" Tod asked anxiously.

"This isn't where we want to be. It *really* isn't."

"Have we gone the wrong way?" Oskar asked.

There was a note of panic in Kaznim's reply. "I must have missed a turning. It was all that drumming. I couldn't think."

Tod was beginning to wonder if they had made the right decision to trust Kaznim. But she was determined to appear calm. "That's OK," she said. "We can retrace our steps."

"The turning is by an old lamp with a snake wound around it."

"You should have told us what you were looking for," Ferdie said sharply. "We went past that ages ago. It was the first one covered in red paper."

"We must go back. This is the Queen's Square. It's dangerous. We must not be here," Kaznim whispered, her eyes wide with fear.

The Tribe of Three exchanged anxious glances. This was not looking good.

# DRUMMED IN

*Tod, Ferdie and Oskar followed* Kaznim as she fled back down the alley. Ahead of them the sound of drumming was growing ever louder and as they hurtled around yet another corner, they came skidding to a halt. They were face to face with the drummers.

Both groups stopped dead. Tod, Ferdie and Oskar found themselves confronting a frightening group of about twenty teens in long cotton robes, all in different shades of red. The *tarra-taa tarra-taa* of the drumming subsided to an ominous *derummmma … derummmma …* as the drummers marked time, expecting Tod, Oskar, Ferdie and Kaznim to get out of the way. Fast. The front three drummers – two girls and a boy – looked wild. Their dark hair, which shone with grease, was gathered into a tall topknot with a spike driven through it. Their skin was caked in white dust and their eyes were lined with kohl, making them look as though they had been dead for some days. The wide pupils of their eyes stared at Tod, Oskar and Ferdie as though they were nothing more than insects upon the ground, while their drums continued their impatient *derummmma … derummmma …*

And then Kaznim was gone. Like a snake slipping into its burrow, she wriggled through a gap between two of the drummers and disappeared. Tod, Oskar and Ferdie went to follow but the drummers closed ranks. Kaznim was one of their own; they would give way to her, but not to strangers – strangers gave way to *them*.

The beat continued and the drummers pushed forward. The Tribe of Three had no choice but to step back. And with every step they took backwards, the drummers took a deliberate step forward: *derummmma-drum* – step, *derummmma-drum* – step. Like the sea nudging driftwood on to the shore, the tide of drummers pushed them remorselessly along the alley and swept them into the square.

The square had filled with people. From each corner through an identical gateway, a team of drummers was emerging – all dressed in red and marking the same beat. *derummmma-drum* … *derummmma-drum* …

A crowd had gathered around the central platform leaving aisles clear for various processions. As they were being marshalled into position by officials, someone yelled out: "Spies! Spies!" The cry was taken up and in seconds Tod, Oskar and Ferdie were surrounded by a group of hooded guards armed with short, broad swords. The guards herded them along the open space at the back of the crowd while the drums rolled to a crescendo. Suddenly the crowd erupted into frenzied shouts and the guards stepped up the pace, forcing their prisoners into a run at sword point. They were heading for a barred gate set into the wall and it seemed to Tod that the guards were desperate to get them there before whatever the crowd was waiting for began. As the gate drew closer Tod grew increasingly certain that once they were inside, there was going to be no way out. She *had* to do something. With no time to think, Tod threw herself to the ground as if in a faint and felt first Ferdie, then Oskar trip over her. She heard the guard commander bark an order and became aware of a sudden silence descending on the crowd. In the distance came a fanfare and Tod risked opening one eye. She had stupidly managed to fall over at the end of an aisle. She had a clear view to the platform, and those on the platform had a clear view of her.

Staring straight at them was the Red Queen. And beside her stood a familiar figure: the sorcerer Oraton-Marr.

# THE RED QUEEN

*A low, tense drumming began.* The rhythm was that of an anxious heartbeat: two beats per second. Roughly, the guards pulled Tod, Oskar and Ferdie to their feet, then stood to attention. Tod noticed that the hands of the guard next to her were shaking. She was not surprised – the Queen was terrifying. A tall, imposing woman with long white hair held back by a simple gold crown, she put Tod in mind of a much older Jenna, but even from a distance Tod could see that there was none of Jenna's humanity about this Queen. She was flanked on either side by two masked figures holding axes and in her hand she expertly held a long sword, the flat of its blade stained with the rust of blood but its cutting edge shining bright silver, thin and razor-sharp from the Queen's expert honing that morning. As the Queen's gaze ranged slowly over the Tribe of Three and they saw her adjust her grip on the sword, a stab of fear ran through them – the Queen was sizing them up with the expert eye of someone who knew the power of her blade – and wanted to use it.

The Queen's axe men shouted an order and the drumming ceased. At each entrance on the corners of the square, just behind the assembled drummers, a great sheet of metal slid slowly down from each gatehouse tower and barred the exits.

The silence in the square became tense with fear. No one knew the reason for the square being sealed and many now feared for their own lives. The Queen raised her sword and pointed at the three captives. All the faces in the crowd turned to stare.

"Sheesh," Oskar whispered. "This is scary."

On the dais, Oraton-Marr leaned over and said something to the Queen. She rewarded him with a frosty stare that would have turned anyone else into a shaking jelly of fear. Oraton-Marr, however, did not notice. He was buoyed by the excitement of the imminent hatching of his Orm Egg and the heady prospect of power. The unexpected sight of the Apprentice being brought to him confirmed to Oraton-Marr that all was going his way. "The one in green is promised to me," he told the Queen. "You can do as you wish with the other two."

The Queen tapped her foot in annoyance. She was honouring Oraton-Marr with a place on the Royal Block and a front-row seat at the morning's executions and now he had the cheek to claim one of her captives. Did he not realise that this was *her* square and all who stepped into it gave themselves over to her? She glared at Oraton-Marr but restrained herself from doing more. She remembered that he had offered her the Queenship of a powerful Castle and thought it wise to humour him – for now. The Queen snapped her fingers at the captain of the guard at the foot of the Royal Block and said, "Bring the child strangers to me. Now!"

The captain saluted, turned on his heel and marched down the aisle towards Tod, Oskar and Ferdie. He had yet to reach them when he heard the thunder of tumbling masonry, and a gasp from the crowd. The captain risked a quick glance and it was only his rigorous training that stopped him from breaking

284

his pace in shock. A monstrous, thirty-feet-tall figure was smashing down the barricade on the south-east gatehouse.

The figure glowed a brilliant yellow like the sun. It was broad as a house, as tall as a tower, with wild hair of gold surrounding a fine pair of horns, its eyes burning with orange fire. In one massive hand it held a chunk of the gatehouse, in the other a sword ten feet long. The ground shook with a deep rumble as the monstrous giant swept away the last remnants of the gatehouse and stepped into the square. A wild scream spread through the crowd and a stampede began, but the captain pushed on through, desperate to obey his order.

But as he lunged to grab Tod, Oskar and Ferdie, a giant yellow finger flicked him aside. As the colonel flew backwards all he could think of was the fate that surely now awaited him. He had failed in his task to bring the captives to the Queen. For which he would pay.

# BOUNDARIES

*The yellow giant flowed along* the alley that led away from the square. In order to keep its hands free it had put Tod, Oskar and Ferdie into one of its deep pockets, but they did not stay there – much as they would have liked to. Slowly, they slipped through the fragile cloth of the robes and when they tried to cling on they discovered they were grasping little more than thin air. They began to drop towards the ground, clutching at what they could. Tod was bracing herself for a fall when the giant slithered into a gap between two houses and sank to the ground like a boneless snake, taking his three passengers with him.

Tod was jubilant. "Jim Knee, you are amazing!"

Jim Knee had never done an out-of-boundary Transformation before. It was a risky thing, for it took the jinnee into an ethereal state where he could be trapped in a receiving vessel once again. Slowly, he gathered himself into his normal boundaries, and resumed his solid state. Jim Knee allowed himself a satisfied smile. He had always wanted to be a terrifying jinnee and now, acting under Septimus's Command to "keep my Apprentice safe", he had done it. However, they were not safe yet. The drumming had begun again and he could hear the distant shouts of the guards. Woozily, Jim Knee stood up. "Time to go," he said.

They ventured warily out into the sunlight of the festooned alley with Jim Knee leading the way. He seemed a little unsteady on his feet but he hurried along with a loping gait, as if, Tod thought, he still had a trace of tiger within. Behind them they could now hear the heavy thud of booted feet, running in step, heading their way. Jim Knee sped up; they ran fast between the striped shadows cast by the ribbons above, following the jinnee, trusting that he knew where he was going. As they hurtled around yet another corner, they saw someone waiting by a lamp post festooned with red, below which lurked the shape of a snake.

It was Kaznim. She gave them an anxious wave but no one returned it. Kaznim had ratted on them.

Jim Knee stepped in. "Now, before we get into any unpleasantness, I would like to tell you three that if the young lady waiting for us had not been brave enough to stop a wandering tiger – that everyone else was running from, screaming – and ask it if it happened to be a jinnee, then you would all probably be in more pieces than you are right now. So just think about that before you say anything. OK?"

"You mean, Kaznim went back to the treehouse and got you?"

"No, no. I was already here. I followed you through the avenue of weird trees. It took a bit of doing – those trees weren't very helpful, I can tell you. You had all gone by the time I got to those funny little huts. The first one I tried I ended up in some ghastly snowy forest. So I tried the next and when I got into the courtyard I saw your footprints. I jumped the wall – it's a wonderful thing to be a tiger – and had a bit of fun with the denizens of this fair city. And then I was approached by this young lady here, who was most insistent that I rescue you. I must do anything I could, she said. And she offered to come with me too. So all is not as it seems. I suggest a few thank yous might be in order."

Neither Tod nor Oskar nor Ferdie felt they could go that far. When Kaznim had left them to face the drummers alone, they doubted she had done it with the idea of saving them. But saved them she had, and they decided to let things be.

Kaznim smiled uncertainly at them all, and then to Jim Knee she said, "I like your hat."

Jim Knee smiled. His hat – which looked like a pile of yellow doughnuts stuck on his head – was something he was very proud of.

"Thank you, kind lady," he said with a small bow. "Now, lead on, Macduff."

"Who's Macduff?" Oskar asked, looking around, puzzled.

"The Thane of Fife," Jim Knee answered.

*"Who?"* said Tod.

"Oh, ignore me," Jim Knee said. "I'm feeling a bit light-headed with all that boundary shifting. It's an old saying from an ancient earl – one of my favourite writers. A misquote, actually. Lead on, Miss Na-Draa. The sooner we are out of here, the better."

Kaznim led the way, taking them confidently around twists and turns and through the narrowest of opes, cuts and paths and passageways. She ran fast and steadily through the maze until, halfway down a dark and chilly corridor between two high walls Kaznim stopped beneath a tall tower. She turned around with a puzzled expression. "I ... I don't know why I came down here," she said.

"What do you mean?" Tod asked a little sharply. She had been wondering where they were going for some time. It seemed a convoluted way to get to one of the main routes out of the city.

Kaznim rubbed her eyes and blinked. She looked quite disoriented. "I don't understand it ..." She shook her head. "This isn't the right way. I *know* it isn't."

"So why on earth did you take us here?" Tod asked crossly.

"Now, now," Jim Knee said. "No arguing. It's easy to get lost here. I'm sure that –"

A sudden scream from Kaznim rang out. A dark, winged animal was falling from the window of the tower and heading for them. Before anyone had time to react, a net had dropped on to Tod and was wrapping itself around her like a snake. Ferdie and Oskar tried to tear it away, and Jim Knee pulled out his flick knife and leaped up to try to cut the rope that snaked down from the window at the top of the tower. But Jim Knee, like Ferdie and Oskar, could do nothing. The rope was like steel and already Tod was being lifted out of his reach. Up, up, up she went, swinging precariously on the end of a thin rope while someone at the top of the tower hauled her in like a fish. The jinnee watched in dismay, knowing there was nothing he could do. His out-of-boundary **Transformation** had exhausted him and he must stay as he was for some hours before he could **Transform** again.

Tod looked down. She saw four horrified faces staring up at her – and then she was dragged through an open window into a cool, round room at the top of the tower. The net opened and she was dumped unceremoniously on to the cold tiled floor.

# The Darke Dart

*Ferdie and Oskar stared up in shock.* A hand reached out from the window; between its finger and thumb was a small but deadly **Darke Dart**. A moment later the **Dart** was winging its way down to the upturned faces below. Jim Knee caught it. The poisoned tips cut through his fingers and he dropped to the ground. Ferdie rushed to help him, but the jinnee shooed her away. "Run!" he said, his voice harsh with pain. "Go back to the Forest."

"We're not leaving Tod," Oskar said stonily.

"On her own," added Ferdie.

"She is not alone. I am here," Jim Knee said hoarsely.

Ferdie, Oskar and Kaznim took a few steps back, but they did not take their eyes off Jim Knee. He looked awful. A blue pallor was spreading across his skin and his face was shiny with sweat. No one liked to say it, but right then it didn't look like Jim Knee would be there for much longer.

"Get out of here. Now ..." Jim Knee gasped. "Kaznim ... knows the way."

"We're not going anywhere with *her*," Ferdie told him. "She set this up."

"She's a double-crossing low-down spy," Oskar added for good measure.

Kaznim looked aghast. "I'm not! I promise you. I don't know why I came here. I *don't*."

"Witch's **Draw**," Jim Knee said weakly. He looked at Kaznim. "I saw it … in your eyes when you turned around. Not … your fault."

"Nothing ever seems to be her fault," Ferdie observed tartly. "But bad stuff always happens when she's around."

"Some people … are unlucky that way," Jim Knee said with fellow feeling. "Now *go*."

"No," Oskar and Ferdie said together. "We are *not* leaving Tod."

Jim Knee did not have the strength to argue. "Very well. But go for now. To the courtyard. When midnight strikes … she will come to you. All will be … as it will be."

"Just because you are a jinnee doesn't mean you have to talk in riddles," Ferdie told him sternly.

"I shall talk how I want to," Jim Knee said sharply. His annoyance seemed to give him strength. He sat up and said, "Now *go away*. What use is your having a jinnee if you won't let him be one? Now just *pop off*, will you?"

An arm shooting out from the window at the top of the tower stopped any more discussion. Reluctantly, they turned and walked slowly back through the chill of the dismal, dark alley.

Kaznim led the way back to Ferdie's dragon, which lay waiting for them in the dust. Oskar opened the door with two quick turns of his lockpick and in a moment they were inside the courtyard.

They stood in the heavy, late-afternoon heat and listened to the stillness broken only by the soft burble of water running in the culvert.

"We'll stay here until midnight," Ferdie said. "And if Tod isn't back by then we're going to go to that horrible tower and rescue her. Whatever Jim Knee says."

"How will we know when midnight is?" Oskar wondered.

"There will be no mistaking it when it comes," Kaznim said.

Ferdie and Oskar glanced at each other. Kaznim's words sounded ominous.

# THE PRISONER IN THE TOWER

*Within the tendrils of the **Darke** net*, Tod shivered. Every spot where the fine strands touched her skin felt like burning ice. She sat absolutely still while Marissa snipped through the net with a tiny, sharp pointed pair of silver scissors, and to her relief, not once did the witch's hand slip. While she sat, Tod had time to work out her strategy. She was very frightened, but she was determined not to give Marissa the satisfaction of knowing it. And so, as the last strands fell to the floor and Marissa trotted over to the window to fix its bar back into place, Tod pushed down her fear and very deliberately replaced it with anger.

When Marissa turned around with a smug little smile she was met with an angry glare. "You pig," Tod said. "You low-down piece of –"

"La-di-da, la-di-da," Marissa trilled loudly, drowning out the rest of Tod's words. "Just calm down. I'll bring you a nice sherbet and some stuffed dates."

"You can stuff your dates where the –"

"Now, now, Alice," Marissa interrupted. "There is no need to be such a grumpy cow. You're lucky – the trouble is, you just don't realise it yet. You're on the fast track to fame and fortune. You'll soon be back at the top of your precious Wizard

Tower with a *much* more powerful boss. Septimus Heap is nothing –" Marissa snapped her fingers dismissively – "compared to His Highness."

"His *Highness*?"

Marissa glanced at the door nervously and dropped her voice to a whisper. "Oraton-Marr. He likes to be called that. See, there's a handy little tip from me. Don't say I don't look out for you." Marissa giggled and pranced out before Tod had the time to fling back a retort. She heard a heavy bolt being slid across, then the tinny sound of footsteps disappearing down stone stairs.

Tod raced to the window to look out. She had watched Marissa drop the **Darke Dart** and was terrified of what she might see below. But there was no one there. *No one*. Tod bit back a surge of disappointment. She had hoped for some friendly faces gazing up at her. But her friends had gone. They hadn't even bothered to wait a few measly minutes.

Tod leaned back against the wall and told herself not to be so silly. To wait beneath somewhere where two **Darke Darts** had been thrown was suicide. She should be grateful that neither Oskar nor Ferdie was lying in the dust far below. However, Tod was not a bit grateful that Kaznim seemed to have escaped too. The more she thought about it, the more obvious it was that Kaznim had led them into a trap. She sighed. Jim Knee was a rubbish judge of character.

Depressed by the emptiness outside the window, Tod slowly began to pace her prison. It was a small, circular room and it took her thirty paces to walk the circumference. She came first to a little door set in the wall about two feet up from the floor. She pulled it open to find a musty cupboard containing a bucket and a shelf with a folded blanket and small, embroidered pillow. Apart from the cupboard the only other details of interest were the door through which Marissa had gone out – ancient wood hard as stone and studded with flat-headed nails – and the window through which she had been dragged, which now had an iron bar screwed into the middle of it. The floor felt solid and was covered with tiny green and blue diamond-shaped tiles and the walls were smooth, reddish stone – as was the ceiling, which curved up into a perfectly round dome. The only ways out were the door and the barred window.

Tod paced the circumference a few more times. She must, she told herself, keep a clear head. It shouldn't be too difficult to outwit a birdbrained, two-timing witch like Marissa Lane. Tod pushed away a niggling thought that Marissa was possibly not as birdbrained as people thought she was and was, in fact, turning out to be a particularly nasty force to be reckoned with. Tod wandered back to the window and did what all prisoners do if they can – she gazed out at the free world beyond. Once again she peered down to see if there was any sign of Jim Knee or Ferdie and Oskar but the alley was deserted. She stared down for some time, hoping to catch a glimpse of someone hiding or watching out for her, but she saw nothing. To counter her feeling of desolation, Tod looked out across the flat red rooftops, many with faded washing spread out to dry in the sun, trying to spot any sign of life. There were a few children playing on a rooftop some distance away and an old man laying out some faded clothes to dry. There was an assortment of cats dozing in the evening warmth and oddly, a small donkey standing patiently on a rooftop. Then once again Tod looked down into the alley below, but as ever it was deserted.

To take her mind off people – or the lack of them – Tod turned her attention to the glimpse of desert on the far right of her view. It, too, was empty. There was nothing to see but sand dunes rolling into the distance like a long, slow swell on the ocean. The very thought of the sea made Tod feel horribly homesick for the village where she had grown up. There had been sand there too, but it had been mixed with grasses, bounded by the ocean and home to a village of tall houses on stilts. The sand Tod now saw was vast and featureless. She watched the sun dipping towards the distant dunes and saw the sky turn as red as the mud from which the entire city seemed to be built.

Marissa kept Tod waiting. It was not until the room was nearly dark that she returned with a tray on which were a small candle, a large jug of sherbet and a plate of dates stuffed with marzipan. "His Highness is dining with the Queen tonight," Marissa said. "He'll fetch you in the morning. You'll find some bedding in the garderobe and a bucket." She sniggered. "Not quite the delights of the Wizard Tower but you'll be back there soon enough. Ha-ha. See ya!" With that Marissa was gone, slamming the door. Once again Tod heard the bolt being shot and the tippy-tappy footsteps departing.

Tod drank most of the sherbet – a sweet, slightly fizzy drink that tasted of a fruit she did not recognise – but she felt too miserable to eat. And then she resumed her place at the window and watched the night-time lights of the city appear.

# ITSY-BITSY SPIDER

*In the time-honoured manner of jinn*, Jim Knee was not as absent as he appeared to be. Lurking in the shadows at the foot of the tower – waiting for the onset of night, when the sharp eyesight of arachnid-eating birds was no longer a danger – was a fat yellow spider. It sat huddled in the dust-filled angle where the foundations of the tower rose up from the alleyway and tried to avoid looking at any of its eight hairy legs, which were folded beneath it in a most uncomfortable manner. Jim Knee had a revulsion for exoskeletons and a difficulty with more than four legs. The spider combined both to an unsatisfactory degree but he could see no other solution to his present problem, which was to obey his Master and keep his Apprentice safe – an Apprentice who seemed to have a remarkable talent for getting into dangerous situations. Jim Knee tried to shake his head but discovered he didn't really have one.

As the shadows of twilight began to deepen, the spider unfolded its legs, stood up, toppled over, untangled the third leg from the fourth, and after three attempts managed to balance on all eight legs. Then it set off unsteadily to find some food. It had a long night ahead.

It was many hours later when the spider returned to the foot of the tower, replete with the liquefied insides of two moths and a baby beetle. All of its eight eyes looked up anxiously at the vertical red wall that rose before it, and like a climber checking his rope, the spider checked its spinnerets and spun a short length of silk. It tickled, but to the spider's frustration it was unable to giggle. It placed two wavering front legs on to the rough red mud of the wall and began to climb, remembering to keep four legs on the wall at all times. *Four legs down … four legs up … four legs down … four legs up …* was the rhythm to which the spider climbed.

Tod did not like spiders. So when a particularly large one sporting a nasty, poisonous-looking yellow body and long hairy legs appeared on the window ledge and began waving its two front legs at her, Tod fought very hard to suppress a shriek. She backed away from the window, where she had been gazing up at the stars, and watched it for some moments, wondering what to do. The thought that the spider might drop into the room and then she would be spending the night with it at large gave her courage. Steeling herself, she ran at it and flicked it off the window ledge.

Jim Knee suddenly found himself flying. Instinctively, he stretched his hairy legs out like a parachute to slow his fall and the spinnerets in his abdomen began churning. He became aware that above him a silken thread was trailing in the breeze, and as the ground drew frighteningly close he felt the thread snag against the rough wall of the tower and his fall was abruptly halted. Jim Knee dangled ignominiously for some seconds as his spider brain struggled to take in what had happened. He swung back and forth like a demented pendulum until a deft twist took one of the swings close to the wall. Jim Knee's spiky pincers at the end of his two front legs (how he hated pincers) caught against the stone, and in a moment he was scuttling back up the wall, trailing the silken thread behind him.

Tod was horrified to see two yellow spider legs waving at her as they felt their way over the window sill. Once again she steeled herself to flick the spider away but this time the spider was prepared. It wrapped its legs around the window bar and Tod recoiled. She watched the spider, wondering what to do. Slowly, the spider unwrapped its legs from the bar and once more waved them around. Tod was dismayed. It was obviously one of those aggressive ones that jumped on people and bit them. Tod made a decision: she was going to have to kill it. She picked up the brass tray that Marissa had left behind and slowly advanced.

The spider saw what was coming and thought fast. There was a flash of bright yellow light and Tod dropped the tray with a clang. She stared at the window where the flash had come from: the spider had disappeared but in its place were two sets of elegant fingers clinging to the window bar. Suddenly Tod understood. "Jim Knee!" she gasped. She rushed to the window to see the jinnee dangling precariously two hundred feet above the ground.

"Kindly desist from attacking me with that tray, Apprentice," Jim Knee said. "I have come to rescue you, if you will allow me to do so."

"I am so sorry!" said Tod. "Can I help ... er, maybe I could pull you inside?"

"No, thank you," Jim Knee said. "Before my plan was so rudely interrupted I intended to leave you a thread." He sighed. "Now I shall have to **Transform** once again into a nasty little hairy thing with too many legs and a bad attitude. I do not like the way a spider thinks, I can tell you. Right then, I will be off."

Tod felt desolate. "Please don't go, Jim Knee. I am truly sorry."

"I'm not leaving you for ever, child," Jim Knee said wearily. "Before my fingers give up, you need to understand what to do. I will leave a thread behind, which will go all the way to the ground. When I am back on the ground I will **Transform** into myself and attach the thread to a cord. You will then pull the thread up and the cord will come with it. You will loop the cord around the bar and drop it back to me. This is important because once you are on the ground we can pull it all down and no one will be any the wiser. Got that?"

Tod laughed with relief. "Yes! It's brilliant. Oh, thank you. And I am *so* sorry about the tray."

"I hope you are. And now I am going to **Transform**, so please try to restrain yourself."

Sheepishly, Tod stepped back. There was another flash of yellow light and once more the spider sat upon the window sill. The next moment it was gone. Tod rushed to the window and saw it flying down through the air, a thin thread trailing behind it, glinting in the light of the torches burning in the alleyway below. She took the fine, slightly sticky thread between her finger and thumb and wrapped it around the bar, just to be sure.

While Jim Knee attached the cord below, Tod went to the cupboard and took out the rugs and the bucket. Then she slipped off her cloak, placed its hood over the bucket and rolled up one of the rugs to form the shape of her body. She arranged her "bed" carefully in the shadows opposite the door and stood back to inspect her work. Tod was satisfied. Anyone taking a quick look – particularly a lazy pig like Marissa – would think she was sleeping quietly. Tod drank the rest of the sherbet, put the dates into her pocket and returned to the window.

Everything worked as Jim Knee had planned. Tod watched the jinnee tie the end of a long length of worryingly thin cord to the spider thread and at a signal from him, she pulled the thread very carefully upwards, holding it away from the rough stone of the walls, praying that it would not break. But the jinn spider had spun a particularly strong silk. Soon Tod had the cord looped around the bar and was running it back down to Jim Knee. Now came the scary bit. She had to wriggle out through the gap between the bar and the edge of the window and *not fall*.

As Tod climbed out of the window, a high, thin bell tolled in the distance. Determined not to look down, she grasped both lengths of the cord, leaned outwards – just as she always used to when climbing down the side of her house in the PathFinder village – and began her descent.

Halfway down Tod very nearly fell off in surprise. A cacophony of chimes all across the city began to strike up. It was the midnight chiming of the thousand Red City clocks – the very moment that Jim Knee had timed his rescue for. The huge variety of chimes filled the air; moderate, mellow tones keeping pace with each other, deep, slow, resonant chimes overtaken by rapid, excitedly tinny chimes. Long and deep, high and fast, doubles and trebles, every clock in the Red City waited twenty-four hours for its moment of glory and made the most of it when it came. They each chimed twenty-four times and were still going when Tod reached the ground.

To the echoes of the last long, low booms, Tod helped Jim Knee pull down the cord. As they slipped away into the shadows, the jinnee allowed himself a smile. "Perfect. No one will have heard a thing with all that racket going on."

In the room at the top of the tower, the door opened and Marissa peered in. "G'night, *Alice*," she said. "Sleep well. You've got an *egg*-citing day tomorrow. Ha-ha!" Marissa stared at the unresponsive form for a few seconds. "All right, sulky brat. Be like that, then." She turned on her heel and slammed the door behind her.

In the stillness of the room, the bucket fell out of its hood and rolled across the floor.

# MIDNIGHT IN THE COURTYARD

*Ferdie, Oskar and Kaznim were* sitting in the chill of the courtyard, wrapped in the discarded wolverine skins. "What's the time?" whispered Ferdie.

"You keep asking that," Oskar said, a little snappily.

A few seconds later a high, clear chime rang through the night air. "That's the midnight Harbinger bell," Kaznim said.

They listened as the sound of the bell died away. "But it's not chiming midnight," Oskar said.

"Just wait," said Kaznim. A few seconds later the midnight peals began. The courtyard turned into a bowl of sound and the three sat suspended within it, entranced. As the last deep chimes faded Oskar whispered, "That was so beautiful."

They sat in the silence and waited. Nothing happened. "I thought Jim Knee said Tod would be here at midnight," Ferdie whispered.

"He did," Oskar said. And as he spoke, the door to the courtyard opened and in walked Jim Knee and Tod.

"Tod!" Ferdie and Oskar shouted together.

"Shh!" hushed Jim Knee. He looked around the courtyard anxiously. "This place gives me the creeps," he said. "Let's go."

No one needed any persuasion.

"Kaznim knows the way," Ferdie told Tod.

Tod was feeling a little edgy. "I bet she does," she said. "Just like she knew the way to the ambush at Oraton-Marr's tower."

"Oh, Tod, that's not fair. Jim Knee explained," Ferdie protested.

"Explained that she double-crossed us? He explained that, did he?"

*"Stop bickering,"* Jim Knee intervened. "Miss Na-Draa was under a Witch's **Draw**. It was not her doing. Anyway, no one is going anywhere with Miss Na-Draa unless she decides to come back to the Forest with us."

But Tod had not escaped from Oraton-Marr's clutches only to run back home. "We're not going to the Forest," Tod told the jinnee. "We're going into the desert to get the Egg of the Orm. You *know* that, Jim Knee."

"I know no such thing," Jim Knee replied. "My Command is to keep my master's Apprentice safe."

"*And* to seek out the Egg of the Orm," Tod told Jim Knee.

"Indeed. But my Master gave me two separate Commands. And if two Commands are incompatible – which these are, for I cannot seek the Egg of the Orm *and* keep you safe – the human safety Command prevails. So I am taking you back to the Forest."

"I'm not going," said Tod.

"Yes, you are." Jim Knee took a step towards Tod only to find his way barred by Ferdie and Oskar.

"Are you Commanded to force me to do something against my will?" Tod demanded.

"Well … no. I am not."

"But I am refusing to go," Tod said. "And if you make me

304

go I will fight you. And because you are much more powerful than I am, I shall get hurt. Which is hardly very safe."

Jim Knee was shocked. "I would never hurt you, Alice," he said. He sighed. "You have the luxury of free will. I do not. I gave that away in exchange for my succession of lives. So I will leave you to enjoy your free will and trust that it all turns out as you wish. Farewell." With that Jim Knee bowed and walked into the centre of the courtyard.

"Wait!" Tod called.

Jim Knee turned. He had expected a change of heart at the last minute. Humans were prone to panicking when left alone, especially young ones. "Yes, Alice?" he asked, a little smugly.

"Will you wait a moment, please? I want to write a note for you to give to Septimus. To tell him where we are. And where the Egg is." Tod rapidly scribbled the note and handed it to Jim Knee.

Jim Knee looked at the note disdainfully. "I am not a Message Rat," he said.

Tod pushed the note into the jinnee's reluctant hand. "This is part of your Command," she told him. "If you give it to him, I will be safe."

With the uncomfortable feeling that Tod had outwitted him, Jim Knee took the note. Then he stepped into the pool of darkness in the centre of the courtyard and disappeared.

# WHISTLING IN THE DARK

*"Kaznim,"* Tod said, *"can* you guide us to your tent from here? Please?"

Kaznim looked at Tod. She did not answer.

Tod was not surprised. Now that they were in Kaznim's territory the balance of power had shifted. The Tribe of Three needed Kaznim to take them to the Egg, but Kaznim no longer needed the Tribe of Three to help her get home. She could do that for herself. Now they were nothing more to Kaznim than three people who would place her sister in grave danger if they got their way about the Orm Egg.

The Tribe of Three exchanged glances. Tod could see that Ferdie and Oskar were thinking the same thing she was. So all were surprised when Kaznim said, "We must follow the stars. Just before dawn, my tent will be beneath the Great Palm of Dora."

"Can you see trees in the dark?" Ferdie wondered.

"It's a constellation," Kaznim said.

"I don't know that one," Tod said, puzzled.

"Our star names are different from yours," Kaznim said. She frowned. "I hope we do not cross the path of the sand lions."

"Sand lions?" Oskar whispered.

"The lionesses hunt all night at this time of year, for their cubs are growing fast."

Oskar and Ferdie exchanged anxious glances. "Maybe we should wait until daylight," said Oskar.

"But we have to get to the Egg as soon as we can," Ferdie said. "Don't we, Tod?"

Tod nodded. "I've got an idea," she said. "We might have to wait a bit, but it will be worth it." She drew out the *Wiz*'s silver whistle and blew. No sound came but Tod could feel the vibrations in her throat. The whistle had worked.

Oskar knew what Tod was doing. "It won't hear you," he said.

"It might," said Tod.

"*What* might?" Ferdie asked.

Tod didn't want to say, in case nothing happened, which seemed very likely. She reached into her pockets. "Anyone want a date?" she asked.

They sat in the darkness of the courtyard, eating the stuffed dates supplied by Marissa and listening to the sounds of the night-time Red City. Once they heard footsteps approaching, but they passed by safely. Another time they heard the shrieks of fighting cats. And then, drifting across the rooftops, came a scream. *"Noooooo!"*

"Was that Marissa?" Ferdie whispered.

"I don't think so," Tod said, uncertain. All screams sounded much the same.

Oskar looked anxiously at the door. "If it was … she'll come looking for you. And this is the first place she'll come."

Ferdie was on her feet, convinced that Marissa was on her way. "Tod, we've got go. *Now*," she said.

"I know, I know …" Tod said. "But please, just a moment longer. It's on the way now, I'm sure it –" Tod was cut short by a flash of silver shooting out from beneath the palm. With perfect timing, the *Wiz* arrived. And behind it, to Tod's surprise, came the *Beetle*. Someone had carefully knotted the sleds' ropes together.

Ferdie stared at Tod as though she had gone crazy. "What do you want those for?" she asked.

"To get to the Orm Egg, of course," Tod said, trying to unknot the intricately joined ropes.

"Tod, those are *sleds*," Ferdie said. "For *snow*. They can't run on sand."

Tod grinned. "Want to bet on it?" she asked.

Ferdie gave her friend a quizzical look. "You know something about the sleds that we don't," she said. "I can tell."

"Well, Oskie knows it too, don't you, Oskie?"

"Knows what?" asked Oskar.

"About the SandRider Charm."

Oskar looked blank.

"It was in that book, Oskie," Tod told him. "The one that Beetle – I mean the Chief – gave us about the sleds' history."

Oskar looked sheepish. "I didn't get around to reading it."

"Well, you missed something really interesting. The Charm for these sleds actually comes from the desert. Ancient sorcerers used huge sleds for travelling across the sands. They called them SandRiders. And the *Beetle* and the *Wiz* are both SandRiders."

"Wow ..." Oskar breathed. "They run on sand?"

"Yes. Even better than on snow."

Oskar grinned. He was suddenly looking forward to the desert a whole lot more. He kneeled down and helped Tod undo the ropes, which were tied in a very complicated knot – the kind that a turtle trader's wife once used to secure her turtle baskets.

# FIND HER!

*Somewhat unsteadily, Oraton-Marr* was on his way back to the
tower. The Queen's banquet had been an exciting taste of many
important occasions he knew were to come and he had made
a few mental notes on it for the life he was planning for himself
in the Castle. He had particularly liked the live ducklings over
which scalding-hot orange sauce was poured before the diner.
This was most definitely a tradition he intended to start. He
could set up a nice little hatchery on the banks of their muddy
little river …

Oraton-Marr's mind travelled back to the earlier events of
the day. He had very much enjoyed the ceremony in the
Queen's Square, even though it had been cut short by that
monstrous jinnee and the Queen had had to postpone the
beheadings. The sorcerer turned his thoughts to another
Queen, far away – Jenna, the Castle Queen. She was, the witch
had told him, no more than a girl living in a ratty old building
that needed pulling down. Well, he'd soon get rid of her and
her crumbling old palace. In fact, Oraton-Marr mused, most
of the Castle could do with being razed to the ground; the
Wizard Tower was the only decent building in it. Once he'd
taken charge of that and got the Red Queen installed in a nice
new palace, he'd make sure she kept the Castle under control

and operating as he wished. He would insist she had a compulsory weekly roll call for all Castle inhabitants to keep them in order and let them know who was in charge. From what he had seen of the Castle in his clandestine visits through a scrappy little arch high above the Moat, the place was a shambles. But the Wizard Tower was another matter. That was very impressive indeed; he certainly would not object to living there …

Oraton-Marr bounced happily along the alleyways, mulling over his plans, looking forward to greeting his Apprentice in her prison. The girl would be quite amenable by now, he thought. He took the narrow ope that led to the side gate of the Queen's guest tower – known as the Hospitable Gard – and let himself in.

Marissa was dozing in a chair in the entrance hall. She jumped guiltily to her feet as the door swung open.

Oraton-Marr frowned. "I hope you have been keeping watch," he said.

"I haven't moved," Marissa assured him.

"Well, you can move now," the sorcerer told her. "I need to sit down."

Marissa stepped aside and Oraton-Marr sank gratefully into her chair. He pulled off his spring blades with a sigh of relief and threw them clattering on to the floor. "My feet are killing me," he muttered.

After Marissa had brought him a restorative sherbet, Oraton-Marr said, "Right then, let's have a look at my little key to all the Wizard Tower passwords."

After a weary climb, Marissa drew back the bolts and stepped aside to let Oraton-Marr in.

"Bucket!" She heard him gasp – and then the metallic sound of the bucket being kicked across the floor. The next moment Oraton-Marr had his hands around Marissa's neck.

"Where *is* she?" he hissed.

"Erg …" Marissa gurgled. The hands were squeezing so hard, she could hardly breathe. Not a moment too soon, Oraton-Marr let go. Marissa swayed with relief. It was all she could do not to fall to the floor, but she understood well enough that to show weakness was dangerous. "It's no good you getting in a temper," Marissa told him hoarsely. "She must be here. She's done some kind of kids' UnSeen. She didn't get out past me, I know that."

Oraton-Marr was furious. "I can tell you, she is *not* here. Are you suggesting I cannot See the spell of a child?" he demanded. Marissa wisely refrained from saying that yes, that was exactly what she was suggesting. She watched Oraton-Marr check the room for an UnSeen Tod, but he knew she was gone. He could Hear no human heartbeat. How she had escaped was a mystery, but that did not matter. The mystery only added to her value; the Apprentice was clearly talented. She *must* be retrieved. He wheeled around to Marissa and screamed into her face, *"Find her!"*

The Tribe of Three and their guide were heading towards the distant light of the two torches burning on either side of the Beggars' Gate, when a high-pitched shriek echoed across the rooftops: *"Find her!"* They picked up speed and hurried on.

★    ★    ★

Inside the Hospitable Gard, Oraton-Marr was – as Marissa observed with dismay – in a panic. How was this sorcerer going

311

to set her up as Witch Mother of the Wendrons if he couldn't even work out where a stupid kid Apprentice had gone? It was obvious to anyone with half a brain. Marissa, however, was far too clever to use those words to Oraton-Marr.

"Your Highness." She coughed tactfully.

*"What?"*

"The Apprentice – I mean *your* Apprentice – will surely have taken the Forest Way back to her home. I can go after her if you wish."

Oraton-Marr tried not to look relieved, even though he felt it. Of course that was where she had gone. Why hadn't he thought of that himself? Oraton-Marr remembered how the Red Queen had proudly told him that every one of her guest towers contained a windowless dungeon complete with nests of scorpions for the convenience of her guests. "Servants," she had told him, "can be such trouble."

"Very well," he said. "Go after the girl. Bring her back and lock her in the scorpion dungeon. That will teach her that she will not trifle with *me*."

Marissa dropped a curtsy and turned to go. Oraton-Marr shouted after her, "Marissa. Before you go, call me a camel, will you?"

Marissa was glad she was facing away from the sorcerer. She fought to gain control of the laugh that was bubbling up. Over the past few weeks there were many things she had thought of calling Oraton-Marr, but a camel had not been on the list. Marissa spluttered and managed to turn it into a cough.

"One from the Queen's stable. With a night desert guide," Oraton-Marr added.

"Yes, Your Highness," Marissa gasped. She ran to the courtyard door, wrenched it open and, at the end of the alley, at last allowed herself to collapse into giggles.

The camel and night guide were duly delivered to the courtyard of the Hospitable Gard, and Marissa hurried off to the Forest Way. She was not looking forward to negotiating the night-time Forest but, she told herself, she probably wouldn't have to. No doubt she would find Tod huddled in the hut at the other end of the Forest Way, too scared to leave. She would be back with her in no time.

But all Marissa found waiting at the end of the Forest Way was a pack of hungry wolverines.

# PART XI

## FIVE AND A HALF HOURS TO HATCHING

# THE CITY OF THE FREE

*The* Beetle *and the* Wiz *swished noiselessly* towards Beggars' Gate. "It will be unguarded," Kaznim had told them. "No one bothers with beggars here. In the Red City, they say that the poorer you are, the freer you become. They call their encampment 'The City of the Free' because the Queen's guards never come here. But really, lots of the people here aren't beggars at all. They just want to not be scared all the time."

They walked through the pool of light cast by the torches, their flames steady in the still night air, beneath the red-stone arch and then were out of the city. They stopped and gazed at the strange sight before them – the ground dropped down into a sea of flickering lights, an earthly reflection of the starlit sky above. They were aware of the low murmur of conversation mixed with the soft snuffles of sleep and knew they were in the presence of hundreds of people.

They followed Kaznim as she walked slowly along the track that curved down to the lights below, and as the track levelled out, Tod heard the whisper of a voice. "Spare a peckrin, miss?" Tod stopped and peered down. An old man wrapped in a swathe of blankets was looking up at her, his hand out-stretched. Guessing that a peckrin was a small coin, Tod said, "I'm sorry. I don't have any money with me."

"Ah, so you've come to join us, have you?" the man asked.

"Er, no. We're ... we're heading for the desert."

"You're mad," came the response. A thin white arm extended from the blankets and pointed into the desert. "There's a pride on the prowl out there. Saw them at dusk. You'll be dead in an hour."

"Oh!" Tod gasped.

"Good thing we've got the sleds, then," Oskar said with a grin. "We'll outrun any pride. Easy-peasy."

Kaznim led them slowly along a narrow, winding path that wandered through the City of the Free. Tod was fascinated by the huge variety of tents, ranging from a simple blanket thrown over bent poles to beautiful circular structures made from embroidered cloth with carved wooden doors. Many tents shone with the warm glow of candlelight, which cast shadows of the people within, sitting talking quietly. The soft buzz of conversation reminded Tod of wandering through her village late at night and she felt a pang of homesickness. An urge to turn around and run almost overcame her, but Tod reminded herself that if she wanted the places and the people she loved to stay safe, then she, Ferdie and Oskar were going to have to go into the desert that night and find the Orm Egg.

Before long the City of the Free lay behind them, and they stood on the edge of the wide darkness of the desert. From somewhere in the distance a long, low roar came drifting across the sands.

# THE YELLOW OWL

*A large yellow owl landed* on the roof of the Manuscriptorium, where it sat for some minutes digesting a particularly bony shrew before it spat out a pellet and watched it roll down into the gutter.

Down in the Conservation basement, Darius Wrenn was dwarfed by four figures. Each one scared him for a different reason. The ExtraOrdinary Wizard scared him because he could turn him into a toad or something. Ephaniah Grebe scared him because he was half rat and Marwick scared him because he reminded Darius of a wolf. But the person who upset him the most was Beetle, his boss. Beetle just looked very disappointed, and that made Darius feel worst of all.

The intimidating group was gathered around one of Ephaniah's worktables, upon which a strange-looking map was spread out. Beetle pushed a list of numbers across to Marwick. "These are the Ways we took the flyers through," he said. He turned to Darius. "Are these the Way numbers that you gave to the girl, to Kaznim Na-Draa?"

Darius nodded.

"You are sure?"

Beetle sounded so stern that it was all Darius could do to squeak, "Yes."

Darius watched Marwick check the numbers against the map. After some minutes Marwick looked up and said, "It goes to the Port of the Singing Sands – to a **Hidden** arch. It's the end of the road."

"Sounds right to me," Beetle said. "I could hear gulls." He grinned. "Actually, I didn't see much. I just dumped the flyers and ran."

Marwick smiled at Darius. "You remembered the Ways well."

"He would have done better to have remembered his Manuscriptorium Promise," Beetle said.

Darius gulped and stared at his shoes. He wished he could disappear. If only he could get through the big door and into the Way, he would run and run and run and never, *ever* come back.

"Ah, well," Marwick said. "I don't suppose he meant to. And he *was* under instructions to be helpful."

Darius cast a grateful glance at Marwick, who was carefully rolling up the map. "Need a guide?" Marwick asked Septimus.

"Yes, please," Septimus said. "If you don't mind leaving Sam?"

Marwick smiled. "Sam needs to sleep. And whenever I go to see him he wakes up and wants to talk, which annoys Dandra, I can tell you. So I reckon I am doing him a favour by disappearing for a day or two. Anyway, I'm intrigued."

"Thank you, Marwick," Septimus said. "That would be a great help. Even when we get to the Port of the Singing Sands, we have absolutely no idea where to go from there."

Darius hardly dared to speak, but he knew he could not possibly make things worse. "Um. Excuse me ..." he said.

"What?" Beetle snapped.

"The girl, Kaznim. She said she lived in the desert in a tent with stars on it. If that's any help?"

"A tent with stars on it …" Septimus mused, wondering why that sounded familiar.

"Yes. Her mother is an … er … Pothy Cary."

Septimus suddenly made the connection. "Dandra!" he said. "*She* lived in a tent with stars. And Kaznim's mother took it over. Dandra will know how to get there."

Beetle was not so sure. "But don't they move the tents around in deserts?" he asked. "It may not be in the same place now."

Septimus was already hurrying along the corridor, heading for the wide white stairs. "It's the only clue we've got! Wait here. I'll be back with Dandra as soon as I can."

"Right," Marwick said as Septimus's purple cloak disappeared around the corner. "We'd better get a few things together. We'll need water, for a start."

"I'll get it!" Darius said. "Do you want it in water bottles you can carry?"

"Yes, we do." Marwick smiled.

"I won't be long," said Darius, and he raced off along the corridor and clattered up the stairs, glad for any excuse to be away from the angry glare of his boss.

Beetle and Marwick watched him go.

"Don't be too hard on the boy," Marwick said.

"He broke the Promise," Beetle replied grimly.

"Then you should give him a chance to mend it," Marwick replied.

★    ★    ★

The yellow owl watched his Master running to the Wizard Tower. The languor of a full stomach began to overtake the owl and its eyes began to close. Its claws uncurled and a tiny tube of paper rolled down the slope of the roof and landed in the gutter. There it unfurled and a gust of wind picked it up and sent it fluttering down on to the pavement below.

As the light of the moon shone down on the piece of paper, the owl on the roof fell asleep. As it closed its eyes, the weakness of too many Transformations in too short a time overcame it. The owl-form left the jinnee and the long yellow figure of Jim Knee lay draped along the ridge of the roof. He rolled over, slipped off, and slid down into the large gutter that lay between the double-gabled Manuscriptorium roofs. And there he curled up and fell deep into hibernation.

Ten minutes later, Septimus and Dandra Draa came hurrying towards the Manuscriptorium. "I can't believe that Alice would go off without saying anything," Dandra was saying. "Something awful must have happened to her."

Septimus was shaking his head. "I don't know, Dandra. I really don't know."

The scrap of paper shining in the moonlight caught Septimus's eye and he stopped to pick it up. "Well!" he gasped. "Another note. How extraordinary." He passed it over to Dandra, who read it. The note said:

*Dear Septimus,*

*We are going to get the Egg of the Orm. Jim Knee will explain and will tell you how to find us.*

*Your Apprentice,*

*Alice TodHunter Moon*

"Oh my goodness!" Dandra gasped. "So where's Jim Knee?" She put her hand on Septimus's arm. "Septimus, you've *got* to ask him. We have to know where she is!"

Septimus shook his head. "Unfortunately, I have no idea where that jinnee has got to," he said. "But at least I now have some idea where my Apprentice might be. With your help, Dandra, we'll get to your old star tent, and with any luck we'll find her there."

Bemused, Dandra shook her head. "But how will Alice get there? How on earth does she know where to go?"

"My Apprentice is a PathFinder," Septimus said. "I am beginning to realise that means she can go pretty much anywhere she wants to." He smiled. "I suppose it's a little like having a cat."

"A *cat*?" Dandra said indignantly as she followed Septimus into the Manuscriptorium.

"You're never quite sure where they go, or why. You just hope they come back to you." Septimus looked at Tod's note and smiled. "The only difference is, cats don't send you regular updates."

As the door to the Manuscriptorium swung closed, a loud snore came from above. But no one heard it. It was only the next day, when Colin Partridge went to investigate the strange noises on the roof, that Jim Knee was discovered, half frozen and delirious. He spent the rest of the winter in front of the fire on the big purple sofa in Septimus's rooms – which was what he'd wanted in the first place.

# THE FORK IN THE ROAD

*Night-time in the desert* is hunting time. It is a time when small, soft-skinned creatures bury themselves in the sands and hope that nothing with teeth, claws or stings will come calling. But that night there were four creatures – not so small but relatively soft-skinned – who were about to brave the hunting ground.

The open desert spread out before them. Above, the clear night sky was alive with stars that seemed so vibrant and busy, they almost took away the loneliness of the empty sands ahead. A feeling of excitement began to creep over Tod. They had left the encampment behind and now stood at the beginning of the road that would take them to the Orm Egg – or to within sight of where it lay. All they had to do was follow the road as fast as they could.

The only thing that worried Tod now was if they were going to get to the Egg in time. "How many more grains to go through in the Egg Timer?" Tod asked Kaznim.

Kaznim took the Egg Timer from her pocket and peered at it, taking care to hold it away from Tod. The grains of silver shone like tiny points of light and there were only three left, which Kaznim knew meant that – depending on how soon the next grain was due to move – there was at the most nine hours to go until the Egg hatched. And possibly, if a grain was about to move, only six.

"Let's have a look," Oskar said.

Kaznim closed her hand tightly over the **Egg Timer**. "It loses energy in the dark," she said. "You can see it in the morning."

"So how many grains are left?" Tod asked again.

"Six," Kaznim lied.

"And how many to each hour?" Oskar asked.

Kaznim was pleased to be able to tell the truth this time. "One goes through every three hours," she said.

"So ... it looks like the hatching is set for sometime tomorrow evening, then," Tod said. "That's good. It gives us lots of time."

Oskar liked to have things planned out. "Time to steal the Egg?" he asked.

"No, time to get there," Tod said. "I've been thinking. We don't have to steal the Egg, all we have to do is be there. As long as we make sure that one of us is the first person the Orm sees when it comes out of the Egg so that we stop it from Imprinting on ..." She dropped her voice to a whisper. *"You-know-who."*

Oskar grinned. "Wouldn't it be great to have a little Orm Imprinting you? I hope it chooses me."

"Don't be so stupid, Oskie," Ferdie snapped. "It's not going to be that easy. Oraton-Marr is not just going to stand aside and say, 'Oh, hello, Oskar Sarn, do you want an Orm all of your own? Go ahead, be my guest and have mine,' is he? Really, Oskar, think about it. This is not going to be a picnic."

Tod knew that Ferdie and Oskar picked fights when they were nervous. She tried to be peacemaker. "It's not going to be easy, that's true," she said, "but we can do it. Tribe of Three, remember?" Tod made the Tribe of Three sign and Ferdie and Oskar returned it.

"Time to go," Tod said.

The *Wiz* and the *Beetle* sat patiently in the starlight, two steeds waiting for their riders. No one spoke. The two riders took their places, then Kaznim joined Tod, and Ferdie joined Oskar.

"I hope Oraton-Marr doesn't have a sled," Oskar said.

"The sorcerer uses **Magyk** and camels," Kaznim said. "But they say, in the olden days, the Red Queen had a beautiful SandRider."

"OK," Tod said, a little nervously. "Ready?"

"Ready!" said Oskar.

Tod leaned forward on the *Wiz*. "Go!" she whispered. The SandRider **Charm** kicked in.

The *Wiz* led the way with the *Beetle* close behind. Both sleds travelled along the tightly packed sand of the road as though they had never known a day's snow. Tod thought the *Wiz* ran even better on sand. She felt more in control and the *Wiz* had a sense of power that she had not been aware of before. It was as though the sled knew that a great expanse of sand was waiting and it longed to run free. For a sled that had always been constrained either by tunnels or tracks, this was heady stuff.

Behind the *Wiz* ran the *Beetle*, edgy and energetic. Oskar felt exhilarated. He loved sand dunes in the same way that Tod loved the sea, and suddenly he was able to travel across them at a speed he had only dreamed of. But Oskar knew that for now Tod must lead the way, so he contented himself with daydreaming about arriving at the very moment when the Orm Egg was hatching. He imagined drawing up on the *Beetle* in a shower of sand just in time to see the tiny creature – which he knew looked like a dragon – come fluttering out of the Egg and land on his hand. He thought how they would gaze into each other's eyes and be together for ever. And then, Oskar thought, he would take his Orm for breathtaking rides through the desert and –

"Hey!" Tod yelled. "Stop!"

Oskar's dreams came to an abrupt halt. In front the *Wiz* had stopped and he was about to crash into it. He slewed the *Beetle* out of the way and skidded to a halt. "What's up?" he asked anxiously.

In answer Tod pointed to a fork in the road. Kaznim got off the *Wiz* and stood looking up at the sky.

"Kaznim's not sure which way to go," Tod said. "She's working it out from the stars."

But Kaznim had no need to look at the stars – she knew exactly which road led to the star tent. She was in fact struggling with her conscience. Kaznim was well aware that she had promised to take Tod, Oskar and Ferdie to the Orm Egg – and she would honour that promise. What she had not said was *when* they would get there. Kaznim knew she could not risk going home until she was sure that the Egg had hatched. Only then would the sorcerer return her baby sister to her mother. Kaznim sneaked the Egg Timer from her pocket, hoping that maybe another grain had gone through. Then she need not deceive anyone any more and could lead them straight to the tent along the right-hand fork. They would arrive in about four hours' time, and by then the Orm would have already hatched and Imprinted the sorcerer, but that would not be her fault. To Kaznim's disappointment there were still three grains of silver left.

"Kaznim?" Tod called across. "Which way?"

Kaznim delayed her answer for just a little while longer. The right-hand road led straight home. They would be back at the star tent in under four hours. The left went deep into the Dunes of Kuniun – sand lion territory. Kaznim fought down her desire to go home and also to be honest with three people she had come to like. But she could not. If she wished her baby sister to still be alive when she finally returned, she had no choice.

"Left," Kaznim replied with a heavy heart. "We take the left."

# SAND LIONS

*The* Wiz *and the* Beetle *travelled side by side* along the wide, smooth road. All were silent as they headed towards the Dunes of Kuniun, each occupied with their own thoughts. Tod and Ferdie were focused on the task ahead, Oskar still daydreaming about "his" Orm. Kaznim was scared: for her sister and of her companions working out what she had done. But her most pressing terror was of sand lions.

The sleds were going beautifully. They ran smooth and fast, and although they were now beginning to climb up into the dunes, the soft *shish-shish-shish* of sand beneath the sleds' runners felt so right that Tod found it strange to think that the *Wiz* also ran on snow.

As they climbed higher the cold night air began to bite, and they took turns to lead so that one was always sheltered. On the back of Oskar's sled, Ferdie found her eyes closing with weariness, but on the back of the *Wiz*, Kaznim was wide awake and very nervous. Once she thought she heard a distant roar. Tod heard it too. She slowed down and said to Oskar, "Did you hear that?"

"No," said Oskar. He was lying. He knew how scared Ferdie was of strange creatures and he saw no reason to panic her. And so they travelled on beneath the canopy of stars, steadily up into the wide expanse of the Dunes of Kuniun.

After many miles the track had petered out and the sleds were now travelling through unmarked dunes, guided entirely by Kaznim's directions. The waning full moon was dropping down towards the horizon, its light silvering the sand that rose and fell before them like waves, the sleds flowing up and down the slopes like boats riding the surf. As they crested yet another rise, Tod drew to a halt and surveyed the scene. She had expected by now to be able to see tents in the distance, but she could see nothing but empty, rolling dunes. A niggle of worry that had been growing ever since the track had petered out became impossible to ignore – *Where were they?*

She turned around to Kaznim. "I thought you said when the road ended you could see your tent."

Kaznim was flustered. "No, I didn't," she said. "It goes to the dunes. And *then* you see the tent."

"That's not what you said." Oskar leaned across to the *Wiz*. "And anyway, we are in the dunes now and I can't see any tents at all."

"Neither can I," Ferdie added for good measure.

"So where *is* your tent?" Tod asked.

"It will very soon be under the Palm of Dora. Like I said," Kaznim replied. She pointed to a constellation straight ahead of them. "Over there."

"That's not the Palm of Dora," Oskar said.

"Yes it is," Kaznim insisted.

"No, it's not," Oskar shot back. "I know where it is, and it's not there."

Kaznim was trapped. There was nothing she could do but lie, and keep on lying. "Yes, it *is*," she repeated.

Tod was getting a bad feeling about this. "Oskie," she said, "do you know which constellation the Palm of Dora is?"

"Yep," said Oskar. "It's over there." He pointed to the west. "It's the one with five stars in a vertical row with a semicircle of stars above."

"Oh, you mean the Anchor!"

"Yep," Oskar said. "That is exactly what I mean."

"Well, there is no way we are heading for that, is there?" Tod turned to Kaznim. "We should have taken the right-hand fork," she said. And then, as Kaznim refused to meet her eyes, Tod suddenly understood what had happened. "But you knew that, didn't you?"

"No, I didn't," Kaznim countered. She had told so many lies now that another did not seem to matter.

"Are you saying that Kaznim has deliberately taken us the wrong way?" Ferdie asked anxiously.

"That's what it looks like to me," Tod said stonily.

Everyone fell quiet – that was what it looked like to Oskar and Ferdie too. And then, the silence of the night was broken by a sound that no one wanted to hear: a long, low growl.

*Sand lions*, Oskar mouthed rather unnecessarily.

Then came another growl – this from a different direction. Oskar had a talent for reading the land and all creatures within it. Like a sand snake, he slipped from his sled and put his ear to the ground. He listened to the sound of the sand and the pad of paws, and he knew it was bad. Very slowly he moved back on to the sled. "We're surrounded," he whispered. "But if we stay totally still I don't think they'll go for us. They need movement to judge their attack."

Kaznim stared at Oskar in horror. This was her fault – and

she knew they knew it. Kaznim felt more alone than she ever had in her life, even more than when she had been waiting outside the Sick Bay. At least then she was only being ignored by strangers. Now she was surrounded by a pride of sand lions in the company of three people who had just realised that she had tricked them. A horrible thought came into Kaznim's mind. There was an easy way for the others to escape; all they had to do was to push her off the sled and leave her behind. The sand lions would find her and they wouldn't bother to go hunting anything else that night. Kaznim's fingers closed around her opal pebble **Charm** – she still had her **UnSeen**. But even as she tried to comfort herself with that, she knew it would be useless. Sand lions hunted by scent, not vision. It was then, in the darkness of Kaznim's pocket, that the penultimate grain of silver in the top of the **Egg Timer** wandered through to join its friends, leaving behind a lonely singleton to ponder what it had done to offend all the other grains. There were a mere three hours left until the Orm Egg hatched.

"Oskie," Tod was whispering. "We have to make a break for it. Which way?"

Oskar knew there was only one way out. "Along the ridge. Towards the moon," he whispered. "We go fast – *really* fast. There are lions on either side, but I reckon they are too far down to get us at first pounce."

"What about second pounce?" Ferdie whispered.

"We don't let that happen. OK?"

"We'll go on the count of three," Tod said. She turned to Kaznim. "Hold on really tight," she told her. "This is going to be *fast*. If you fall off I won't be able to come back to pick you up, do you understand?"

"Yes, Tod," Kaznim meekly replied. "I understand."

Tod began the countdown: "One … two … three!"

The standing-start practices for the sled race stood them in good stead. The *Wiz* and the *Beetle* shot along the ridge in a shower of sand that flew into the air and landed on the lions lying in wait on either side. The animals were so shocked that they did not get a chance for a first pounce – let alone, as Ferdie had feared, a second. She risked a glance back and saw not the lions themselves – who were perfectly camouflaged – but their moon shadows, long and dark, loping effortlessly after them. "They're coming after us!" Ferdie shouted in dismay.

Oskar had hoped that the shock of their escape would confuse the pride and they would not bother to follow. But he did not know that the pride had not eaten for days and the heady smell of human cut through all confusion. One thing Oskar did know was that, unlike their cousins, the great lions of the plains, sand lions had tremendous stamina. They were small, lithe creatures, built for travelling long distances to find prey in the emptiness of the desert. There was no hope of them tiring fast and giving up the chase. Oskar knew they must outrun them. "We have to go faster!" he yelled. "*Much* faster!"

Tod could feel the reserves of power within the *Wiz*; she knew the sled could easily go faster, but she was not sure that the *Beetle* could. And there was no way she was going to leave Oskar and Ferdie behind. "You go first, Oskie!" she called back. "Go as fast as you can. We'll follow!"

The *Beetle* drew ahead and once more the two riders were in a race – but this time it was for something a little more important than the Apprentices' Cup.

# Transport

*Oraton-Marr stood on the rooftop* of the Hospitable Gard looking at his **Egg Timer**. With a sense of excitement he saw that now there was only one remaining grain of silver. His Orm Egg would hatch in three hours' time. He put his **Enlarging Glass** to his eye and scanned the sky. He was searching for the Palm of Dora.

In the courtyard below, a camel from the Red Queen's stables, accompanied by the Red Queen's spy authentically swathed in smelly camel-driver robes, waited impatiently. Oraton-Marr was not quite as stupid as Marissa had assumed. He had no intention whatsoever of taking the camel to the Orm Egg. The Red Queen's heavy hints at the banquet that she knew of his "buried treasure" in the desert had put him on guard. He had had no choice but to accept her offer of a camel and guide, but he had no intention of using them.

While the spy irritably scratched her camel-flea bites and the camel dribbled down her neck, Oraton-Marr located the Palm of Dora. He moved the Glass down the vertical line of stars and beneath he saw the tiny but unmistakable shape of the star-strewn tent. He fixed the position in his mind and put the **Enlarging Glass** away.

Right now, he thought, his sister would be making the long

trek from their ship to the Egg tent. With her would be the Mitza woman and the hostage toddler brat. Oraton-Marr smiled to himself. He liked to think he was a man of his word, and he would prove it by returning the child as promised – but only if all went as he wished it and he got his Orm. If the Orm did not hatch successfully or the creature did not **Imprint** him, he would at least have the pleasure of drowning the child in the pool beside her mother's tent. The child was his guarantee that one way or another, there would be something he would enjoy about the coming day.

With these happy thoughts, Oraton-Marr began his **Magyk**. He narrowed his dark green eyes and fixed his gaze on the exact point on the horizon just below the Palm of Dora and prepared himself. While it was not strictly necessary to see the place to which he was planning to **Transport**, on such an important occasion the sorcerer was taking no chances. He focused his mind on the flat rock beside the pool. Thirty seconds later all that remained of the sorcerer on the rooftop was a lingering purple haze and an unsettling aura of smugness.

# SPEED

*The average speed of a sand lion* in for the long chase is thirty-five miles an hour, although it is perfectly possible for it to top fifty miles an hour in a quick spurt. The lions now settled into their hunting rhythm, each leader dropping back after some minutes to allow a fresher lion to take its place and keep the pride's pace steady.

The lions easily followed the sleds as they ran along the top of the ridge, and every time she glanced around, Tod could see that little by little the pride was gaining on them. But there was nothing she could do. There was no way she was going to take the *Wiz* up to full speed and leave Oskar and Ferdie behind.

Oskar did not glance back; he could feel the padding of the lions steadily growing stronger and he had no wish to see them as well. Ferdie, however, could hardly take her eyes from the scene behind. The dark shapes of the lions and the glassy glint from their eyes terrified her; she held on tightly to Oskar and wished she could do something – *anything* – to make the *Beetle* go faster. And then it occurred to Ferdie that she could. If Oskar could will the *Beetle* faster, then surely she could too.

Ferdie remembered what Oskar had excitedly told her when he had first been picked to ride in the Apprentice Race. "You have to imagine that you actually *are* the sled," he had said.

Ferdie knew that Oskar had expected her to laugh at him. But she had simply asked him how he did it, because she wanted to know. There was so much Ferdie wanted to know. Her brother, like Tod, was learning so many new things and Ferdie sometimes felt a little bit left behind – but there was no way that she was going to let that happen now.

And so, saying nothing to Oskar, Ferdie focused on the small wooden sled beneath her as it travelled steadily along the sandy ridge, closely tailed by the *Wiz*. In her mind, Ferdie became the *Beetle*. She felt the slip of the sand beneath her, the resistance of the cold night air before her; she became fast and sleek, full of energy, power and speed.

To Oskar's shock and delight, with a tremendous kick, the *Beetle* suddenly shot off, spraying sand over a surprised Tod. Ferdie and Oskar felt as though they were flying. Far below, the desert lay before them like the ocean; above, the immense indigo sky seemed to sing a high, thin tune as the stars whistled by. Only the greatest willpower stopped Ferdie from shrieking with exhilaration as the *Beetle* reached the end of the ridge and went barrelling down the slope, heading for the wide plains lying before them.

At the foot of the dune, Oskar slowed the sled to allow the *Wiz* to catch up. His eyes were shining with excitement. With Kaznim clinging on to the back, covered in sand, Tod brought the *Wiz* alongside.

"Oskie ... that was brilliant!" she said, breathless. "I never knew the Beetle could go so *fast*!"

Oskar grinned. "Neither did I!" he laughed.

Ferdie just smiled. "Look at the lions," she said, pointing to the top of the dune.

Lined up along the ridge, silhouetted against the sky, was the pride of sand lions looking mournfully at the two sleds. They were exhausted. Even the tasty scent of four small humans was not enough to risk good energy on a chase they were never going to win.

Twenty-one pairs of mirrored eyes watched the *Beetle* and the *Wiz* set off at a steady speed across the desert plain, their course set for the Palm of Dora.

PART
XII

ONE HOUR
TO HATCHING

# THE DRAGON ON THE DUNE

*Oraton-Marr arrived exactly where he* had planned. He stood for some minutes to allow the effects of his Transport to fade and as the last wisps of purple evaporated into the night air, he walked over to the encampment. He opened the door flap of the Egg tent and stepped inside.

The Egg Boy jumped to his feet and stood to attention. He had been dreading this moment and had not slept all night. "All in order, sir," he said.

"I'll be the judge of that," Oraton-Marr snapped – secretly gratified that not only was the Egg Boy still afraid of him but that he did appear to have done a good job.

In the shadows of the tent, the Apprentice Mysor watched warily. No one wanted the Egg hatched successfully more than he, so that the sorcerer would go away and leave them alone. Even so Mysor disliked seeing the sorcerer getting what he wanted. He watched Oraton-Marr kneel down, lift the furs from the Egg and place two proprietorial hands on it and run them across the Egg's smooth, leathery surface. When they reached around to the back the long, questing fingers found what they were looking for.

"The Egg Tooth bulge," Oraton-Marr whispered excitedly. He looked at the Egg Boy and gave a thin smile. "You have done well." The Egg Boy almost fainted with relief.

Oraton-Marr knew that the most prudent course of action was to keep the Orm Egg within the tent, so that when the little Orm emerged it could not escape. But Oraton-Marr had not put in years of planning, violence and intimidation to have no one witness his moment of triumph. He would never admit it, but he wanted his sister to see how clever her big brother really was.

And so, as dawn began to break over the desert, Oraton-Marr watched Mysor and the Egg Boy stagger out of the tent with the Orm Egg and lay it gently on the sand. Then, under instructions, they lit a fire on the flat rock beside the pool and brewed coffee. Oraton-Marr settled down to gaze at the Egg and enjoy the moment. Soon the key to an endless supply of lapis lazuli would be in his grasp.

The smell of coffee woke the Apothecary, who had only just fallen into a fitful sleep. She emerged from the star-strewn tent, haggard with exhaustion and fear for her two daughters. She saw the sorcerer sitting beside the fire, drinking his – or to be accurate, her – coffee. In the sand beside him was the hateful Egg, still unhatched, but clearly not for much longer. Even from a distance, Karamander could see the lump of the Egg Tooth bulging in the smooth ovoid.

On his last visit to the star-strewn tent, Oraton-Marr had gleefully informed Karamander that he now had custody of Kaznim too. At first Karamander had been ecstatic to hear that Kaznim was actually alive, but her joy had soon been replaced with fear for her daughter's safety in the clutches of such a wicked man. Karamander Draa stood still and took three deep, slow breaths of cold morning air. She must calm down, she told herself. She must *not* run screaming at the sorcerer, punch him in his smug face and demand the return of her children – she must *not*. She had only to wait a little longer and all would be well. The Egg would hatch, Oraton-Marr would get his stupid Orm and then he would give her back her daughters. Wouldn't he?

\*　　\*　　\*

From the top of the long dune, Spit Fyre watched the proceedings below. He had not eaten for twelve weeks, and even though a dragon is a beast built for endurance and he still had reserves left, Spit Fyre was not feeling his best. He didn't look too good, either. He was no longer the shining green dragon that had once glittered in the skies above the Castle. Sand had settled over him, sticking to his scales, which had been dried and roughened by the sun, so that his brilliant colour and sheen had long gone and he now looked as though he were carved from sandstone. The only glimpse of colour was in his eyes, a deep emerald ringed with red.

Some weeks previously a rumour had spread around the encampment that the dragon had turned to stone. Spit Fyre had heard the mutterings and decided to encourage the idea by moving only at night and making sure he resumed the same position at daybreak. One of Oraton-Marr's guards had eventually ventured up for a closer look. Spit Fyre had remained immobile and had not reacted even when the guard had given him a vicious jab in the belly with the end of his charred FireStick. The guard had returned with the news that the dragon had indeed turned to stone. And on his next visit Oraton-Marr had taken the glory of the awesome feat of turning a dragon into stone.

From his vantage point Spit Fyre now saw all. Below to his right, he saw the Orm Egg lying on the sand, surrounded by people whose hopes and fears rested on its hatching. To his left on the plain that stretched all the way to the Port of the Singing Sands, Spit Fyre saw a small group of people making their way towards him, a long trail of foot- and hoofprints stretching out behind. A large woman swathed in blue rode a small, grumpy camel. Behind her came a dumpy woman on a donkey carrying a small, sleeping child upon her back and in front walked a man with a long stave, leading the way.

Spit Fyre also was aware of two fast-moving objects on the plains some distance behind him. There was something familiar about them. They had, he thought, a feel of the Castle to them. He had at first wondered if it was his much-loved Imprintor, Septimus. But as they drew closer he could tell that sadly, it was not Septimus. Spit Fyre was intrigued. There was an air of Magyk about them and they were hurtling towards him at a surprising speed, but the dragon resisted the temptation to turn and look. He must remain immobile for now. He did not want to draw attention to himself. Not yet.

With an unblinking eye, Spit Fyre watched the man lead the camel and donkey with their burdens up the dune. They stopped at the top and the travellers looked at him warily. The one in blue stared hard. "So he *did* do it," Spit Fyre heard her say in an awed voice. "He really has turned a dragon to stone."

Spit Fyre felt the near-irresistible urge to yawn that always came before a breath of Fyre. How he would have loved to have aimed a blast at the shiny blue one and seen it shrivel up to a crisp. He put the thought from his mind and allowed his right eye to follow the group as they made their way down the dune towards the little group gathered around the Egg.

344

The minutes passed slowly. After spending so long waiting so very patiently, Spit Fyre found it hard to contain his excitement. He longed to fly down and retrieve the Egg *right now* but he dared not risk it. He knew he was weak from lack of food and stiff from lack of movement – he could not risk a fight that he may well not win. His advantage must be in surprise and perfect timing. He had to get it right the first time. There would be no second chance.

# THE PRODIGAL RETURNS

*A lightening of the sky* in the east told Tod that the night was nearly gone. The Palm of Dora was beginning to fade but in its place, at the foot of the vertical line of stars, was the dark shape of a tent. Sitting behind Tod, Kaznim saw the same. A thrill of excitement ran through her at the sight of her home, quickly followed by the terror of what she might find there.

With the threat of the sand lions gone, the sleds were now travelling at a comfortable pace. The sand no longer stung the riders' eyes and cut at their faces, and Tod and Oskar could actually see where they were going. They had now reached the beginnings of the gentle swell in the sand that rose up to form the ridge of the long dune above the star-strewn tent. A short conference between the riders – in which Kaznim took no part – led to the decision to head to the top of the dune. Tod hoped to be able to see the Egg from there. Oskar hoped for a quick descent, giving them the advantage of surprise.

Ferdie was keeping watch on Kaznim. She did not trust the girl at all, but she could not entirely blame her. Ferdie knew that if the safety of her own little brother was at stake, she suspected that she might well do as Kaznim had done.

They ascended to the ridge of the long dune and coasted quietly along the top. Soon the stone-still shape of Spit Fyre came into view. Tod turned to Oskar and Ferdie. "There's a dragon up ahead," she whispered.

"A stone dragon," Kaznim said. And then wished she hadn't. How stupid could she be? It would be much better if they were too afraid of the dragon to go any further. She quickly added, "It belongs to the sorcerer. It is there to protect the Egg. It will come alive if anyone but the sorcerer Imprints the Orm."

Tod, Ferdie and Oskar exchanged glances. No one knew whether to believe Kaznim. "Do we risk the dragon?" Tod whispered.

"If it's stone, then surely we're safe," Ferdie said. "It can't become a live dragon in just a few seconds ... can it?"

Tod was not sure. She had heard many things about Darke Magyk and not all of them made sense. But a sudden change in the balance of the *Wiz* and a gasp from Ferdie drove the conundrum of stone dragons entirely from her mind – Kaznim was off and running fast.

Skidding, sliding, hurling herself forward, Kaznim took the steepest part of the dune, which was too sheer for any sled. "Ammaa!" she screamed out, her voice piercing the silence. "Ammaa! *Ammaaaaa!*" The sounds fell away as Kaznim hurtled out of sight.

The Tribe of Three stared at one another in dismay. Their only advantage was surprise and now that was gone. There was no doubt in their minds that Kaznim would very soon be telling everyone exactly who was on the dune – and why.

Throughout their long ride across the sands, Tod had been thinking about what they would do if they were seen too early. She knew they needed a back-up plan, and her brief stint as Oraton-Marr's prisoner had given her an idea, but it was not a pleasant one. It was to use only as a last resort – and the last resort had arrived unexpectedly fast. "I'm going after her," Tod said.

"We're coming too," said Ferdie at once.

"No," Tod said. "It won't work if you come too."

"Why not?" Oskar asked.

"Trust me, it *won't*. OK?"

"OK …" Ferdie and Oskar agreed reluctantly.

"We're here if you need us," Ferdie said.

"Ready and waiting," added Oskar.

Tod set off on the *Wiz* with a heavy heart. She took a diagonal route across the face of the long dune, keeping well below the dragon. Halfway down the dune, the encampment came into view. She saw the faded silver stars stitched across the roof of a large, circular tent. She saw the smaller tents gathered around it. She saw the dark, mirrored water of the pool beneath the long dune, the flat rock in front of the pool on which a fire was burning and people were gathered around. And then she saw the Orm Egg for the very first time – as large as a small child, deep blue, lying quietly in a dip in the sand, unaware of all the fuss it had caused. And was still causing. A flash of light from the rising sun touched the surface of the Orm Egg, which shimmered like water. Tod caught her breath with excitement. The Egg was beautiful. And even better, *it was unhatched*.

The *Wiz* continued its downward path towards the encampment. It felt so wrong to be coasting along in full view of everyone, but Tod steeled herself to act the part she had set herself to play – and to act it well. Ahead of her she could see another party on a small camel and a donkey stumbling down the long dune, and as the *Wiz* drew slowly closer, Tod's heart began to race with fear. She was heading towards two people she had hoped never to see again – the Lady and her tormenter of old, her mother's stepsister, Aunt Mitza. Tod's instincts screamed at her to turn the *Wiz* around *right now* and head away as fast as she could. But she resisted. She must keep going. For the sake of all the people she loved, she must get to the Orm Egg and then, when it hatched, she must Imprint it. That was all that mattered. And so Tod let the *Wiz* saunter nonchalantly down the long diagonal, drawing ever closer to the nest of vipers below.

Suddenly Tod saw the tiny figure of Kaznim Na-Draa hurtle out of the shadows behind the star-covered tent. Her shouts of "Ammaa! Ammaa!" were closely followed by her mother's answering screams of joy. Tod saw a woman in red robes lift Kaznim into the air and swing her around and around in utter delight. An unexpected twinge of sadness for what she had lost when her own mother died caught at Tod. She pushed the feeling away and allowed the *Wiz* to trundle on.

And then, as Tod knew it surely would, the sled caught the eye of Oraton-Marr.

# AN ORM IS BORN

*The* Wiz *coasted to a halt beside* the Egg of the Orm. Oraton-Marr looked down at Tod with an expression of annoyance. "Where have you been?" he snapped.

Hating the thought of what she was about to do, Tod forced herself into role. She got off the *Wiz* and stood meekly before Oraton-Marr. "I am sorry," she said. "I disappeared from your tower by mistake. I was … I was bored so I was playing around with some **Magyk**. It was a stupid thing to do, because I really do want to be your Apprentice. It is such a wonderful opportunity."

Oraton-Marr was impressed by Tod's acquisition and mastery of a **SandRider** and her obvious talent for **Magyk**. His arrogance was such that he found it very easy to believe that Tod truly did want to be his Apprentice. "It is indeed a wonderful opportunity for you, Apprentice," he told Tod. "However, you are very late. I shall expect better timekeeping in future."

"I came as fast as I could," Tod said. "And you were hard to find."

"Do not answer back!" Oraton-Marr snapped. He glared at those gathered around the Egg – Mysor, the Egg Boy, the three guards and an open-mouthed Kaznim, clutching her mother's hand. Oraton-Marr now addressed them equally severely. "The

Orm Egg is about to hatch. When it does you will all look away. You will *not* catch its gaze. If the Orm Imprints on anyone else I shall *kill them*. Do you understand?"

There was silence. They understood.

Oraton-Marr took advantage of having an Apprentice. He left Tod beside the Egg – with the instruction to fetch him at once if the Egg Tooth broke through – and he went to meet the party on the camel and donkey who were heading wearily towards the tents. Oraton-Marr greeted them and irritably beckoned the guards to help Drone get his sister off the camel.

Horribly fascinated to see her step-aunt again, Tod stole a few glances in their direction, but as Aunt Mitza waddled towards the fire by the pool, Tod stared stonily down at the Egg and refused to catch her eye.

With much fuss the Lady was settled on some cushions from Karamander's tent. Karamander's sleeping baby daughter was lifted from the papoose on Aunt Mitza's back. Oraton-Marr instructed Aunt Mitza to stand beside the pool with the child in her arms and then he addressed them all. "If anyone gets between me and my Orm – *anyone* – Mitza Draddenmora will drown the child immediately."

Karamander suppressed a gasp, but Kaznim did not supress anything. "No!" she screamed. "No! Not Bubba!"

"I will *not* have any disturbance," Oraton-Marr told Karamander. "Take your daughter to your tent and stay there." Karamander led Kaznim away and as they disappeared into the star-strewn tent, an excited cry came from the sorcerer. "Breakthrough!" he shouted out. "Breakthrough!"

Like a baby's tooth pushing through the gum, a white point gleamed wetly at the top of the bump on the Egg. It was the

Egg Tooth. It had pushed its way through the leathery skin of the Egg, and a serrated edge now revealed itself. Slowly, the Egg Tooth of the Orm began to cut its way along the length of the Egg.

"All of you, turn around! Close your eyes!" Oraton-Marr barked.

His sister, his servant, Drone, Aunt Mitza, the three guards, Mysor and the Egg Boy obediently turned away towards the shadow of the dune and the darkness of the pool.

Oraton-Marr's hand descended on Tod's shoulder. "As my Apprentice, you will stay with me beside the Egg," Oraton-Marr said. "You will close your eyes until I tell you otherwise. Do you understand?"

"I understand," Tod said meekly.

A tense silence fell. Head bowed, Tod discovered that she could raise her eyelids just enough to see the whiteness of the Egg Tooth as it sawed back and forth, its sharp teeth glinting in the firelight. She saw Oraton-Marr crouch down, put his hands on the Egg and lean over it, like a small child keeping a favourite toy for himself.

The Egg Tooth slowly cut a slit along the length of the Egg, then it stopped moving. It wobbled for a moment, then it fell out like a milk tooth and lay wetly on the sand. For a few long seconds the Egg was still and all was suspended, motionless, while Oraton-Marr stared into the Egg, seeking the gaze of the baby Orm.

Like a midwife at a difficult birth, Oraton-Marr was now leaning right over the Egg, intent on the stirrings inside. Safe in the knowledge that the sorcerer's whole being was fixated upon the Orm, Tod dared to open her eyes a little more. She saw that the cut along the length of the Egg was beginning to gape and beneath she glimpsed something moving. Tod knew that any second now the Orm would hatch.

Her heart beating fast, Tod readied herself. As soon as the Orm emerged, she would throw herself at the sorcerer and send him reeling. She would Imprint the Orm and then ... Tod remembered Bubba clutched in Aunt Mitza's iron grasp beside the pool. She swallowed hard. She could not think about what would happen next.

A thin wail of pain came suddenly from Bubba – Aunt Mitza had pinched the child to stop her wriggling. And with the wail, Tod's resolution evaporated. If Bubba drowned it would be because of her actions. *What should she do?* Tod no longer knew. She wished that Ferdie and Oskar were with her. Or Septimus. Or Dandra. She needed to talk about what was right. But there was no time for that. She was on her own.


Tod was not quite as alone as she thought. After some discussion, Ferdie and Oskar had decided that whatever Tod might have said, she needed back-up. They were now creeping through the shadows at the foot of the star-strewn tent and the Orm Egg had just come into view.

*Tod's there*, Oskar said to Ferdie in PathFinder signs.

*Is she OK?* Ferdie signed.

*So far*, was Oskar's reply. And then he added, *I'm going to go for the Orm.*

Ferdie frowned. *Tod said to let her do it on her own*, she replied. *Anyway, they'll see you coming.*

*No they won't*, Oskar signed. *They're facing the other way. And he told them to close their eyes.* With that Oskar set off.

Petrified, Ferdie watched Oskar pad noiselessly across the sand, heading for the Egg. Not one person reacted. She saw him reach Tod and blithely confident, she saw him tug at Tod's tunic. Surprised, Tod swung around. Oraton-Marr caught the movement and glanced up.

And then it happened.

There was a flash of brilliant blue and a glistening, wet tail flipped out of the Egg. Oraton-Marr grabbed hold of it and pulled. Oskar was shocked. It was cruel to pull a creature out of its egg before it was ready. But Oraton-Marr did not care – he had the tail of the Orm in his own hands. The sorcerer leaned back to get more traction, and pulled as hard as he could.

"Don't just stand there, Apprentice," he snarled. "Help me pull! And you, boy," he snapped at Oskar. "Pull!"

"But you'll hurt it," Oskar protested.

"Rubbish!" Oraton-Marr grunted with the effort. "It's an Orm, for goodness' sake. It eats *rock*."

But Oraton-Marr *was* hurting the Orm. Its tail felt as though it was being wrenched from its body, and the little Orm, still inside its Egg, quite reasonably became convinced that something was trying to eat it. It switched into attack mode.

No one wants to be near a young Orm in attack mode – let alone holding its tail. Suddenly the casing of the Egg flew apart as though an explosion had happened from within. Oraton-Marr went staggering backwards but he did not let go of the tail. The Orm – five feet of slippery, spiky, wriggling, snapping fury went flying through the air and arced up, taking Oraton-Marr with it. As it went, its little wing bones began to flap and the soft membrane between them opened out like a parachute.

But the dead weight hanging from its tail was pulling it down and so the Orm did the only thing it could. It dropped its tail. Oraton-Marr plummeted to the ground and lay senseless on the sand, a cold blue tail clutched to his chest.

The Lady heard the thud. She sneaked a look, staggered to her feet and set off towards her brother. "Orrie, Orrie!" she screamed.

Tod and Oskar raced after the Orm, which, with no tail to balance it, was flying erratically away, dipping and soaring. "Hey!" Oskar yelled. "Hey! Ormie, Ormie! Look at me! *Look at me!*"

Karamander Draa rushed from her tent. She saw the sorcerer unconscious on the ground and the woman in blue hovering over him like a giant, predatory butterfly. She ignored them and raced to the pool. The woman with Bubba wheeled around and Karamander saw the flicker of fear in her eyes as she strode towards her. She took her baby with no resistance whatsoever. Then she turned her back on the woman and walked quickly away to the tent. "Kaznim!" she yelled as she went. "Come here. Take Bubba, please!" Kaznim came running and in a moment she had her baby sister in her arms and was watching her mother stride over to the stricken sorcerer.

Karamander Draa had come prepared. She knelt down beside Oraton-Marr, elbowed the Lady out of the way and sent her reeling backwards on to the sand where she lay stranded like a beetle, yelling for help. No one came.

From her pocket Karamander took a vial of black liquid labelled: "HeadBanger. Maximum strength." With a long pipette she dropped the liquid into Oraton-Marr's mouth, then she held his nose closed until he swallowed it. Brushing the sand off her robes, she stood up. "Get out of here," she told the Lady, who was struggling to her feet. "And take your filthy sorcerer with you."

"You've killed him! You've killed my Orrie!" his sister wailed.

"I do not kill," Karamander told her. "I have sworn to uphold life. He is asleep. He will sleep for seven days. And when he wakes he will have the worst headache imaginable. I have something that will cure it if he wishes to ask me. But he will have to come to me in person and ask very, *very* nicely indeed." With that she turned and went over to her Apprentice.

"Mysor," she said. "See these people off the premises, will you?"

Mysor smiled. Nothing would please him more.

# Imprinting The Orm

*The tailless Orm lurched away* into the desert on a roller-coaster flight, heading towards the rising sun. Leaping uselessly up into the air, arms reaching for the Orm, Oskar followed the shimmering, oddly truncated scrap of blue. It was *his* Orm; he had loved it at first sight. No one else could Imprint it – *no one*.

From somewhere far behind him, Oskar heard Ferdie yell, "Watch out! Watch out!"

But Oskar – intent upon his dance with the Orm – took no notice. It was only when the shadow of the dragon fell across him that Oskar looked up and saw two great taloned feet heading, it seemed, straight for him.

It was not Oskar but the little Orm that Spit Fyre wanted. However, he got both. As Spit Fyre's huge feet curled gently around the body of the Orm, Oskar at last timed his leap perfectly and grasped the Orm. It was slippery from the Egg and gritty with sand. Oskar wrapped his hands around its belly and the next thing he knew he was shooting vertically up in the air, looking into the irritated eye of a dragon. It was then that Oskar had second thoughts, but it was too late – he was now dangling fifty feet off the ground and far below he could see Ferdie and Tod running around like a couple of demented ants. He pushed away his fear and concentrated on the Orm. He must get it to look into his eyes. *He must.*

"Look at me!" Oskar yelled. "Please, Ormie, please. *Look at me!*"

But the little Orm took no notice. It only had eyes for its mother – or the creature the Orm assumed to be its mother: the creature who had rescued it from the animal that had tried to eat it and the other animals that had chased it. The little Orm gazed into the eyes of Spit Fyre and Imprinted the dragon deep into its flat little reptile brain. It loved Spit Fyre for ever. And then, realising that one of the animals that had chased it was still holding on to it, it turned around and spat at it.

The Orm spit stung viciously. Oskar's hands flew up to his face and he fell.

Ferdie screamed.

Human-Imprinted dragons like Spit Fyre have a reflex called Rider Retrieve. Even though Oskar had merely hitched a ride on another passenger, the reflex kicked in. As Oskar plummeted to the ground, the dragon fell even faster. The split second before Oskar would have hit the ground, Spit Fyre let go of the Orm – which was perfectly capable of flying for itself – grabbed Oskar and took him up into the air.

Spit Fyre landed a shocked Oskar gently beside the fire and then flew off to catch the Orm. He plucked the tiny, spiky, gritty creature out of the air and, watched by all below – bar Oraton-Marr – Spit Fyre flew up and over the top of the long dune.

And then the sky was empty. Dragon and Orm were gone.

# A LINE IN THE SAND

*Back at the fire beside the pool*, Tod and Ferdie stood staring into the sky, hoping that the dragon might come back. Oskar, stunned from his fall, lay beside the pool with his hands over his eyes. He was bereft: he had lost his Orm.

Tod, however, felt relieved. She may not have been about to return to Septimus in triumph with the Orm, but Bubba was alive and the sorcerer had not got the Orm either. It could, she told herself, have been a lot worse. As she squinted up into the blue of the sky, out of the corner of her eye Tod saw a small figure in red approaching. Kaznim came hesitantly, nervously even, and when she reached Tod she kneeled on the sand before her. "I betrayed you," she said. "I beg your forgiveness."

Tod felt embarrassed. No one had ever kneeled to her before. "Oh! Um ... well, that's OK," Tod mumbled. "I understand why you did it. Please, please get up." And she pulled Kaznim to her feet.

Karamander joined them. "I wish to thank you all," she said. "Kaznim has told me what you did for her. My tent is your tent. Please come inside and rest." A sudden bellow from the camel interrupted her. "Excuse me for a moment," Karamander murmured. "My Apprentice needs some help."

The Tribe of Three watched Karamander and Kaznim help Mysor despatch their unwelcome guests. The Egg Boy was sent to look for Aunt Mitza, who had disappeared. The Lady was heaved on to the camel, and the unconscious Oraton-Marr, still clutching the Orm tail, was slung over the donkey with a distinct lack of respect. Suddenly Oskar was on his feet and staggering away, heading for the donkey. Unsure of what harebrained plan Oskar might have now, Ferdie went after her twin.

Tod was watching Ferdie arguing with Oskar when a low, malevolent voice came from behind her. Tod swung around and found herself face to face with Aunt Mitza.

"Alice," said Aunt Mitza. "We do bump into each other at the strangest of times, don't we?"

Mitza reached out and placed a heavy hand on Tod's shoulder. Tod swept it away as though swatting a fly. "Don't touch me!" she growled.

"All right, I won't." Aunt Mitza chuckled. It seemed to Tod that she was laughing at a private joke. "Just like I never touched your mother," she said.

"What do you mean ... my *mother*?"

Aunt Mitza was enjoying the effect she was having. "I mean the dear, saintly, beautiful Cassandra who everyone loved, especially my Dan."

"Your Dan?" Tod asked, puzzled.

Aunt Mitza leaned in so close to Tod's face that she could smell fish on her step-aunt's breath. "Your father. He was meant for me. Not *her*. She always took everything I wanted. *Everything*." Aunt Mitza spat on the sand. She gave Tod a cold smile. "You want to watch out for sand flies, you know. There are some very nasty ones about. *Very nasty indeed*."

Tod was too shocked to speak. She watched Aunt Mitza walk away, her broad back impervious to anything she might wish to hurl at her. Tod was still watching when Ferdie brought Oskar back. Oskar was clutching the Orm's tail. "Oraton-Marr is disgusting," Oskar was saying angrily. "He hurt a defenceless little Orm."

Ferdie looked at Oskar's singed eyebrows and the livid streak of red down his cheek where the Orm spit had burned him. "Not entirely defenceless, Oskie," she said.

They watched Oraton-Marr's entourage trail away up the dune. Tod stared long and hard at Aunt Mitza as she plodded wearily up the slope behind the camel. She could not get her step-aunt's words out of her head. Tod was not sure of their exact meaning, but she was sure of one thing: they were laden with hate. There was no doubt about it – whatever Aunt Mitza had meant, she had not meant well.

# NEW FAMILIES

*Later in the morning* Karamander Draa emerged from her tent after settling a disturbed Bubba down to sleep. She surveyed the group of young ones — Mysor, Tod, Ferdie, Oskar and Kaznim — who were playing a game in the sand involving twelve scooped-out dips and numerous pebbles, which Kaznim called "Village Chief". It was causing much laughter and noise. Karamander smiled. She enjoyed the company of the young.

But Karamander was worried. The three children from the Land of the Castle were confident of getting home, but she knew it was not as simple as they thought. As soon as they stepped inside the Red City, they would be in grave danger. Karamander had seen Oraton-Marr's entourage change direction at the top of the long dune and she knew they were now heading not for the port but for the Red City. She suspected that as soon as they reached it, the sorcerer's minions would scuttle off to the Queen and seek revenge. Karamander knew that revenge was something the Red Queen understood very well.

Karamander watched Mysor laughing as he scooped up the last of the pebbles. She would let them have their fun for now, but she must plan what to do. The Castle children were not safe with her, but where could they go? The weary

362

Apothecary retreated into the cool of her tent to think – and fell into a deep sleep.

She was awoken by screams.

Karamander leaped from her chair. Dreading what she would find, she threw back the door flap. She stared for some seconds, trying to make sense of the scene before her. There was a dragon. There was a tail-less Orm running around, snapping at everyone's ankles and a small boy with short fair tousled hair standing apart from the group, gazing at the tent with an expression of wonder. The rest of the young ones were bouncing up and down as though they were on springs – apart from Mysor, who was too cool to bounce. In the middle of the melee were three travel-stained young men and … *No, it couldn't be.*

But it was.

Karamander steadied herself. She had told Kaznim to make things right with Tod, and now it was her turn to do the same. Unnoticed by all, Karamander walked slowly across the sand. She reached the strangers and took a deep breath. "Dandra Draa," she said.

Dandra turned and bowed her head briefly. "Karamander Draa," she returned.

Karamander began to kneel, but Dandra caught hold of her hands and stopped her.

"Forgive me," Karamander said.

"Forgive *me*," replied Dandra.

There was silence and then Dandra said, "Your daughter Kaznim. I, er … I have something that belongs to her." And from a sling beneath her robes, Dandra brought out the tortoise.

Karamander smiled. All was indeed forgiven.

★    ★    ★

"So *this* is where you got to," Septimus was saying to Tod. "I suppose I shall have to get used to my PathFinder Apprentice turning up in strange places."

Tod looked sheepish. "I'm sorry," she said. "I thought it was the best hope of getting the Orm. But it didn't work quite as I planned."

Septimus smiled. "You will find that things rarely do." He looked over at Spit Fyre, who was licking sand off the baby Orm. "But one of the reasons I wanted you to be my Apprentice was that I knew you would think for yourself. You would work out what you thought was best, and then you would be brave enough to do it."

Tod felt as if a weight had been lifted from her shoulders. She realised how worried she had been about doing the wrong thing and disappointing Septimus, but now she understood. She could be an Apprentice and be herself too – *and he thought she was brave*.

"So, it's all worked out pretty well, don't you think?" Septimus was saying.

Tod smiled. She thought it had worked out very well indeed.


Karamander plied her guests with a feast. As they sat inside the dim coolness of the tent escaping the fierce heat of the midday sun, Septimus, Beetle, Marwick and Dandra discussed the journey home. Dandra did not think it wise to wait until nightfall. "The Red Queen has spies at the Port of the Singing Sands," she said. "We must get there before they are alerted."

"Rest and eat first," Karamander told them. "There is time to do both."

Outside the tent, Spit Fyre and his new baby kept watch. The Orm – or the Ormlet, as people were now calling it after

Tod made a lame joke about breaking eggs – kept glancing up at Mother Orm. Every now and then Spit Fyre gave the tail stub of the Orm a rasping lick. Already a new barb was forming and it would not be long until a fresh tail would begin to grow.

Leaving the older ones to talk, the younger ones drifted outside and went to dabble their toes in the cool spring that bubbled up beside the flat rock. With them was Darius Wrenn, pink from the sun, his eyes shining with excitement. "You look a bit different from the last time I saw you," Tod said, remembering the worried, pale boy who blinked a lot.

"Marwick made them let me come too," Darius said shyly. "He said I could carry the water bottles and help him read the map and make myself useful. And I *did*." He watched his feet in the green of the water and then said very quietly, "I *love* it here."

"So do I," Kaznim said. She smiled at Darius. "Do you want to play Village Chief?"

Darius blinked in surprise. "Play what?"

"It's fun. I'll show you." As Kaznim began to scoop out hollows in the sand, Tod got up and left them to it. She walked back to the star-strewn tent, feeling a little nervous. There was something important that she wanted to ask Beetle and Karamander Draa.

It was hard to leave when the time came. In the midst of the partings and the promises to meet again, the small figure of Darius Wrenn stood wide-eyed as ever, too excited to speak. One of the people in the amazing ExtraOrdinary Apprentice Spell – he thought it was probably the one named Tod – had done something wonderful. She had gone into the tent in that confident way that he wanted to have one day, and then, she had emerged with Beetle and the Apothecary. Darius had watched them walk around the outside of the tent and had heard the murmur of them talking. And then the Apothecary had come over and she had asked him *to be her Apprentice*. And to live in the tent with her and her daughters, just like *a real family*. Darius still could not believe it. And what had surprised him almost as much was that Beetle had said that he would really miss Darius and that he would be very welcome if he ever wanted to return to the Manuscriptorium.

But Darius didn't think he ever would.

★   ★   ★

That afternoon, Tod and Oskar became SandRiders once again. They took the *Wiz* and *Beetle* back to the Port of the Singing Sands. With no fear of sand lions or a missed Egghatching, it was a thrilling ride. Above them flew Spit Fyre, ferrying Beetle and Marwick to the Port of the Singing Sands.

As the sun began to sink over the sea, Marwick, Tod, Beetle, Ferdie and Oskar met up outside the Hidden arch. Led by Tod and Marwick, they entered the Ancient Ways. They walked through nine Hubs until at last they found themselves behind the Manuscriptorium door, which was quickly opened by the faithful Ephaniah Grebe. He had not left his post for a second.

Back at the star-strewn tent, Septimus was saying his farewells. His hand held tightly by Karamander Draa, Darius Wrenn watched the ExtraOrdinary Wizard climb on to his dragon, shift the baby Orm out of the way, get nipped on the arm for his trouble and then lift off into the starlit sky. Surrounded by his new family, the small boy watched the beautiful green

366

dragon wheel around and set off into the night. Darius looked up at Karamander and smiled. His new life was about to begin.

★    ★    ★

It would be a long flight home, but Septimus did not mind at all. His Apprentice had done well, the Castle was safe and, best of all, he had his dragon back. Septimus didn't even mind that he was going to have to share Spit Fyre with a jealous little Ormlet, who possessed very sharp teeth – *ouch* – and was not afraid to use them.

The next morning at the Castle, Tod, Oskar and Ferdie were waiting in the courtyard of the Wizard Tower, at the front of the huge welcoming party for Septimus, Spit Fyre and his baby Orm. As they saw a distant sparkle of green appear over the snowy treetops of the Forest, a hush fell over the whole Castle. Word had spread that the ExtraOrdinary Wizard was bringing his dragon home at last and people had gathered on the rooftops, watching for the return of what they thought of as their dragon too. As the impressive sight of the ExtraOrdinary Wizard flying his dragon drew close, a ripple of applause began to spread, until a tumult of clapping filled the air.

Spit Fyre landed expertly in the courtyard to the background of cheers and whistles of encouragement. Septimus leaped down from the pilot seat and, curled around the dragon spine behind him, Tod saw a twist of blue – the sleeping baby Orm.

Septimus gave Jenna a quick hug and hurried straight over to Tod, Oskar and Ferdie. "We did it!" he said. "Thanks to you three, we have the Orm. Our Castle is safe."

Tod exchanged smiles with Ferdie and Oskar. They knew that from now on it would always be "*our* Castle".

LOOK OUT FOR THE NEXT
TODHUNTER MOON
ADVENTURE

OUT IN OCTOBER 2016